CITY OF SEVENS

ELIZABETH COLEMAN

VOID BUNNY

Cover artwork by Augusto Silva @_.augustosilva._

ISBN: 979-8-9873902-1-4 (paperback)
ISBN: 979-8-9873902-0-7 (ebook)

Library of Congress Control Number: 2022922052

Published by Void Bunny
San Francisco, California

Printed in the United States of America
First edition

For Sam

Any sufficiently advanced technology is indistinguishable from magic.

—Arthur C. Clarke's Third Law

PROLOGUE

Rune was ready to kill.

As he relentlessly jabbed at the black leather punching bag hanging in the corner of Myst's gym, he imagined he was punching Miles Kirkpatrick's face. It felt good to let out that anger. They'd been beta testing Myst's new augmented reality game, Veil, and Rune had thought they were safe from Miles stealing his ideas. But once again, Pact had scooped them. It was almost like there was a mole at Myst. There was no way Miles and Pact would have gotten into AR otherwise.

Rune's cell phone chimed.

RUNE. SOS. 911. WRU??

Piero Bellini, the VP of talent management, was a harlequin prone to theatrics.

WU?

Artemis room. Need u NOW.

BRT

Myst's headquarters buzzed with early morning productivity as Rune moved quickly through the converted industrial warehouse space sprinkled with open coworking stations. When he reached one of the glass-walled conference rooms on the ground floor, he noticed the opaque screens were activated, shrouding the room in privacy. Rune pushed the door open.

Piero threw up his hands in relief, looking flustered despite his immaculately pressed, salmon-colored suit. "Thank the Light you're here." He gestured to a seer. "This is the situation."

Strands of the seer's bleached blonde hair covered her face as she leaned forward in one of the leather conference room chairs around the table. The Veil team gathered around her as she stared passively at the floor, rocking back and forth slightly. A full glass of water sat on the table in front of her. She looked up at Rune with glassy eyes.

"Do we need to call a healer?" asked Rune, glancing at Carson Ross, the wolf-shifter head of engineering.

Carson scratched the back of his neck with a furry hand. "I don't think so. She's in some sort of psychic trance, though."

"What happened?" demanded Rune.

"I'll tell you what happened," said Piero. "We were going through the usual vetting questions for seers—predicting sports outcomes and news headlines and that sort of thing. She seized up and started talking gibberish! She was talking in Aramaic or something. Kept saying 'Veil' over and over." He gave Rune a pointed look. "Dealing with malfunctioning Sixers is *not* part of my job description."

"So far, she's mentioned things about demon attacks, Myst, and Pact," said Carson. "Half of what she's saying is somehow coded in C-plus-plus." Carson waved a notepad at Rune. "I'm trying to decipher what she's saying, but it's all garbled."

"I think we should call a healer," said Piero. "Or an exorcist. I've never seen a Sixer convulse like that, even during a psychic episode. What if she's possessed?"

Rune shook his head. "The wards prevent it. Even if something were hitchhiking without full-on possession, she wouldn't have been able to cross into the building."

Rune bent down to look at the seer. Taking her face gently, he peered into her eyes and sent out psychic probes to examine her mind. Static. "Everything is clouded, like a thick fog. I can't see anything inside."

"You," said the seer in a faraway voice. She stared at Rune. "You."

"Whoa, freaky." Piero shuddered.

"You seek salvation, redemption," said the seer. "The making of your true Soulwish."

All eyes turned to Rune.

"Make any Soulwishes recently?" Carson raised an eyebrow.

"I doubt she means me," said Rune, frowning.

"Heed me, Rune Christiansen!" the seer cried.

"I guess we know who she was talking about," Piero whispered loudly to Carson behind his hand.

The seer grabbed Rune's hand and pulled him down so she could speak directly in his ear. Her voice was low, barely a whisper. "A raven-haired woman will ensnare you with a ring of fire. When the great dragon rises, you will know it is she who you have been seeking."

The seer convulsed, her body shaking. Rune shot up, stumbling backward in surprise. Piero and Carson grabbed the woman, steadying her so she wouldn't fall out of the chair. After a few seconds, the seer stilled and looked up. Her blue eyes were clear.

"Sorry, I must have spaced out. It happens sometimes." She glanced at Piero, who looked stunned. "What were you asking about the Warriors game?"

Rune took a step back. He turned away before the others could see the expression on his face. Closing his eyes, he forced his heart to calm, taking deep, steady breaths.

He tried to focus his emotions and recognize what he was feeling—frustration, anger, confusion, excitement. But there was one emotion he hadn't felt in a long time.

Hope.

Chapter 1

Nadia stood in the middle of her upended bedroom, the culmination of her twenty-three years surrounding her in half-packed moving boxes.

She wanted to burn it all.

She picked up books and shirts and shoes and continued haphazardly filling boxes. She swept the contents of her medicine cabinet in with her slutty Halloween costumes and water coloring supplies. She tossed her perfume collection into a big black trash bag along with childhood stuffed animals and hair products. She threw the silver-framed photos of herself and her friends, smiling and happy, into a duffle bag with her jewelry and tennis racket.

Nadia would pay for that disorganization later when she was trying to find things, but for now, she didn't care. She was done with this life. Done with Washington, DC and the lame, entry-level customer service job she had landed straight out of college. Done with her cheating scum of an ex-boyfriend and duplicitous best friend, both of whom she had found the previous day in bed together. Done with putting her dreams of working in the arts on the back burner. She was moving to New York City, and her new life was going to be amazing.

The doorbell rang.

"Zoey!" Nadia called out to her roommate. "Can you get that?"

When Zoey didn't respond, Nadia stomped over to the front door, unfastened the door chain, and ripped it open.

No one was there.

Instead, she found a twine-wrapped package sitting on the ground. A dark-red rose was tied to the top of it. She pulled it out and inhaled the rich, damask scent. Elegant script on the brown paper wrapping read: "To Nadia Winters. Happy Birthday."

Nadia felt a tingling sensation, like someone was watching her. A couple of people strolled down the street outside her Foggy Bottom flat, but she didn't see anyone who looked like they had left the package. Annoyed at the interruption, she locked the front door as she returned inside.

Back inside her room, she ripped the brown paper away and turned over the gift. It was some sort of fitness tracker or smartwatch called a Myst Psionic. The M of the Myst logo looked like two misty mountains. There was no note or any sort of clue about who had left it. Nadia clasped the purple band to her wrist. She tapped the screen, looking at the face.

Strange multicolored images that looked like alchemical symbols flashed on the screen, followed by numbers. The numbers changed, and then told her she was a "Level 0." It seemed to be a gamer watch.

Nadia tapped on the glass again until she got to the screen that was measuring her heart rate, a small red heart flashing on the left next to the number eighty-six. Nadia tapped the LCD screen again, and the images changed as she tapped and swiped the device, rotating through its various screens. The watch had GPS, a world clock, numerous apps that synced with smartphones and other Bluetooth devices, and basic fitness tracking. She downloaded the Myst Psionic app from the website listed in the manual and attempted to sync the phone to the watch.

"Device already registered to an account."

Figures. Someone had given her a stolen smartwatch. But who?

Nadia didn't have time to figure it out. She got back to work, dumping her crap into bags and boxes. She felt herself getting worked up again as her thoughts kept spiraling back to her dickwad ex-boyfriend and best friend.

"Nice rage-packing," said Zoey.

Nadia glanced over to her roommate, who stood in the doorway in her underwear and a T-shirt. Her strawberry-blonde hair was up in two mini buns, which irritated Nadia for some irrational and probably petty reason. Zoey was eating a bowl of Cocoa Puffs, her pixie features frowning at the disaster zone that was Nadia's bedroom. Nadia stuffed her black leather high-heeled boots into a garbage bag.

"Seriously, it looks like Chernobyl in here." Zoey carefully picked her way through the space like she was walking through land mines and took a cross-legged seat on the bed after nudging over a pile of old paperbacks with her bony hip. Zoey went into therapist mode, adopting a serene, neutral expression on her face, and watched Nadia work.

"I don't want to talk about it," Nadia snapped.

"Evidently."

Nadia pulled out her bedside table drawer and dumped it into a cardboard box. It clanged and rattled with the sound of glass breaking.

"Can you chill out for just one second?" asked Zoey. "Your energy is seriously harshing my vibe. And that lotion bottle you just threw in there is open. Here, have a bite of cereal." She held out the bowl. "Chocolate helps everything."

Nadia's stomach twisted. She'd been drinking vodka on an empty stomach while she packed. She accepted the bowl and spooned a bite into her mouth, taking a seat on the bed. "You know the worst part about it all? They both were supposed to help me pack today, and instead, I'm stuck here, trying to finish this all at the last minute!"

Zoey nodded sympathetically but didn't offer to help.

"They've already made it Instagram official. It's literally been one day. One. Freaking. Day." Nadia forlornly looked at the piles in her bedroom, losing steam now that she was sitting.

"But weren't you going over there to break up with him?" asked Zoey gently. "You didn't want to be in the relationship anymore either. Everyone knows long distance sucks donkey balls."

"*Still.*" The betrayal stung, but at least she no longer had to pretend. She had met Keith and Hailee in college at William & Mary, and after graduation, the three's relationships had run their course. Turns out, Keith's frat-bro mannerisms and Hailee's incessant weeknight partying weren't that cute or welcome away from campus.

"Hey, what's that?" asked Zoey, pointing to the smartwatch on Nadia's wrist. "New Apple Watch?"

Nadia held out her wrist for Zoey to examine. "Whoever left it didn't include their name. Thought it might have been an apology from Keith, but it said 'Happy Birthday' on the package."

"Creepy. Meet any stalkers lately?"

"I know, right? I'm really hoping they just forgot to sign their name and that I'm not going to end up on a true crime show."

Zoey jumped up from the bed. "Speaking of birthdays, now that you're free tonight, you should come out." Nadia had planned on just taking it easy and ordering a pizza with her boyfriend and best friend after packing all day, but now that plan had gone to hell as well.

"There's this super cool band playing in Georgetown," continued Zoey. "A bit hipster, but the bassist is hot. I'll text you the address. I promise we'll keep the birthday shots to a minimum. I know you need to get all this"—she waved her spoon around the room—"finished by Sunday."

"I'll think about it," Nadia said, just to appease her.

"Oh, don't wear those suede heels you like to wear dancing," said Zoey as she walked out. "They're calling it the storm of the century. Can you believe it? It's June, for crying out loud."

Nadia eyed the disaster in her bedroom, trying to gauge how much more she had to do that evening before she could consider meeting up with Zoey for drinks. Determined to shake her bad mood, she put on one of the viral chart playlists on Spotify. An indie rock song blasted out as she started sorting books. She put a few of her favorites—including *Gone With the Wind* and *Pride and Prejudice*—into a fresh, lotion-free box.

The music switched to a dark tribal house song, and she glanced at the name of the song: "Roots and Chains" by a DJ called The Mighty Troglodyti. She hit the thumbs-up before tying her long dark hair up into a ponytail and getting back to work. She pulled down the *Les Mis*, Lizzo, and Degas posters from her wall and packed them away, a bit more carefully than she did the other items before. Before she knew it, the sky was dark out through the window next to her bed.

Her cell phone rang. It was a 212 area code. New York City.

Nadia quickly answered it before it could go to voicemail. "Hello?"

"Hi, Nadia? This is Carolyn with the Gagosian. I'm so sorry to call you after hours, but I knew you were moving this weekend, and I wanted to reach out as soon as possible. There was a mix-up with the paperwork, and I'm afraid we are going to have to rescind your job offer."

Nadia's heart leaped into her throat. "I'm sorry, I must have misheard you. Did you say you were 'rescinding' my offer?"

"Yes, unfortunately."

"I . . . I don't understand. I already signed all the paperwork. I'm starting next week. How could this happen?"

"Very unfortunate. A mix-up like this does occur occasionally."

"Wait, what kind of mix-up? Is there someone I can talk to?

What about Mr. Stanley? I'm supposed to report to him. Can't he do something?"

"It's out of my hands. I'm so very sorry."

"Wait, I—"

The woman hung up.

Surely, this was a joke. A friend playing a prank. This was her dream job, a foot in the door of the art world, a fresh start.

And all that had just been ripped away.

Nadia's eyes darted around, failing to focus on anything. All the air rushed out of her lungs. She was on fire, burning up. There was a rumbling, like a volcano was erupting from her core. The world spun around her, and she had to close her eyes. The tracker on her wrist beeped frantically.

She barely noticed it.

Her hands shaking, she called her dad. Straight to voicemail. She left a quick message telling him what happened and asked him to call her back.

Her parents were driving her to New York on Sunday. She had just leased a new apartment. New York was happening, job or not. She closed her eyes, fighting back the tears. Crying would not help the situation.

But a night out on the town would.

A call from her grandmother popped up on her cell. She sent it to voicemail.

Nadia quickly changed out of sweats and pulled on jeans and a tank top. She slapped on some makeup, ran a brush through her hair, and threw on a pair of heels. It *was* her goddamn birthday, after all. She was going to wear heels and maybe make out with a cute random guy she never had to see again—maybe even that bassist from the band—and forget everything else.

She grabbed a rain jacket, an umbrella, and her purse. Three missed calls from her grandmother. Strange. They hadn't talked in years. Maybe she'd remembered it was her birthday and was trying to make up for missing all the others. Nadia would call her back when she was in the mood to deal with small talk and could pretend everything in her life was going fine.

Her phone lit up with another call from her grandmother. She ignored it.

The storm was in full force by the time Nadia reached Georgetown Waterfront Park. The rain came in thick sheets; the wind threatened to rip the umbrella from her. The Potomac River was a glassy ribbon, heavy raindrops pummeling the dark surface. The park was empty, the normally busy tree-lined paths and grassy knolls deserted in the storm. Nadia suddenly felt stupid for even going out. She should focus on coming up with a plan to get her life back on track, not drown her sorrows in alcohol and hot guys to numb her misery.

As Nadia walked on the slippery pavement, she mentally cursed herself for wearing heels (though not the suede ones) instead of practical flats or boots. Her foot went out from under her, snapping the heel off. The umbrella went flying off into the void. She fell and smacked her knee painfully on the pavement. Blood and gravel covered her scraped-up palms.

Tears welled up in her eyes, and she sat up slowly to assess the damage. Her right knee was bleeding a rather alarming amount, her jeans torn. Blood trickled down her leg. Her palms were raw with road rash. She tried picking out the bits of concrete and dirt in her knee, wincing at the pain.

"Here, let me help you." The voice was male, British. Aristocratic.

A black-gloved hand appeared in front of her. She hadn't seen anyone on the paths, but she grabbed her purse and took his hand. She brushed away tears and mascara, sniffling. Her long hair was plastered to either side of her face. She was sure she looked like a wet rat or that chick from *The Ring*.

Nadia looked at her savior for the first time. Light from the streetlamp above them cast long shadows on his pale features. He looked to be in his late twenties, decently attractive, though his face was a bit thin. He wore a long black overcoat with a wide lapel over a ruffled dress shirt, like maybe he was part of a theater troupe. Rain soaked his dark hair, running in rivulets down long sideburns. Nadia wished he would stop staring at her so intensely, like he already knew her. He looked wistful for a second before his thin lips turned up in a small smile.

"That was quite the tumble you took, Nadia. Are you okay?"

"H-how do you know my name?"

His smile turned thick and serpentine. Small creepy fangs descended from his canines. Nadia took a faltering step back, wobbling on her broken heel.

"I know many things about you. Many happy returns of your birthday, my dear."

She backed away from him, clutching her purse. *What a fucking weirdo.* She didn't know how he knew her name or that it was her birthday, but she was not about to get mugged by some freaky wannabe vampire who liked to hang out in parks at night, scaring women.

The smartwatch on her wrist beeped repeatedly. He chuckled, a strangely delighted look on his face. "You don't have to be afraid of me. I'm not going to hurt you."

Nadia turned quickly and fled, limping on her broken heel as fast as she could. She cast a few worried glances over her shoulder in case he decided to follow her. She had taken some self-defense and Krav Maga classes in college, and she started digging in her purse for her house keys or something else sharp she could use to stab him in the balls or gouge him in the eyes if he tried anything.

She blinked, and he disappeared behind her. Before she could even gasp, he appeared in front of her on the concrete path with a puff of air and a small pop. Adrenaline pumping, she turned to flee, keys forgotten. He appeared in front of her again like a pop-up jack in the box, waving back and forth to corral her in.

Nadia couldn't run on her broken heel. Her breath came in shallow gasps. She couldn't believe this was happening to her. "What do you want? Money? Here, take it!" She pulled out the few bills from her wallet and thrust them at his chest.

He threw back his head and laughed: a rich, cultured sound. Nadia's mind flashed to memories that weren't her own. Disjointed images of men in an old boys club, mahogany paneling, and green velvet drapery. Brandy being poured, the smoke from cigars snaking into the air. Gambling with dice and cards. A hidden card up a sleeve.

Nadia shook her head in confusion. The images cleared.

"Put your money away," he said, chuckling.

Nadia's cell phone suddenly rang. The man tipped his head with a flick of his wrist at her purse. "I believe that will be your dear grandmother, Marina. Do tell her hello for me." Nadia stared at him dumbly. He flicked his wrist again. "Go ahead and pick it up."

"Nadia! Is that bastard there?" Her grandmother's words came out in a rush. "Tell him if he so much as hurts a hair on your head, I will string him up by the balls and—" The man snapped his fingers, an irritated scowl on his face. The line went dead.

The phone rang again. Nadia jumped at the sudden sound. With a roll of his eyes, the man sighed dramatically. "Fine. You can answer it. Tell the old witch I won't hurt you. I just want to talk."

Nadia pressed accept. "H-hello?"

Her grandmother spoke fast. "Thank God! Okay, listen, Nadia, something has happened. I tried to stop it, but I failed. You have special abilities. Magical abilities—"

"Wait, hold on. What? I don't understand what you're saying."

"Let me talk to her," said the stranger, his voice tinged with annoyance. Nadia's phone flew out of her hand in a graceful arc. He caught it in midair. "Hello, Marina. Guess who I found?"

That was it. She was done here. Nadia kicked off her heels and ran.

"Help!" she cried out as she ran out of the park to K Street. The street was empty of pedestrians, and she tried to flag down passing cars, crossing her arms back and forth over her head, but the cars merely honked and swerved around her, sending up splashes of muddy puddles that hit her in the face. She looked around wildly at the underpasses and buildings and streets and spied a portly man out walking his little dog, coming toward her on the sidewalk. Nadia ran to him, waving an arm in front of her. Startled, he picked up his dog and clutched it to his chest under his umbrella.

"Help! There's a man trying to hurt me." Nadia pointed back at the creepy stranger who was walking toward them across the grass in a leisurely fashion, like he didn't have a care in the world. His long black coat whipped about him in the wind.

"Nadia," the stranger called out playfully. "You can run, but you can't hide."

The man with the little dog looked around Nadia and frowned, skepticism on his face. "I don't see anyone. Do you want me to call the police?"

Nadia gestured to the stranger. "What do you mean? He's right there. He made my phone fly through the air! And he has fangs!"

The man with the little dog narrowed his eyes at her before shaking his head and muttering something about "damn junkies." He pushed past her quickly, like he was trying to get away from her. Nadia turned to gape at him, stunned at his lack of sympathy for a woman clearly in distress. The man hurried right past the stranger, stepping into the street to give him a wide berth. The man's little dog growled and yipped as they passed him, but the man didn't even look at him, like he wasn't even there.

"We can do this the easy way or the hard way, darling. It's up to you," the stranger called out as he continued to approach.

She wasn't about to stick around and find out what the hell that meant. She turned and ran.

Nadia didn't stop running until she reached a crowd of people at nearby Washington Harbour. She ran up to the fountain, gasping for breath, a stitch in her side. Her bare feet were dirty from running through puddles. Her leg throbbed from where she had smacked it on the pavement. Luckily, the rain had let up for a bit, coming down in a light drizzle versus the monsoon from earlier. She rummaged through her purse in a panic. That fucking weirdo had her cell phone. A small price to pay to not be mugged. Or worse.

"Nadia, are you really going to keep running from me?"

She shrieked at the sound of the stranger's voice. The British man was sitting on the concrete lip of the fountain, looking extremely calm and collected, the antithesis of Nadia's flustered self on the verge of hysteria.

"What do you want?" she exploded. A few people who were walking nearby cast worried looks in her direction.

He chuckled. "Keep your voice down. Nobody else except you can see me."

Nadia suddenly felt woozy. "Are you real? Am I imagining all this?" She leaned back on the lip of the fountain a few feet away from him.

"I'm very much real. I'm just casting a glamour right now to be invisible to everyone except you." He took out some papers and started rolling a cigarette.

"I think I'm going insane," said Nadia, detached. Her vision swam, her world fishbowling for a second. The smartwatch beeped, and she took deep breaths, trying to calm her thumping heart. She rubbed her hands down over her thighs, a nervous tic she had developed in college during stressful situations. Her jeans were soaked and torn, the gash on her knee still bleeding a dark cherry red. "What's going on? How do you know my grandmother?"

"Marina and I go way back. I'm rather fond of the old bat. Pain in the arse at times. Let's just say, we are associates."

Nadia scanned the plaza. Couples strolled hand in hand under umbrellas, the pavement reflecting the streetlights from the recent rain. Waiters brought over food and drinks to patrons sitting in the windows and outdoors at restaurants with nice little hedges and manicured trees in pots. *And here I am, talking to an invisible person.*

Questions bubbled up into Nadia's mind, and she tried to order her thoughts and think rationally and logically. "My grandmother said something about special abilities. What was she talking about?"

"You, my dear, are what they call a Sixer."

"A what-er?"

"A Sixer. You have the sixth sense, also known as psychic ability, to see spirits and supernatural creatures. And you most certainly have some other latent magical powers from the seventh sense, evidenced by your little episode earlier this evening." A flame lit up from his palm, and he lit the cigarette, taking a long drag.

Nadia blinked. "What's someone with the seventh sense called? A Sevener?"

"The term is Septer, but you 'catch my drift,' as they say."

The smartwatch beeped.

"Are you enjoying your birthday gift?" asked the stranger. "I thought you might like it."

Realization dawned on her. "Have you been tracking me?" Her fingertips itched, and she had the urge to fling the smartwatch across the plaza.

"A slight invasion of privacy, I admit. But I had to be sure of what I was dealing with here and what you are capable of."

"What are you talking about?"

He leaned toward her, a glint in his dark eyes. "What if I told you that centuries ago, one of your ancestors was a witch, and she made a Blood Oath with a vampire—an oath in perpetuity—that passes down through the matrilineal line?"

Nadia narrowed her eyes. "Is this a joke? Did Zoey put you up to this?"

"No, my dear. The Blood Oath is no laughing matter." He looked serious, his face almost statuesque. Nadia got ready to run again.

The man noticed. "Humor me, Nadia. Suspend your disbelief for just a few minutes while I explain."

Nadia looked down at her dirty, bare feet and knew she couldn't outrun him. He looked at her pleadingly, and she said, "You've got two minutes."

The man flicked his cigarette to the ground. "To cut a long story short, your ancestor made an oath that she—and her female descendants—would have immense power to cast spells and harness the energy and power of the universe in exchange for serving a powerful vampire master. Your ancestor had Sixer powers naturally, as some humans do. But the Oath gave her magical, Septer abilities."

Nadia studied the man's vampiric face and couldn't help the skepticism that slipped out. "Are you trying to tell me you're this guy?"

He bit out a short bark before raking his eyes up and down her body in a decidedly lascivious manner designed to make her uncomfortable. She scowled at him and hugged her arms to her chest to cover herself.

"As lovely as that sounds," said the man, "I am not your master. I *work* for your master, Lord Mercurio. I am not a vampire . . . I am a demon."

Oh, wonderful. This nut job was trying to tell her that one of her ancestors basically sold her soul to a devil, and he'd sent his minion to do his bidding. No, thank you. She was done here. She stood up.

"Listen—"

"Thomas Drake. At your service." He stood up and took a deep, theatrical bow.

"Mr. Drake. This has been real, but I'm out of here. I don't believe in magic, or demons, or vampires. I've been under a lot of stress recently. You aren't real. I'm just having some sort of psychotic, hallucinogenic episode that will pass." She started walking away, and he appeared again in front of her with that small pop.

"Would you quit doing that?" she hissed, glaring at him. People around them were giving them plenty of space, almost like they were being repelled.

"This always happens." He sighed to himself. "Okay—what will it take for you to believe me?"

She crossed her arms, sizing him up. "I don't know. Do something . . . fantastic. That others can see."

A mischievous grin spread over his face. "As your wish commands."

"Isn't that what a genie says?" She snorted.

He closed his eyes, his palms turned down toward the earth. The ground beneath them started shaking like there was an earthquake. All around them, people started screaming, outdoor tables at the restaurants on the plaza toppled over, people ran in a panic for cover. Dizzy from vertigo, Nadia fell to her side, looking up at him in horror.

He seemed to have grown, his muscles bulging under the coat. His face morphed, twisted into a wicked look of satisfaction. Horns protruded from his hair, his eyes inky black pools. A monstrous shadow hulked over him. The earth cracked, and a giant fissure zigzagged through the plaza out to the river, swallowing up the fountain where they had just been sitting. Explosions and fire and steam spewed up from the crack, sending rubble and fiery pieces of earth flying into the sky with a thunderous boom.

Nadia screamed, covering her head as she curled up into a ball. The watch beeped rapidly on her wrist.

He stopped. The ground ceased shaking.

She looked up at him, the color draining from her face. All around them, people were still screaming. Bits of rubble and fire littered the plaza, the steam from the fountain water hissing as it evaporated into the fissure. People were emerging and looking around at the ruined waterfront buildings, dazed. A man walked over to the fissure and looked in before running back to safety next to a streetlamp on a tall pole.

Thomas held out a hand to her. She stared at it dumbly, unable to move. When she didn't take his hand, he leaned down and picked her up from the ground like she was a ragdoll, setting her up on her feet. He waved a hand toward the fire and chaos, and the plaza returned to normal.

"I feel like you need a drink," said Thomas as he clasped a hand to her arm and dragged her away.

CHAPTER 2

"So, what if I don't want these powers?" Nadia asked Thomas a bit later, after a few drinks. "Can't I just give them back and not have to serve anyone? This Mercurio guy and I can go our separate ways. No one has to owe anyone anything."

They sat in the back of a small bar off one of the side streets of the plaza. The bar was mostly empty, save for what looked like a few crusty regulars and one boisterous group of frat boys. On the large flat-screen TV on the wall, the local news was already reporting about a mass delusion where witnesses had seen the gates of Hell erupt in Washington Harbour. Aerial shots of the scene showed firetrucks, police, and paramedics swarming the area, with no sinkhole or lava in sight.

Thomas had bundled Nadia into the corner of the bar, lending her his jacket and mumbling something about "feeble humans" when he saw her shivering in her bare feet and wet clothes. The bartender had distractedly served them drinks before turning back to the TV and watching with the others. Warm with his thick overcoat around her shoulders, Nadia absentmindedly twirled the tiny red straw in her vodka soda, grateful not for the first time for the numbing effects of alcohol.

"I wouldn't do that if I were you." Thomas took a sip of his whiskey soda. "Mercurio is a very powerful vampire, and you should be honored to serve such an esteemed lord and master."

"Calling him 'master' is a little chauvinistic and outdated, don't you think?" Nadia knew she was being flippant, but she didn't care.

Thomas ignored her attitude. "You're taking this all rather well. I'm impressed. Most people by now are blubbering fools, begging God for redemption."

"I'm not most people. And I don't believe in God."

"I'm sure up until an hour ago, you didn't believe in demons or vampires either."

I'm not sure I believe any of this. The more plausible explanation was temporary insanity.

"So, what does this Mercurio guy want me to do then?" She shifted uncomfortably in her seat, her half-dry jeans chafing and sticking to her thighs.

"He will call on you from time to time to aid him, but for now, you must move to San Francisco so your grandmother can train and prepare you. There is a special job for you there, one I will tell you all about once you get settled in and start learning about your powers."

Nadia shot him a contemptuous look. "I am *not* moving to San Francisco."

"Yes, you are."

"No, I'm not! I have a life. Plans. I'm moving to New York."

"Not without a job, you aren't." He said it so innocently, she almost didn't catch it.

"*You* did that, didn't you? You made me lose my job!" The bartender and the regulars looked over at her outburst. Thomas shushed her.

"A minor interference, I admit. But, please, who are you kidding? You didn't want to work there anyway, shackled to a desk instead of creating the art yourself. And that boyfriend of yours was a real wanker."

Nadia gaped at him, realization dawning on her. "Did you make Keith cheat on me?"

Thomas shrugged. "Hardly took any mental coercion. I think he'd given her a poke before. In any event, I merely cut the ties you had to make this whole thing easier for you. Really, you should be thanking me. I'm helping you fulfill your destiny. Isn't that what all you kids dream about nowadays?"

"And I suppose being Mercurio's errand boy is *your* dream life?" Nadia huffed. "Pot, kettle, black?"

Thomas's countenance hardened. "I am doing you a favor here, Nadia. There are other 'errand boys,' as you so charmingly put it, who would simply haul you back to him without letting you get your affairs in order." Thomas stood. "I'll get us more drinks."

Nadia watched as he charmed the bartender with a wave of a hand. Thomas hopped over the top of the bar, swatted him on the ass to move aside, and started pouring himself drinks. The bartender and the other patrons all watched with goofy expressions on their faces.

"Don't be like that," said Thomas as he handed her a vodka soda. "I promise you, your life is going to change for the best. See"—he wagged his drink at her playfully—"you'll never have to pay for a drink again!"

"Wow, such a perk." The smartwatch on her wrist beeped. "What's this thing, anyway? What's it measuring? Have you been tracking me with it?" She tapped the screen. It blinked "Level 1."

He chuckled. "A company called Myst makes them. You'll learn more about it when you move to San Francisco." Nadia shot him a withering look at the mention of San Francisco, but he continued, "It's like your basic smartwatch, but with a few extra features. It detects mood and emotional levels, measures different types of energy to help train humans and Numinals to be more effective spellcasters. Think of it like training wheels until you become familiar with your powers. I needed to test and measure your potential, even dampened, to know if you were worth the hassle of bringing you in. And lucky for me, you are. Mercurio will be very pleased to have you back as an asset."

Nadia's stomach tightened. "What do you mean?"

"Your grandmother tried to stop your fate. Before you were born, she throttled your powers. Tried to change your destiny. Stop you from having to fulfill the Blood Oath. I recognize remnants of her spell signature all over you. She hid you from Mercurio.

"But last week, I found you. I've been watching you since then. I wasn't sure if you had enough control over your emotions and intentions to undo your grandmother's meddling, but the watch helped you. It focused your energy and allowed you to cast a spell that razed the bindings she had put on you. Birthday magic—solar returns, if you will—are very powerful for changing personal destinies and life trajectories. Congratulations"—he smirked—"you managed to return yourself to a life of servitude."

Nadia shrugged off his coat. "Listen, I've gotten by twenty-three years without having any sort of special 'magical' powers. I think I can get by the rest of my life without them. Take them back." She unclasped the smartwatch from her wrist and tossed it down on the table where it skidded to a stop in front of Thomas. "I will not serve some vampire. And neither will my daughters or any of their children." Nadia grabbed her drink and downed it in several gulps, slamming the glass back on the table.

Thomas tried to hide his smile but failed. "Oh goody. This is my favorite part. Instead of completely stripping you of your powers, I will offer you a trial run. I will strip them from you for twenty-four hours. If you still want to go through with it, then I will respect your wishes, strip your powers, and erase your memory of ever meeting me. Mercurio has no use for servants who don't want to serve him."

"Such a generous guy," Nadia huffed.

"He can be. Your mother returned her powers."

Nadia's breath caught in her throat at that bit of information.

"There are plenty of others," Thomas continued, "who would kill, literally, for the chance to serve Lord Mercurio." He fingered the smartwatch on the table, glancing at it. "Do you agree to twenty-four hours without your powers? We'll use the watch as consideration."

She nodded.

"I need you to say out loud that you agree, so there is no ambiguity in the pact."

"Fine. I agree to twenty-four hours with no powers."

"In exchange for Thomas holding on to my watch for safekeeping," he prompted. She repeated the words.

Thomas waved a hand in front of her face. A shudder ran through her, and she convulsed, suddenly feeling empty. Like a part of her, something very core to her being, was gone.

"The feeling will pass." He shrugged. "Most fill it with booze or drugs or sex."

"I'll be fine. Thanks for caring." Nadia stood up, grabbing her purse. She turned to leave, but then remembered something. She turned back and held out her hand. Thomas fished her cell phone out of his pocket and plopped it into her hand with a smug smile.

"Sweet dreams, dear Nadia."

"Yeah, whatever. Don't follow me."

Nadia could feel his eyes watching her as she quickly made her way out of the bar and back into the night.

Zoey was still out by the time Nadia returned to their apartment. There had been numerous text messages wondering where she was. Nadia texted Zoey that she had gotten caught up with packing and then had fallen asleep. A lame, easily seen-through excuse, but Zoey's feelings weren't exactly high on Nadia's priority list right about then.

There had also been a voicemail from her father saying not to worry, that she was smart and beautiful and that he would find her another, better job. Good ol' Dad, with his blanket platitudes and empty promises. No mention of her birthday. There were also several missed calls and voicemails from her grandmother. Nadia ignored it all, powering off her cell phone after she showered and climbed into bed.

Nadia lay there for a long time, her mind turning over everything that had happened that night like she was trying to figure out a Rubik's Cube. Except Rubik's Cubes were logical and made sense. None of this made sense. She had powers? If so, why did her grandmother stifle them? Why would Mom give back her powers? What did her grandmother have to do when that Mercurio guy called on her? Nadia had always been open-minded, but she didn't want to think about having to participate in some weird, gothy, sex-cult shit with Satanic, goat-murdering weirdos.

She examined all possible explanations. Maybe she was delusional. Or maybe Thomas or her grandmother was delusional. Or this was some sort of cult thing, a way to trick people into believing some nonsense about magical powers just so they would give some sham guru all their money, like a multilevel marketing thing where she would have to recruit others to the fantasy.

Only a tiny part of her allowed herself to consider that what Thomas said was actually real. Maybe, just maybe, magic was real. Vampires and demons were real. And she had magical powers! She stared at her still raw and scraped hands, wondering if all those times she had what her therapist had called "episodes" were something more. But if it was all real, she had done the right thing trying to get out of a life of servitude. Most definitely. Thomas had talked about freeing her from a life shackled to a desk, but what was he offering except new shackles, this time to a vampire for chrissakes? No, she had done the right thing. The most important thing in your life is freedom, isn't it? America was built on that principle! She wasn't about to sign up for a life of enslavement, powers or not.

She tossed and turned for hours, finally falling into a fitful sleep in the early hours of the morning.

Nadia awoke to Thomas's face staring into hers. She tried to scream, but nothing came out. She tried to sit up but couldn't. With dawning horror, she realized that she was paralyzed, completely at his mercy. Her eyes flicked back and forth. She was still in her bedroom, the pale moonlight pouring in through the window and illuminating the figures in her room. Thomas stood next to the bed on her right. Two shadowy orbs floated in behind him, hazy in the air like thick smoke.

"Wakey, wakey, Nadia. You said you wanted to experience life without your powers. I'm here to give you a taste of that."

Nadia tried to scream again, failing. She could feel her heart beating in her ears, fast, like a trapped rabbit.

Thomas's voice was low and menacing. "You cannot move because I've paralyzed you. Most people know this as sleep paralysis. But what you don't know is that when this happens, demons are feeding on you." The two shadowy figures behind him moved forward, one on either side of the bed. They crawled under the covers with her, flanking Nadia with their smoky tendrils.

"Most of the time, demons feed when humans are sleeping," Thomas continued, his mouth close to her ear. "Their psychic defenses are down, and they have the most *delicious* subconscious energy. But now and again, a human wakes up, and we have to paralyze them so we can finish feeding." He stood up, trailing a finger down her cheek.

The two shadowy orbs wrapped themselves around Nadia, caressing her skin. She struggled to move, to scream, to fight. But she couldn't manage anything more than muffled moans. She was completely powerless. Tears pooled in her eyes.

"You said you wanted to know what life is like without your powers," Thomas said. "See, if you had your powers right now, you would have defenses against this. Even untrained, you would know how to break my spell on your mind and protect yourself. But you said you wanted to forgo the master's protection and abilities bestowed on the women in your family."

Thomas leaned in, whispering, "This, my lovely, is what life is like without Mercurio's protection. I promise I will make it torture. I will send demons to you and your family and your friends each and every night until they suck you all dry. Shriveled up and used. Husks of your former selves. Demons can take a life like *that*." He snapped his fingers. "But I will draw it out, a little each night, until you all wither away, and finally give up on life and die. Or just kill yourselves to make it stop." He licked her temple and shuddered in bliss. "Boys, if you will."

The two shadowy figures started feeding, sucking off Nadia's life energy. She could feel it leaving her body, draining through the punctures at her neck to her aura, being pulled from her like the pith from an orange. She closed her eyes, wishing that this was some horrible nightmare that she could wake up from. But it wasn't. It was real, and she was dying.

Nadia felt like she was being deveined, and all that would remain would be a sack of bones and blood. Her entire existence narrowed into fear and pain. She started getting sleepy and fought to stay awake, forcing her heavy eyes open. If she fell asleep, she was sure she would die. She could sense the orbs' pleasure, and they started fondling her breasts with their tendrils. She tried to fight, but all she could muster was a sad little moan. Thomas's eyes went wide as he realized what they were doing.

"That's enough!" Thomas barked. The shadowy figures fell off her like ticks full of blood. They disappeared from her line of sight. Thomas hovered over her prostrate form. He looked guilty, like he hadn't meant for it to go that far.

He opened his mouth like he was going to say something but stopped himself, cringing. Without another word, he turned and fled.

Nadia woke the next morning to the sun playing across her face, streaming in from the open window. She stretched, sleep still clouding her mind, and she took a minute to luxuriate in the bed's warmth, the softness of the pillows and sheets, and the lovely ache in her body.

Ache in her body . . . what the? She shot up, fully awake. Her body was sore, like she had run a marathon. Images from the night before burst into her mind. The phone call, the plaza, drinks with a demon, the nighttime visitors. *Being fed on.* She paled, running her hands over her face and chest as if to convince herself she was still there and not dead.

Pulling the covers back to examine her legs, her arms, her feet, and her hands, she seemed to be in one piece. Nadia gingerly touched fingers to either side of her neck, expecting to feel gaping wounds from fang bites. Nothing. She must have dreamed the whole thing. It was too insane, too crazy for any logical explanation.

She lay back in bed, clutching the blankets to her chin. She must have imagined it all. It was the byproduct of stress, no longer having a job or boyfriend, and basically freaking out about her life plans being derailed. It had to be.

The sun was already high in the sky, but she closed her eyes, determined to get more shut-eye before she had to figure out whether she was still moving to New York.

But then, she thought of something. She forced herself to look at the nightstand.

There, laid out in a circle, was the Myst smartwatch, the sun reflecting off its glassy surface. Propped up next to it was an envelope, her name written in elegant calligraphy on the front.

Her hand shook as she pulled out a piece of parchment.

Dearest Nadia,

Please do let me know what you decide about the Oath. I don't want to keep my promise, but I will.

— Thomas Drake

Chapter 3

Marina Nichols's house was a grey two-story Victorian walk-up with a red door. Overgrown bushes flanked the sides of the wooden stairs leading up to the aged front porch. Bright magenta, pink, and purple bougainvillea blossoms climbed up and covered the front of the house; the thick, unruly vines twisted around wrought iron balconettes under bay windows like coiled serpents. Nadia shivered a bit in her yoga pants and light zip-up jacket as she pulled her suitcase out of the taxi and set it on the curb. The air was cooler than it had been on the East Coast.

As the taxi drove off, Nadia stood for a minute and scanned the neighborhood. People were out and about, pushing strollers and walking dogs. Out front of a bodega, an old woman bought a box of oranges from a shopkeeper. A man wearing AirPods jogged by and nodded to Nadia in greeting. She smiled back out of habit; strangers always liked to talk to her. That made her think of Thomas, the last stranger who had decided to talk to her, and her smile faded.

Nadia dragged her suitcase behind her as she made her way down the twisting stone pathway toward the front steps. Orange and copper wildflowers sprang up on either side of her and swayed in the breeze like the flames of candles. Although Marina's house might look like the other aged Victorians on the block, there was something dark and wild and distinctly gothic about it, like it was perched alone along a remote cliff overlooking the sea instead sitting smack in the middle of a dense neighborhood in San Francisco.

Nadia hauled her luggage to the top of the weathered wooden porch. On the front door was a wrought iron symbol: a circle with a blossoming, fractal center. Some sort of sacred geometry pattern, no doubt. She rang the doorbell. Wind rustled the leaves of the giant maple tree next to the house making shadows and light dance.

After a minute, the red door opened with a long creak. A lanky man in his early twenties stared at her. He looked a bit like a surfer bum, with his bare feet, baggy cargo shorts, and unbuttoned flannel shirt. He cocked his head in a rather inhuman way, like how a dog tilts its head in question, and looked her up and down. He tucked a strand of dirty-blond hair behind his ear.

Nadia's mind flashed to images of regal palaces and gardens, laughter and violins and flutes, children chasing one another through dense rose gardens and hedges. She shook her head, trying to shake the strange fog that had settled over her brain. She knew that the memory flashes that weren't her own were related to whatever had happened on her birthday.

"Can I help you?" he asked again in a bored tone when she didn't answer him the first time.

"Oh, sorry. Does Marina Nichols live here? I'm Nadia, her granddaughter."

He frowned, and Nadia thought he might slam the door in her face from the way he hesitated, but he merely stepped to the side and motioned for her to enter.

Nadia had to stop herself from letting her jaw hit the floor. The inside looked like a curio shop had exploded: various antiques and eclectic furniture mixed with taxidermy and skulls and Victorian occult art on red-papered walls. Down the hall, gilded mirrors and picture frames reflected low light from a side window where a row of ceramic pots full of plants grew toward the sun. A Moroccan-patterned rug covered the hardwood floor, with strings of Christmas lights twinkling around the edge of the ceiling. Nadia tucked her suitcase off to the side and realized she knew way less about her grandmother's life than she had initially thought. This didn't look like the house of someone related to her mom. Everything in Nadia's childhood home was tastefully decorated by a professional design team in a neutral, color-coordinated palette.

"Avery, who is at the door?" Marina's strong, raspy voice called out. Nadia followed the young man into the living room. Her grandmother was sitting cross-legged on a purple yoga mat in front of a large brick fireplace. Another yoga mat was next to hers. Like in the hallway, various bric-a-brac, hanging plants, and ceramic pottery littered the room along with an array of candles, crystals, and mystical décor.

"Hi," said Nadia, suddenly shy.

"There she is." Marina rose to her feet, arms outstretched, and rushed toward Nadia. Her grandmother looked like Nadia remembered, in the gauzy, half-memories she had: an older woman with long dark hair, though now liberally sprinkled with grey, blue eyes lined with kohl, billowy hippy clothing. Her grandmother pulled her into a slightly strangling embrace. Nadia pulled away quickly. She wasn't much of a hugger. Not with relatives she barely knew. And especially not with ones who may have majorly tampered with her life, in some form or another.

Marina took a step back, holding on to Nadia's shoulders, and looked at her like she was an appraiser inspecting a rare gem at auction. "My, my, what a beauty you've become. You look so like your mother when she was your age. Except I can tell you need to use more sunblock. I have some cream that will fix those lines around your eyes right up."

"Uh, thanks." Nadia extracted herself from the woman's grasp.

Marina's eyes flashed. "Thomas. What did he tell you? I'm going to kick his snivelly little—"

"Marina," Avery cut in smoothly as he stepped around from behind them. "How about some tea? I'm sure Nadia could use a little refreshment after her journey."

"Yes, yes, of course." Marina winked at Nadia. "There's a couple of things that always help a situation: a strong cup of tea and a shot of whiskey. How about both?"

The three of them settled into the living room around a weathered coffee table. Marina splashed a generous amount of liquid courage into their teacups. Nadia suddenly felt uneasy. There was an elephant in the room, a great, big one with "Blood Oath" written on the side of its body, and Nadia was ready to grab a gun and test the line of sight.

Nadia shifted in her seat. The springs in the old velvet armchair squeaked. "Grandma Marina, maybe we should speak privately?"

"Please. Call me Marina. I haven't heard someone call me 'grandmother' in quite some time." She forced a laugh. "And Avery should stay. I hold no secrets from him."

Avery regarded Nadia with a cool gaze, the slightest hint of a smile tugging at the corner of his mouth like he knew he had won some minor battle against her. Avery 1, Nadia 0.

"Fine." Nadia took a deep breath. "I don't know where to start with all this . . ." How do you launch into the whole "Demons and other magical creatures walk among us and you have special powers" talk? Or maybe even harder, the "I'm totally batshit insane and I'm dragging you into the delusion" talk?

Avery reached over the side of the couch and picked up a ukulele, like he was suddenly disinterested in the conversation. He picked out a few notes. But despite his nonchalance, Nadia could tell he was listening intently.

"How's Helen?" asked Marina. "I should call her and let her

know you're here. You should have called when you landed. I would have picked you up at the airport."

Nadia shrugged. "Mom's fine. They're both confused about why I decided to move here instead of New York."

Nadia took a sip of her tea and eyed the whiskey enviously. An uncomfortable silence fell on them. She looked back and forth between Marina and Avery, waiting for one of them to say something.

"So, are we going to talk about all this, or what?" she asked finally.

"Yes," said Marina. "I suppose it is time to tell you."

The air around her crisped in anticipation of whatever Marina would say next. Nadia's arms broke out in goosebumps. Marina looked at her intently, focusing on her like a crow on a shiny gleam of light. "Nadia," she said. "You are a witch."

Nadia blinked. The tension in the room broke as Nadia let out a deep breath. "Okay," she said slowly. "What does that even mean? Like a *witch*-witch? Like broomsticks and pointy hats and black cats?"

As a girl, Nadia had dabbled in the occult: séances with Ouija boards at sleepovers, performing love spells on her crushes, playing "Light as a Feather, Stiff as a Board," creating candle-filled altars. It had been the trend of the moment, the Instagram aesthetic that Nadia had always thought held a deeper meaning, but that she had always been too afraid to dive into and fully explore. After a while, the shallow waters had proved to be boring. Nadia had grown out of her witchcraft stage, instead focusing on mastering sports and boys and school before condensing all those individual goals into the general concept of "leveling up" in life.

As if on cue, a black cat jumped onto the coffee table. It flicked its tail back and forth as it watched Nadia through slanted yellow eyes.

Marina shooed it off the table. "Get down, Monday." The cat

jumped to the floor, where it proceeded to sit down like a little sphinx.

"I know this is a lot to take in," said Marina. She leaned in, looking like Sophia Loren letting someone in on a secret. "But you come from a long line of witches. Real witches, not that shit you see on TV or the internet. This isn't some sort of self-help, law-of-attraction bullshit. I'm talking *real magic*."

Marina continued, the cadence of her voice changing like she was reciting a rehearsed or memorized speech, "I don't know how else to tell you all this, except the way I learned it. Sixers, those with the sixth sense of clairvoyance, telepathy, and precognition, can sense spirits and the supernatural and pierce through the glamours that those creatures cast. Some Sixers also can cast minor spells and perform magic, if they have the aptitude for it, but for most, Sixer magic happens by accident. By chance, they'll put together the correct ingredients to effect change, or their spell works like an offering to a Numinal or a spirit, who then effects the magic. To practice true magic, a witch needs to have Septer ability, the seventh sense of knowing how to bend reality to her will."

Nadia's head swam with what Marina was telling her. "Okay, so a Septer is . . . like a wizard or something? I'm just trying to wrap my head around what exactly you're telling me."

Avery strummed another note on his ukulele.

"I suppose if you want to look at it like that, then a Septer is more akin to a magician. Traditionally, Septers were the right hands to the kings and queens in the world. They were the trusted advisors. The priests and the alchemists. Carrying out the wishes and the will of the ruling elite, hiding their magic in religion or superstition. Septers were the 'scepters,' literally: the mechanism that royalty could lean on to carry out royal decrees."

Nadia's heart sped up. This was it! Magic was real, and she was a witch. Or a Septer. Whatever. It was like someone finally let her in on the secret to her life that she had been missing. The thing she'd been searching for. Willy Wonka's Golden Ticket to life. Her own personal Holy Grail. She had always secretly thought she was special, that there was a greater destiny out there for her. Some written in the stars, Hollywood-worthy fame and fortune. And now, her grandmother was telling Nadia that she had been right all along, that there was a greater story, a bigger mystery out there. It wasn't like leveling up. It was like discovering an entirely new game.

It seemed too good to be true.

"Thomas mentioned something about magic powers, but I'm not sure that I believed him. I mean, it's just . . ." She opened her mouth, then closed it again, unable to articulate how unbelievable it all was.

"I'm sorry you had to find out this way. Please trust me that I wanted to tell you, but I couldn't."

"Why couldn't you?" Nadia could hear the resentment in her voice.

Marina leveled her gaze. "Most people have their powers since birth, but they don't manifest until the witch is ready to receive them, usually during puberty. I cast a spell before you were born to hide you and throttle your powers. I tried to give you a normal life so you wouldn't have to serve Lord Mercurio. I thought I would have found a way by now to sever the Blood Oath that binds our family to the generational curse. Unfortunately, I haven't found a way."

"You had no right to make that decision for me!"

"I was doing what I thought was best at the time," said Marina. "Now, in hindsight, I'm not sure that springing this on you was the right thing to do. I thought you wouldn't be able to break my spell, but I was wrong about that as well."

"What about Mom? Thomas said that she gave back her powers?"

Marina's expression dropped, a flash of pain registering on her face. "Your mother refused to serve Mercurio. She didn't want anything to do with her magic or the Craft. She went to him before you were born and returned her powers so she wouldn't have to serve him when I die. He erased her memory. She has no idea now about our lineage. I thought the Blood Oath would stop with her, but then she had a daughter—you. We never anticipated that there was a loophole in the bargain that would allow the Blood Oath to pass on.

"When Mercurio sensed your mother was pregnant with a girl, he claimed you. After I hid you, he thought you had died at birth. I hoped and prayed that any powers had skipped over you, but you came into your powers during puberty, as most witches do. Do you remember your thirteenth birthday? When I visited you in DC? I had to re-up the bindings. Even with my spell to bind your powers, I could tell they manifested and were trying to break free."

Nadia felt slightly ill. "Okay, so why can't I just go to Mercurio and give my powers back like Mom did?"

"Part of your mother died when she lost her powers. I didn't want that to happen to you. Trust me that this was the only way I could think of to give you a normal life."

"Fine, but why would you do this to me in the first place? Why couldn't I just serve Mercurio like the other women in our family have? Like you have?" Nadia tried to keep her voice calm, but she could hear the tension in it.

Marina sighed. "There was a big movement in the '90s to free witches from their bindings to dark lords. I got caught up with the radical rebellion. I was young and stupid. I thought I knew what was best. When you get to be my age, you learn that there are forces in the universe larger than you that you can't control. The Blood Oath is one of them. You can either fight the tidal wave or learn to swim. I wish I had learned that earlier. I would have never put you in this position."

Nadia felt the anger in her boiling up at Marina's nonchalant attitude. This woman, this *stranger,* had interfered in her life because of some radical hippy whim. She had made decisions for her that had long-lasting, life-changing impacts on her abilities and natural right to magic. It stunned Nadia into a seething silence. The Myst Psionic on her wrist pinged.

Avery motioned to Marina with a nod of his head. Marina nodded, agreeing in a wordless conversation.

"Is that a Myst training watch?" asked Marina.

Nadia looked down at the LCD screen on her wrist. "Thomas gave it to me as a birthday present."

Marina looked thoughtful. "It's very expensive. It seems Mercurio sees you as an investment. He never paid much attention to me. I barely have any Septer abilities. Never had the interest or aptitude for rote practice to grow my skills. I wonder what Mercurio has in store for you."

"You seem awfully blasé about my future," Nadia huffed.

Marina stood up and went over to an ornate wooden cabinet off to the side of the room. She pulled open the doors and rummaged around inside. Nadia took this minute to look around the room, studying bits and pieces of this woman's life. Over the fireplace was an altar. Candles and crystals, bits of witchy knickknacks. Bottles of what looked like homemade elixirs. Several framed pictures were scattered around the room, pictures of Marina and Avery and people Nadia didn't recognize. In a black-and-white picture that looked to be from the '70s, Marina was jumping up and down with a tambourine on a stage, wearing a top hat and looking very much like a young Stevie Nicks.

Marina returned with sage and a copper bowl, digging in the pocket of her billowy pants for a lighter. Nadia watched as the edges of the fragrant sage bundle crisped and smoldered, the smoke snaking into the air as Marina waved it around her, wafting the smoke up toward her face. Avery absentmindedly gave the cat's belly a scratch. Marina fanned some of the smoke toward him and then at Nadia. Nadia sneezed.

"Okay," said Marina. "I've cleared the air of any lingering energy that might cloud your vision. I can tell you're angry. That's okay. Be angry! Lord knows that all society does is tell us women to stop being emotional, to calm down. But channel and focus that energy into something productive instead of letting it slip away, okay? Look at Avery and tell me what you see. Let's figure out what we are dealing with here since Mercurio has such an avid interest in you."

Nadia looked over at Avery. What, exactly, was she supposed to see? She shook her head. "I don't understand."

"Avery, if you please," said Marina. They shared another wordless conversation. Marina raised an eyebrow at him.

Avery sighed dramatically and set the ukulele down on the couch next to him. "If I must."

Nadia turned to Avery, wondering what was going to happen. He stood up to his full height, throwing his shoulders back and jutting an arrogant chin. As she watched him, he started changing. Transforming. His face became even more beautiful, his cheekbones higher. His ears elongated into points. His skin radiated, glowing from within. From behind him, translucent, mother-of-pearl wings unfurled and expanded out like those of a giant insect. The room pulsed at the sudden influx of power and energy.

"Holy shit!" Nadia exclaimed. She wanted to jump behind the couch and hide, but she was riveted to the spot. It was one thing to have seen Thomas during his little demonstration in the plaza when he had gone all demonic on her in the panic and chaos. It was quite another to see a magical creature in its full glory in her grandmother's living room, having tea and whiskey with her.

"That's enough. You're scaring her," said Marina. Nadia blinked, and then suddenly Avery was back to normal, the wings and pointed ears gone. He sat down, picking up the ukulele, once again uninterested in Nadia. The energy in the room was dampened once more.

Nadia looked from Avery to Marina and back. "Okay, what the hell just happened? You—your face. Your ears. They changed!"

"I lowered my glamour so you could see me," he explained in a bored voice.

"Look at him again," said Marina. "Concentrate and try to see through the glamour."

Nadia looked back at Avery, and her vision started flickering. She could barely make out the image of his elongated ears, his higher cheekbones. It was like there was an overlay on top of his image, a duality that her measly brain couldn't quite comprehend.

Her eyes widened.

"Most of the time magical creatures—collectively called 'Numinals'—wear their glamours so that humans cannot see them, blending in with mankind or remaining invisible altogether. But with the sixth sense, you're able to see through the glamours. You can't fully see them as if the glamours were lowered, but you can sense them, so to speak. Like imagining something in your mind's eye." Marina looked at her expectantly. "I'm sure you have some questions now."

Boy, did she ever.

Nadia's new bedroom was on the third floor: a cozy attic room under a sloped ceiling. It was only about ten feet wide, with a small bed covered with a pillowy white comforter tucked in the corner next to a wooden nightstand. Ivy branches had crept in on the side of the distorted glass windowpanes that overlooked the street, the vines crawling up the powder-blue wall like veins. Tucked in one corner was a wooden dresser with chipped paint. In another, there was a Tiffany floor lamp with a cracked shade. An antique cherry armoire rounded out the furniture. As Nadia looked about the room, she wondered how they had gotten all of it up the narrow stairs that led up to the attic from the second floor.

"Magic," said Marina, as if reading her thoughts.

"Hey!" Nadia turned at her.

Marina held up her hands in mock innocence. "Tonight, as soon as you're settled, we're going to work on defensive mental shield training. Witches usually master this in their first year of coming into their powers."

Nadia bit back a retort at why she was so ill-prepared.

Marina tsked. "You'll thank me later when someone or something tries to seize control of your mind, and you have the power to block them."

A shiver ran down Nadia's spine.

Marina fluffed the pillows on the bed. A fine layer of dust flew up in the air. "I know it isn't much, but with Avery here, I don't have an extra bedroom anymore." Marina went to the window, unlatched it, and pushed it open to air out the room. "Bathroom is downstairs."

"I have some boxes that I shipped here before I left. They should be here in a few days. I won't stay long. I'll find a place as soon as I can."

"Rent prices are absurd in the city, even after COVID. You're welcome to stay here as long as you need. It's the least I can do."

"Thank you. I appreciate that."

"I'll let you get settled, then." Marina paused at the door before she started down the stairs, her hand resting on the antique brass doorknob. "Oh, Nadia? I know you're still processing everything, but I'm glad you're here. I feel like we never had a chance to have a real relationship, but now that can change."

Nadia forced a smile. She knew her grandmother was trying to be nice, but she still wasn't sure how she felt about the woman. Marina nodded once with a crooked smile and then left, closing the door behind her. Nadia was thankful. More real talk about family secrets and lies was more than she could handle.

She spent some time getting settled into her tiny attic room, beating the dust out of the comforter and unpacking her things. It didn't take long. Restless, she looked about the room.

Nadia spied a white pillar candle on the nightstand next to the bed. She climbed onto the comforter, sitting cross-legged on the musty white blanket, and made a mental note to go shopping for new décor and bedding ASAP. Nadia stared at the candle. If this whole magic thing was real, if she really was a powerful witch or Septer or whatever, she needed to test her powers. But she had no training. She didn't know any spells. She didn't even know if you needed spells to make it all work, or if you could just think something and *poof*, magic would just happen. She hoped it was the latter. Insta-gratification would be a really useful life skill.

She cleared her mind, thinking of her therapist's insistence on practicing mindfulness and meditation. She stared at the candle, willing it to light, imagining a flame bursting to life. *Flames. Fire. Burning. Light, goddammit. Just flicker, at the very least. Or maybe just a spark, please?* She wasn't sure exactly who she was talking to, but she hoped they would give her a sign of what she was supposed to do if they were listening. She thought she would go cross-eyed looking at the thing. But nothing happened. Not even a wisp of smoke.

Finally, she gave up. This was pointless. She might have Sixer powers, but it was clear she was practically a squib when it came to Septer powers. Marina had said she wasn't very talented. Maybe the magic was dying out in their family. The thought comforted her for a moment. Maybe Mercurio would release her from any servitude. Surely, he wouldn't want a defective witch around, would he? Spiraling, self-defeating thoughts plagued her mind. Maybe she wasn't even a witch. Maybe none of this was real. Whatever she had thought she had seen with Thomas's horns and Avery's wings was some sort of hypnosis or delusion or drugs. What was in that tea, anyway?

"Fuck you," she muttered under her breath to the candle and flipped it off.

The candle exploded.

It was like a bomb had gone off. Melted wax flew everywhere. She ducked for cover as splatters hit her and the bedsheets and the wall. She froze, her heart racing.

It was real.

Chapter 4

The next day Nadia walked down Valencia Street, window shopping as the sun, high overhead, burned away the remnants of the crisp morning fog. Full of funky boutique stores, thrift shops, Mexican restaurants, and coffee shops, the Mission District neighborhood was—as Marina had put it—a perfect way to be introduced to the city.

That morning after a breakfast of mushroom quiche and wild strawberries from her garden, Marina had kicked Nadia out of the house, telling her that she didn't want her hiding up in the attic all day. Nadia had a strong suspicion that her grandmother was reading her mind again; that was exactly what she had planned on doing.

On her way out, Nadia had seen Thomas skulking outside the wards in front of the weathered Victorian. He had been pacing back and forth like an impatient suitor, which would have been comical if Nadia had been in the mood to deal with him. Instead, she had slipped out the back door. Marina had told Nadia that she had wards and seals up around the house to keep demons and other unwanted creatures out of her property and had shown her how to sense the boundary line outside. If Nadia squinted and tilted her head at just the right angle, she could barely make out a dome of shining fractal patterns and woven occult symbols that undulated slightly like heat waves on pavement around the house, a slight ringing in her ears as her perception lined up to reveal the shields. Marina assured her that soon, it would all come as second nature.

In fact, the more Nadia practiced, the better she was getting at sensing magic. After Thomas returned her powers, the floodgates had been opened and they were growing with a vengeance. Even after one day of Marina's tenuous guidance, she felt more in control of herself and her body. Magic rippled through her blood, a powerful undercurrent ebbing and flowing with her emotion and mood.

She smiled to herself, reveling in the power, feeling a small sense of self-righteousness and entitlement. She had been tried and tested and had come out the other side unscathed! And then, as quickly as her pride came, it evaporated as she brushed by a husky man wearing a bowler hat. She blanched, realizing he was an ogre-like creature.

Nadia ducked into the nearest doorway to escape. Her heart pounded in her chest. Painted above the door was the same symbol as on Marina's front door. She rushed inside. A bell jangled. She removed her sunglasses, her eyes adjusting to the dark interior. Lines and squares and shapes started to appear. The air was thick with the musty smell of old paper: a used bookstore. Perched on a large piece of driftwood in the window, a Komodo dragon watched her. Its pink tongue flicked in and out.

"Welcome to This Mortal Coil," said a voice. For a second, Nadia thought the giant lizard was talking to her. But the voice belonged to the man at the cash register with tanned skin and a dark pointed beard. He gestured to the shelves of books. "Please, let me know if I can help you find anything."

His image flashed in her mind's eye as Nadia pierced his glamour. A small set of golden horns poked out from his mass of tangled curls. She guessed he was a satyr from his appearance, though she hadn't seen any hooves. Yet.

Nadia ducked her head. "Thanks," she mumbled.

She took several deep breaths, calming herself. After a minute, she felt more in control. She started browsing the books, occasionally glancing toward the man at the counter, like he might explode or go full goat on her. He hummed to himself as he worked, a melancholy tune reminiscent of Greek temples and pan pipes.

In the "zine" section, Nadia found a small chapbook of what could only be Numinal poetry, the few poems she skimmed full of references to various mythical animals and creatures. Nadia tried not to stare at the Numinal man as he rang up her purchase, instead reading the newspaper headlines along the rack in front of the counter.

The *San Francisco Chronicle* caught her eye. "Violence on the Rise." Nadia picked up the newspaper, trying to look normal.

"At least it's not vampires, like in Santa Cruz," said the man.

Nadia glanced up quickly. "What do you mean?"

He handed her back her credit card. "Demons. They are easier to deal with than those rabid bloodsuckers."

The man must have seen the shocked expression on her face because he looked at her strangely. "You're a Sixer, aren't you? I know you can see me. You have that look in your eye."

Nadia grabbed the chapbook and shoved it into her purse, giving the man a weak smile as she rushed out of the store. Once back outdoors in the daylight, Nadia hurried along the street, weaving in and out of other pedestrians on the sidewalk as they meandered along. She tried to push the strange encounter with the satyr out of her mind, but she couldn't stop thinking about what the man had said about demon attacks. Marina hadn't warned her about it being unsafe to walk around the city.

Nadia stopped to buy an overpriced pour-over coffee. While she waited for the barista to make it, she pulled out the chapbook and opened it to a random page.

A Perfect Circle
By F.C. Suri

A perfect circle does not exist here
Except in our minds
Incomprehensible Numinous
The closest is the circle her mouth makes
When she comes

I would die a thousand times over
For that feeling of being complete
Cut off from home
Life on Earth is but a pale shadow
I crave your essence

Sometimes I close my eyes and pretend
I am whole
A perfect circle, no beginning, no end
I am beyond time, beyond space
A ring that I reach for but can never grasp

After she got her coffee, Nadia continued on as she thought about the words she had just read. The sentiments in the poem resonated with her. Maybe she wasn't so different from Numinals after all. Maybe their worlds weren't so far apart. Maybe she could not only handle the hand she'd been dealt but maybe she could even play it well. Maybe everything happens for a reason, and there was some great, big life for her out there, filled with love, laughter, happiness, and magic. Big magic.

Nadia stopped for a moment at Valencia and Twentieth Street to glance at her reflection in a store window. She was wearing a white blouse tucked into denim shorts, with ankle booties and a black fedora. Her dark hair tumbled down her back in glossy waves. Her mother had always told her that she should look her best even in the face of adversity. She lowered her large sunglasses to check out the window display.

In the reflection, she caught the eye of a cute guy riding a bike. He smiled and winked at her as he passed. Maybe San Francisco wasn't so bad after all, even with demons and vampires and lord knows what else around. She smiled inwardly and added a little extra oomph into her step, her hips swaying as she strutted down the street.

And then she ran smack into Thomas.

"Jesus Fucking Christ!" Nadia jolted at the collision and spilled hot coffee all over her pristine white blouse.

"Good to see you too, darling," he purred. "I've missed you. If I didn't know any better, I would think you're avoiding me."

"If I knew a way to avoid you," Nadia muttered darkly, "I would have done it already."

"Touché."

Nadia looked around for a napkin and spied one in a nearby taco shop. Thomas watched in amusement as Nadia grabbed a handful of napkins from the dispenser on the table and dabbed in vain at the giant blotch on her boob.

"What do you want, Thomas? I don't have all day." Nadia crossed her arms, giving up on the stain.

Thomas was dressed differently than before. Instead of looking like some sort of Victorian dandy or demonic Liberace, he was wearing a black T-shirt and jeans, with a silver chain hanging around his neck. He looked like a Vegas street magician. Nadia wondered if others could see him.

He smiled coyly, like he could read her mind. She quickly put up shields like Marina had taught her.

"Don't worry. I'm a normal boy today."

"Get on with it," she hissed.

Thomas smiled, revealing his small fangs. "Mercurio requests your presence. He has a favor to ask of you."

"What if I don't want to do him any favors?" she snapped. She glanced down at her ruined shirt.

Suddenly, Thomas slammed her up against the side of a brick building. The back of her head hit the wall and her teeth clacked together painfully. He grabbed her by the collar of her coffee-stained blouse.

"Hey, what the fuck!" she shouted. Two girls gave her a strange look as they walked past. Thomas must have gone into invisible mode. She looked like a coffee-stained crazy person throwing herself against walls and screaming to herself. Wonderful.

"Do I have to remind you of the consequences with another nocturnal visit?" he asked in a low, steady voice.

Nadia squirmed against the wall, twisting back and forth, and tried to break free. "Get off me! Marina has wards and seals around the house, so you can't get in anyway."

A slow, disturbing smile broke over his face. "Those can be broken."

"Get. The. Fuck. Off. Of. Me." Nadia wrenched free with a twist, glaring at him as she smoothed down her clothes. He popped back into corporeal existence and offered her his arm like a gentleman.

"Walk with me."

"No."

"Stop being a childish bore."

"Stop being an insufferable creep."

"If you don't take my arm, I won't tell you what Mercurio's special plan is for you."

She sucked in her breath. He had her there. She needed to know more about Mercurio and what he had in store for her if she was to survive it.

"Fine." Nadia linked her arm with Thomas's, scrunching her nose up in disgust like she was being forced to deal with something highly unsavory.

"You know the startup, Myst?" Thomas looked down at her with a grin on his face, like a cat that had gotten the cream.

"The company that made the smartwatch?"

"The very one," said Thomas. "It's a supernatural startup. It has a wide variety of projects, but it focuses on finding meaningful employment for supernatural beings by finding them work on various consulting projects, odd jobs, and occasional gigs. Helping humanity solve problems through iPhone apps. All that goody-goody 'save the planet through innovation' rubbish that seems to be *en vogue* at the moment."

"Odd jobs and iPhone apps? Like a TaskRabbit for supernatural creatures?"

"Cute. Yes, it employs creatures with special abilities like that Hire-A-Bunny, or whatever you humans call it. There are several supernatural startups in the city. Myst is the largest. They have a couple of apps, some games too. Very popular."

"Okay, so how does this involve me?" Nadia asked as she stepped over a pile of what she hoped was dog feces on the sidewalk.

"Mercurio would like you to get a job at Myst and report back." Thomas stopped at an intersection and let a car drive by before they continued on their walk.

"You want me to be a spy."

"Spy is such a loaded word," said Thomas. "We would merely like you to just observe and report what you see."

"That sounds like a spy to me." Nadia's tone was flat in her ears.

He flashed his fangs and grinned down at her. "I knew there was a reason I liked you, Nadia. You're quick. I like that in humans." He reached his hand over to their locked arms and clamped down on her elbow so she couldn't escape. "Hold on, please."

And with that, they were teleported across town.

One minute they were in the Mission District, and the next, they were outside a large grey warehouse with tall glass windows at the corner of Eighth and Folsom Streets.

"I think I'm going to throw up." Nadia lurched backward, her stomach rising to her throat. Thomas caught her and steadied her on her feet.

"Breathe. Watch me," he said, taking her by the shoulders and breathing deeply. She didn't want to look him square in the eyes like that. It was too weird, too intimate. Instead, she closed her eyes and took several deep breaths until the urge to vomit had passed. She wished this were all just a bad dream.

"Okay, that's good. One, two, three, deep breaths. Now there. Better?" he asked. He actually looked concerned for her.

She took a step back as soon as the nausea had passed. "What the hell did you just do to me?"

He looked cocky, a smug smile on his face. Nadia wanted to punch it off of him.

"Public transportation is so tedious. I merely hastened our journey."

"By teleporting me? You could have warned me!" Nadia was tempted to flag down one of the passing cars and try to escape. She was in fight-or-flight mode, her senses heightened, her muscles tense. The sidewalk smelled like urine. The sound of the rushing traffic was deafening. Across the street, a homeless man sat on the sidewalk next to a shopping cart full of blankets and electronics, watching them. Nadia wondered if he had seen them suddenly appear.

"We call it folding. Some Numinals can fold space to move quickly through it. And if I had warned you, it wouldn't be as much fun for me, would it? Now"—he grabbed her wrist and snuffed out any chance she had of running away—"Mercurio would like an audience with you."

Thomas led her through the protective wards circling the building and stopped before an unmarked metal door. He pushed it open, revealing a dimly lit flight of stairs, and dragged her through, keeping a firm grip on her as he walked quickly down the steps. At the bottom, they entered a warehouse nightclub called Alchemy—its name glowed from a red neon sign behind the bar. As the club wasn't yet open, the overhead lights were on, exposing a large empty dance floor flanked by corrugated metal and unfinished wooden beams. The club had an industrial, bondage vibe, with cages for go-go dancers hanging from the tall ceiling and stripper poles jutting up from the center of elevated platforms.

Thomas pulled Nadia across the empty dance floor, her heart pounding. She looked up at the lofty ceiling. A matrix of strange tubes and pipes and wires crisscrossed across the top before disappearing into the wall. Behind the bar, a grizzled bartender with curved black horns and leathery bat wings wiped down the counter with a dirty rag, a cigarette hanging loosely out of his mouth. He looked up at the sound of their footsteps across the empty room and nodded his head in greeting at Thomas. Nadia felt a strange sense of detachment. The whole thing was surreal. Thomas and Avery kept their glamour on around her, and despite her Sixer ability to sense Numinals, seeing one out in the open like that was unsettling.

Nadia tried to loosen Thomas's grasp on her arm. "Ouch, you're hurting me." She dug in her heels, trying to prolong their time in the club before she had to meet Mercurio. She looked around for an escape.

"Hurry along now." He wrapped an arm around her shoulders as he pushed her toward the back. "Mercurio waits."

The warehouse in the back was dimly lit, with tall ceilings and rows of crates and boxes organized off to the side on industrial pallet racks. A few workers were moving boxes out of a semi, loading them onto dollies and small forklifts while a dozen or so creatures sat or stood around a long baroque dining table. A yellow Lamborghini, a red Ferrari, and several other turbo-charged classic cars were parked in a circle behind them. It was like stepping onto the set of *The Fast and the Furious*.

Conversation came to a halt. All eyes turned to them. Nadia felt like a tropical fish in an aquarium, on display for everyone to see. About half the men and women gathered at the table were Numinals, their glamours lowered to reveal horns and tails. If they had all been human, they would have been a strange mash-up of DJ types, jail-hardened criminals, used car salesmen, Mafioso-looking guys, supermodels, and tech groupies. Nadia caught flashes of fangs and filed teeth, teardrop tattoos and brass knuckles, iPhones and Beats headphones.

One of the Mafioso types, sitting in a baroque throne chair at the head of the table, stood out as the boss. Mercurio. There was something magnetic about him. Dark, elegant, and old-worldly, he exuded a sense of quiet power, dressed in a simple black button-down shirt with the sleeves rolled up. He looked to be in his early forties, but it was hard to tell; there was no grey in his chin-length dark hair. His face was unlined, his mouth a cruel smirk. A woman wearing leather leaned in and said something to him and he laughed, his sharp canines flashing in the low light. Despite his easy manner, something was rippling under the surface, like he could easily snap at any second.

Thomas pushed her to the table, one hand on either of her shoulders, as Mercurio looked her up and down. Nadia was suddenly self-conscious of the coffee stain on her blouse. Instinctually, she leaned in closer to Thomas. Not really a palatable option, but he was the lesser of two evils and would have to do. Thomas squeezed her shoulders as if he was reassuring her that everything was going to be okay.

"What do you want, Drake?" asked Mercurio. He had a faint Eastern European accent. His voice was full of disdain.

"My Lord," said Thomas. "May I present Nadia Winters?" He

said it like he was giving a gift to a king, waiting for approval for the offering. A couple of the others around the table sniggered.

"Who?"

Thomas cleared his throat. "My Lord, if you recall, this is the one I recovered for you. To be placed at Myst. The pretty one?" Nadia stiffened. What did her looks have to do with anything?

Mercurio nodded slowly, like he was remembering, and stood up. Moving with preternatural speed, he was suddenly in front of her.

Nadia tried to keep her eyes lowered—vampires hypnotize their victims, right? She tried to focus on his black leather pants and expensive Italian leather shoes, but he lifted her chin with the crook of his finger and inspected her face, turning it to catch the light like she was a doll—or, more aptly, a slave he had just purchased at auction. She couldn't tear her gaze from his face. His eyes were cold inky pools. Power rolled off him in heady waves. Nadia didn't dare breathe. Her heart pounded, a heavy drum. She was sure he could hear it, her pathetic mortality ripe for the taking.

He dropped his hand. "Ah yes. I remember now. She is very pretty, like you said, Thomas. I think she will do nicely." Mercurio smiled at her, like he suddenly remembered he was supposed to be pleasant and sociable and not deathly terrifying. He wrapped an arm around her shoulder. Nadia flinched. A look of hurt crossed his face.

"I'd like to be friends, Nadia." He said her name with a lover's tenderness. "I like to be friends with all my employees. Wouldn't you like that?"

Nadia nodded, her mouth dry. Part of her wanted to run. The other part of her basked in the attention he was giving her. Maybe it was the knowledge that he controlled her fate, maybe he was using some sort of vampire magic, but Nadia found herself strangely drawn to Mercurio.

"I'd like to show you something." He led her over to the tall aisles of crates and boxes. Thomas followed them at a respectful distance, looking smug.

They stopped halfway down one of the rows. Mercurio snapped and pointed at a crate. His gold and ruby pinky ring gleamed. The nearest demon worker handed Mercurio a small wooden box and scuttled back, bowing his head in fear. Mercurio slid the lid off and held the box out. Inside was a pale-blue gemstone, about the size of a goose egg, in a bed of fine salt. Mercurio plucked the gem out, blew on it to clear the salt, and held it to the light.

"This is a Resonance Stone. It amplifies and clarifies frequencies of energy."

Nadia wasn't sure why he was showing her this. She looked to Thomas for help, but he held up a finger to her and answered his cell phone. She was on her own.

"What is it used for?" Nadia's voice sounded more confident than she felt.

Mercurio looked delighted at her question. "Ah, well, I have many clients with very unusual tastes. Resonance Stones can read and distill those specific . . . essences. It's all very complicated. Pretty, isn't it? Here, hold it for a minute." He placed the gem into her hand. It vibrated slightly, warming to her touch.

"Myst is working on an augmented reality technology in one of their mobile games—I believe it's called Veil—that could disrupt my current business model," said Mercurio. "I need you to just keep an eye on everything there. Let me know where this technology is headed. I've heard that it can cast a spell around a creature to pierce their glamour, and I need to know how that works. All you have to do is simply report back to Thomas. He will relay any pertinent information to me. You can do that, can't you?"

Nadia didn't want to nod, but she forced herself to. The gem turned murky brown.

Mercurio's face changed for a split second, and Nadia glimpsed his inhuman nature lurking beneath the surface. Blue veins ran under his pale skin, his cheekbones high and pronounced. Fingernails pointed into claws.

Mercurio's dark eyes bore into hers. He licked the tip of one of his fangs. Nadia thought he might bite her.

"The Resonance Stone can also read a person's frequency," said Mercurio. "Their mood, if you will. It appears you are feeling resistant. Let's change that, shall we?" He smiled an understanding, almost paternal smile and snatched the stone back, tossing the box to a worker.

Mercurio walked back toward the others. Not knowing what else to do, Nadia followed.

He dropped gracefully into his chair and plucked a cigar from the hand of one of the Numinals seated next to him, kicking his feet up on the table. He puffed on the cigar a few times before blowing out the smoke above his face. "You know, I was very disappointed in your grandmother. What's her name?"

"Marina Nichols," called out Thomas as he hurried over.

"Ah, that's right. Marina. I was very disappointed in her for hiding you from me. I'm surprised she had the gumption. Not many people, let alone *mortals*, dare to defy me. And to think, after all these years, how *good* I've been to her. Really, it's remarkable how people take advantage of my generous, kind nature. You give them an inch, and they take a mile." He glanced about himself for confirmation. Mercurio's gang agreed wholeheartedly.

Thomas laughed uneasily. "A wild streak. Nothing that can't be broken and controlled."

"It better be." Mercurio uncorked a crystal bottle on the table and poured himself a drink. He took a sip of the strange dark liquid and swirled the taste around.

"Nadia, I will make you a deal. I am offering you everything your little heart could ever want. I can make all your wildest dreams come true. What do you want? Money? Power? Happiness? A sense of purpose? I can give you all that and more. In return, you give me your obedience. Simple as that. It'll be a win-win for both of us. I don't like employees who don't want to be here. Your mother, if I remember, returned her Septer powers. That's fine. That was her choice. And I want you to have the same choice as well."

Nadia's eyes darted to Thomas. He hadn't made it seem like she had much of one when he came to her bedroom in the middle of the night and had his demon lackeys molest her and feed from her.

She leveled her gaze at Mercurio. "I was under the impression that I was a servant, not an employee."

"I prefer the term employee when it comes to those who serve me. But I do need your commitment. We are a team here, and I need all my employees to be team players.

"But I want you to know what you are getting into. There are no tricks here. Just good, old-fashioned loyalty and obedience. Now and again, though, one of my employees steps out of line. Like Thomas here. Thomas, you *lingău!*"—Mercurio looked like he couldn't decide whether he wanted to squash Thomas like a bug or buy him a beer—"I appreciate the enthusiasm, but I'm a little disappointed that you brought her here without my permission. What if I had been in the middle of some important business? Maybe you need a bit of a reminder so that Nadia here doesn't get any ideas about crossing me."

A burly, blue-skinned djinn stood up and raised his palm. Thomas shrank down, falling to his knees. Nadia jumped back, startled.

"Please, My Lord," Thomas begged. "It was a foolish thing to do! I thought it would please you to meet her."

The djinn muttered something, and a blast of energy shot out from his hand. It morphed into a two-headed black asp that slithered toward Thomas and coiled itself up and around him. Thomas screamed and fell to his side as the snake squeezed him, wrapping around his throat, cutting off his air so only gurgles came out. Thomas looked like he was moments away from passing out, twitching and kicking on the floor. His eyes rolled back in his head.

Nadia choked back a sob at the horrible sight and tried to shrink even smaller.

Mercurio flicked two fingers in the air and the djinn released Thomas. The two-headed snake dissipated like smoke. Thomas rolled back and forth on the floor, moaning and clutching his sides while his pallor returned to normal. Nadia had the urge to see if he was okay, to help him from the ground, which was ridiculous. Thomas was on Mercurio's side. He was the one who brought her there. She shouldn't have any sympathy for this cretin bounty hunter who got her into this mess in the first place.

Mercurio smiled. "Just a little test of your loyalty. Don't worry about Thomas. He'll be fine. I just wanted to demonstrate what happens when you misbehave. But you wouldn't do that, would you?"

Nadia felt like she was choking. Her vision narrowed until all else fell away except Mercurio.

"As I said earlier, Nadia, I want you to *want* to be here. I want your full commitment. I want you to be excited to join the team and learn what we are doing here." He waved his hands around at the warehouse. "This, this is just the beginning. I have big plans. You, and all my people, will be part of destiny, my journey. And in the process, you will become wildly rich and famous and powerful. Your work will have meaning. *Real* meaning. Won't that be wonderful?"

He clapped his hands. "Now, I need you to swear allegiance to me. This is one hundred percent your choice right here, okay? You can give back your powers like your mother did, or you can swear allegiance right now. Your grandmother serves me now. We both hope she has a very long, happy life and dies a natural death, don't we? We wouldn't want anything to cut her life short. After all, your grandmother is a crone, past her prime. Her magic wanes. But you, my dear, are still a maiden. Much more powerful and useful to me. But, as I said, this is completely your choice."

Nadia swallowed. *Some choice.*

"Now, Nadia, do you agree to abide by my wishes and do you vow obedience?"

She forced herself to nod.

"In exchange for your obedience, you will have my protection against all Numinals if you need it. And all that happiness and riches stuff, too. But if you don't obey my commands," he said, looking at the demon next to him, "what do you think should be the punishment? How about . . . your firstborn will be mine? A bit Rumpelstiltskin-ish, but why reinvent the wheel, right? Sound okay to you?"

"Yes," said Nadia, her voice barely a whisper. A shudder ran through her.

"Great! Welcome to the team, Nadia," said Mercurio. He took a puff of his cigar. "Thomas will show you out."

CHAPTER 5

Nadia pushed open the red front door to Marina's house and slammed it behind her. She slid the deadbolt into place. Marina and Avery were in the kitchen, and she ran up the creaky wooden stairs to her attic bedroom before they could intercept her and ask how her day was going.

Once in the room, she threw her purse on the bed, a wave of panic rising. Her breath came in shallow gasps. Her nails dug painfully into her palms as she made a fist. She fought back tears. She would not cry. Crying would not solve any problems. She needed to think logically and rationally.

She had vowed allegiance to Mercurio. He had told her it was her choice, but really, she didn't see any other option. His veiled threats against Marina, torturing Thomas, the fact she was bound to Mercurio already and would have to serve him through the Blood Oath. It all led to one conclusion: returning her powers and walking away from Mercurio was not an option, now that she knew demons were real and fed from humans at night. She'd had sleep paralysis before. She needed to protect herself. And if living a life bound to a vampire master was the best way to defend herself, she would do it.

She didn't like the shackles that she had donned, but a life of being fed on at night by creatures in the shadows was not a life of freedom.

It was a literal nightmare.

She thought back on what Mercurio had promised: happiness, money, power. A sense of purpose. It was like he knew exactly what she had been searching for her entire life—like he could sense what made her tick, what got her juices flowing, and played right into it. It was almost ridiculous how easy this decision was for her; of course she would get a job at a supernatural startup that made cool magical gadgets like her watch! It's not like she had anything else going on, now that her New York plan had been derailed. If she had to pass on a bit of information now and then to keep her vampire overlord happy, so be it. Really, she was the victim here, caught up in the web of fate. She didn't have much of a choice in the whole thing. She was doing the best she could, and that's all she could ask for in life, right?

And Mercurio didn't seem *too* bad. Sure, a little terrifying, a little patronizing, but he was a visionary! A powerful business mogul with an empire to maintain and expand. The Steve Jobs and Elon Musks of the world weren't exactly the Mr. Rogers types, themselves. Really, this was a great opportunity for her. She could learn so much from him. It was like a dream internship on world domination.

Nadia pulled out her laptop from her canvas backpack and set it on the bed. She quickly changed out of her coffee-stained blouse and into yoga pants and a tank top before settling in under her freshly washed white duvet. With a strange sense of detachment— she didn't dare get excited about all this yet—she googled Myst and clicked through articles and webpages.

Myst might have been a supernatural startup, but for all intents and purposes, it appeared like any other Bay Area startup. Gizmodo and TechCrunch even profiled it. She clicked through to Myst's website, its iconic M logo—the same one that had been on the packaging of her watch—looking like misty mountains, and browsed around their website. As Nadia would discover, there wasn't much tangible information about what exactly the company *did*. In the "About" section, Myst's description of itself was awfully vague.

WE CREATE INNOVATIVE NEW TECHNOLOGIES
TO SOLVE THE WORLD'S TOUGHEST PROBLEMS.

That sounded promising. She scrolled down.

Myst is a conglomerate that focuses on solving the world's biggest problems by pairing radical new technology with the brightest minds in the world. By using cross-industry innovation and collaboration, Myst harnesses the power of synergy to deliver unique solutions that align with our vision of creating lasting, positive change.

She clicked on the icon for "Explore Our Projects," and the following links appeared:

How can solar panel kites be used to help rural communities?

How can we provide clean, safe drinking water to developing nations?

How can geothermal energy be used to reduce greenhouse gas emissions?

How can we build a self-sustaining, long-term colony on Mars?

How can new technologies incorporate privacy protections against mass surveillance and unlawful data collection?

Impressive. She wasn't aware of too many companies that made it their mission to actually improve the lives of others. Most companies she knew of made token efforts at charity through the occasional donation or sponsorship, but it appeared that philanthropy was core to the values of Myst. Nadia wanted to spend more time learning about the various projects and bookmarked the page to come back to later.

Back on the main page, Nadia scrolled down to one of Myst's divisions.

Myst Labs incubates and fosters new ideas and efforts, like the Developer's Edition Myst Psionic Smartwatch, and Veil, our exciting new augmented reality game that brings the magical and fantastic to life. Myst Labs encourages its inventors to build and launch technology that has a direct impact on humanity's quality of life and advances human potential.

She clicked on the tab for "Explore the Myst Psionic," glancing at her watch as she read.

The Developer's Edition Myst Psionic is not your everyday smartwatch. Using proprietary technology, the watch not only contains core fitness and smartwatch functionality but also monitors mood and emotion to train users in Mindfulness-Based Stress Reduction (MBSR) in a fun, intuitive platform. We get it. Life is stressful. But your smartwatch doesn't have to be.

Under the tab for "Explore Veil," Myst had screenshots of the game. From what Nadia could tell, it looked like users completed various quests in their neighborhood by interacting with magical creatures.

Veil is Myst's new augmented reality game that blends technology and live role-playing for an unbelievably real experience. With the Veil plug-in that works with all smartphones, virtual 3D objects interact and are layered with the physical world, seamlessly blending virtual reality and the real world for a next-level gaming experience that allows users to explore unusual aspects of their community and find the magic in everyday life. Veil is currently in beta testing. Watch for its general release soon!

Back on the main page, Nadia continued to read about Myst Foundation, the charitable arm of Myst.

Myst Foundation supports and curates a large museum collection and prides itself on promoting the understanding and appreciation of art and antiquities. The Foundation focuses on the application of ancient art and technology to modern cultures and issues.

"Wow," mouthed Nadia as she skimmed through Myst Foundation's art collection. With Nadia's art history background, she was well-versed in museum science, and Myst's collection appeared to be extremely extensive. She bookmarked that page to return to later.

At the bottom of the main page, she read the Myst news headlines that linked to blog posts, which included: "Myst Foundation Launches Grant-Giving Program for Technology and the Arts," "CEO Rune Christiansen Recognized at San Francisco Giants Game for Community Efforts," "Myst Pairs with Golden State Warriors and Chan Zuckerberg Initiative to Build New Children's Infectious Disease Ward at UCSF," and "Myst Labs Looking for Game Testers to Beta Test New Augmented Reality Game, 'Veil.'"

At the bottom of the page was a link for "Careers at Myst."

Mystics, as they are referred to here, are an eclectic group of people who share a bright vision for humanity and the future. Our mission is to elevate humankind by using technology in innovative and creative ways. We seek out diverse perspectives and unique backgrounds for our various projects and teams. We don't believe in predefining job roles; instead, we examine how prospective talent can best fit in with the company, and customize each position to the skills, expertise, and interests of the employee to best unlock each employee's potential.

LIKE WHAT YOU SEE? APPLY NOW!

Next to the "Apply Now" button was a picture of a drone taking what looked like medicine and supplies to an impoverished community. Nadia blinked, realizing there was an image within that picture: a virtual palimpsest that was only visible if you pierced the glamour magically hiding the image underneath. She squinted, sensing the image of Leonardo da Vinci's *Vitruvian Man*.

Nadia took a deep breath, chewing on her bottom lip. On one hand, with its commitment to philanthropy, art, and innovation, working at Myst would be a dream come true. Even if it didn't work out in the long run, it could be a stepping stone for her to get back to her old life and move to New York. But on the other hand, Mercurio wanted her to spy for him and pass on insider details about Myst, something that she knew was morally wrong. She quickly scrolled back through the pages once again, but by then, her mind was made up. She knew what she had to do: she would get the job at Myst but figure out a way to keep Mercurio at bay.

Shaking slightly from both excitement and nervousness, her Psionic pinging at her shift in mood, Nadia quickly wrote a cover letter that highlighted her internship experience with auction houses and museums and tied her interest in the position to match Myst's vision and mission statement. Then, she uploaded her already-prepared resume and the cover letter to the application portal, after answering several essay-style questions and prompts that included "Describe your career ambitions and reason you want to work at Myst"; "Who do you most admire and why?"; and "Explain a moment in your life that you failed and what you learned from it."

The very last question on the application was: "Explain the symbolism of the image on the job portal as it relates to Myst's vision." This had to be the question they used to weed out normal humans from Sixers and Numinals.

Her hands shook as she wrote her answer:

Leonardo da Vinci's Vitruvian Man *is a symbol of the marriage of science, technology, and art. The image symbolizes the embodiment of humanity and human potential, a body in peak physical condition, exhibiting perfect symmetry. The workings of the human body are a symbol of the workings of the universe. It is a fractal based on the Golden Ratio. This relates to Myst's vision that local action leads to global reactions. Like the flapping of the wings of a butterfly, a tiny, seemingly inconsequential action sends ripples out to the world and can cause monumental change. As above, so below.*

She hit the final "Submit" button before she could stop herself and doubt her answers. She closed her laptop and exhaled a deep breath.

Having a mission, a tangible goal to get the job at Myst, helped. Nadia's hands were no longer shaking.

"If you are a supernatural or magical creature or whatever," Nadia asked Avery a bit later, "then what *are* you exactly? You have wings. Does that make you a faerie?"

They were sitting around the kitchen table. Half-empty take-out containers and fortune cookies littered the wooden picnic table in the candle-lit, farmhouse-style room. All around them, pots and pans and bottles filled with strange liquids and pickled items lined the cupboards. Bundles of rosemary, thyme, and other herbs hung from drying racks. Baskets, bowls, and jars of spices and other ingredients like rattlesnake and scorpion tails were haphazardly thrown on the shelves in no discernable order.

Avery gave Nadia a contemptuous look. "It's a bit rude to make generalized assumptions from one's appearance. Didn't your mother ever teach you manners?"

"Avery," warned Marina.

He rolled his eyes. "Fine. I am High Fae. One of the Seelie, if you insist on labels."

"Seelie," Nadia echoed.

"Yes, Seelie. Faeries. The Fair Folk. Tinkerbelle. Any of this ringing a bell?"

Nadia narrowed her eyes. She focused, barely able to discern Avery's real appearance underneath his glamour. "No need to get snarky. I know who the Seelie are." Nadia had done her fair share of reading on Ancient Celtic myths and legends during an art history and mythology class in college. While it had been a while, she remembered learning about races of mythical creatures, including the Seelie and Unseelie.

Myth-ical being the operative word. Or at least, she had thought it was.

"Okay, so what other mythical creatures—Numinals—are there?" asked Nadia. Her mind spun. She hoped they would say Pegasi. During Halloween dressage shows, she'd always dressed up her pony Skyfire with wings.

Marina dumped more lo mein onto her plate before offering the container to Nadia, who declined. "Well, Thomas is a demon. Mercurio is a *strigoi*, a vampire from the old country. Avery here is Seelie. But there are numerous other species of Numinals. All myths have their origin in truth, in some form or another. They all stem from the Numinous."

Nadia shook her head. She still didn't understand.

Avery looked like he was losing his patience at having to explain everything. "Numinals are named for their connection to the source of magical power and energy in the universe, the Numinous. San Francisco has an especially large Numinal population."

"Why here?" Nadia cracked open a fortune cookie: *A ship in a harbor is safe, but that's not why ships were built.*

Marina shrugged. "San Francisco is an informal test city, a sort of experiment for Numinals and humans to live together in a symbiotic relationship. San Francisco has a big enough counterculture that they blend in easily. Humans turn a blind eye to strange things they see. Chalk it up to the Burning Man community, street kids on Haight, the homeless population. In return, Numinals inspire technological advancement and creativity. A lot of Numinals work in the tech industry."

"Mythological creatures working in tech? This is, like, the biggest kept secret in all humanity or something."

Avery drummed his fingers on the arm of his chair. "It's one of them."

Nadia sat back, her mind reeling.

"San Francisco has always had ties to the occult and magic," continued Marina. "It was practically built for Numinals and Septers to tap into their magic and the Source, with so many ley lines that cross through the Bay Area. It isn't a coincidence that the city is seven square miles by seven square miles—the city was originally built on seven hills, seven mounds of power. Seven is a very magical number."

"Is that why you moved here? To enhance your power?"

A smile crossed Marina's face like she was remembering a fond memory. "No, I came to San Francisco in the Summer of Love, in '67, when I was seventeen. I had run away from home, determined to get the last bit of living that I could before I had to serve Mercurio. He wasn't based in San Francisco yet. I was in a band. We drove around the country in a beat-up VW van. It was the best time of my life."

Nadia couldn't help but grin. "I saw those pictures in the living room of you singing."

"Yep. We sure knew how to rock it. We weren't very good, but man, did we have spirit."

"Do you still sing?" asked Nadia.

"No, no. That's all behind me."

"She has an amazing voice," cut in Avery. He looked angelic, a halo of light pouring from him as he looked at Marina. Marina gave him a doting smile back. The cat jumped on the table, bumping into Avery's arm with a purr, like she wanted to join the love.

"You said earlier that you never advanced your Septer abilities. Why not?" asked Nadia, interrupting their moment.

"I will teach you everything I can," said Marina, "but I just never had much of an aptitude for it. Sure, I know the basics . . . wards, charms, a bit of defensive magic and hexing, and I can do some pretty useful party tricks . . . mix up a decent margarita, string lights in the trees, self-rolling joints, that sort of thing. But I only ever learned the things that I needed. I lived a pretty good life, Nadia. I never felt the need for more."

Nadia shook her head. That idea was foreign to her. She couldn't understand why Marina wouldn't want to learn everything she could about magic. She was capable of so much more. Nadia would never settle for average—not when she could be *extraordinary*.

"A lot of the spells that were passed down through my coven have become moot, anyway," added Marina. "You don't need a spell to make fire when you can have a lighter that works just as quickly . . . *and* doesn't drain your energy. You don't need a spell to send a message to someone when you can just text or email. Some sorcerers still invent new spells to do more complex and specific things, but honestly, I've heard that those spells are so convoluted and layered that often it's more hassle than it's worth to cast them. That's my two cents on it. You should, of course, figure out what type of magic interests you and pursue that. I've always been drawn to healing magic and herbal spells, myself."

"So," Nadia asked, "what sorts of things does Mercurio make you do? Does he make you do healing magic?" She hoped that her grandmother wasn't about to divulge anything about sex cults. Mercurio had made servitude seem more like a corporate team-building exercise than anything else.

"Well, Mercurio is a very powerful *strigoi*—a vampire. He's very rich and famous in the Numinal community. Over the centuries, he's amassed quite the empire. He owns several properties around the Bay and is involved in numerous business ventures. But fortunately, he mostly leaves me be. Since I don't have very advanced Septer abilities, I'm not very useful to him. It's been about five years since he's called on me. Now and then someone like Thomas checks in or tasks me with various spells or rituals that require knowledge of witchcraft as opposed to some type of Numinal magic."

"What's the difference? Isn't all magic the same?"

Marina shook her head.

"Some Numinals have magic," said Avery, "and some merely *are* magic. For the Numinals who have magical abilities, each kind of magic is like a different language. Witchcraft is like the human translation for Sixers and Septers, but most Sixers have no idea what they're doing."

"Thomas told me once that Mercurio didn't want to be associated with the Blood Oath," said Marina. "I got the impression that using witchcraft and calling on humans to do Numinal bidding is somewhat looked down on in their community nowadays." That made sense. Mercurio had acted like he wanted to keep Nadia in his back pocket, not overtly call on her daily.

But Nadia still felt like she wasn't getting the entire picture. That feeling niggled at her brain. "But he can just order me to do whatever he wants, right? Because of the Oath?"

"Well, technically, you won't serve him until I die," said Marina. "You can't be compelled until the Oath passes to you."

"Wait, what?" Nadia exploded, jerking forward and hitting her knee on the side of the table. She winced, rubbing the sore spot. She had vowed obedience to him. Did that mean she could have waited? Could have delayed the inevitable for a while?

Marina's expression softened. "He still controls the Oath that binds our family, even if it hasn't passed to you yet. I tried to shield you, to hide you from him. But they found you. Mercurio has a network of demons like Thomas working for him. Thomas is more or less harmless. An annoying lackey that gets sent around to do Mercurio's bidding."

"He's like a cockroach," Avery added. "Always scuttling around in the shadows."

"I'm not sure how he managed to find you, but in any event, you undid my binding spell without any formal training or knowledge of spellcasting, proving your innate power and value to Mercurio as a Septer. It would be impressive if it wasn't so unfortunate."

"Lucky me," Nadia muttered.

Avery floated a fortune cookie toward himself. It unwrapped itself in the air and then broke in two with invisible hands. "Nadia, you need training. Not learning about your abilities for twenty-three years might have allowed you to have a normal life until now, but it also hindered you. You shouldn't have been able to undo that binding spell, but you did. We need to teach you to control your powers before you mess something else up. You're a loose cannon and a liability."

"Well, good thing I have the watch to help me then," Nadia said tightly. "Oh, by the way, I applied for a job there. At Myst."

Marina nodded encouragingly. "Oh? Why there?"

Nadia shrugged, trying to look nonchalant. "It looks like a cool place to work."

CHAPTER 6

Myst's headquarters were located on the San Francisco Bay in an industrial warehouse on Pier 70. The enormous brick front of the building, punctuated by several arched windows, rose to meet a pitched roof. Despite the hustle and bustle surrounding it, the massive multistory brick-and-steel warehouse with its large reflective glass window siding—some broken and covered in soot, grime, and graffiti—looked abandoned. It definitely didn't look like the type of building to house a tech startup run by Numinals.

Nadia stood in front of the building and glanced about herself. Moms jogged on the sidewalk pushing baby strollers. People walked their dogs down the street. No one gave the building a second glance. Nadia realized that the building was magically glamoured and warded to not draw attention to itself and to keep people away. Even the squawking seagulls overhead seemed to avoid the building. If Nadia squinted and turned her head slightly, she could see the wards. They looked like the ones around Marina's house but far more complex. Golden alchemical symbols, shimmering in the light of the late-morning sun, sat in a faint, fractal web around the building like a geodesic dome. Even though it seemed to repel people away, Nadia didn't have a problem crossing the boundary line once she sensed where it was.

Only two days ago, Nadia had sent her resume to Myst. The next morning, she received a phone call inviting her in for an aptitude test and interview. The HR manager had been thrilled with her art history background and cataloging experience. Apparently, the director in charge of Myst's antiquities and library collection was leaving soon, and they were eager to find a replacement, even temporarily, to carry on day-to-day activities.

The position would focus on maintaining Myst Foundation's extensive collection, as well as working with other departments to help them use the antiquities and knowledge from the library in their projects. The HR manager had also subtly asked about Nadia's powers as a witch—probably part of the initial screening process. After it had been established that Nadia was a Sixer, the HR manager told her that Myst only hired humans who had Sixer abilities. Nadia hadn't told the woman about her Septer abilities; she was too new to it all, too unsure about her newfound skills to broadcast those powers to a potential employer.

After her Lyft had dropped her at Pier 70, it had taken Nadia about ten minutes to find Myst's headquarters. The building was entirely devoid of signage, apart from a sacred geometry symbol etched into the wall above the door: a circle with a blossoming fractal center like the one on Marina's front door and the one that had been above the doorway to the bookstore with the satyr. Nadia suspected that it was a symbol for the Numinous: the God power of the universe. A secret glyph to tell people that the building was a Numinal-safe zone. The only indication that she was at the right place was Myst's mountain logo painted on the front door below the symbol.

Nadia rang the buzzer. A short gruff security guard answered. He peered out from behind the heavy metal door, and she sensed he was a Numinal. His glamour shimmered in her vision. He looked like a bridge troll, his face wrinkling, his nose changing shape into something looking like a lumpy potato. His name tag, pinned to the front of his rumpled uniform, read "Arne." It was not visible without piercing through his glamour with Sixer abilities.

He stared at her without expression.

"Is this Myst?" Nadia asked. "I'm here for a test and an interview."

"ID," he demanded. Nadia fished out her wallet from her bag and handed him her driver's license. He inspected it as he checked something on his phone. Satisfied that she had an appointment, he pushed the door open and let her enter.

Nadia walked into an antechamber. A security desk sat in the corner of an otherwise bare part of the industrial warehouse. Nadia followed the guard to a small plain room off to the side.

A test packet and pencil were lying on a small elementary school desk in the center of the room. The guard ushered her inside, grunted at the packet, and slammed the door, leaving her alone in the windowless space. Nadia looked around. She was sure they were watching her.

Nadia was no stranger to standardized testing. Her academic career was liberally sprinkled with all sorts of exams, ranging from admissions tests to prep schools, the SATs, various APs, and even the LSAT when she briefly considered going to law school before she decided that was a horrible idea. She took a seat at the desk and picked up the paper, scanning the questions. It appeared to be a logic or IQ test mixed with a personality test, focusing on game theory, critical thinking, and psychological assessment. She picked up the pencil and started answering the questions.

There was only one question that appeared to measure Sixer ability: *What was the security guard's name?* She wrote Arne on the line provided.

After about thirty minutes, she reached the last question, filled in the bubble, and put down her pencil. She wondered if she should somehow signal she was finished. After a few moments, Arne returned, furthering her impression they had been watching her. He grabbed the test and left again. Nadia waited patiently at the small school desk, her hands clasped in front of her, until he came back several minutes later.

"Okay, you passed. Come with me." He beckoned her with a lumpy hand. She grabbed her purse and quickly walked after him. Her heels clicked on the concrete as she hurried to catch up. He led her back through the antechamber to a secure door next to the security guard station, scanned his keycard, and opened the door to the lobby.

A woman looked up from behind a large desk. The Myst sign and logo were prominently displayed behind her on a partition with blue and purple lights. Over the sound system, an electronic downtempo song played. The strong beat thumped out in time to the pulsing multicolored LED light canopy on the ceiling. Arne led Nadia through the waiting area around mid-century modern leather couches and chairs and past eclectic abstract art on the walls. Next to the front desk was a magnolia tree in a large pot, the blossoms giving the room a pungent, floral smell.

"She passed," said Arne gruffly as they stopped in front of the desk. He handed the striking blonde receptionist the test. Nadia sensed she was a Numinal as well—a type of sexy nymph creature if Nadia had to guess. Normal humans definitely weren't born with those Kate Moss cheekbones.

"Wonderful! I'll let Vega know. Thanks, Arne," said the nymph.

Arne turned to Nadia, grunted, and walked away.

The receptionist pushed a button on her Bluetooth headset. "Vega? It's Anya. I have," she said, reading Nadia's name from the top of the test, "a 'Nadia Winters' here. Yes. She passed. Okay. Great. I'll bring her to you."

Anya handed Nadia a guest badge and walked around the desk, revealing golden-tan legs in a red leather mini skirt. She showed off a dazzling smile. "Ready?" She motioned for Nadia to follow her around the partition and down the hall.

Nadia gasped as they entered the main floor.

The space was huge, even bigger than it had looked from the outside. There was some sort of spatial trickery going on to make the inside larger than the outside. About sixty or so employees—mostly magical creatures interspersed with a few Sixer humans—bustled around the open coworking spaces on the floor, holding team meetings and going over specs. Some Numinals still had their glamours on, but many of them were freely exposed, revealing their true form. A troupe of tiny green faeries trailing pixie dust flew over Nadia's head, startling her. A garden gnome in a pointy red hat argued with a banshee with long white hair that floated up around her face like she was underwater, the banshee's voice rising to shrieking levels as they debated something about a WishSeed app, which Nadia realized must be the app she had described to Thomas as a TaskRabbit for magical creatures.

Anya led Nadia around the first floor's perimeter. Glass-encased conference rooms and offices lined the sides adjacent to the open floor in the main area. In the back, a giant steel staircase wound up from the first floor to the second-floor balcony that lined the perimeter of the space. Nadia was surrounded by faeries with bright, translucent wings, squat goblins with large pointy ears, shifters that were half-changed into animals, sprites and elementals with bodies that dissolved into the air as they moved, and centaurs with mohawks and dreadlocks wearing Hawaiian shirts. Nadia fought the urge to stare and tried to keep her face impassive like it was every day she saw this many supernatural creatures in an office environment, battling copy machines, playing foosball, and typing away at laptops, but her head swiveled left and right as she tried to take everything in.

One corner of the main floor had a café and lounge area next to a huge indoor oak tree that was crawling with goblin-like creatures serving up snacks and drinks. Employees sat at tables and on bean bag chairs eating lunch, while others played foosball and ping pong in a gaming area lined with retro arcade machines. On the wall, giant flat-screen TVs alternated news broadcasts with calming images of nature and sacred geometry. Over the sound system, the music changed to a chillwave electronic song. Several employees started dancing as they worked at stand-up desks. Others bobbed their heads as they sat in front of their laptops. A harlequin wearing a cream-colored suit and rose-tinted sunglasses looked up and flashed her a peace sign as she passed. Nadia grinned, flashing him the sign back.

A giant mural covered an entire wall on the ground floor, and Nadia stopped for a second to admire it. It was like a Hieronymus Bosch / street art mash-up, complete with graffiti goddesses, immortal deities, and the battle between good and evil playing out in a vibrant tapestry of reds, purples, golds, and blues.

Anya noticed Nadia's head swiveling about as she tried to look at everything. She chuckled. "Sixers always lose their minds the first time they come here."

"How big is this place? It doesn't look like all this could fit in here from the outside."

"Bigger than you would think. There are several floors underneath this one as well, where the innovation lab and vaults are located."

Nadia hurried to catch up with Anya's long strides. "Do non-Sixers ever come inside? I think they might notice this isn't exactly your normal work environment."

"Oh, sure. But we warn all the employees over the Godspeaker so they can put their glamours on before a muggle enters."

"You actually call them muggles?" Nadia asked. Anya laughed.

They climbed the giant metal staircase to the second floor, and Anya led Nadia to one of the glass-walled conference rooms that lined the perimeter.

A kind-looking woman in her fifties, with a mane of dark unruly curls loosely pinned up on top of her head, rose to her feet when they entered, a set of tiny translucent wings vibrating behind her. She was wearing a pink pantsuit and floral neck scarf, which made her look vaguely like a real estate agent. She floated over and shook Nadia's hand warmly, giving off a distinct "house mom" vibe.

"You must be Nadia. Please, take a seat," she said with a benevolent fairy godmother smile, gesturing at one of the chairs around the conference room table. "I'm Vega, the HR manager. We spoke on the phone a few days ago." Tattoos peeked out from under her jacket sleeves as the woman sat down and clasped her hands. Nadia took a seat, poised on the edge of the chair with perfect posture, and folded her hands in her lap.

"Well, to start off," said Vega, "I'd like to congratulate you on passing Myst's aptitude test. We know it wasn't easy. But as I mentioned, we only hire humans for full-time positions if they have Sixer abilities and if we think they would be a good fit for the unique personality of the company."

Vega shifted around some papers in front of her. She held up a pair of gold-rimmed spectacles to her face as she read from one of the sheets. "As I told you on the phone, your background is exactly what we're looking for at the moment. Imogen McKenna, the director of Myst Foundation, is returning to Dublin at the end of summer. We're planning on finding a long-term replacement, but for now, we need someone to oversee the daily functions of the collection."

"Well, as I noted in my resume, I have extensive cataloging experience with various museums and auction houses." Nadia leaned forward, trying to look eager and intent. "It's a passion of mine, as crazy as that sounds. I just love finding the proper home for pieces in a collection."

Vega nodded approvingly. "Your most recent position after you graduated wasn't in the arts, though. Why the shift?"

Nadia took a deep breath. "My experience in the arts was all unpaid internships. There aren't a lot of paid positions, and most of the time, you have to continue as an intern until a position opens.

I would have loved to get a job working for a museum or gallery, but I didn't have that option with student loans and bills to pay. I always intended to pivot back." Nadia didn't mention that she could have continued as an intern, taking the money her father had offered her when she graduated. But she had wanted to prove that she didn't need him and could make it without his help or the strings that came with it.

"Understandable. I myself took many strange jobs over the years until I found a career at Myst," Vega said with a sympathetic smile. "Are you familiar with Myst's onboarding structure? New employees come on as 'Unassigned.' After working on several projects and with different departments, we develop a position and title that is customized to their interests and skills. It looks like you have some experience interacting with artists?" Vega picked up her glasses again and squinted at the resume.

"I interned one semester during school for a gallery in Virginia Beach. The owner had a very collaborative approach to running the gallery. I helped a lot with artist management and cultivating relationships with not only the clients but with the artists as well. It was very . . . illuminating to learn the people side of running a gallery."

Vega's tiny wings fluttered behind her. "Excellent. Our VP of talent management is looking for an assistant on some upcoming projects and that could be a good fit for you as well as with the Foundation."

Nadia leaned forward slightly. "I'm definitely interested in that as well."

Vega nodded. "Hobbies include horseback riding, sailing, field hockey, reading, chess, and volunteering. Sounds like you're pretty active. Myst has a few sports teams that play other startups in local leagues. If you are picked for the position, you should look into those."

"That would be great. I played on several intramural teams in college."

"Wonderful." Vega shuffled her papers together, collecting them into a folder. "Well, that's it for me. I think you're very qualified and would be a good fit here. Our CEO, Rune Christiansen, interviews all candidates, though, before we extend any formal offers. Normally, you would have to come back for a second interview with him, but I want to expedite this process since Imogen is leaving. I'll go see if he's available right now."

Vega flitted out, leaving Nadia in the conference room.

Alone, Nadia started to grow nervous. The Myst Psionic smartwatch on her wrist beeped at her change in mood. She smoothed down her blouse and slacks and ran a hand over the top of her dark hair that she had pulled back into a neat bun. Nadia squared her shoulders and took deep breaths, willing her racing heart to calm. In her mind, she practiced her interview smile and handshake, imagining how the encounter would go.

After a few minutes, the door opened. Nadia rose to her feet. Her mother had always said you only get one chance to make a good impression, and Nadia wanted to win over the CEO. This job was going to be hers.

A tall man with broad shoulders walked in. He wore jeans and a grey Henley shirt and held a two-pronged manila folder. He looked up from the papers he was reading. Nadia flushed.

Before her was the most beautiful man she had ever seen.

He looked to be in his early thirties, with dark hair swept back from his face and piercing sapphire eyes. Nadia's own eyes roamed freely over his chiseled jawline and sensual lips. Everything about him screamed sex, from the way he moved with a casual, primal grace to the way he looked at her, like he was a predator assessing his prey. Without thinking, Nadia stood up straighter and pushed her shoulders back and her chest out. He flashed a smile, revealing a row of perfectly white teeth that contrasted sharply with his tanned skin. He was a Numinal, most likely High Fae, but his glamour was too strong for her to see through. He was powerful, brimming with strong magic in a dark, dangerous way.

"You must be Ms. Winters," he said in a deep, silky voice. He held out his hand, and Nadia somehow had the sense of mind to reach over and shake it. "I'm Rune Christiansen." His touch was electric. Her fingers tingled at the contact. "I've reviewed your resume and test scores. Very impressive."

Nadia had a momentary flash, a rogue fantasy, of Mr. Christiansen pulling her to him and grabbing her like he owned her, dipping his mouth to hers in a possessive, claiming kiss.

Nadia gave herself a shake. What the hell was that? She tried to push all inappropriate thoughts about Mr. Christiansen from her mind. He was ridiculously, unfairly attractive, but she had to focus on the interview.

They took a seat at the conference table kitty-corner from each other. Their knees brushed as they sat down. Nadia's breath hitched. She quickly pulled her legs away. The room suddenly seemed too warm, her conservative, high-necked blouse too constricting. A trickle of sweat slid down between her breasts.

Nadia cleared her throat. "You can call me Nadia." It came out a little harsher than she had intended.

He looked up at her from under long lashes. Nadia's heart did a little flip-flop.

"Nadia it is, then. So, tell me a bit about yourself."

Nadia launched into her background in art history and experience working at museums and auction houses, highlighting her cataloging skills and business experience. She mentioned the various classes she took in college related to ancient myths and artifacts and told him about the passion she felt for antiquities. She also mentioned her experience managing artists while she had worked for an art dealer. Nadia could tell he was impressed, nodding as he took notes on her resume.

Nadia knew that she had nailed the interview, but as Mr. Christiansen walked her down the hall, he stopped at the top of the stairs.

Regret tinged his deep voice. "Ms. Winters, I must be frank with you. While I appreciate your interest in Myst, I'm going to pass."

Nadia's heart leaped into her throat. "What? Why?"

Mr. Christiansen studied her for a few seconds. "I can tell you have a lot of relevant experience and a certain"—he paused, searching for the right word—"*zest* for antiquities, but I'm afraid you're just not a good fit for Myst."

Nadia felt like she'd been kicked in the stomach. This was *not* how this was supposed to go. Panic started rising, but she squashed it down and steeled her composure.

"Listen, Mr. Christiansen. I'm perfect for this position. I have experience with both ancient artifacts and talent management. You aren't going to find another Sixer with my unique qualifications. I know I'll fit in here. I'm adaptable. Like a chameleon." She glanced over the balcony at the scene below, the Myst employees busy and unaware of the conversation above them.

Mr. Christiansen smiled slightly, pityingly. He shook his head. "I'm sorry, but my mind is made up. I'll walk you out."

Nadia needed to get this job. And she wanted it, not only because her vampire overlord was forcing her to get a job at Myst to pass along insider magic and tech secrets. She thought she could be happy at Myst and make a difference. She needed an anchor, something to tether her down and give her life direction. Everything had gone so unexpectedly wrong the last few weeks, completely gone to shit. And suddenly, Myst had come into her life, a shiny carrot dangling in front of her. The ring she was reaching for on the merry-go-round of life. She needed a rudder, something to guide her and give her something to work toward, or she was going to implode.

He started heading down the stairs. "Wait!" she cried out as she held up her palm. Without knowing how it happened, a blast of reddish-pink energy shot from her hand and wrapped itself around his bicep like a vise made of lightning. Mr. Christiansen froze, stunned. Nadia froze as well, trying not to panic.

Mr. Christiansen moved first. Slowly, he looked down at the thin ribbon of energy before he flexed his bicep, his hand tightening in a fist. The vise disintegrated into the air like wisps of cotton candy. Nadia's measly little attempt at casting a spell was clearly nothing he couldn't handle.

"You're a Septer?" His face was a mask of anger and disbelief at her lame attempt to bind him.

"I think so? I'm not really sure."

He shot her an incredulous look. "An untrained Septer, at your age?"

"I'm new to the whole Sixer and Septer thing. It's kind of a long story, but I just found out about Numinals and magic." The words came out rushed. The Myst Psionic pinged, and she held up her wrist. "See? I'm trying to learn. I have the smartwatch and everything. My grandmother is a witch too, and she and her Seelie roommate are teaching me about my powers."

His eyes flicked back and forth over her face. She could tell he was trying to calculate the risk she brought to the table.

"Where did you get the Myst Psionic?" He gestured at the smartwatch. "We only released a limited number."

She shrugged, trying to look nonchalant. "A friend gave it to me to help with my training. I promise I'm doing everything I can to control my powers."

The seconds crawled by. Nadia held her breath, waiting. Mr. Christiansen's dark sapphire eyes assessed her.

Finally, he spoke, his voice cold and matter-of-fact. "You have issues with emotional control. This is extremely dangerous for a

Septer. To control your magic, you need to control your emotions and tap into them at will."

She gaped at him, shocked at his overfamiliar evaluation of her mental state.

He continued, not breaking eye contact with her, "The moment you saw me, you lit up like a disco ball. Your scent, the pheromones you were emitting, were palpable. I can't have that sort of"—a nerve in his temple fluttered—"*distraction* in my company. For any of my employees. It's hard enough balancing out all the strong personalities here without worrying about some human who can't control her magic interfering with productivity and employee safety. Half the demons in the city would be at our doorstep the second you lost control, trying to get to you."

"What do you mean?"

He stepped in closer to her, his head dipping down. "When you light up like that," he said, his voice low, "it's like a beacon for demons to come feed. You are pulsing, glowing like a little star, *leaking* energy and emotion all over the place. It makes you an easy and attractive target."

Nadia paled. Suddenly, he seemed menacing, looming over her like that. She stood her ground and jutted her chin, not wanting to show him that he intimidated her. She was tired of men using their power and position to threaten her.

"I didn't know that. Listen, if you give me the job, I'll work extra hard to control my magic. I'm already getting better. I know I'm the right person for this job. Please, just let me prove myself. You won't regret it. Please."

Mr. Christiansen closed his eyes, considering her words. In her mind, she cast a spell, silently mouthing *say yes, say yes* and throwing the full weight of her desire to get the job behind it. If she had any real magical ability to bend reality to her will and sway the outcome of events through manifesting intention, now was the time to try.

After what felt like an eternity, he opened his dark eyes and stared intently into hers. She couldn't look away, knowing that if she did, she would lose this chance.

"All right," he said, a tinge of uncertainty still in his voice.

"All right?" she asked, hopefully.

"I don't like this, but we could use someone with both Sixer and Septer powers. It's rare, and you could be very useful if you learn to master your abilities. Plus, Imogen *is* leaving soon, and I do need someone with experience to temporarily manage the vault. You can have the job. On a test basis," he added.

A grin broke out over her face. A warm feeling of excitement and relief flooded her body. The Myst smartwatch pinged at her change in mood.

He frowned at the watch. "But only on the condition that you agree to train with me to learn to control your abilities. I can't have you lighting up like that again and attracting half the demon scum of the city here."

"Absolutely. When do I start?"

"Monday."

She'd done it. The job was hers.

Chapter 7

Today is the first day of the rest of your life, Nadia told herself as she took a deep breath and stepped into Myst's lobby. As she walked through the waiting area, she glanced up at the LEDs on display on the installation on the ceiling, the lights pulsing in rhythm to the music streaming throughout the room. Nadia's steps fell in sync with the beat.

The blonde nymph receptionist Anya looked up. The Myst logo shined brightly behind her.

Nadia smiled brightly. "Hi, I'm Nadia Winters. It's my first day."

Anya's eyes lit up in recognition. "Welcome! I'll let Vega know you're here. Take a seat." She gestured to the mid-century modern couches. Nadia thumbed through a *Wired* magazine as she waited. Myst was profiled in the magazine's list of the hottest startups to watch out for.

After seeing what other employees had been wearing when she had been in for the interview, she had ditched the business look. Instead, she had opted for a more casual outfit of skinny jeans, cheetah print flats, and a form-fitting beige cashmere sweater. She had tousled her hair into long waves, pulling it back into a messy yet chic ponytail, and dabbed her lips with baby-pink lipstick after two coats of black mascara. She looked trendy but capable. Perfect for her first day when impressions mattered the most.

She had already blown that with the CEO. Her lame attempt

at binding him topped with some cringe-worthy groveling and desperate pleading had made her determined to make a better impression on everyone else going forward.

"Nadia." She looked up at the sound of her name. Vega wore a bright-yellow pantsuit, her frizzy hair pulled up on top of her head. Her translucent wings buzzed behind her. "You're here early. Great. I have us set up in one of the conference rooms upstairs. Let's go get your picture taken for your employee badge, and we can begin the onboarding process."

"Sounds good."

Vega gestured for Nadia to follow.

"We have some paperwork we have to do, pick out your benefit options, all that. And then I'll give you a brief orientation and overview of the company before I hand you off to Maya Wren, your 'Myst Buddy' who will show you around and take you to lunch in our café."

Vega led her through the main floor. Like before, the room hummed with Numinals, some meeting in groups, others working with headphones on in the coworking space, hanging out in the break areas, or riding Segways and skateboards through the halls.

Nadia tried not to stare, but it was difficult.

The morning went by in an overwhelming blur. After getting her badge and handling the HR paperwork, Vega gave Nadia an overview of Myst's different divisions and subsidiaries, the company's history, and Mr. Christiansen's vision for finding meaningful work for magical creatures to live among humans. Myst's core tenet was from Arthur C. Clarke's three laws: "Any sufficiently advanced technology is indistinguishable from magic." That statement was plastered everywhere around the building, including painted in giant letters on the wall opposite the brightly colored, Bosch-like mural in the main coworking space. Myst's divisions were all centered on this philosophy. The MystOS system, which humans believed was a proprietary algorithm, was actually fueled by magic. The human customers believed that Myst's technology and algorithms were so far advanced they had the predictive capabilities and analytical abilities to solve issues and provide guidance.

They had no idea the whole thing was magic. They had no idea that Myst was acting as a mechanical Turk that shielded humans from the knowledge that magic was real.

Myst's headquarters contained all the necessary ritual rooms, magical tools and equipment, artifacts, and talismans to create intense magic to fuel a wide array of projects for their clients. The main division, a SaaS company called Mystos, was built on the MystOS operating system. Other divisions included WishSeed, an app that connected service and good providers with customers, Myst Labs, which created the Myst Psionic smartwatch, and Veil, Myst's augmented reality game that they were beta testing for both Ocular Rift and via app. Nadia had read about it all online, but she started to really understand the organizational structure of the company after Vega handed her a chart that labeled Myst's different divisions and showed how they interacted with one another.

"Are you overwhelmed yet?" asked Vega with a smile after she had finished the morning orientation session.

Nadia nodded, slightly dazed.

She chuckled. "You'll get the hang of everything. Most Sixers take a bit to get accustomed to the company. Numinals, of course, seem to pick things up quicker. No offense to humans," she added.

"None taken."

Vega handed her a thick, spiral-bound book. "Here's your copy of the employee handbook. It has more information in there. Please take the time to read Myst's policies and procedures. Even though we didn't go over them all today, we still require you to adhere to them." She stood up. "I'll email you all the orientation material from this morning, as well."

"Thanks." Nadia grabbed her bag and tucked the book under her arm.

"Now I'm going to drop you at your Myst Buddy Maya's desk. She'll give you a tour and take you to lunch."

Maya turned out to be a willowy Numinal who looked to be in her mid-twenties, with dark skin and a septum piercing, her long dark hair braided. With her army-green cargo pants and drapey black tank top that revealed a neon-orange bralette underneath, she looked like she was on the way to a rave.

"Welcome to Myst. How's your first day going so far?" Maya grinned up at Nadia from her desk, which was covered in activist and eco-warrior pictures, including a photograph of herself chained to a giant redwood tree. She ducked under her desk and came back up holding a pair of combat boots, pulling them on. She tucked her hair behind delicate, pointed ears covered in stretched hoops and piercings.

"There's a lot to take in," Nadia confessed.

"I know it's overwhelming at first. Especially for humans. But you'll get into the groove of things." She checked her copy of Nadia's schedule. "I think I'm supposed to give you a tour right now and show you where your habitat is. We call our assigned desks 'habitats.' Ready?"

"As I'll ever be." They started walking toward another cluster of coworking spaces. Nadia immediately knew which spot was hers.

Nadia's desk was embarrassingly decorated and overflowing with Myst swag: T-shirts and hoodies, coffee tumblers and mugs, pens, pencils and notepads, stress balls, and a backpack with the Myst logo. A giant cluster of balloons tied to her chair was the icing on the cake.

"Is this all for me?" exclaimed Nadia. She could get used to being spoiled rotten. At her last job, the best perk was lukewarm coffee.

"Yep! We like to make a fuss over the new hires." Maya picked up an MP3 player and handed it to Nadia. "Here. It's preloaded with a bunch of my music. I'm Myst's resident DJ, on top of my job as a developer, and help write the music that we use in the apps. You might have heard of me—The Mighty Troglodyti. My track 'Roots and Chains' is number two on the global charts right now."

"No way! I love that song."

A brilliant smile lit up Maya's face. "I put some new stuff I haven't released yet on there. Let me know what you think."

"Maya, there you are. I've been looking everywhere for you." They turned to the deep voice, which turned out to belong to a ruggedly handsome man in his early thirties. He was tan and muscular, like he spent a lot of time outdoors. Dog tags hung around his neck. His neatly trimmed beard gave him a distinct mountain man look when coupled with his plaid flannel shirt.

He discreetly sniffed the air. Nadia sensed he was some sort of shifter, the animal inside him quickly assessing her.

"Carson, this is Nadia. Nadia, Carson." Maya waved her hand between the two of them. "Carson manages the engineers."

"Nice to meet you." Carson nodded at Nadia briefly before turning back to Maya. "Do you have a minute? I want to pick your brain on this issue I just discovered with Veil."

Maya sighed. "What now? We aren't going to have to push back the release again, are we?"

Carson looked toward the heavens and shook his head. "Rune is going to kill me if we have to. I don't think it's serious, though. But if it is, I want to get in front of it."

"We were just about to take a tour. Walk and talk?"

"After you, m'lady." He gestured toward the pathway around the inner perimeter of the building.

Nadia fell in behind Carson and Maya as they discussed the issue with Veil. Maya interrupted Carson periodically to show Nadia something or introduce her to people.

"The employee perks here are great. We have a basketball court, a gym and sauna, an indoor atrium, rain forest, and botanical garden, as well as our on-site bar, the Bell, Book, and Candle," Maya explained.

"You have an on-site bar?"

"Yup," said Carson. "Those who drink together, work better together."

A guy with shaggy blond hair, wearing a Grateful Dead T-shirt and expensive high tops, drove by on a Segway.

"Yes! Let's do it!" he shouted. "Let's crush it, guys!" He whooped in the air and gave Nadia a high five as he passed them.

"Who was that?" Nadia asked when the guy was out of ear range.

"Oh, that's just Kevin," said Maya. "He's one of the game testers. He's cool, he's just . . . enthusiastic about startup culture."

"He's a menace, and you should stay clear of him and his inane ideas," said Carson with a growl. "He's not even a Sixer. We have to erase his memory every night. The guy isn't quite 'all there,' if you get my drift."

Maya punched Carson's arm. "Oh, stop! He's fine."

"I'm serious. If I have to hear him say 'crushing it' one more time, I'm going to eat him." He flashed his fangs and wagged his eyebrows at Maya.

"If he's not a Sixer, then what does he think when he sees the others here without glamours?" Nadia asked as she watched Kevin across the room. He was showing card tricks to a group of Numinals. Even at a distance, Nadia could see the eye rolls and groans as he flubbed the magic trick, a hidden card falling to the ground.

"He's high, like, every day," said Maya. "Microdosing is big in the startup world right now."

"LSD?" Nadia asked.

"Yeah, except ol' Mindfreak over here"—Carson jerked a thumb in Kevin's direction—"doesn't understand the concept of 'micro.' Any horns or tails he sees just register as part of his trip."

They stopped in front of a lavishly decorated habitat, full of gold gilded desk accessories, framed paintings, and vases full of red and pink roses. Instead of the blonde wood desks most of the other employees had, this habitat had an antique writing desk and chair. A framed *Turandot* poster hung on the wall next to it. Lined up on the desk were several brightly colored Venetian half masks.

"Now where did he go?" Maya scrunched up her face and looked around the office.

"Who are we looking for?" Nadia asked.

"Piero. He's the VP of talent management. You'll be working with him, right?"

Nadia nodded. "Vega said he will be my direct supervisor."

"He probably left for lunch early," remarked Carson. He eyed a large black hat outfitted with a foxtail that was lying on the opulent chair.

"Out of my way, out of my way." A man's voice rang out over the floor. A harlequin in a bright-blue suit with a yellow checkered tie hurried toward them. People scurried out of his way like he was a bowling ball hitting pins.

He stopped in front of Nadia. "Are you my new neophyte?"

"That would be me," she chirped. "Hi, I'm Nadia. Nice to meet you." She stuck out a hand.

"Piero Bellini. Charmed, I'm sure." He squeezed her hand before looking around her at Carson, who had picked up Piero's hat and was sniffing the foxtail. "Drop it, Dog. I don't want your wolfy paws touching all my things."

Carson threw the hat back down with a growl. "Can it, Clown."

"Listen here, you animal . . ." Piero raised a finger at Carson.

Carson stepped forward so that he was towering over Piero. "What are you going to do about it?"

"Whoa, whoa, whoa." Maya stepped in between them and

placed a gentle hand on Carson's arm. "Come on, children. Let's all play nice. We don't want to scare Nadia."

They all turned to her. "Hmm. You're right. She does look a little traumatized," said Piero.

As if in response, the Myst Psionic pinged.

"You have a Psionic," commented Maya. "That must mean you're a Septer." She looked impressed. "How do you like the watch? That was Carson's pet project before we started on Veil."

"It's great. I, uh, just came into my powers, so it's really helping."

Carson looked smug. "It was a bit of a passion project for me. I wasn't sure if Rune was going to let me run with it, but he believed in my vision to basically hack magic. Make it more accessible to everyone. Right now, the Psionic integrates with the WishSeed app so that users can buy spells, but we are working on the next version that will integrate with Veil so that users won't need to carry their phone with them to play the game."

"Can you help me customize it?" asked Nadia. "I haven't had the chance to explore all the widgets yet."

Carson glowed. "Most definitely."

Piero gathered up his fox hat and settled it on his head with an evil glare at Carson. "All right, kiddies, as fun as this has been, I have a business lunch I'm late for at Gary Danko's. Time to turn on the charm and land the big fish." He straightened his tie, looking in a gilded mirror on his desk as he checked his teeth.

Maya looked dubious. "Literal, or metaphorical big fish? Must be someone important if Rune's letting you use the corporate card at Gary Danko's. Wasn't he pissed when you ran up that two-thousand-dollar bill at Benu last month?"

"Literal fish. Rune wants to enlist the talents of the Namazu catfish to do some underwater mountain moving in a new bid we are putting together for Halliburton." Piero glanced back at them over his shoulder. "And Rune knows that the only way to attract the top talent is to spend a buck wining and dining."

"I thought we weren't doing any more offshore drilling projects," said Carson, frowning.

"He told us we weren't after I threw a fit last month." Maya crossed her arms over her chest.

"Rune thinks our involvement will minimize the environmental impacts. Better us than Pact. Lord knows they will just come in with magical guns blazing and destroy the site like they did with BP." Piero turned to Nadia. "I will see you after I get back from lunch, and we can sit down and figure out how to use that pretty face of yours to land us some business. Ciao!" He waved goodbye before he strolled off.

Soon, it was lunch. As Maya and Carson led her over to the café, Nadia noticed Mr. Christiansen across the room, deep in conversation with several Numinals. He noticed her watching him, and she looked away quickly, blushing.

"This is the café and lounge area." Maya waved a hand around as they approached. Nadia glanced about herself in awe. To the left was a large café where chefs were serving up delicious-smelling dishes; Numinals lined up to order at the different counters. To the right was a large lounge area full of couches, chairs, and tables that opened up to an outdoor seating area with wooden picnic tables, stone fire pits, and several blossoming patio trees strung with lights.

"Meals are subsidized," explained Maya. "Just swipe your badge when you leave, and the meal will be charged to your employee account. Most of the food is human food: salads, sandwiches, soups, etcetera, but you should probably stay away from the 'special dishes.' They're marked with a symbol."

"What's in the special dishes?" Nadia asked.

"You don't want to know," said Carson, looking grave.

"Seriously?" exclaimed Nadia.

Maya punched him on the arm. "Stop it. It's just faerie food."

In the center of the café was a giant oak tree, about twenty or so feet high, covered with twisted whorls and knots. Scattered throughout the gnarled tree were several little irregularly shaped doors with wooden pathways and bridges wrapped around the tree like a mess of ribbons. About a dozen or so little goblins worked, baking and cooking, chanting a work tune as they prepared snacks on their porches and inside their little homes. On the side of the tree was a walk-up chrome counter and a handwritten menu where employees could place orders for snacks. A goblin with a face like an Ewok sat at the front, looking grumpily out at the employees on their lunch break.

"This is the Keebler Elf Tree," said Maya. "We just call it that to piss off the goblins. They can be a little prickly."

"The goblins were going to lose their home because of deforestation," added Carson. "Rune had the entire tree moved into Myst to save it. The goblins provide us with snacks in return. Sometimes they act like its indentured servitude"—he rolled his eyes—"but Rune pays them well."

Interesting. So, Mr. Christiansen had a definite philanthropic streak to him. And was apparently very powerful. How much magic had it taken to move an entire tree and its inhabitants permanently inside the startup?

"Feel free to just grab a snack from them, anytime. Snacks are free." Maya led them into the café, where Nadia ordered a turkey sandwich from the automated touchscreen menu. Maya opted for a salad, while Carson ordered a large steak, very rare.

The special dish of the day looked like glowing neon-blue mushrooms. Nadia stayed away from it.

"I don't know how you can eat that sort of thing," Maya said later, as they sat outside on the patio eating lunch under a large red umbrella. She wrinkled up her nose in disgust at Carson's steak. "I'm vegan," she explained to Nadia.

Carson took a large bite of his bloody steak. "I am what I am, baby. Take me or leave me."

Nadia looked out over the patio to the edge of the wards at the boundary line. They looked like a faint, shimmering net full of ancient symbols that vibrated with power. On the other side, people milled around, some walking dogs or riding bikes, oblivious to the Numinals within the wards.

Maya caught her gaze. "No one can see us in here. It's glamoured to be invisible."

"No one accidentally wanders in?"

"Nope," said Carson, matter-of-factly. "Can't happen. Normal humans are repelled. You have to be a Sixer to sense how to cross over the wards by yourself."

"Unless it's Firmament Night," Maya corrected. "Then the wards aren't repelling humans."

"What's Firmament Night?" Nadia asked.

"Once a month, we have a pop-up restaurant called Firmament in the dome off to the side of the café," said Maya. "It's open to the public. We bring in a guest chef from around the world and each month is a different theme tied to their specific culture and cuisine. Rune started it as a way to inject cultural diversity into the city's foodie scene." Maya stabbed a piece of lettuce and held it up in the air with her fork, waving it at Nadia to make a point. "A lot of Myst's projects are aimed at diversifying the status quo, both with humans and Numinals. Most of the Numinals in the startup world are from Western cultures, unfortunately. Rune's always trying to bring in more of a global perspective."

"It's awesome," added Carson. "The whole dome gets decorated with AR and magic. We use the dining experience to help beta test our systems to ensure that humans are getting the full sensory experience from our tech and the magic and that the two are blended seamlessly."

Maya took another bite of salad. "So, once a month during the pop-up, Rune moves the boundary of the wards so guests can find the restaurant."

"The wards can discriminate and only let specific people through. Rune also keeps out certain kinds of Dark Numinals who don't play nice with others or who have pissed him off and have been blacklisted, through the use of seals in the wards." Carson bit off another huge chunk of steak.

"The Myst headquarters is the safest place in the city," Maya added. "If anything were to ever happen, Myst would be safe for a very long time, hidden from the outside world."

"What kind of thing would happen to need to go on lockdown like that?" Nadia asked. She thought back to that headline about increased violence in the city.

"Zombie apocalypse." Carson's expression was grim.

"Zombies are real, too?" Nadia nearly choked on her sandwich.

Maya and Carson burst out laughing. "No, of course not!" Maya wiped the tears from her eyes. "You should have seen the look on your face. Priceless."

Nadia smiled sheepishly at her naiveté. "Okay. No zombies. Got it."

"You sure you're a Septer?" asked Carson. "Even most Sixers aren't this, uh—" He broke off, struggling to find the correct word.

"Clueless." Nadia shrugged. "It's okay. You can say it."

Maya smiled apologetically. "You said earlier you just came into your powers. That's a little strange. Most Septers figure it out around puberty when they get all hormonal and start accidentally lighting stuff on fire or casting love spells that actually work."

"My grandmother cast a binding spell when I was little. I somehow undid the spell, and now here I am. Sans training." Nadia didn't mention the whole part about the Blood Oath and vampire overlord. Obviously.

Maya sucked in her breath. "That's some serious magic. I hope she had a good reason to do that."

Nadia shrugged again, changing the subject. "So, what about you guys? Do you have magical abilities as well?"

Carson cringed. "We have got to get you up to speed on Numinals."

"What?"

"It's just that it's a little rude to ask," explained Maya. "It's kind of like asking what someone got on the SATs or how much money they make."

"Oh, shit. Sorry."

"It's okay," Maya said quickly. "You didn't know. Yes, we both have basic magical abilities . . . but we aren't advanced. Numinals all are born or created with a certain innate amount of magic."

"Some *are* magic, and some *have* magic," said Nadia, thinking back to what Avery had said.

"Exactly," said Maya. "Those who exhibit a proclivity to spell-casting then can train and advance in a specific school of magic."

"There're schools of magic?" Nadia asked. "Like . . . colleges for magic?" Nadia wondered if she should look into those. The structure of a graduate degree sounded like a pretty good way to learn about everything.

Carson nodded. "A few. But they are super elitist, and hardly anyone gets in. Most people are self-taught or have a mentor or group they study with. I think Maya meant school in the sense of a certain style, like how there are various styles of martial arts." Carson jutted his chin toward Nadia's Psionic. "Let me see the watch. I'll make sure all your settings are correct."

Nadia unclasped the watch and handed it to him. He started fiddling around with the settings.

"Well, no wonder you're having issues," said Carson. "You have it set to Advanced Mode. Looks like you're only a Level 2, from the readings."

"I'm not sure what it's doing."

"Okay, check it out," said Carson, leaning over so Nadia could see the LCD screen. "The theory behind the Psionic is that the only thing a user needs is his or her own mind to power the spell. We've started with a handful of basic training spells and distilled them down—hacked the magic—so that extra equipment or tools aren't needed. All that's needed is the caster's emotion and intent in alignment with the spell. Assuming they have enough casting energy, that is.

"There are three modes. In Easy Mode, the Psionic casts the spell for you. See this graph here? It's measuring where your emotions are. You need to align your emotion in the acceptable casting range for that particular spell, and then the Psionic does the heavy lifting for you. In Intermediate Mode, the user has to say the words and cast the spell themselves, but the Psionic helps you focus and gives you a push. Advanced Mode strips away all the safety nets so that the Psionic works like an extensive grimoire or database of spells and information."

"Well, that does make things easier," said Nadia.

"Not all the spells are programmed for Easy Mode, though," continued Carson. "We started with a handful of basic spells that Rune thought everyone should have access to."

"Rune believes that magic shouldn't be in the hands of the few elites," added Maya. "For centuries, arcane knowledge was a closely guarded secret known only to a handful of Septers and Numinals. But Rune believes magic is a basic right and doesn't believe in limiting access to knowledge. The Psionic even helps Sixers and regular humans cast, if they have the mental agility for it."

Carson nodded. "It's the same argument for open source. The quality of the spells drastically improves when we can leverage people's abilities. Most of the spells in the database are crowdsourced from users. Spells and charms are peer-reviewed, and users can curate lists and upvote the best spells so that the Psionic grimoire reflects the current magical trends and tastemakers in the magical community."

"Wow, that's awesome," said Nadia. "It's sort of like a Reddit for magic."

"Exactly," said Carson. He handed the watch back. "And each spell is tagged with a level of difficulty so that users know if they will be able to cast it or not depending on their skill level."

"Carson's a big D&D nerd," Maya added.

"I feel so behind. I don't know anything about magic yet."

"Give yourself more credit! I've never been very good at magic," confessed Maya. "It just doesn't come naturally. I can do the basic glamouring, can do a bit of healing magic, charms, some light conjuring or repelling, that sort of thing. Nothing too fancy. I think most of us here are like that. The watch helps me cast, but I just can't do the mental acrobatics required for advanced spellcasting. Many of the consultants we have, though, possess a lot of magical talent for our projects. Numinals or Septers who practice magic can also use talismans or amulets or other items to help boost and focus their power."

"Rune is probably the only one here with true power," added Carson. "He's constantly surprising me with the insane amount of magical ability and knowledge he has. I think he has studied every school of magic there is. Guy's a genius. He hardly uses it, though. Tries to live as close to humans as possible. I'm pretty sure we've never even seen his true capabilities."

Nadia finished her sandwich and crumpled up the wrapper to throw it away. "Why? If he's so powerful, you think he would use it all the time."

Maya shook her head. "He wants to set a good example for the rest of us. Myst's mission is for Numinals to integrate into human society. Many think that with each generation, the magic is dying out. At some point, something's gotta give. Numinals will either die out, or we will fully integrate into society."

"Most Numinals are mixed blood," said Carson. "We've been working on some DNA projects here, looking into the biological process that turns humans into Numinals. Tracking different genetic variations. Even if a human was turned into a specific type of Numinal, they might possess some other types of magical blood from the way or where they were turned, or the human's heritage. No one really knows how it works, but we're studying that too."

Nadia smiled. "That's rad. Like your own Ancestry.com."

"More or less," said Carson. "I'm a wolf-shifter, but it turns out I also have a bit of Earth spirit among other things in me too. Probably from when I was turned. It was on native land."

Maya rolled her eyes. "It's *all* native land."

"Did you do the DNA sequencing too?" Nadia asked Maya.

Maya shook her head. "I don't believe in all that shit. A Numinal is a Numinal. Trying to pinpoint lineage is counterproductive and elitist." Her tone was crisp.

"What do you mean?" asked Nadia.

"Historically, there was this split between 'dark' Numinals and 'light' Numinals," said Maya, making the quote signal with her fingers. "The age-old battle of good and evil, white and black. It was simplistic. Numinals were polarized. Fae were good, demons bad. But as Numinals evolved and interbred, it wasn't so clear anymore which side of the line they were on. People and creatures were lumped into categories, stereotypes and assumptions were made. Wars were fought, and it wasn't clear who was the enemy and who was family based solely on blood.

"It's a much more modern view to look at the individual. Every group is going to have its bad eggs, but that doesn't mean you can or should paint with such broad strokes. It's much more nuanced than that. Morality isn't black and white. Numinal morality is more orange and blue than anything else."

Carson looked skeptical. "I mean, stereotypes exist for a reason. If you're dealing with a demon, ninety-nine percent of the time, they're going to be bad. They just aren't wired to be good. It's not in their nature. They promote sin, for crying out loud! Turned ones are better, of course—they have some humanity left—but still."

Maya looked at Carson with contempt. "I have some demon blood in me. Does that make me evil?"

"It probably accounts for some behavioral traits," he countered. "I have some púca blood in me. God knows I'm no saint."

Maya stood suddenly. "I have to get back to work." Apparently, they had hit a touchy subject.

Nadia stood as well. "I should probably get back too."

"You know I'm right!" Carson called out as they made their way inside.

Maya left Nadia at her habitat to get acclimated. After settling in, arranging her desk, and raiding the office supply closet for extra Post-its and pens—she wasn't quite ready yet to delve into the magical supply closet—she booted up the laptop Myst had given her to read emails and go over the information that she had received in orientation. While she was going to be working with both Piero and Imogen, Vega had explained that the first couple of days were more about getting settled into Myst and learning the systems than actually working.

After a couple of hours, Nadia needed a break. She stood up, stretched, and looked over to Piero's desk. Empty. She headed over to the lounge. A few others were there, sitting on brightly colored couches and bean bags. To the side, in a large open area, a tree spirit in an ephemeral blue sari led a yoga session for some of the other Mystics, the tree spirit weaving through the group and stopping occasionally to correct someone's downward dog.

"Um, hello?" Nadia stopped in front of the gnarled oak. A small goblin, about a foot or so tall, looked over. He wiped his hands on his apron and waddled over to where she stood at the counter.

"What do you want?" he asked gruffly. Nadia suppressed a smile. Maya was right; the goblins were prickly.

"I'd like an apple, please." Nadia eyed a basket of red apples sitting in a wooden bucket behind the counter. They looked like Christmas ornaments, perfectly shiny.

The goblin turned and grabbed a chocolate chip cookie from a plate in the display window, placed it on a plate, and smacked it down on the counter. "Next."

"Oh, wait. I'm sorry. I said I wanted an apple, not a cookie."

His head swiveled to her, and he stared at her blankly. "You get cookie."

"Excuse me?"

"All rookies get cookies. That is rule."

She opened her mouth to argue when she heard a voice behind her.

"Grudax," he said. "Are you picking on our new hire?"

Nadia turned around to see Mr. Christiansen standing behind her. His gaze flicked down to meet hers. Nadia stumbled backward a bit into the counter, grabbing it for support.

"Oh, hi," she said awkwardly. It wasn't clear where exactly where they stood since their last conversation where Nadia had basically tried to magically bind him and then pleaded for him to hire her. Not her finest moment.

"Good afternoon," he said smoothly. Today he was wearing denim jeans and a black T-shirt with the Myst logo on the front, stretched taut over his muscles. His dark hair was damp, and a little mussed. A clean, masculine scent rolled off him, like he had just showered after a heavy workout. Nadia squished herself back farther against the counter, trying to think of herself as a vacuum to attempt to control any pheromones she was accidentally leaking.

He looked back up at Grudax. "I believe Ms. Winters here asked for an apple."

"Oh, you can call me Nadia," she started, but Grudax cut her off.

"Rookies get cookies," he said forlornly in a last-ditch effort.

"Yes, that's true. But they also can have apples. Or anything else they ask for, for that matter." He winked at her with a slight smile before looking sternly at Grudax again, and Nadia locked her knees so she wouldn't swoon.

Grudax sighed. "Fine." He placed an apple on the counter.

"I'll have this cookie though, if you don't mind." Mr. Christiansen grabbed the cookie. "Hope your first day is going well." He turned to walk away.

Nadia had to say something. She was uneasy, unsure of how to act, unsure of what he thought about her. She couldn't make another first impression, but maybe she could salvage the one she had. They had to work together now, after all. "Mr. Christiansen—Rune. May I call you Rune?" He stopped for a moment, and Nadia continued in a rush, "I wanted to thank you for uh, you know. Giving me the job and everything."

Nadia felt exposed and transparent.

Without saying anything, he nodded and walked away.

Well, that was awkward. It was clear that Rune was still unsure about her. She couldn't blame him. She took her apple and went to find a couch and watch TV.

"Hey, new girl!" a voice called out.

A pink-haired woman sat on a high table, dangling her fishnet-covered legs over the edge. She wore a Kawaii-goth style, leather and chains mixed with cutesy pastel Hello Kitty accessories. Nadia checked for a glamour, finding none. Human.

She had been watching Nadia for a bit, it appeared. She jumped down from the ledge, shrugging up her leather jacket, and sauntered over like a cocky alley cat.

"So, you're the new Sixer," she said. Her smile didn't reach her pretty, dark eyes.

Nadia stuck out her hand, smiling brightly. "Hi, I'm Nadia Winters."

She chuckled. "Well, aren't you just so *perky?* I'm Sophie Lu. Those shoes are totally beast, by the way."

"Oh, thanks." Nadia looked down at her cheetah print flats, unsure if the woman liked them or not.

"You'll be working with Piero and Imogen, right? Fab. I'm in HR. Let me know if you need any tips or advice. You know, the ins and outs of working here—who to get to know, who to stay away from. I was the first Sixer they hired. I had to figure out the inside scoop all on my own."

"Oh, thanks. It would be awesome if we could get a cup of coffee sometime." Nadia smiled.

"Sophie!" Piero's voice trilled out as he bounded over. "Baby girl, there you are. I landed the fish. I had to drink *gallons* of champagne to do it." He giggled, swaying. "It's true what they say about how fish drink. I need you to expedite the paperwork, bring him on board, stat."

Sophie high-fived him. "Dude! We're totally going to land that Halliburton bid now."

Piero did a little happy dance. "Rune promised me a large signing bonus if I got him. Let's go to The Bell. Drinks on me."

"Wanker." Sophie laughed. "Drinks at The Bell are always free."

"Want to come, Nadia?" asked Piero. "The Bell, Book, and Candle is right downstairs." He nodded over to an elevator in the corner of the room, lit up with the bar's neon sign and a red blinking arrow pointed toward the floor.

"Oh yes!" Sophie said, a bit too forced. Nadia knew she didn't want her there. "I was just offering to give our new Sixer some survival tips."

"She's actually a Septer." Piero hiccupped.

Sophie's icy gaze swiveled over. "Is that so?"

"Guilty as charged," said Nadia, raising her hand.

Sophie regarded her with the newfound knowledge of her

abilities. A slight frown tugged at her lips. "Well, my mistake. As a Septer, I'm sure you'll do just fine."

"Nadia, I am so sorry." Piero shook his head dramatically. "I know we haven't had the chance to sit down yet, but I am deeee-runk. Hazard of the job. Let's talk tomorrow, 'kay?"

"Let's get that bevvy now." Sophie steered Piero away, arm in arm.

Nadia wasn't sure if she should follow them or not. She stood for a few seconds before deciding that getting drunk with her boss and another coworker on the first day was probably a bad idea. With a sigh, she returned to her desk and continued reading through emails.

A couple of times she looked over to Rune's office and caught him watching her as she worked.

Chapter 8

What a day! thought Nadia as she stood at the Muni stop near Myst. She rubbed her shoulders, trying to massage out the tension she felt. She made a mental note to ask Marina to help her out with some healing magic.

Nadia glanced at the other people standing or sitting on silver benches on the raised platform, heads bowed over smartphones. The summer sun was still well above the horizon despite the hour. Nadia checked the time on her watch. Seven o'clock. She stifled a yawn with the back of her hand. To her left, two women were discussing the rise of violent crime in San Francisco, blaming the tech industry and gentrification.

"How was your first day?" asked Thomas as he manifested out of thin air on the other side of her.

"Goddamit!" Nadia jumped. The Psionic pinged at her sudden spike in blood pressure. She took a deep breath, steadying her heart. "I really wish you would stop doing that." The two other women looked over, worried expressions on their faces, and moved down a bit away from her.

Thomas wore jeans and a black moto jacket. He looked like James Dean, with his dark hair slicked back, showing his sideburns. If he hadn't just appeared on the sidewalk out of nowhere, you could almost mistake him for any other guy getting off work in the city.

"But then I wouldn't get the pleasure of making you scream." His dark eyes sparkled at the thinly veiled innuendo. Images of Thomas partaking in some sort of orgy—writhing limbs and flesh slicked with sweat—suddenly flooded Nadia's mind. She shook her head, trying to get them out.

He cocked his head to the side with a dirty smile. "Ah, your Sixer powers grow. See anything you like?"

"Get out of my head!" she hissed, pushing past him as she tried to escape. He paced her as she crossed the street.

"Sixers have different powers. Most can sense Numinals and spirits. Some are clairvoyants, while others have precognition. It appears you can read minds and see memories."

"Lovely. How do I stop it?"

"You'll be able to control your abilities in time. Now, tell me . . . how was your first day?" He said it in a singsong voice like it was her first day of school and she was supposed to give him the rundown.

"It was fine." Nadia kept walking. She knew she couldn't outrun him. But damn if she wouldn't make him work for it.

"Nadia, please. I think you can do better than that. Anything unusual happen?"

Nadia snapped. "Unusual? The whole thing is unusual! I'm working at a startup that manages magical talent, and my supervisor is some sort of harlequin clown who got drunk with a giant magical catfish. I don't even know how the catfish can be on land, let alone go to lunch at a nice restaurant. The whole thing doesn't make any fucking sense to me!"

Thomas looked concerned. "I think you need a drink."

"What I need is a fucking lobotomy!"

He grabbed her by the shoulders. "Get a grip on yourself, woman."

And like before, they were teleported across town.

"Not again," Nadia mumbled. She lurched into a bush and

vomited. After the day she had, she didn't have the control to keep the contents of her stomach down. Thomas handed her an embroidered handkerchief. She glared at him as she wiped her mouth.

"May I take you to dinner?" He gestured at the restaurant in front of them. "After you, my dear."

Nadia didn't want to enjoy herself, but she did. The restaurant turned out to be one of the hottest new places in town, a Michelin-starred Indian fusion restaurant that specialized in curry cocktails and dosas. Without a reservation, the modelesque hostess tried to turn them away, but Thomas waved a hand, the spicy tang of his demon magic in the air, and the hostess showed them to a table.

Nadia figured if he was paying, she was eating.

Much to her annoyance, Thomas was utterly charming. Nadia found herself forgetting he was a demon who had caught her and forced her into serving a vampire business mogul. Instead, she felt like her old self: the confident Nadia on a date with a cute guy who was witty and charming and who could provide a satisfactory level of verbal sparring.

Thomas and Nadia even started playing a drinking game to get to know each other better. As with most drinking games, the rules devolved quickly so that Nadia just took a drink whenever she felt like it.

"Okay," said Thomas. "Childhood traumas. Go."

"My mother is an emotionally unstable alcoholic, and my father is a narcissistic philanderer." Nadia took another sip of her cocktail. "Your turn."

He grinned. "My mother was a whore, and my father a hedonistic libertine."

Nadia raised her glass to his. "Sir, I think you take the cake on that one."

"It's true, though."

She hiccupped slightly. "A libertine, eh? When were you born?"

He spooned more curry onto his plate. "In 1734. I was turned when I was twenty-nine."

"I know other Numinals were turned but were some demons too? I thought you guys came from the bowels of Hell or something." Nadia grabbed the basket of dosas. Thomas had ordered for both of them, asking her to trust him, and he did not fail.

He chuckled. "A common misconception. Humans are turned numerous ways—through magical rituals, or if they spent too much time in a demon realm, to name a few—but the most common way is that they obsess about something to such an extreme that they open their minds to demonic possession. The possession eats away most of the humanity inside them. Turns them into something else."

"That's horrible." A shudder passed through her. "So that happened to you? You were turned through possession?"

"Yes." His eyes softened for a moment. Nadia felt a pang of sympathy for him. It was clear that Thomas had past trauma in his life, and she wondered what he had obsessed over so much that it opened him up to demonic possession.

They lapsed into a comfortable silence. Thomas checked his cell phone while Nadia studied him. He didn't seem evil, though Nadia wasn't sure she knew what evil was anymore. Never in her wildest imagination would she thought she would be having cocktails and dosas with a demon. She wondered how he had gotten wrapped up with Mercurio, who seemed to unfairly treat Thomas like a bumbling idiot of a servant. Nadia wondered why she was feeling so sympathetic toward him and decided it was because Mercurio was the common enemy of them both.

Thomas looked up from his phone. His expression hardened at her soft gaze toward him, like he knew what she had been thinking. He snapped for the waiter. "Coffee. Would you like some?"

Thomas didn't even ask Nadia about her first day at Myst until after they had finished coffee and dessert. But when Nadia had finished her espresso and licked the last bits of carrot cardamom cake from her fork, he finally asked.

"So, how was your first day at Myst?" He said it so innocuously, Nadia had to fight to remember that this entire dinner was a setup so that she would tell him what had happened. Suddenly, she felt sleazy and used. She was a spy, a traitor. She tried to hold on to that thought, that knowledge that what she was doing was wrong. It was proving harder than she thought it would be.

"It was great." Nadia tried to keep her tone light.

"Tell me about it."

Nadia looked around the restaurant with its wooden chairs and tables, geometric wall hangings, and paper lanterns hanging from the ceilings, and tried to center herself. The light buzz of conversation from the other diners hummed around her. Couples leaned in toward each other. Friends drank cocktails and laughed. Nadia felt very alone. She caught her gaze in a mirrored reflection across the room: a dark-haired girl with pale-blue eyes, looking a little unsure and out of her element. Nadia steeled her composure, drawing in on her reserves. She sat up a bit. She was strong. A survivor. She could do this.

"I met my new boss and the team. I'm doing a job rotation, starting with the talent management team and Myst Foundation, working with the antiquities in their collection in the vaults. They haven't sent me to the vaults yet, though."

"Fascinating. Anything else?" There was a hardness in his voice. The niceties were over. They were all business now.

"I met the CEO. He's—" Nadia struggled to find a word that summed up Rune. Interesting? Enigmatic? Standoffish? She settled on "compelling."

A vein pulsed in Thomas's neck, but his features remained entirely controlled. "The CEO?"

"Yes. Rune Christiansen. I know he's a Numinal, but I can't get a read on him. His glamour's too strong."

"I see." Thomas fingered the little handle on his espresso cup, looking down like he was thinking. "Continue."

She wasn't sure what else he wanted to know. "Rune said he was going to train me. As a condition of my employment."

"Train you how?"

"I . . . I'm not sure." Nadia's eyes darted around as she thought back on the day. She realized she had no idea what he had in mind for her. "He knows I'm a Septer or a witch or whatever, and untrained. He said unless I was trained, I was a risk to the company."

Thomas's face was entirely composed, but his hand was fisting the napkin, crushing it. His fist shook. He looked close to snapping.

He regained his composure and smoothed out the napkin. An invisible wall had gone up, and he was hiding behind it.

"And what about the office itself?" he asked. "How many floors? What's it like inside? Where's the CEO's office? Is he among the others?"

Nadia paused. "Uh . . . it's, like, an open floor space plan. Rune's office is upstairs on the second floor. Most people sit downstairs in the common area."

"Are there elevators or stairs to get to the second floor?"

Nadia narrowed her eyes. "Why are you asking?"

"I'm just trying to paint a mental picture of your day."

Nadia doubted that, but answered truthfully, worried this was a test of her loyalty and he knew the answer already. "There's both. An elevator and stairs."

This seemed to appease him. "Thank you, Nadia. You're doing very well. Mercurio will be very pleased."

Nadia met his eyes. But they were scary and cold. Suddenly, she was very aware of the lack of humanity in him. She needed to remind him they were having a good time. She worried he could suddenly turn on her.

"Thank you for dinner. This was amazing."

He settled back, preening at the praise. "I'm so glad you liked it."

Thomas took her hand in his. Nadia wanted to snatch her hand back, but she didn't. She couldn't. She merely smiled, pretending.

Nadia was good at pretending. She slid the mask down over her face, so all that Thomas saw was a grateful, attentive dinner date.

If Numinals could have their glamour, so could she.

Chapter 9

The next morning at work, Rune and a Fae woman appeared next to Nadia's desk as she was getting settled in for the day. The woman was a striking redhead with a smattering of freckles and pale, creamy skin. She wore a pin skirt and heels. She looked like she had stepped out from a scene in *Mad Men*.

"Good morning!" the woman said brightly in a thick Irish accent. She held out a hand. "I'm Imogen, the director of Myst Foundation. Rune here tells me you're helping with the collection after I leave."

"Nice to meet you," said Nadia, shaking her hand.

"If you'll follow us," said Rune, "we'll show you the vaults and get you set up down in the library."

Rune and Imogen escorted Nadia across the main floor to the shiny chrome doors of the back elevators. Rune pressed the call button, and the doors opened silently. They stepped inside, and Rune swiped his key card and pressed the elevator button labeled "V." The doors slid shut, revealing their reflections. Imogen's eyes met Nadia's, and she smiled. Nadia caught Rune's eye and tried to smile at him as well, but he just stared at her with intense, dark eyes until she looked away.

Rune cleared his throat. "The library in Myst's vaults is highly specialized. We have an immense amount of historical and proprietary knowledge, and it would be a disaster if it fell into the wrong hands. As an employee, you are permitted to use the library for studying. But please do not remove any information without checking it out so we can track it and have it returned if the item is needed."

The elevator doors opened to a dark, subterranean room. They stepped out of the elevator, and motion sensors activated the lights, illuminating the space. It looked like it had been carved from bedrock. The air was cooler than it had been above. In front of them, flush against the rock wall, was a giant circular vault door. The gold metal on the rim shone in the light. There were three other giant circular vault doors, one in each quadrant of the rectangular room, with the elevator shaft in the middle projecting up to the tall ceiling.

"Employees and contractors have access to Vault One," explained Imogen. Her heels clicked as she walked, echoing in the chamber.

"What's in the other vaults?" Nadia asked.

"It's restricted access." Rune stopped in front of the giant round door to Vault One. He patted the door. "These doors are class three Orichalcum and steel, linked to the magical wards around the building that put the vault on lockdown in the event of an emergency. These vaults are designed to withstand a nuclear blast or any sort of magical attack."

"Orichalcum, like from Plato's *Critias*?" Nadia's heart sped up. The Myst Psionic pinged. She placed a hand over the watch, trying to stifle any other noises it was going to make as her mood shifted to excitement.

Rune looked impressed with the reference. "I'm surprised you know of it. Not many humans do."

"I wrote a paper on Atlantis when I was at school. It's the magical substance that covered the walls of the Temple of Poseidon."

Imogen glanced at him. "Maybe I can get back to Trinity sooner than later. It looks like I am going to leave you in capable hands."

Rune's expression darkened.

"We'll talk about it later," said Imogen quickly.

There was an access point next to the giant door. Rune took Nadia's hand and laid it palm down on the small screen. "Now, whenever you need to get access to Vault One, just place your palm here, and it will read your psychic signature. It only works through intention. If you placed your palm here but didn't want to get in, it wouldn't let you. An extra security measure."

After he punched in a series of numbers to program in Nadia's access, the vault unlocked. Rune turned the chrome ship handle on the door, and the seal broke with a hiss. They stepped back as the heavy vault door swung out toward them. Nadia gasped at what she saw.

Inside the vault was an immense baroque library with two floors. A gilded balcony lined the perimeter. Rows and stacks of books lined the walls, with a long black-and-white tiled corridor extending down the middle of the room to what looked like safety deposit boxes and metal stacks in the back. On the ceiling were frescoes of allegorical motifs, cherubic angels, and various mythical Numinals. As they walked into the room, Nadia couldn't keep herself from brushing the rich velvet armchairs with her hand.

"This place looks like the Klementinum in Prague," she murmured as she gazed at the rich wood and gold finishings.

"It was modeled after the Klementinum. I studied there for a bit and am rather fond of it." Rune looked up at the ceiling. "But that was a long time ago." He sounded wistful. Rune motioned for them to follow him to the back. He spun an antique globe on a brass stand as he passed it.

They walked down the lofty corridor toward the back of the room and passed brass telescopes, astronomical clocks, and musical instruments. Early airships and flying machines hung above them from the ceiling like steampunk kites, and Nadia couldn't help but marvel at the extensive museum-quality displays of artifacts and technology. The room was her dream library, better than any library-porn she had seen on Pinterest.

They stopped at a study table in the back of the room in front of shiny chrome safety deposit boxes that were compressed together in rolling stack shelves. Imogen picked up the iPad propped up on a stand on the table and turned it on. The Myst logo rotated on the screen before it disappeared to reveal the search page.

"All Myst's books and artifacts are cataloged in this database. It's searchable by keyword. Part of your job will be to cross-index new acquisitions and expand the current index of items. Books are located in the library here, and any physical artifacts will be found in these safety deposit boxes. The library items will have an identifying classification number, and the artifacts will have a button to retrieve."

She handed Nadia the iPad. "Okay, do a Boolean keyword search for 'medieval' and 'scroll' and see what comes up."

Nadia typed that in and hit search. Numerous book entries came up, as well as nine artifact entries. She clicked on the first entry, which was for an artifact:

Twenty-five Bodhisattvas Descending from Heaven, Japan, Kamakura period c. 1300. Pair of hanging scrolls; gold and mineral pigments on silk. On loan from the Kimball Museum. The painting expresses belief in the compassionate grace of Amida. Used in spells to transfer the soul of the deceased to heaven.

"And then, if you hit the request button," said Imogen, "it will move the stacks and open the drawer containing the object so you can inspect it."

Nadia hit the button. In front of them, the compact stacks moved on a rail system anchored to the floor with a slight buzz, moving all the compressed rows over to access a specific row of the safety deposit boxes. They walked over to the now-open pathway and found the open drawer marked D-2769. Rune stalked silently behind them, observing.

"We're going to start you out doing collections cataloging," said Imogen. "We have some new pieces that we just acquired that haven't been cataloged yet."

"Sounds easy enough. I have a ton of experience with that."

"Most of the data we have on the items is analog," interjected Rune. "You will need to go through the source data to verify its authenticity."

"I'm sure Nadia knows how cataloging works," said Imogen. "I'll finish up her training, if you don't mind. It's probably better if I just deep dive into all the nuances of the job."

Rune looked like he wanted to stay but merely nodded and left.

Imogen clasped her hands together with a smile. "Shall we?"

To get Nadia up to speed and familiar with the collection, Imogen started her off with auditing the records, ensuring that books and artifacts were in their proper location and indexed in the database. It was tedious work, but relatively easy, and allowed her to peruse the extensive collection of ancient tomes, relics, and mythological artifacts that Myst housed. The entire place was chock-full of books and scrolls, magical weaponry and armor, amulets and treasure, jewelry and art, musical instruments, chalices, and cups—anything you could possibly need for a spell or to enhance magic. Staff and consultants could browse the collection and check out books or tools to complete projects. Imogen told her that Rune encouraged many of the Mystics to use the collection to learn various new magical techniques and spells through self-study.

While Nadia worked doing inventory in the back of the library, Imogen sat at one of the tables with her laptop and chatted with her as she answered donor emails, telling Nadia about the Foundation and the classes she taught at Trinity. Imogen told Nadia that her Seelie family members disapproved of her work.

Nadia got the impression that Seelie were kind of uptight. While Avery seemed to be a Fae slacker or bum, she had noticed a few hoity-toity mannerisms from him.

"But when I heard about Rune's mission, I knew I had to get involved in the Foundation, even temporarily. The Seelie are an ancient, proud race of High Fae. But times are changing. We need to find ways for the Fae to live among humans. Most of the Seelie are back in the Light Court in the Fae Realm, of course, but it's not just a Fae issue. It's a Numinal issue."

Nadia wasn't sure what she was talking about with realms and all that. "My grandma's roommate is Seelie," said Nadia. She pulled up the index for a draconite stone.

"What's his name? There aren't many Seelie. I probably know him."

"Avery Thornwood."

Imogen looked thoughtful and confused. "I'm not sure that I know him. That's strange. The Seelie community is tight-knit. I thought I knew everyone here."

Nadia shrugged. "So, what's the Light Court?"

Imogen laughed before she saw the confused expression on Nadia's face. "Oh, I thought you were joking."

"Uh, no. Sorry, I'm new to all this." Nadia waved a hand in the air, irritated at Marina for keeping her in the dark all those years. She had so much to learn.

"Oh well, let's see. You know about the Collapse, I assume?" Imogen arched a pretty eyebrow in question.

"I don't think so."

"Oh! Well, I am sure we have a history book around here somewhere that you can read, but the CliffsNotes version is that about seven hundred years ago—around the time of the Black Plague—something, some great catastrophe happened, closing and locking the Realm Gates so that Numinals can no longer travel between

Earth and the Other Realms. The Light Court is home to the Seelie."

"Ah okay, I see." She didn't. Not really.

They continued in silence.

"Can I ask you a question?" Nadia asked.

"Sure."

"What's the best way to impress Rune? I really want to do a good job here."

Imogen sighed. "Rune can be difficult. He's an extremely powerful and influential Numinal, especially in the Fae community."

"Rune is High Fae, like you?"

"Basically." She stood up and started packing away her things. "He's extremely smart, innovative, and driven. He holds himself up to an impossibly high standard. Luckily, he doesn't hold the rest of us up to that same standard. The best way to impress him is by being genuine. He values honesty and integrity. Admit when you make a mistake. We all make them. But he appreciates employees who take ownership of those mistakes and learn from them."

Nadia's mouth went dry. "That makes sense."

"I need to handle some things above. Are you okay here by yourself? Just lock away all the items you called up when you leave."

"Thanks. I'll be fine."

She listened to Imogen's heels click on the marble floor of the library and fade away until she was left alone with just her thoughts to keep her company for the rest of the workday.

Nadia arrived at work early the next morning. On the way over to her desk, she spied Maya and Carson in the lounge area having coffee, and she waved at them. Maya waved back. Carson looked preoccupied as he reviewed several printouts, pointing something out to Maya who was disagreeing, shaking her head.

Kevin flew by on an e-scooter, nearly hitting her, and she jumped out of the way as he careened into a troupe of tanukis like a bowling ball. The shapeshifting raccoons scattered like pins, snarling and shouting obscenities. One of the tanukis jumped onto Kevin's head in retaliation and tea-bagged him with a mischievous glint in its eye.

"Oh good, you're here," said Piero as he bounded over to Nadia at her desk. "I have a special project for you."

Nadia dropped her bag next to her chair. "What's going on?"

Piero leaned against her desk and crossed his arms, adopting the air of an FBI agent briefing a situation. "We're getting a pitch ready for Mystos. The US government invited us to bid for a tsunami-and-extreme-weather early warning system. My sources tell me Pact is also putting a bid in for this one, so we need to make sure it's airtight."

"Pact is the competition?"

"Correction," said Piero. "Pact is the enemy. They are Bad News Bears. Everything they touch is tainted and evil."

Nadia chuckled. "Okay, so what's the plan? How can I help?"

"The plan is to not only put into place an early warning system for extreme weather using our seers, but we also want to influence the weather to prevent disasters from happening in the first place. Pact never incorporates preventative measures, so this will really make us stand out."

"How do we influence the weather?"

"That's up to the team to decide. But with the catfish I just brought on board as the cornerstone of the project, I'm assuming it will involve heavy weather and ocean spells. We tell clients its proprietary trade secrets, and we can't reveal our methods. We've done similar projects like this before."

A large stack of papers zoomed through the air like a flying carpet and stopped in front of Piero. He reached up, grabbed them, and dropped them into Nadia's outstretched hands. "We need to expand our current talent pool to deal with specialized weather knowledge for this project. This is the slush pile of resumes. Flag anyone who has experience with oceans, weather, and wind, do a background check on their qualifications, and then write me up a report highlighting the top candidates and their credentials."

Nadia glanced down at the voluminous stack of resumes. The whole project seemed entirely out of the realm of her experience and expertise. "How am I supposed to do a background check on their credentials?" she asked, dubiously.

"In the library, of course." Piero poked her in the middle of the forehead with his index finger. "Use that brain of yours. Research what they list as experience and cross-check it against the myths and history books in the stacks. I would help, but I'm just too slammed right now."

Nadia shifted the papers in her arms. "Sorry, I'm just not understanding. You want me to look up myths? How does that complete a background check?"

"Listen, this isn't an exact science here." He grabbed the resume off the top of the pile and scanned it. "Okay, take a look at this one: Magus Stormwatcher. Magician. Experience includes controlling the wind and storms, breaking droughts. Representative projects include Tibetan rain dances and calling lightning through celestial manipulation. So, you would look up Tibetan rain dances and lightning spells and see if his experience holds water. No pun intended. Got it?"

Nadia frowned at the papers.

Piero placed the resume back on top of the pile. "This will be a good experience for you. We all have to wear different hats here and pitch in where we can." He glanced at his watch. "Oh shit. I'm late for a coffee meeting. You got this?" He looked at her expectantly. She nodded. "Great! I expect the report on my desk by the end of the week."

Nadia took a seat and started scanning the resumes as she waited for her laptop to boot up. The breadth of experience was astounding. The candidates were all experienced magicians, sorcerers, druids, witches, and Numinals with magical powers and abilities. One resume was from a candidate who had gone to not only medical school but also veterinarian school and some sort of magical post-doc program. He specialized in animal-human hybrids and shapeshifters, several of which Nadia had never heard of. It would take hours to figure out what myths and folklore those were from to do the background check, and that was from one resume. She had a huge pile to go through, each just as complicated.

Nadia got up to grab herself a latte from the café. Caffeine would definitely be needed.

Chapter 10

Nadia's first week at Myst flew by. Between Piero's project of going through the resume slush piles and Imogen's work getting her up to speed on the library and collections, Nadia had her work cut out for her. But it felt good to work. It was a welcome distraction. The more she worked, the less time she had to think about her life and what was in store for her as one of Mercurio's employees.

By the time Friday rolled around, Nadia was exhausted and looking forward to a quiet night of Netflix, Ben & Jerry's, and a bottle of wine. As she was packing up her habitat, Piero strolled over.

"Where do you think you're going?" he demanded.

"Uh, home?" Nadia glanced at her Psionic. "It's six. Do you need me to stay late?"

He rolled his eyes. "No, of course not. I'm cruel, but not that cruel. It's happy hour. I wanted to take you out to celebrate you surviving your first week."

"Oh, that's okay." Nadia tucked a strand of hair behind her ear before she picked up her bag and swung it over her shoulder. "I should be getting home."

"Nonsense! It's tradition."

Sophie and Maya joined them in front of Nadia's habitat.

"What's the good word?" asked Maya as she shrugged on an

army-green coat with patches pinned all over. "Happy hour at the food truck park?"

Nadia tried to rouse interest in going . . . and failed. "I'm pretty beat after this week."

"You *have* to go," said Maya. "As your Myst Buddy, I insist."

"I know of something better than the food truck park." Sophie fished her cell phone out of her back jeans pocket and started scrolling through email. She held it up so they all could see the screen. "It's a 'Fuck Me, I'm Funded' party for Kami." Sophie swayed slightly on her heels. Apparently, she'd already started happy hour.

Piero's eyes lit up. "We have got to go. Everyone who is anyone is going to be there."

"What's a 'Fuck Me, I'm Funded' party?" Nadia asked. In college, she'd been to her fair share of theme parties, but that was a new one.

"Kami is another Numinal startup based out of Tokyo. They have an office in San Francisco. They just got their Series A and are throwing a huge party in Japantown." Sophie looked at her phone, squinting. "Cocktails started at six. Shall we?"

Carson strolled up. He clapped his big hands once and rubbed them together. "Who's headed to the Kami party? Want to ride together?"

Piero linked his arm through Nadia's and steered her toward the front. The others followed. "Guess you're coming out with us," said Piero, grinning.

The Kami party turned out to be in a nightclub and lounge called Tokyo Drifter. After they all piled out of the Lyft, Nadia gazed up at the pink neon sign that made the club seem more like a cheap karaoke joint rather than a venue that could host a lavish party.

"Have you been here before?" Maya asked her as they walked toward the entrance. Nadia shook her head. Maya's eyes lit up.

"Oh, you're in for a treat. It's awesome. It's decorated like a Yakuza nightclub from the '60s."

And indeed, it was. Nadia followed the others in through swinging doors, past big Numinal bouncers, past velvet ropes, and down plush red carpets to enter a hopping cocktail hour, pop music blasting over the sound system.

They took some selfies at the selfie station near the front, striking various hilariously awkward group poses as they tried unsuccessfully to all do a "serious one" and a "fun one." They uploaded the pictures to social media, tagging the pictures. #Kamibot #FuckMeImFunded #CantStopWontStop #WorkHardPlayHard #MysticsDoItBetter

Nadia hoped that Keith and Hailee and all her old friends would see her looking like she was having the time of her life out in San Francisco. It had been a small consolation to tell them all she was working at a hot new startup in California while they all were pushing papers at their lame entry-level jobs back in DC.

"I need a drink," said Sophie as soon as they were done at the selfie station. Piero was vogueing for Nadia as she laughed, taking photos of his clowning around, but Sophie grabbed Piero's hand and disappeared with him into the crowd.

"There's the CEO of Kami. I want to pick his brain on how they're handling the API." Carson ushered Maya toward a crowd gathered on the other side of the room. Maya gave Nadia an apologetic smile and mouthed "be right back" over the blaring music as he dragged her away.

And suddenly, Nadia was alone.

She stood at the front entrance, feeling slightly foolish for coming. But, she figured, free food and drinks. Might as well hang out a bit and check out the scene. Netflix and the Boys—that's what she called Ben & Jerry's—could wait.

Nadia scanned the crowd. The club was spacious, with what looked like several side rooms all playing different music. The main space was playing clubby J-Pop and had Harajuku imagery and art on the walls. On either side, black leather couches and chairs flanked the sides with large mirrors paneling the wall. Go-go dancers in mod outfits and thigh-high boots danced on elevated platforms. It was the type of place Zoey would have loved.

Nadia suddenly had a pang of missing her old life and friends. She hadn't talked to many people since the move. Everybody was so busy, off living their lives. And she had completely cut Keith and Hailee from her life. Nadia snapped a picture of the room and shot it off in a text to Zoey.

Check this place out. Miss you xoxo.

Nadia made her way through the throngs of Numinals and humans to check out the other rooms. One was set up like a casino, people gathered around poker and craps tables throwing dice and spinning wheels. Another was more of a lounge area, with beds and pillows. Another had karaoke, while a fortune teller was set up in a covered booth. And weaving throughout everyone were small white humanoid robots, about three feet tall, serving drinks and sushi to guests.

Still looking for the others but not finding them, Nadia got a glass of champagne at the bar and then headed over to the sushi station, where one of Kami's robots was slicing fresh pieces of sashimi. It was wearing a sushi chef coat and a little hat with Kami's symbol embroidered on the front. Its hands transformed into cutting knives like Edward Scissorhands as it sliced and diced the fish. Her stomach rumbled, reminding her she hadn't eaten dinner yet. Nadia ordered toro, hamachi, and kampachi from the cute little robot and found a seat at a nearby table to eat and people-watch while she scouted for the others. She popped a piece of toro in her mouth with chopsticks and then texted Piero to ask where everyone was.

"You know, you are ruining that sushi by drinking champagne with it." The man's voice was playful and slightly mocking.

Nadia looked up. Standing in front of her was a good-looking man in his early thirties, with short wavy blond hair. He was wearing a striped seersucker jacket with jeans and had a pair of Warby Parkers tucked into his shirt collar. He looked very East Coast, like he took a wrong turn from his garden party in the Hamptons. In one hand was a bottle of sake; in the other, a plate of sushi and two little cups.

"Care for some sake?" He raised the bottle at her, waving it back and forth slightly, and grinned like the Cheshire Cat.

"I'm okay, thanks." Nadia returned her attention to her phone.

Instead of taking the hint, he sat down at the table. He poured two cups of sake and placed one in front of her. She looked up at him, surprised at his boldness.

"It's clear you are new to this whole thing," he started, waving a hand about himself.

"This whole thing, meaning . . . ?" She was unsure if he meant startups, or Yakuza-themed Fuck Me, I'm Funded parties, or Numinals in general, or—

"Sushi."

Nadia suppressed a laugh at his earnest expression. "Oh?"

"Yes. It is very apparent from your choices. You are playing it safe with those fish. You need to be adventurous and try new things." He gestured to his plate. "Now this, *this* is a real piece of fish. This here is blowfish."

"You mean fugu?" She smiled sweetly at him and took another sip of her champagne. She was going to need another drink stat to deal with this knockoff Jude Law trying to neg her.

His blue eyes lit up. "You *do* know your sushi. But why on earth would you ruin it with *that*"—he waved another careless hand toward her drink—"when you could pair it with *this*?" He picked up a piece of nigiri from his plate with his hands and popped it into his mouth before shooting the sake in one gulp.

"You know you are supposed to sip that, right?"

He grinned and poured himself another cupful. "I guess you could say I'm a nonconformist when it comes to my drink and my women. Here's looking at you, kid." He raised the other sake cup and shot it back.

Nadia cringed. "Does that line actually work for you?"

"You'd be surprised. Most people aren't Bogart fans and have no idea what I'm talking about, and the others who recognize it think I'm just being clever." He held out his hand over the top of the table. "I'm Miles, by the way."

"Nadia." They shook hands.

He smiled. "I think this is the beginning of a beautiful friendship."

Nadia laughed, shaking her head at his lame joke, and then kicking herself for falling for it.

"So, what brings you here?" he asked.

"Besides the sushi?" Nadia leaned back in the booth. "Just hanging out with coworkers, who happen to have gone missing at the moment."

"Well, it's a good thing I swooped in to save you and keep you entertained, then. I would hate for someone as lovely as yourself to be lacking company."

"Are you always this . . ."

"Charming?"

"I was going to say 'forward.'"

He laughed. "Fortune favors the bold."

"Fortune favors the foolish."

He laughed again, placing his arm over the back of the booth casually. "Touché."

A small humanoid robot with large round eyes walked over with a tray of champagne. Nadia downed hers before she grabbed another and placed her empty glass on the robot's tray.

"The robots are a nice touch," she said as it walked away. "I don't know that I've ever seen ones like that before. Their movements are so fluid. I would say they're almost real."

He eyed her suspiciously. "Are you a Sixer, by chance?"

She looked at him sharply, mentally kicking herself for not checking for a glamour on him earlier. She checked now, finding none. Human.

"You must be one as well then," she replied.

"Guilty as charged."

"What if I wasn't a Sixer?"

"Then you'd probably have no idea what I was talking about. But almost all humans who are in the Numinal startup scene are Sixers. Are you familiar with Kami's business model?"

Nadia shook her head.

"Ah, well, let me enlighten you," said Miles as he poured himself another shot of sake. "These newest models are basically like personal assistants. But instead of AI, Kami uses *yōkai. Tsukumogami,* to be exact. They are so much more dependable."

"Sorry, did you say that the robots, these robots"—Nadia gestured to one standing nearby—"are *Tsukumogami?*"

Nadia had taken a class on Japanese art and mythology in college. *Yōkai* was the term for spirit in Japanese, and *Tsukumogami* was the term for household objects that obtained a spirit after a hundred years. The art depicting animated brooms, fans, and lanterns had always reminded Nadia of *Fantasia.*

Miles nodded. "Kami transplants *Tsukumogami* into the robots and gives them a new life. There isn't much need for sentient antiques, but personal assistants are high in demand."

"Wow." Nadia took another look at a nearby robot, trying to figure out what *Tsukumogami* it used to be.

"Kami is rather ingenious," Miles continued. "Unlike some of the other local startups around here."

"Oh?"

He shrugged. "In the startup scene in the city, there are only a few that stand out. But most are just not up to snuff. Take Myst, for example." He gestured at Nadia's watch.

"What's wrong with Myst?"

He waved a hand dismissively in front of his face. "Total lack of focus. They have too many projects and divisions. One minute they have a gig-based app, the next, they are doing mobile games. They're all over the place."

"But they all sort of tie together, don't they?"

"Barely. The CEO tries to do too much with too little."

From the corner of her eye, she saw Piero, Carson, and Maya storming toward her. They stopped up short at the black leather booth where she and Miles were seated.

"Hey guys," said Nadia.

Piero looked at her, then looked at Miles, then looked back at her. "Nadia, there you are. We've been looking everywhere for you." His normally jovial tone came out clipped and short.

"These are your coworkers?" asked Miles in surprise. "You work at Myst?"

"She does, and if you excuse us, we have to go." Piero grabbed Nadia's arm and started to haul her up out of the booth.

"Carson Ross, right?" asked Miles, eyeing Carson. "I'm surprised to see you here. Rune must have let you slip the leash tonight." He glanced about himself, a self-confident smirk on his face. "Where is he, anyway? I should have known you guys would try to ride on the coattails of Kami."

Carson took a step toward Miles with a growl, but Maya grabbed his bicep.

"Enough!" she said. "We don't want to make a scene. There are reporters everywhere here."

Piero started to pull Nadia away as Maya grabbed Carson.

"Lovely talking to you, Nadia. I hope to see you around," Miles called after her.

"I fucking *hate* that guy," said Carson through clenched teeth when they had moved into a corner in the next room. All around them, people danced, bopping to the music and waving glow sticks in the air.

Piero whirled on Nadia. "Why on earth were you talking to Miles Kirkpatrick?"

"Whoa, easy there," said Nadia, leaning back in surprise at Piero's outburst. "He just came over and sat down. Who is he, anyway?"

"He's the CEO of Pact!" Maya exclaimed. "He's a notorious playboy and loves to steal all Myst's ideas. He probably was after information from you."

"What did you tell that meatbag?" demanded Carson, his fangs extending. The tips of his ears and the back of his hands sprouted fur.

"Watch it, Romulus," said Piero. "You're looking a little wolfy there."

Carson growled, but he gave himself a slight shake with a self-conscious glance about himself. The fur receded.

"I didn't say anything," said Nadia. "He didn't even know I worked at Myst until you guys came over."

Piero, Carson, and Maya looked visibly relieved.

"You should stay away from him," warned Piero. "Seriously. Nothing good can come from talking to Miles Kirkpatrick."

Maya looked over to the doorway they had come through. "There *is* something off about him, but I can't put my finger on it."

"Come on, guys. He wasn't that bad. Sure, he used some pretty lame pickup lines, but that hardly makes him a leper."

"He and Rune hate each other," said Piero, leaning in conspiratorially. "Like, mortal enemies sort of hatred. I'm glad Rune isn't here, or else there definitely would have been a scene." Piero rubbed her arm supportively. "Sorry for the fire drill, but when we saw you over there, we assumed the worst."

Nadia shrugged. "It's fine." She looked around at the dancing crowd. "Where'd Sophie go?"

Piero stood on tiptoes, glancing about. "She's around here somewhere."

"She's over there." Maya nodded toward the far corner. Through the crowds of people, they could see Sophie talking to some techie-looking guy in a hoodie and jeans. Sophie was flagrantly flirting with him, touching his arm and flipping her pastel-pink hair about.

"What's she doing?" Nadia asked.

Piero shrugged. "Looks like she's finally talking to that guy she likes."

"Doesn't she like that guy, Peter?" asked Maya.

Carson shook his head. "That's not Peter."

Piero's head waved back and forth as he tried to get a better look through the crowd. "Then who the fuck is that guy?"

As they were watching her, Sophie made an animated, wild gesture with her arm, sloshing the drink she was holding all over the guy. He leaped backward, knocking into a LED light display on a table behind him which tumbled to the ground with a loud crash.

"And that's our cue to leave." Maya made a circle in the air with her finger. "Round up. Let's get her out of here. I'm over this party."

The moon was high overhead as they exited Tokyo Drifter. A few people were standing around the front smoking JUULs and clove cigarettes, including a group of three female *yōkai* spirits. As Piero flagged down a cab, Carson and Maya flanked Sophie, holding on to either arm so she wouldn't topple over. Nadia watched as a tech guy walked up to the *yōkai* and tried to hit on them, failing miserably. The *yōkai* laughed at his attempt and then dismissed him, one of them telling him to "get lost, nerd."

"Hey, new girl," Sophie slurred, raising her head as she looked at Nadia with glassy eyes. "You're a Septer, right? Do some magic."

"That's enough of that," said Piero sternly. "There are muggles everywhere." Piero looked apologetically at Nadia as a cab pulled to the side of the road.

"What?" said Sophie. "She's a Septer. She should prove it. I bet she can't even do anything."

Nadia bit down on a petty comment. She wasn't trying to make an enemy. Piero opened the cab door and he and Carson shoved Sophie into the backseat.

"She'd better not be sick back there," said the cabbie, frowning as he looked back dubiously at Sophie.

"She's fine," called out Piero into the cab. "I'll tip you extra."

"Make her do magic!" yelled Sophie. She crawled to the window. "Pull a rabbit out of a hat!" She laughed manically, suddenly way more animated than she had been when she was nearly passing out a minute ago.

Maya touched her two index fingers together and quickly twisted her hands together in a series of rapid hand and finger maneuvers that Nadia recognized as some sort of spell. After the spell had been charged up, she pinched her thumb and index finger together. Sophie suddenly went quiet mid-laugh, glaring at Maya. She tried to speak, opening and closing her mouth, but no words came out. Nadia laughed, surprised.

Maya shrugged. "What? She was getting on my nerves."

"What spell was that? I need to learn that one."

She grinned. "It's a silencer charm. Comes in super useful, but it only lasts a couple of minutes. You should stock up on a few innocuous charms. Speeding up people in the checkout line at the grocery store, repelling weirdos on BART. Totally makes navigating the city easier."

"No shit? That's awesome. I'm definitely going to do that." Nadia watched as Sophie continued to try to talk, frustrated.

"Staff meeting first thing on Monday." Piero climbed into the back of the taxi. "It's mainly for team leads, but the entire Veil team will be there to give Rune an update. Nadia, you should sit in.

It will be a good opportunity for you to learn more about the other projects going on." He glanced at Sophie. "I'd better get Drunky McDrunkerson here home before we all end up splashed on the front of TechCrunch." Nadia got the impression this wasn't the first time he'd taken a too-drunk Sophie home.

Sophie tried crawling over Piero's lap to the window. Her heels flew up in the air as she toppled over.

"Oh lord, she's kicking like Seabiscuit now," said Piero, shoving Sophie off him. "Okay, we are out of here."

Nadia suppressed a chuckle as she slammed the car door. Piero slapped the back of the passenger side headrest twice. "Onward, cabbie! Tally-ho!" The cab driver shook his head, muttering something about tech weirdos, and pulled away from the curb.

Maya and Carson turned to Nadia. "What did you think of the party?" asked Maya.

"I've never been to anything like it," confessed Nadia. She shivered a bit, wishing she had on a heavier jacket. Nights in San Francisco were colder than in DC.

Carson checked his phone. "My Lyft is almost here. Maya, you're on the way, right? Want to split?"

She nodded and then hugged Nadia. "Do you want us to wait for you?" asked Maya as the Lyft pulled over to the curb.

"Naw, I'm fine. I'll see you on Monday," said Nadia as they climbed into their ride. Maya waved out the window as the car pulled away.

Nadia stood out in front of the club, watching as others stumbled out, laughing with their friends and coworkers, and she suddenly felt very alone. She scrolled through her phone, looking for someone to text. Thinking about how Miles had reminded her of Keith, she hovered over Keith's name, wondering what she could text him to say "hi" but not sound desperate or like she forgave him. They hadn't exactly left things on the best terms after she told him to go fuck himself. Luckily, before she could text him, her phone vibrated, letting her know her ride was arriving soon. She opened the app and concentrated on that instead.

On the way home, nestled safely in the backseat of the car, Nadia's cell phone pinged. It was Zoey.

Miss u 2. Looks like ur living it up!

Nadia sighed, and put her cell phone back into her purse, closing her eyes to fight back the tears that threatened to fall.

Chapter 11

"Good morning, Miss Studious," said Piero the following Monday. "Don't you just look adorable, with your notebook and pencils. Are you wearing plaid? How very vintage Britney of you." Piero, dressed in a grey pinstripe suit with a checkered bowtie, flipped his bangs out of his face as he checked out Nadia's outfit and sat down next to her at the conference table.

Nadia looked down and realized that she had subconsciously dressed similarly to her prep school days, with a plaid mini skirt, knee-high black socks, and a fitted sweater. It had been her power outfit when she was younger. It gave her confidence. Academia was familiar and comfortable; all her life she had good grades and had been at the top of her class. If she could turn this entire situation of suddenly working for a supernatural startup into a research exercise, she knew that she could handle it.

The others poured into the conference room, late for the weekly status meeting. Nadia was beginning to learn that startup time wasn't real time, as everybody seemed to come into the office whenever they felt like it and were perpetually five minutes late for meetings. Nadia, of course, had been on time; she had sat alone at the conference table, wondering if she was in the right room.

While they waited for the meeting to start, the Mystics poured themselves coffee and what looked like a steaming green potion from the pots and bottles on the side tables. Nadia hadn't met most of the other Mystics yet, but she recognized a few, including a forest nymph who trailed footprints of moss and blossoms wherever she walked and a leprechaun in green overalls who winked at Nadia when he entered the room.

Sophie breezed into the room wearing dark aviator sunglasses. Her hair that morning was purple. She took a seat across the table from Nadia, ignoring her as she chatted to Carson. Maya entered, headphones on, smiling brightly, and waved at Nadia. Carson moved over to give Maya room next to him.

Rune entered. Everyone quieted and looked up at him expectantly. He was wearing a grey zip-up sweatshirt and wire-rimmed glasses, making him look exactly what Nadia always thought a startup CEO would look like, if CEOs looked like *GQ* models. She pushed that thought away, trying to focus and control her thoughts and emotions. She really needed to get a grip on herself when she was around him.

Nadia held her pen over her pad, ready to take notes. Rune scanned their faces, nodding slightly as if he was taking inventory of everyone. Nadia thought she saw the corner of his mouth twitch when he saw her there, looking like the eager student, ready to write down everything he was going to say, but he launched into the meeting.

Rune went over the status of current projects in the pipeline, including putting together a bid on a consulting project for a branch of the federal government responsible for anti-terrorist initiatives. "Here's the deal," he said. "They already use Palantir, but it isn't cutting it. Their predictive technology isn't one hundred percent accurate."

"But neither are our seers," interjected Piero. "We are hitting ninety to ninety-two percent accuracy at best right now with our current talent pool."

"Better than Palantir, though," said Rune. "The problem is with human behavior. Humans are mostly predictable creatures that the algorithm can figure out, but they need better to take into account the anomalies and outliers. They need to see the future. I told them we can give them that with our forecasting 'technology.'"

"Do we know if Pact is putting in a bid on this as well?" asked Imogen. "I can see what artifacts we have that Pact doesn't that will boost the seer's accuracy." Imogen sat by Rune's side, taking notes. She was dressed fancier than others in a pin skirt and white blouse, her red hair pulled back into a bun. Nadia felt a pang of self-consciousness at her outfit that had only moments before given her confidence. It was hard not to compare herself to the woman whose Louboutins she would have to fill.

"Rumor has it that they are." Rune rubbed the stubble on his chin absentmindedly.

While Imogen and Rune had a sidebar conversation, Piero leaned in toward Nadia, speaking in a low voice. "Pact uses black magic. Like, real bad, dark stuff with the intent to harm. The clients don't know it, thinking their technology is just an advanced algorithm like they think ours is. But often Pact ends up with more bids because of the types of projects they will take on and the methods they use to complete the projects."

"What kind of projects?" Nadia whispered.

"Sometimes, some of the consulting project requests are ones we have to turn down because it would take black magic—something that Myst doesn't tolerate—to work. Like last week, we had a corporate intelligence request where a big oil conglomerate wanted their competitor's fleet to mysteriously be out of commission. They don't want to know how we're going to do it; they just want it done. The week before that we had to turn another down where a well-known political figure wanted us to dig up dirt on their competitor in an upcoming election, and when we couldn't find anything, to plant something. You know, pictures with hookers, or a men's bathroom toe-tapping debacle. That sort of thing."

"I'm surprised they're so candid in their requests," Nadia said.

"The requests, like the bids and the results, are all confidential. People come to us when their current systems or fixers—ones like Palantir or consulting firms like Bain or Blackwater—can't do the job. They don't know and don't want to know *how* we do it. Pact is way more lenient in its methods than we are. We expressly forbid our talent pool from using black magic, but Pact allows it. Sometimes even encourages it."

"I see," she said, not really understanding at all.

Rune continued going over the status of current projects. After an hour or so, Nadia's hand was cramped from taking so many notes, her head spinning. She felt like she would never get up to speed.

During a short break, the goblins came in with a snack cart and passed out treats, including freshly baked muffins and neon-glowing smoothies. Grudax handed Nadia an apple after a stern look from Rune.

"All right," said Rune, clapping his hands. "Let's get back to it. Let's hear from the Veil team. How are we doing with the release?"

Carson started discussing the results of the latest beta test of Veil. From what Nadia understood, users ran around the city gaining points by having adventures and live role-playing interactions with magical creatures. Except the creatures in Veil were real, magical beings that could earn extra money by posing as creatures in the game, basically combining AR and real-life role-playing games into one. The AR plug-in—which was a small flat plug that connected through the power source on a cell phone—would cast a spell that allowed the user to pierce the glamour the creature was wearing, so the user would think that the game was just an advanced augmented reality system that was giving actors an overlay or skin.

Mercurio had mentioned "Myst's game, Veil." He had seemed especially interested in the technology they used to cast a spell around a user to pierce the glamour of magical creatures. Nadia wasn't sure exactly why he was interested in it, but she sat up in her chair, determined to learn everything she could. Whether she told him anything, well, that was a different story. She wondered if she could twist any details, so it just looked like she was spying without actually betraying the company.

"What is the status of the battery design?" Rune scrolled through his phone, checking his notes.

Carson pulled up some specs and projected them across the screen. "The main issue we're having is that the technology to cast the spell that pierces the glamours is eating up the battery life at too fast a rate. So far, we're only getting about twenty to thirty minutes tops before the battery dies."

"No good. Let's keep working on that. Maybe revisit some of the old battery and efficiency specs to see if we can salvage any of that work." Rune leaned back in his chair. He threw a pen in the air and caught it.

Nadia whispered to Piero. "Why can't they just 'spell' the battery to last longer? You know, use magic?"

Piero gave her the side-eye. "You know magic has limitations, right? You can't just go 'hocus-pocus' and make things work. I'm not in the tech department, but my understanding is there is an issue with entropy. The amount of energy needed to power the AR plug-in is being eaten up at too fast a rate."

Maya had been listening to their conversation and cut in. "We've been working on a way to supplement the batteries with alternate sources of energy, like kinetic or thermoelectric energy on wearable devices, but it's unstable. That's those specs that Rune was talking about. So, we're working on other ways to make tiny long-lasting batteries."

Nadia leaned back in her chair, pretending that she understood. She was doing a lot of that recently.

The meeting was almost over, people starting to pack up, when Vega cleared her throat.

"There's one last thing," said Vega, drumming her Barbie-pink nails on the table. Her translucent wings fluttered behind her. "It has to do with the safety of the actors." Groans erupted. "I know, I know. No one wants to talk about HR issues, but it's important. The beta testers are responding well to the game, but they keep trying to grab the actors, especially those who give out coins. We just had a user try to wring coins out of a Redcap. It required a lot of hazard pay and a replacement pikestaff after he broke it fending off the user, who has since been dealt with through the usual memory extractions."

Rune leaned back in his chair with his hands behind his head, looking up at the ceiling as he thought. "What about the safeguards? Don't we have a magical barrier up for the actors so users can't touch them?"

"Doesn't stop them from trying," chimed in Sophie. "And sometimes the actors are caught unawares without the guards up, like they forgot to turn off the app when they went on break."

"Earlier this week, we had a complaint from a faerie that the user was being inappropriate with her," continued Vega. "Lewd gestures and attempts at inappropriate touching. We put the user on probation and smoothed it over with the faerie with hazard pay. But this is a major harassment issue."

Rune sighed. He took off his glasses and rubbed the bridge of his nose before replacing them. "We can't keep putting actors in situations that warrant hazard pay. How do we fix this?"

Nadia cleared her throat. "How about in the high-risk situations, the Numinal is virtual instead of real?" All eyes turned to her. It was the first time she had spoken up all morning.

Sophie rolled her eyes. "That goes against the whole point of the game. We're employing magical creatures to replace virtual ones for a more authentic experience, newbie. If we wanted to make a virtual reality game, we would've done that."

"Sophie," warned Rune, silencing her with a glance. Her cheeks reddened at his tone.

"I think Ms. Winters might be on to something here," said Rune, slowly. He looked thoughtful. "What if the Numinals involved in those specific interactions that lead to users getting coins are virtual reality? We can use the Redcaps and other Numinals with that function somewhere else in the narrative. We can't cut out the coins altogether. Veil is incentive-based. Users need to gain coins to unlock new aspects of the game."

"Most of the issues we've had have been with those Redcaps," admitted Piero. "People get excited like they're gambling and start getting grabby with the coins as they pop out."

"So then make some sort of virtual treasure faerie instead of using the Redcaps. Rewrite the Redcaps' plotlines to be a fortune-giving situation. Problem solved," said Rune.

"But I feel like this undermines the mission of the game, which is to employ Numinals," protested Sophie. "We shouldn't be using virtual creatures."

Nadia sat up straighter in her chair. "Isn't part of the mission to find ways that Numinals and humans can interact? Safely? I think until humans know about the existence of magical creatures, having part real and part virtual makes sense."

If looks could kill, Nadia would be dead with the look Sophie gave her. "Listen, newbie—"

"The name's Nadia." Her watch pinged with her sudden shift in mood to anger.

"You two, my office, now," said Rune, curtly. The room was silent, watching the interaction.

Nadia's cheeks burned as she rose to her feet, glaring at Sophie. She felt like she had just been sent to the principal's office.

Rune's office was on the second floor of the building, a large bright room with glass walls overlooking the main coworking space. One side of the office was flanked with a large bookcase filled with antique books and collectibles, ranging from brass telescopes and astrolabes to signed baseballs and photos of Rune hanging out with various celebrities on yachts. On the other side were a tan leather couch and live-edge wooden coffee table. The walls were covered in bright, modern pop art that depicted various Numinals—mermaids, hippogriffs, wolpertingers, unicorns, and other human and animal hybrids—adding a rich texture to the Scandinavian minimalist look in the rest of his office.

Sophie and Nadia sat side by side at his desk, their arms crossed, sulking. At least Nadia was. Sophie just kept throwing hostile glances at her. Nadia couldn't believe she had been dragged into all this.

Rune sat across from them in an expensive-looking, custom leather chair. He gazed at them as if he was contemplating what to say, his fingertips pressed together in a steeple. Finally, he spoke. "I can't believe I even have to have this conversation. I don't expect all my employees to like one another. But I do expect all my employees to operate with respect and civility. And that means listening to different opinions with an open mind, even ones you might disagree with. Do you understand?"

They both mumbled, "Yes." Great, thought Nadia. A week into the job and already she'd been branded disrespectful. She wasn't sure why she was acting so immaturely. There was no reason to sink to Sophie's level and break out the drama and cattiness.

"Sophie, you've been here two years. I expect more from you. I don't care if your uncle is on the board. I don't tolerate this sort of behavior. And you, Ms. Winters, you know how I took a chance on you." They both nodded. Heat flooded Nadia's cheeks from shame. "You can go."

They stood and started leaving.

As they approached the glass door to Rune's office, Sophie stepped in front of Nadia, cutting her off, and muttered, "Bitch."

Nadia couldn't help it. She lost it.

She thought about shoving Sophie. Something rumbled up from inside her core, and before she even knew what happened, a furious blast of red energy shot out from her raised palms like water from a firehose. It slammed into Sophie's upper back and tossed her forward with the force of a wave crashing on rocks. Sophie fell, stumbling into the side of the doorframe with a strangled grunt.

Rune was at their side in an instant. He grabbed Sophie to steady her before she could fall. He peered into her face as she gasped for breath. "Are you hurt?" he demanded.

Sophie was shell-shocked, stunned by the blow. Hell, Nadia was sure she looked the same.

Sophie glanced at Nadia warily. "I'm—I'm fine," she stammered when she had recovered.

Rune took her face in his hands and stared into her eyes. The look of distrust vanished, replaced by confusion.

"Be more careful, Sophie. These floors can be slippery." He stood back up to his full height and stepped back.

Sophie nodded, the confused look still on her face, and walked away.

Rune turned his attention to Nadia. She wanted to curl in a ball and hide under his intense stare. She wasn't sure what had just happened, but by his expression, it wasn't good.

"Ms. Winters," he started.

"You can call me Nadia." She forced a friendly, disarming smile. Or at least, she tried her very best.

Rune's dark sapphire eyes were stern. "Ms. Winters. We talked about training as a condition of your employment."

"I remember."

"Well, it appears that it is more crucial than ever. We can't have you accidentally attacking your peers because you get into an argument with them and can't control your reactions. It just so happens that I have the perfect idea of how we can begin your training. And you gave it to me.

"I was impressed with your idea in the meeting today to use virtual creatures instead of the Redcaps. Once you have mastered the basics of spellcasting, I'd like to see if you would be useful in certain Mystos engagements, ones that require thinking outside the box. Be here, six a.m. tomorrow. We'll start then."

"Okay." She started walking away, eager to get away from Rune's piercing gaze.

"Oh, Ms. Winters?"

Nadia stopped and turned back to the doorway.

"Your Psionic," said Rune. "Leave it with me today, and I'll load extra training materials and spells onto it. I will also email you a list of texts from the library that I want you to start studying. You have a lot of catching up to do, and I expect you to adhere to a rigorous self-study plan to master the fundamentals. Do you understand?"

"Yes, sir."

"No need to call me sir. Rune will do."

"Yes, sir. I mean, Rune, sir." Nadia blushed and took a deep breath. "Rune. Thank you." She unclasped her watch and handed it to him.

He nodded once, took the watch, and returned to his desk.

Nadia escaped downstairs quickly and avoided Sophie for the rest of the day.

Chapter 12

Six a.m. was really fucking early.

Avery had agreed to drop Nadia off at work that morning but clearly resented the fact, mumbling obscenities under his breath and demanding coffee after she had knocked on his bedroom door and woken him up. She suspected that he rarely emerged from his room before noon, adding to her impression that he was the Fae equivalent of a wastoid or slacker.

"I'm only doing this as a favor to Marina," he grumbled as he started her car in the garage. Marina's car was a teal 1956 Cadillac Eldorado that looked like it belonged in a museum instead of on the street. It sputtered for a second, and Avery banged on the dashboard with a bit of magic and some choice expletives. Sparks flew into the air as the car purred to life. Avery winked at her at this show of his powers—a cigarette hanging from his mouth—as he backed out at an alarming speed down the driveway, barely missing the trash cans and recycling containers at the corner.

Avery was wearing sweatpants, an unbuttoned pink bowling shirt, and Crocs. He had pulled his blond hair back in a messy bun and didn't bother with the heavy glamour. He caught Nadia looking at his ears and hissed at her, "Take a picture. It'll last longer." As he sailed majestically through the streets of San Francisco in that giant boat of a car—not paying attention to traffic signs, lanes, or any sort of agreed-on societal traffic or safety rules—Nadia gripped the side of her seat and made a mental note to take a Lyft next time. Luckily, there were hardly any other cars out that early in the morning.

"Tell me again, why we didn't fold over to Myst?" Nadia asked, bracing herself after he hit a pothole in the road.

Avery glanced at her, frowning. "How do you know about folding?"

"Thomas showed me. He said some Numinals have that power."

"Show-off," muttered Avery under his breath. "Some Numinals do know teleportation magic. But all magic comes at a cost. Each spell depletes your energy reserves. Not me, of course. I'm very powerful." Nadia rolled her eyes. "Normally, I could get you there in a blink of an eye. My full powers, however, are temporarily dampened, so we are forced to use human transportation."

"Why are your full powers dampened?"

"None of your business," he snapped.

She let it drop.

"Have you ever thought about working at Myst?" Nadia asked. "They're always looking for new talent. I could put in a good word for you."

He glanced at her out of the corner of his eye, taking a drag of his cigarette. "Not my scene."

"What is your scene?" Nadia braced herself as he hit another pothole.

"You're sure full of questions this morning."

Nadia clamped her mouth shut, taking the hint.

After stopping for coffee and donuts at a twenty-four-hour café in SoMa, he pulled up short in front of the Myst offices. The tires squealed as he braked to a hard stop. Nadia took a sip of her coffee, trying not to spill it or scald her tongue.

"All right, get out," said Avery, looking at her over the top of his sunglasses. Nadia grabbed the bag of donuts and her coffee. "Wait, hold up. Pay the toll." He pawed at the donut bag before he shoved a cruller into his mouth, muttering, "It's no faerie food, but it will have to do."

Nadia stepped out of the car, thankful to be alive and able to walk the earth once more.

"Thanks for the ride. I'll see you later."

Avery shot her a V sign, gesturing "word," and then peeled off, leaving her outside Myst alone. She checked the time. Five fifty. She was early, which was good. She could settle in and prep herself for whatever training Rune had in mind.

Nadia swiped her key card on the access port on the building. The doors opened with a click. Arne wasn't at his post this early in the morning. Pushing the heavy front door open, she stepped inside. It was dark, but the lights were on a motion detector and turned on as she walked through the antechamber into the lobby and down the hall to Myst's main floor.

It was strange being there without the hustle and bustle of Mystics at work. Nadia passed the lounge area, where the light snores of Grudax and crew, fast asleep in their tree, filled the air. She wove in and out of desks and chairs, her soft footsteps padding on the concrete floor. The sound seemed louder as it echoed in the silence of the lofty building.

Nadia set her things down at her habitat and glanced up to the second floor to Rune's office. No light. She sat at her desk as she waited, sipping her coffee and drumming her pearly, manicured nails on the desk. Patience was not one of her virtues.

After a few minutes, she went to go find him. He was around there somewhere.

She found him in the gym.

He was shirtless, sweaty, and clearly had been there for quite some time. So much for being early.

Nadia watched from the doorway as Rune moved through a training pattern on the mat, cutting and slicing the air with a large sword that looked like some sort of samurai weapon. He moved with deadly precision, stalking around the mat like a panther, completely absorbed in his movements. Her stomach did a little flip-flop watching him. He was bigger, more muscular than any college boy she'd ever seen at the gym. In fact, he wasn't a boy at all. He was a man. A perfect specimen of man, built like Adonis. She couldn't believe she had to train with him. It was intimidating.

She tore her eyes away to examine the gym itself. It was large, more like a training facility than a normal gym. Free weights, exercise equipment, and aerobics machines were located on one end, with a large mirror and barre on the other. Various martial arts weapons were stacked in weapons racks and display cases, with a large blue sparring mat in the center of the room where Rune was working out. Behind a glass partition were a basketball court and a handball court. A loud metal song blasted out over the sound system, drowning out all other noise.

He sensed her watching him and brought his movements to a halt, turning the booming music down with a small wave of his hand in the air. Nadia gave herself a bit of an inward shake. He was her boss, she was his employee . . . one he must've thought was a bit of a charity case, at that.

"Ms. Winters," Rune called out. He pushed his dark hair off his forehead.

"Nadia," she corrected. She wove through racks of free weights and machines over to where he stood.

"You're late. I said six a.m., did I not?"

Nadia glanced at the clock on the wall, noting it was 6:03, but said nothing.

Rune grabbed a small white towel and wiped down his face before running it over his shirtless body, his muscles glistening in the light as he flexed. His torso was crisscrossed with strange tattoos and cut with scars—old ones, but still visible, like he had been whipped at some point in his life.

Nadia looked down, flustered. Her eyes danced around the floor as she tried to find something else but him to focus on. "Sorry. I didn't realize when you said training, you meant we were going to be physically training. I thought you meant, like, mental training. You know, to control my emotions and powers and stuff."

"Emotions *and stuff* are held in the body. The body is not separate from the mind; they are intricately linked on a cellular and metaphysical level, informing one another. To be successful at controlling your emotions and your magic, you need to be in top physical shape. We will start each session with a workout, before moving on to mental and magical training. You received the list of texts I emailed you, yes? Good. I expect you to work through those on your own and report back to me on your progress."

Nadia looked down at her blue jeans, flats, and green and gold William & Mary Tribe tank top. "Can we skip the workout today? I'm not exactly dressed for it."

"If I were you," said Rune, "I would be trying to impress me with your commitment to this process."

They stared at each other.

"Okay then." Nadia kicked off her shoes and tied back her hair in a ponytail.

"Do you have any martial arts training?" Rune watched her pull one arm and then the other across her body to warm up.

"Sure. I know the basics," she lied. She cracked her neck and rolled her shoulders.

He gestured to the center of the sparring mat. She stood, feeling the slight squish of the foam between her toes, while he went for the weapon rack on the wall. Nadia had done a bit of fencing in high school, but she didn't have any experience with sword fighting. Rune chose a weapon—a slim, slightly curved steel blade with a rope-wrapped handle—and plucked it from the wall. He walked back over to where Nadia was standing and flipped the sword so that the hilt faced her.

Nadia took it from him. The sword felt lighter than she had

thought it would be, given its size. Rune picked up the sword that he had been training with. Nadia brought her sword into position in mimicry of his, holding it in front of her with both hands so that the weapon tilted toward him. He looked bigger, his muscled frame more menacing once he was holding a weapon. Nadia suddenly felt very small, like a mouse next to a lion. She would have to make up for her lack of strength and skill with quickness and agility.

She lunged with a small involuntary cry, thrusting the sword toward him. He blocked it and parried with a graceful circular maneuver as he assessed her with a critical eye.

And then he struck. His sword crashed down on top of hers in a blur of strength and steel. She flew backward with the impact and landed hard on her butt. The sword went flying.

Nadia lay on her back and wheezed. After a couple of breaths, she opened her eyes. Rune towered over her.

"Again." He did not look impressed.

She was stuck frozen, stunned.

"Up, Ms. Winters!" he shouted out over his shoulder. Nadia's cheeks reddened at how quickly he had beaten her. It was a joke. She was a charity case, for sure.

"All right, all right." Nadia gingerly climbed to her feet and retrieved her sword from where it had gone flying. Warily, she watched him as he swiped the blade through the air, testing the sword's balance. The muscles in his back rippled with the movement.

Rune brought his sword back up. He cocked his head slightly, a glint in his dark eyes. "Seems like your martial arts skills are a little rusty, Ms. Winters."

Nadia struck at him with a downward blow before he had the chance to strike her first. Their swords clashed, clanging loudly. Rune sidestepped and twirled so that he was close behind her. His sword was at her throat, caging her in.

Nadia froze, not wanting to even swallow, her head tilted slightly back, her neck exposed. With a small chuckle, he stepped away. Nadia let out a deep breath. She could tell this wasn't going to be a fun training session.

She was right. It wasn't. With each harsh repetition, each complete failing on her part to master the sword stances and attacks, the punches and the kicks and the blocks, she became increasingly frustrated with his stoicism and indifference to her. He was like a brick wall, a cold, detached automaton, merely ordering her to repeat the movements each time she fumbled. With each comment on her inability to perfect the motions, he systematically eradicated all attraction that she might have initially felt. It was clear he thought of her as a clumsy nuisance: basically inept, someone he had to train himself so as not to be a liability to Myst. He barked at her until she was glaring at him like he was a drill sergeant and she was a rookie private in the military who had gotten in way over her head and was beginning to realize this was all a horrible mistake, and please could she just go home?

After practicing the martial arts "basics," Rune made Nadia run sprints back and forth before leading her through grueling strength training and conditioning exercises that included weighted frog jumps, burpees, push-ups, squats, and pull-ups. She was still wearing jeans, which had become damp with sweat and constricted movement to an extremely uncomfortable degree, chafing her thighs where the fabric rubbed. He was like a predator playing with its food, torturing her for fun, as he assessed each clumsy movement with a critical eye, correcting her form and technique. He made her repeat each exercise until she completed a set that satisfied his insanely high standards.

Only after she collapsed mid-plank did he finally take pity on her.

"Get some water. Let's move on." Rune pulled on his T-shirt

and then dragged two chairs over to the mat. Nadia watched him from where she lay on the ground, unable to get up.

"I think I'm dying." Nadia rolled onto her back and pulled her sweat-soaked shirt away from her body, trying to fan herself. She stared up at the lights on the ceiling. They blurred as her vision went in and out of focus.

Rune placed the chairs across from each other on the mat. "No, you aren't. You're fine. Mind over matter. Refuse to give in to the pain."

Nadia closed her eyes and took deep breaths as she tried to bring her heart rate under control. "I can't do this. I'm just not cut out for this."

"Yes, you are."

She opened her eyes. He was standing over her, eclipsing the lights on the ceiling. He crossed his arms over his chest as he regarded her pathetic body in a heap on the floor. "It's your first day of training. It will get easier."

"No, seriously. I can't do this."

"Get up. You're tougher than this."

She shook her head. "I don't want to."

"Get up."

"No."

"GET UP."

Nadia's body moved not of its own volition, and she jumped to her feet, the tang of magic in the air.

She turned and stared at Rune, her eyes wide, her heart pounding in her chest. "What the hell was that? Did you just *compel* me?"

He regarded her coolly. "I can make you run circles around here, but I won't do that. You need to have the mental toughness and grit to compel *yourself*."

Nadia jabbed a finger into Rune's chest. "Fine, but there are other ways to make your point that don't involve *my* loss of personal and physical autonomy. Seriously, that's not cool. I don't care what kind of liability or risk you think I am. Don't. Do. That. Again."

They stared at each other. A muscle in his jaw fluttered. "You're right," he said finally. "I crossed a line. I won't do it again."

"Promise?"

"Yes. You have my word."

Nadia rolled her shoulders and swung her arms around, trying to shake the strange feeling—the remnants of his magic—that still coursed through her veins. It felt somehow simultaneously alien and familiar, the tail end of a meteor shooting through the sky.

She glanced back at him. He was still watching her. "Is that compelling stuff something I can learn?" she asked. Maya had mentioned she should stock up on charms to navigate through the city easier. Compelling people to move out of her way whenever she wanted would take that exercise in convenience to a whole new level.

The corner of his mouth curled up. She must've amused him. "In time. I can tell you have an immense amount of raw power. But you need to learn how to control it before you can master the art of spellcasting."

"Is there a way to protect against that? I mean, if people could just make others do whatever they want, all hell would break loose. People would be, like, robbing banks and stuff."

Rune gestured for Nadia to sit in one of the chairs. "Only very magically advanced Numinals and Septers have that sort of ability, and most use it within generally understood codes of morality. It's a rare skill, and difficult to master. But yes, with mental training, you can make yourself less vulnerable. Right now, your mind is weak, easily manipulated."

"Gee, thanks," she muttered as she took a seat.

Rune sat down opposite Nadia. He flicked his wrist, and a glass of water appeared out of thin air. She blinked, still surprised whenever she saw magic in action. Rune handed the glass of water to her, and she gulped it down. Rune flicked his wrist again, and the glass vanished.

"Let's work on building mental shields."

Nadia crossed her arms, leaning back in the chair. "My grandmother has been teaching me that."

"Good. Show me."

Nadia closed her eyes. She settled into her body, feeling the hard plastic chair under her, the soreness in her muscles. She took deep breaths, regulating her heart rate. Once she was grounded, she went into her mind. She imagined herself building a shield, stacking shining silver blocks like a bricklayer building a fortification. She worked fast, stacking the pieces together as they seamlessly fused into a strong mental shield that protected the inner workings of her mind.

"Again," Rune commanded. "You need to be faster."

Her eyes fluttered open. He was watching her, unimpressed with her efforts. Nadia sighed and closed her eyes again.

She erased the shield in her mind and started over, laying each of the pieces faster and faster. She practiced repeatedly, challenging herself to get a bit better each time and to double and triple the layers. It was like she was on fast-forward speed. Each time Nadia built a shield, she fortified it stronger and bigger, until layers of shields cocooned her entire body. The strongest one protected her third eye like a shining silver walnut shell.

"I'm going to try to break it down now," said Rune, after a bit. "Brace yourself."

Nadia quickly built layers of strong mental shields. They were stronger than any other that she had built before, thick and silver in her mind like a shining dome.

Rune shattered them instantly, the shields crumbling with the force of his psychic attack. Nadia cried out in pain and clutched her head. Waves of power reverberated through her body like shockwaves.

She glared at him as she regained her composure. "Are you going through my mind right now?"

Rune shook his head. "No. I could, of course. But that would be an egregious violation of your privacy. I don't do that to my employees. Everyone is entitled to their own secrets. I have a shield up now to filter out your thoughts that I am sure you are broadcasting. I don't need or want to hear them."

She nodded, relieved.

They practiced building mental shields for a bit more before Rune checked the time. "It's eight. I want to try one last thing today, and then I will let you go."

He stood up. Slowly, she stood up as well, wary of what was next.

Rune magicked Nadia's Psionic from somewhere and handed it to her. "I've loaded extra training materials onto your watch. Please do go through them all and make yourself acquainted with the program.

"During the interview, you attempted to cast a binding spell. I want to see if you can do it again."

"I don't know how I did that," Nadia confessed. "I wanted you to stop, and then poof, out came red lightning."

"Magic works in mysterious ways. Sometimes intention doesn't manifest physically the way we want. There is usually a logical connection, though, that you can trace back. You wanted me to stop, and you created a ring of fire." He paused, a strange look on his face. "A red lasso out of lightning, if you will. Red for stop. Lasso to bind. Lightning for a show of power, I assume."

She nodded slowly, the dots connecting in her mind.

He continued, "This is why it is so important to master and control your emotions and mind. You need to set your will to the correct emotion to cast a spell that has the intended outcome. The Psionic will help with this, but I want to see how you innately cast to know how to best teach you. Septer ability is closer to Numinal magic than it is to witchcraft. Most witches are Sixers and rely on tools and well-practiced spells to channel and focus their energy. Of course, if you use tools or rituals, your magic will be stronger, the intention focused."

Rune held out his arm and made a fist to flex his sizeable bicep. "Try to bind me like before."

Nadia shook her head. "I don't know what I'm doing."

"Just try. You might surprise yourself." He tapped his bicep with his other hand. "Okay. Right here. Just focus."

Nadia held out her palm toward him. "I'm telling you; this isn't going to work."

Rune raised an eyebrow. "I didn't peg you as the quitting type."

Nadia narrowed her eyes at him. "I'm not."

"Then prove it."

Nadia sighed, and then focused. She tried to imagine lightning whips shooting out of her palm.

Nothing happened.

Nadia gave herself a little shake and danced around like a boxer psyching herself up for the ring. Rune watched with an amused look on his face. She stilled and took a deep breath. She brought her hand back up as Rune flexed his bicep again.

Nadia tried again. Nothing happened.

"Slow down," suggested Rune. "Focus your intention. You need to translate mental desire and will into physical action."

"I'm trying," she snapped.

Nadia held her hand up again and tried to see the lightning erupt from her palm in her mind's eye. It was all static, like white noise. Her nose itched, breaking her attention. She rubbed a hand over her face.

"This is pointless," said Nadia. "I clearly can't do this." She looked up at the ceiling, fighting back the tears stinging in her eyes. She would not cry in front of Rune. She was stronger than that.

"Hey," he said gently. Nadia lowered her gaze to meet his dark eyes. "You can do this. You have to *really* want it. Feel the power inside you. Try closing your eyes and focusing." He paused. "Focus on me."

Nadia closed her eyes and let the desire to succeed and bind him wash over her like gentle waves lapping at the shore. She raised a hand, the palm facing outward. In her mind's eye, images and colors appeared in the white noise, fuzzy and undefined. She brought them into focus. The image sharpened and crystalized until she could see herself standing in front of Rune, lightning shooting out from her palm and wrapping around his bicep. She held both ideas—reality and her desire—in her mind simultaneously and superimposed the images so that she was seeing both at once on top of each other. Slowly, her mind as sharp as a diamond, she started to pick out the shimmering threads of reality, the barely visible lines pulsating with energy, and rewove the threads to become the image in her mind's eye. It was like she was mending a hole in a worn tapestry. She wove faster, picking out the vibrating strands and refastening them in a different time and space so that the images became one. Nadia could feel it working. Power coursed through her blood. She felt on fire, the spicy tang of dark magic on her tongue, in her lungs, and in the air.

Nadia lost herself in the rush of immense power. She felt like she was standing on the edge of a cliff overlooking a dark ocean, waves crashing violently against the rocks, wind whipping about her face and her hair. Lightning bolts flashed down from the heavens in a rain of fire like the gods were giving her magic. She felt free; the shackles of what she thought possible melted away by flames that danced around her and inside her like a living thing. Nadia heard her name echoing all around. She reluctantly came back into her body. Rune was shouting at her.

"Nadia, stop!" his deep voice called out. She opened her eyes.

In front of her was a semicircle wall about ten feet high of gold and red fire, frozen into flames of glass. Rune looked distorted through the glass, his palms outstretched as he spelled the flames solid. The glass cracked and burst into tiny pieces. It rained down in chandeliers of crystal that fell around her like raindrops, tinkling as it hit the floor.

Nadia looked down. Fire marks covered the floor of the gym, the foam of the blue sparring mat brown and blistered. She stood, mouth agape, and realized what she had just done.

She had just tried to light her boss on fire.

"Are you okay?" Rune's voice was full of concern. He took a step toward her. Nadia instinctually stepped back, shrinking from him.

"Don't get near me!" she snapped. "What did I just do? Are *you* okay?"

He held up his hands like he was calming a spooked animal. "Everything is okay. I'm fine. The gym is fine. You just got a little carried away with the spell."

She looked at the melted mat covered in shards of broken glass and crystal. "Oh, God! I could have killed you."

The corner of his mouth turned up in a wry smile. "It takes a little bit more than a fireball to kill me. I'm fine. I have protection against that sort of thing, and I countered your spell to stop it before you burned the gym down. It's not a big deal. I've heard that these things happen to Septers when they are coming into their powers." He gestured to the melted mat below his feet. "I needed a new mat, anyway."

Nadia shook slightly, her breath coming fast. "You're just saying that to be nice."

"It's true. Septers coming into their power do all sorts of disastrous things."

Nadia's mind danced to her past. A dinner party for her parents. Wine bottles shattering. AP Chemistry. Glass beakers popping one by one as she walked past. Opening a rejection letter from Yale. Tires squealing in a horrible crash as a car hit a lamp post.

"I used to explode things when I was a teenager," said Nadia. "I told myself I was just clumsy or that it was my imagination."

Rune nodded. "The mind tries to rationalize that which it cannot explain."

"But my grandmother put a binding spell on me. Stifled my powers. I only broke it a few weeks ago." Nadia exhaled, feeling lighter at the confession. "How did I still manage to explode things? I thought I was imagining it all."

"You must have had moments where you loosened the bindings. Weakened the spell." He paused, narrowing his eyes at her. "But why would your grandmother do that to you? I have never heard of a blood relative binding a witch's powers."

Nadia bit back the full truth. "She said she wanted to give me a normal life."

Rune cocked his head, considering this. Nadia realized how close she had come to revealing too much.

Finally, he nodded. "It is natural to want to be like everyone else. To be *normal*." His voice was rough, his expression grave. "But in some cases, you will *never* be like everyone else. You will never be normal. Normal is boring and weak and powerless. The faster you realize that about yourself, the faster you will come into your own, and be able to master your true inner power."

"All I've ever wanted to be is normal."

"I used to be the same," confessed Rune with a wry smile. "Until I realized it's much more fun to be extraordinary. To do extraordinary things. To travel, see the world, and accomplish things, *hard* things, beyond your wildest imagination. Normal people don't do that. They don't push themselves to be better, to succeed, to pick themselves up after every failure. I've failed more times than you can count, until one day, I didn't. One day you're going to look back and wonder how you ever wanted to be like everyone else."

Nadia wanted to ask him what things used to be beyond his wildest imagination, but he turned away from her. "We're done for the day."

From the side of the mat, she gathered her shoes and cell phone, still shaking slightly.

"Oh, and Ms. Winters?"

Nadia looked at Rune, wondering what he would say, what wisdom he would impart like a balm to her scared, confused soul.

"Next time, wear something more appropriate for working out. We have extra Myst shirts in the locker room if you need to shower and change before work."

Her expression hardened. She nodded in thanks, turning away and limping out to the locker room to shower and clean herself up before the day started.

Chapter 13

Nadia glanced out the bay windows in the front parlor of Marina's house. Over the last few weeks, that spot next to the window had become her favorite study location; she could simultaneously watch the world outside and fill her mind with the wondrous myths and legends—that she was learning were, in fact, Numinal history. The current book she was reading was one she had checked out from the Myst vaults, though she was alternating with a smutty paperback romance of Marina's that she had found in the living room. She could only handle so much otherworld study before she needed to take a break and lose herself in a story that wasn't her own.

Outside, the world was awash in a pale yellow. The boundaries of the wards around Marina's house shimmered in the late-afternoon light. Thomas paced back and forth beyond the boundary line like a cat outside a mouse hole. He had been out there for several hours, skulking around trying to get Nadia to come outside. Occasionally, she would look up from the book in her lap, her legs kicked up on a footstool, and wave at him or give him the finger. Thomas had given up motioning for her to come outside, instead just glaring at Nadia each time she looked up from her book, smiling insolently at his pathetic efforts.

Once Nadia knew that neither he nor Mercurio could compel her to do anything, the Blood Oath still resting with Marina, she decided that they weren't going to scare her. She was too valuable an asset. They needed her to spy for them. And for whatever reason, Nadia had become Thomas's pet project. He had vouched for her to Mercurio. Mercurio was the threat if there was one.

But that didn't mean she wouldn't make Thomas's life difficult.

Nadia heard Marina down the hall. The old floors in the Victorian creaked as she walked.

"Yes, yes. She's here. Studying actually. I think that new job is keeping her busy." Marina appeared in the doorway to the front parlor, phone pressed against her ear. She was wearing overalls, her hair in two long braids that hung down on either side of her face. Blotches of red and blue paint covered her hands and arms, with a pink stripe on her cheek like war paint.

"Nadia. Your mother is on the phone." She held it out to her as she walked over. Nadia swung her feet down from the footstool as she slid her notepad into the book to save the spot where she had been reading about the Collapse.

"Hey, Mom."

"Hey there!" Her mom's voice was slightly slurry.

"It's a little early to be drinking, isn't it?" Nadia asked, worried, and glanced up at her grandmother. Marina shrugged and shook her head.

"Oh. I only had a couple with Whitney and the girls at Sunday brunch." She paused. "So, how's this new fancy job of yours? Your grandmother says you're putting your degree to work. That's wonderful! You know, your father and I were a little worried about the sudden move to San Francisco, but it seems like you are doing just great out there."

Nadia had told her parents that she had gotten a job helping catalog artifacts at a startup that worked to advance technology by learning from the past. It was more or less true.

Nadia only felt slightly guilty for lying.

"It's going really well. I'm learning a ton. I'm still getting up to speed, of course, but Mom, everyone is so creative and innovative out here." Nadia picked at the corner of one of Marina's bohemian-patterned pillows next to her on the couch.

"That's wonderful." Nadia's mom paused, her voice muffled in the background. "Honey, your father wants to say hello."

Nadia's dad's voice boomed out. "Hey, kiddo. How's the new job? Marina tells us that you're mopping the floor with all your co-workers and that you're going to run that company in no time flat."

Nadia forced a laugh. "Yep. Just you wait."

She looked up at Marina, who had just noticed Thomas outside the wards. He was sending up red and orange magic flares to get their attention.

How long has he been out there? Marina mouthed silently at her, pointing to Thomas.

Nadia shrugged like she had no idea. "Yep, the weather is great, too. Not hot at all like DC. Uh-huh. No, it's super casual at work, Dad. People wear, like, jeans and stuff."

Marina looked murderous. "I am going to kick his weaselly little ass," she whispered. "He knows he isn't supposed to be here. This is harassment. Why isn't he just sending the proper signal?"

"What was that?" asked her dad.

"Oh, nothing! Marina thinks a weasel is trying to get into the yard." Nadia shrugged at her. "Hey Dad, I gotta go. I'll call you soon, okay? Love you."

Nadia quickly hung up the phone.

Marina stood fuming at the window. She gave Thomas the bird.

"Marina!" Nadia shot out a surprised laugh. Like grandmother, like granddaughter.

She shrugged. "Sorry. I need to work on controlling my temper."

"What is the commotion now?" Avery padded into the parlor, barefoot, buttoning a loud red-and-blue Hawaiian shirt.

Marina gestured toward Thomas, who was now doing some sort

of jig to get their attention. "Drake is outside. He didn't send the proper signal. He's just . . . *loitering* outside the ward boundaries."

Avery cracked his knuckles. "Want me to go deal with him?" There was an evil glint in his eyes. "Been a while since he and I got in a row. I think we are due for one." Brass knuckles etched with Celtic knots appeared on Avery's clenched fist.

Marina grabbed Avery's arm. "No, no. I need to go deal with this."

Avery looked like he didn't want to stop, but he put up his hands after a look from Marina. "Fine. But there are rules for a reason. He knows he isn't supposed to come by without the signal."

"What's the signal?" Nadia asked.

"When Mercurio wants me for whatever reason, I feel it. The universe gives me the message. I feel it in my bones, in my blood. And when I try to resist, things start forcing me to comply."

"Whoa, freaky."

"You're telling me. The universe strives to give me the message. Corrals me into listening and obeying, so to speak. It's easier to comply than to resist. Resisting causes unnecessary disaster."

Nadia shuddered and pushed thoughts of how that would feel to the back of her mind. Thomas was now juggling what looked like fluffy bunnies the size of bowling balls. He mimed dropping them and glanced over to see if it caught their attention. When it didn't, he lit them on fire.

"I'll go deal with him." Marina stormed out of the parlor. Her braided pigtails flew behind her as she marched down the front steps. A string of profanities tumbled from her mouth.

"I hope the neighbors aren't watching." Nadia picked up her book and kicked up her feet again on the footstool.

"She's going to work herself up again," said Avery.

Nadia looked up. "What?"

Cool eyes flicked down to hers. "She gets emotional. Must run in the family."

Nadia scowled at him. "I don't know what you're talking about." She turned back to her book, trying to find her place again where she had been reading about how the Realm Gates between the worlds had suddenly closed, trapping all the Numinals on Earth. She read for a few more minutes before she heard the front door slam.

"Nadia." Marina's voice was flat. "Thomas would like a word with you." She stood in the doorway to the parlor, her face furious.

Nadia flushed as she replaced her notebook to save her spot in the history text. She slipped on her flip-flops and shrugged on a sweatshirt, trying to act calm. But she knew she was busted.

Nadia stopped up short before she crossed the boundaries of the wards and out of safety. The shimmery barrier flickered between them. Thomas had a smug expression on his face.

"What do you want?" Nadia demanded.

"I just wanted to know if you wanted to come out and play." He said it in a singsong, mocking voice, smiling his serpentine smile. "Do come outside the wards. It will be so much easier."

"Fuck off." Nadia turned to walk back up to the house, but his voice stopped her.

"I just discovered that your dear grandmother didn't know of the pact that you swore to Mercurio."

Blood drained from Nadia's face. "W-what pact?"

He chuckled. "That whole obedience or else your unborn child dies pact? Ring any bells?"

Her heart leaped to her throat, threatening to choke her. "I didn't make any pacts. That was just a vow. Like a promise, right? I thought that bit about the unborn child was just flourish or something. He wouldn't actually . . ."

"Oh, but you *did* make a pact." His dark eyes glittered. "If you get something in return for the promise, it becomes a pact. You are getting your riches and happiness and sense of purpose you wanted. You started your servitude early, without the Blood Oath yet passing to you naturally! And also, I am really, truly touched by your concern for me, a demon. I knew you were a good, upstanding human with a true moral compass, but that was more than I would have expected." He placed a hand over his heart. "Really, top-notch stuff. The type of thing that"—he pointed one hand up toward the heavens, the other gesturing mock secrecy—"the big guy up there, if you believe in that sort of thing, really looks highly on. It's such a shame then that you don't believe in anything *Numinous* like that. Demons, faeries, God, gods. None of it." His mouth was a grim line that threatened to explode into laughter.

"I'm going to fucking kill you." The Myst Psionic beeped rapidly. "You asshole! You tricked me!" Nadia prepared to leap at him and throttle his double-timing demon neck.

He jumped back and magicked a barrier of brick in front of him so that she could only see his face behind it. "Whoa, easy there, champ. Where's that control that ol' goody boy Rune has been teaching you?"

Nadia fisted her hands. Her nails dug into her palms, drawing blood. She tried to calm her racing heart, to grab the reins of her out-of-control emotions, the pendulum swinging wide as her mind replayed everything that had happened with Mercurio. Her fire boiled within, threatening to take over. She took several deep breaths until she felt in control enough to open her eyes.

Thomas's eyes were wide, his mouth open in shock. Nadia looked down at her feet, where she stood in the center of a bare patch of earth, the ground smoking where she had burned away the grass.

He shook his head in amazement. He waved a hand, and the illusion of brick disappeared. "Well, well, well. It seems your powers grow even more. Tell me, have you caught anything else on fire?"

She glanced back at the house where Marina and Avery stood watching out the window. Marina's hand covered her mouth in horror. Avery looked like he was trying to get her attention.

Nadia bit the inside of her cheek. The sharp, metallic taste of blood fueled her anger. "What do you want, Thomas?"

Thomas looked like he was enjoying himself immensely. "Mercurio is very pleased with your progress at Myst. But he wants you to get close to the CEO."

Nadia looked at him sharply. "Why? Why does Mercurio care?"

"Rune Christiansen is a threat to Mercurio's business. He simply wants you to get close to him. To find out his weaknesses. He likes pretty brunettes, like you."

"I'm not some goddamn honeypot spy," Nadia bit out.

He threw his head back, laughing. "Are you quite sure?" Seeing her expression, he softened. "Oh, come on. I didn't say you should shag him. Actually . . . please don't." A strange, angry expression crossed his face. His voice hardened. "Mercurio just wants you to get close. Figure him out. Tell us the details. That's all. It's hardly malicious. Very aboveboard, if you ask me."

A rogue tear slid down Nadia's face, and she wiped it away quickly with the back of her hand. Drops of blood dripped into the dirt from where she had punctured her palms with her fingernails.

She took a deep breath, steeling herself. "And if I don't?"

"Then you break the pact, and your firstborn is Mercurio's."

Nadia exhaled, suddenly exhausted.

"I trust you will make the right decision. I'll see you soon." He folded out, leaving her out alone at the boundary of the wards.

"What kind of ignorant, dumb witch child would make a pact with a *strigoi*? And to get nothing in return? Rookie move, Nadia. Rookie move!" Marina paced up and down the kitchen, twisting an oven mitt in her hand in despair. Next to her, Avery perched on the kitchen island, watching with seemingly detached interest at her theatrics. But Nadia knew better. His eyes traced Marina's every move. Nadia scrunched up her nose in disgust. The whole *Harold and Maude* thing was really starting to get to her.

"I'm not getting *nothing* in return," protested Nadia. "He said if I obey him, I will have riches and happiness and a sense of purpose."

Marina looked at her, exasperated. "He cannot give you that. He cannot change the way you feel and think about things. All he can do is give you wealth. Whether that makes you happy and fulfilled is up to you."

"Marina, it's not your fault." Avery's gaze flicked to Nadia's. "Genetics aren't guaranteed. Sometimes there is just dumb blood that runs in the lines."

"For the last time, I didn't know! This is ridiculous." Nadia muttered to no one in particular.

Marina shot her an icy look. "Even if you didn't know about the Blood Oath, which you did, why on earth would you *ever* make a deal with a dark creature unless it was a last resort! Hasn't this whole situation with our family taught you anything about the consequences of such an act?"

"They tricked me. Mercurio and this big blue djinn guy were torturing Thomas. It was horrible." Her voice broke.

Marina threw her hands in the air.

"Thomas is a demon," Avery said, his voice like ice.

"So?"

"Demons like pain," said Avery. "They like vice. That's why they promote it in humans. They egg you on so you feel those dark desires, the dark energy, the immorality and sin. Demons are both sadists and masochists, all at the same time. To them, pain is pleasure. Unless they were using a spell that specifically causes pain in demons, anything you saw probably was little more than a tickle to Thomas."

"Fine, but Mercurio was hinting that he would kill Marina to make the Oath pass to me faster if I didn't obey him."

Marina shook her head. "He can't."

"What?"

"He can't harm me. His protection includes protection from himself. It's built into the Blood Oath."

Nadia sucked in her breath. "What are you saying?"

"They played you!" Marina yelled, sobbing, as she sank into the ground in front of her.

Nadia sank to the ground as well, wishing that what she was saying wasn't the truth.

"So, what do I do now?" Nadia slurred. She shook out the last drops of the tequila bottle into her shot glass. Marina sat across from her on the living room floor. The crystal glass next to her was empty. Marina had gone for the tequila immediately. Mouthful by mouthful, they had drunk all the alcohol in the house. Avery, of course, looked fresh and spry as ever. He sat on the couch, plucking out a slow Celtic ballad on his ukulele, which he had magicked out of thin air.

Marina's eyes rolled to hers. "It's obvious. You have to do what he wants. At least he can't compel you yet; thank God for that. What has he ordered you to do so far?"

Nadia cringed. "Nothing."

"Don't lie to me. I'll wrangle the truth out of you one way or the other."

Nadia sighed and glanced around the room. Candles. Her grandfather's picture. Her eyes settled on a heavy brocade tapestry on the wall. "You know my job at Myst? I'm supposed to spy for him. Report back on company secrets and all that."

"Then that's what you will do," Marina pronounced, smacking her palm on the coffee table.

"I'm not a spy! I'm betraying the company."

"You don't have a choice. You pledged your unborn child." Marina shook her head. "Rookie mistake. Never pledge the life of another. Everyone knows that. Mercurio is dangerous," added Marina, "but he will mostly forget about you. Don't act up. Don't give him a reason to notice you. I don't like this any more than you do, but you're going to have to do it. It won't be so bad. Watch out for Thomas, though—he's a conniving little wiener. I can't figure out what he's up to, but he seems to have taken an interest in you, for whatever reason. Just be wary of him."

Nadia lay back on the carpet, staring at the ceiling as the room started spinning. "I just hope I don't get caught."

Chapter 14

"Ms. Winters?" Rune's low, silky voice called out the next day.

Nadia looked up from the papyrus scrap she was hunched over on the wooden study table in Vault One. She felt a pang of irritation at having her concentration interrupted. She was trying to decipher the faded hieroglyphics on the delicate paper and then translate the spell it contained into English.

She bit back the correction of "Nadia" on the tip of her tongue, instead smiling sweetly, and tried to control her temper and the pounding headache she had from all the tequila the previous night. Marina had given her some sort of nasty herbal tonic that morning that had helped, stopping the vomiting, but the pressure in her temples still lingered. "Yes?" she asked, with deliberate civility.

Rune looked flustered. He was wearing jeans and a black zip-up hoodie, the unofficial uniform of startup CEOs and millennials who still lived in their parents' basement, but Rune managed to make it look trendy. He pushed up his Armani glasses with his index finger. Most Numinals had excellent, supernatural vision. The frames were merely part of his attempt at human appearance.

But despite the careful detail of clothing and mannerisms, you could never mistake Rune for human. He was too otherworldly; his presence too powerful.

"I'm looking for Imogen. Is she around? Ah, never mind." Rune's eyes lit up as Imogen appeared from around the corner of the stacks. Nadia went back to reading the papyrus, lamely attempting to translate the text.

Nadia didn't mean to eavesdrop. She really didn't. But the acoustics in the library and vaults amplified everything so that she could hear their conversation perfectly. Nadia kept her head down, appearing to be studying the text, but her ears burned.

"I can't do Friday. I'm sorry," said Imogen. Her heels clicked on the marble floor as she walked, restacking books and artifacts.

"Imogen," he said gruffly, trying to keep his voice low, "this has been on the books for months now. Myst is expected to make an appearance. We're one of the sponsors of the event, after all. And especially now, with everything. We need to keep up appearances."

"I know, I know. But I have a conflict, and I just can't go. You're going to have to fly solo."

"You know how I hate these things. I merely tolerate them for the company." His voice dipped even lower, barely audible. "Please." It didn't sound like he said *please* very often.

Imogen's voice fell to a whisper. "I'm leaving next week to go back to Dublin. You need to let go. Move on. We talked about this. I have to go back to . . ." Imogen's voice became muffled, mixing with Rune's low baritone, and Nadia lost what they were saying. There was a pause, and then Imogen giggled. "Cut that out, mister. Your seduction techniques won't work on me."

Nadia wanted to crawl under the table and die. She *so* should not be hearing all this. She contemplated tiptoeing out but didn't want to remind them that she was still there.

"Why don't you take someone else?" Imogen whispered. She paused, the volume of her voice rising. "How about Nadia?"

Nadia shot her head up at the sound of her name, like she hadn't been listening to their every word. "Hm, what?" Rune moodily trailed behind Imogen as she walked over to Nadia.

"There is this event on Friday, but I can't make it. It's a charity auction to support the arts. Myst is one of the sponsors. Rune hates going to these things alone. Can you go? It's mostly just rubbing elbows with donors and potential talent. It will be good exposure for you." Imogen said it like she was trying to sell the event to her.

"I'm not sure that's a good idea," said Rune between clenched teeth. He shot Nadia a look, shifting uncomfortably. "She hasn't been to one of these before."

Mercurio wanted her to get closer to Rune. This was the perfect opportunity.

"Actually, my mother was on the board of several charities. I've been to numerous galas."

"It's not really a gala, *per se*—" Rune began before Imogen cut him off with an excited clap of her hands.

"See?" she exclaimed. "It's fate!"

Imogen picked a piece of lint from Rune's shirt and smoothed her hand down over his chest. "Don't worry. I'm sure Nadia will be the perfect company for you."

Imogen excused herself and headed back to the stacks. Rune stood there a moment, staring at Nadia. His dark eyes were hard, his gaze unreadable.

Nadia stared back. "Did you need something else?"

He cleared his throat. "I suppose we could make this a training exercise."

"Oh?" she arched an eyebrow at him. She was already training with him in the mornings. She wasn't sure how she felt about extra sessions.

"There will be a significant number of other Numinals at the gala. So far, our training has revolved around defensive mechanisms. I want you to start going on the offensive, see if you can break down any psychic shields in a person's mind."

Nadia's breath hitched at the idea of trying to enter someone else's mind.

Rune noticed. "I'm not talking about rewriting someone's

essence or even reading their memories. You are expressly forbidden from even going there. All Myst employees have been trained not to broadcast their thoughts, but there should be plenty of others at the event who lack that sort of training. This would be a good opportunity for you to test your powers. In a safe, controlled way, of course."

She crossed her arms over her chest. "So, you're keeping me on a leash?"

Rune looked startled. A flash of emotion played over his face before he quickly collected himself, his expression stoic once again. Nadia recognized the emotion.

Lust.

She licked her lips before she could help herself.

He cleared his throat. "No one could ever put you on a leash, Ms. Winters. Some creatures are not meant to be tamed."

Her cheeks flamed, but she merely nodded. He turned to leave but paused for a moment, cocking his head in question.

"Do you have a dress to wear?"

Rune sent Nadia a dress. She didn't know if she was more weirded out that he sent her a dress or that it fit perfectly.

It was gorgeous. A champagne-colored silk dress, with snakeskin chainmail panels that glistened like ripples on water. The built-in Victorian corset had a deep, plunging neckline with a high-necked collar on the back of the dress that was not quite Elizabethan, not quite *Star Trek*. When she walked, a high slit up each side exposed her thigh. As she turned around, examining her reflection in the mirror in her tiny attic bedroom, she felt like a stranger. Like she was living someone else's life.

And she liked it.

Nadia had curled her glossy dark hair so it hung in waves down her back, and she had tied small rings of gold to match the chainmail into her hair. Imogen had explained it was a black-tie Burning

Man event, so the crowd would be a mixture of, as she described it, the "uber-rich, neo-bougie, hippie dust bum." Not knowing exactly what that meant, but getting a rough idea in her mind, Nadia paired the dress Rune had sent her with black leather boots and a fringed leather necklace that somewhat covered her cleavage and gave her the illusion of, if not modesty, then perhaps a slight concern for public decency.

The doorbell to Marina's house rang. Nadia's heart skipped, causing the Myst Psionic to beep. Go time. She tugged off the smartwatch and set it on the small bedside table. She didn't need the watch distracting her. And it didn't go with the dress.

She grabbed her black leather clutch and quickly hurried down the stairs to the foyer.

Rune and Avery were in a standoff at the front door with Marina trying to intervene, tugging on Avery's shoulders and trying to wedge her small frame in front of his.

They all turned to her as Nadia walked down the creaky stairs, holding on to the railing for support.

Marina caught her eye, a mischievous expression on her face. "Nadia. Your date is here."

Nadia cringed. Her eyes met Rune's, and he looked away quickly. Neither of them wanted to make this more awkward than it already was.

Rune was immaculate in a fitted black blazer over a black shirt, his broad, muscled shoulders under the leather and metal stud coat narrowing down into a trim, fitted waist. He had slicked back his hair and shaved so that his normal five o'clock shadow was gone. In short, he looked like a Mad Max version of James Bond.

Nadia pretended to laugh and caught Rune's eye. "Don't listen to her." Nadia plastered a look of mock concern on her face. "Nana. I think it's time for your medication, okay?" Avery caught on and tried to suppress a smile. Marina looked both outraged and confused.

Nadia skipped over quickly to Rune and placed a hand on his arm. "Let's go." She hoped her expression conveyed her desire to leave, quickly. Next to her, she could sense Marina and Avery having a wordless conversation.

Avery stopped them as they turned to leave.

"I know you from somewhere." Avery magicked a cigarette out of thin air. He took a drag and blew the smoke in Rune's face.

Rune's expression didn't waver at the insult. He stared at Avery, unblinking. "I'm not sure I've had the pleasure. Rune Christiansen." The two men shook hands, weighing each other's grips.

Avery took another drag of his cigarette and blew the smoke again into Rune's face.

Nadia grabbed Rune, dragging him away by his suit before things could escalate.

"We're late for the charity event. Bye! Don't wait up."

"Wait!" Marina called out.

Nadia urged Rune to go on ahead. "Sorry. I'll just be a minute." Rune looked happy to escape.

"What?" she hissed at Marina and Avery. "You're embarrassing me in front of my boss."

A cold expression crossed Avery's face. "I don't trust him. There's something not quite right with him."

Nadia glared at Avery. "Why are you acting like some overprotective big brother? You don't give a fuck about me." She knew she was being a brat, but she didn't care.

"Stop it, you two," warned Marina.

"Fine, fine," huffed Nadia.

Avery looked her up and down and took a long drag on his cigarette. He blew a stream of smoke in her face as he exhaled. "Have fun with your boss. I'm sure your little party will be great."

And with that, he slammed the door in her face.

Well fuck you, too. She clopped down the wooden stairs in her boots, hitching up the side panels of the gold dress, and followed

Marina's winding stone path in the front yard to the street. Rune was waiting at the curb, leaning back on his car. Impatience was plastered across his beautiful features.

Nadia searched his face, imploring him to understand she was balancing a lot of life things at the moment, including a crazy family situation. And then her eyes focused on the vehicle behind him, the sexy lines of the car leading her eye away.

Her jaw dropped. It was a McLaren. Sleek, black, and powerful, the car looked like it belonged on a showroom floor or a racetrack. It didn't look like it belonged outside Marina's house, waiting to pick her up.

"Ms. Winters?" Rune opened the passenger side of his car. The winged door tilted up like the Batmobile.

"Mr. Christiansen." Nadia tucked herself into the supple leather seat, taking in the interior's craftsmanship and features. The car looked like it had been customized to his tastes and size.

"Sorry about my grandmother and her . . . roommate," Nadia started as Rune climbed in the driver's side. He started the ignition, revving the engine as he peeled off from the curb. Her apology was lost in the sound.

Nadia snuck glances over at him while he drove. His strong jaw. The casual way he held himself. His complete sense of confidence. It was intimidating.

She told herself that she would exude that sense of confidence as well. She sat up straighter and took a deep breath. She'd been to charity galas before. This was no big thing.

Nadia turned on the audio system. She was curious to know what kind of music a guy like Rune listened to while he drove.

A dark metal song blasted through the speakers.

Rune gave her a sideways glance. "You aren't a fan of metal?"

"No, I am. I'm just surprised you are, that's all."

Rune downshifted as they climbed one of San Francisco's steep hills. "There's a lot you don't know about me, Nadia."

He had called her Nadia and not the more formal Ms. Winters he usually used.

For a moment, she panicked. Was this a date?

She pushed that thought to the back of her mind—her favorite self-preservation trick—and cleared her throat. "So, what exactly is this event? Imogen said it was like a Burning Man charity event. But it's black-tie?"

Rune slowed at an intersection, allowing pedestrians to cross. "It's called the Festival of Lugh. The Burning Man organization puts it on every year. It's burner black-tie, which is a little different than your mother's charity events."

"The Festival of Lugh, like Lammas Day?" Nadia asked.

The corner of his mouth turned up in a wry smile. "You seem to know a lot about mythology."

"I told you I was the right person for this job."

He chuckled. "Apparently so. The wicker man was tradition- ally associated with Lammas Day, also known as La Lughnasa, the pagan harvest festival that marks the beginning of the harvest month on August first. The original Burning Man festival began as a Lammas festival where they burned a figure in effigy."

"Lugh was the sun god. One of the Tuatha Dé Danann. Burn- ing the effigy represented sacrifice and rebirth," Nadia added as she turned down the music a bit.

"Precisely. Now, Burning Man is later in the month at Black Rock Desert, but the org still celebrates with a black-tie charity gala and auction to raise money before the festival. Myst is one of the sponsors."

"And a lot of Numinals go to this event?"

"Yes. It's very popular. Half black-tie, half costume, like a mas- querade. Numinals can lower their glamours a bit and look like hu- mans dressing up. It's freeing for them to walk among people and not have to hide."

"Are you going to lower your glamour?"

He shot her a dark look. "Ah, no."

She chewed on the inside of her cheek. "Why not?"

He returned his gaze to the road, his hands gripping the steering wheel. "I never lower my glamour." He turned up the music, effectively cutting off the conversation.

They rode the rest of the way in silence as the music blared from the sound system. Nadia wondered if she had said something wrong.

They pulled up to the valet at City Hall. The regal building was lit up for the gala, the lights projecting gold on the building's outside walls with floodlights rotating in the air. Men, women, and Numinals dressed in a mixture of black-tie, Edwardian, steampunk, and forest creature costumes stopped on the red carpet as photographers took their pictures.

The McLaren's door opened upwards, and a valet put out a hand, helping Nadia out of the car.

Suddenly overwhelmed, she stood at the curb for a moment, watching an elf dressed in a blood-red satin gown and hooded cape make her way up the stairs with a man wearing a furry wolf mask, tuxedo, and tail. A man with long dreadlocks, a steampunk top hat, and goggles bumped into her, apologizing briefly before he found his friends: a woman with a blonde mohawk, fake purple eyelashes, and a feathered neck collar, and a tall horned faerie wearing chainmail and sequins. They all air-kissed and then walked past a creature on four stilt-like legs with a hunched back full of spikes.

"Ms. Winters." Nadia started at the sound of Rune's deep voice. He jerked his head toward the entrance. "Let's go."

As they made their way up the red carpet, they stopped to pose for pictures. Rune's arm fit naturally around her waist as they smiled for the camera. Nadia leaned further into the curve of him. Rune stiffened. She jumped away quickly and mentally tried to control any leaking pheromones.

Snap out of it, Nadia! she told herself. *This is your boss. And this is a training session, not a date.*

Good luck telling yourself that, said the other part of her brain.

Lavish gold and ivory accents decorated the main hall. The interior of City Hall was gorgeous, even without decorations, with its gilt accents, white marble floors, and sweeping grand staircase. To the side, members of the San Francisco Symphony played an orchestral accompaniment to a dark electronic song, blending the heady beats with classical instruments. Waitstaff dressed as woodland nymphs threaded through the crowds with tiny hors d'oeuvres and glasses of champagne.

"Care for a drink?" Rune nodded toward the bar.

"Yes, definitely." Nadia suddenly missed the Myst Psionic. Among its many features, it tracked alcohol consumption by reading blood alcohol content from skin contact like a breathalyzer. She would have to count drinks the old-fashioned way tonight and try not to drink too much in front of Rune.

They wound their way through the crowd. Rune stopped to say hello to a few people he recognized. In the middle of the dance floor, Numinals lined up for court dances, twirling and jumping as they moved in sync through a complicated pattern. When they finally made it to the bar, Rune ordered two shots of chartreuse on top of his bourbon and her glass of champagne. He handed her the shot.

"To good company." They clinked their shot glasses and downed the green liquor. It was strong but smooth, with a definitively sweet herbal taste.

"I didn't think you would be a chartreuse drinker." Nadia set the shot glass back on the bar.

Rune smiled slightly. "As I said earlier, there's a lot you don't know about me."

They mingled in the crowd, sipping drinks and chatting with people. Rune pointed out some people he thought Nadia should know about, including various Numinals and humans who were important in the tech community and to Myst Foundation.

A brunette woman in her mid-forties wearing a beaded head-dress grabbed Rune's arm as they passed.

"Rune, darling!" They air-kissed. She was wearing a slinky black flapper outfit, her breasts spilling out over the top.

The woman looked up and down at Nadia with a sniff. She turned back to Rune, dismissing Nadia as a non-threat to her. Nadia stifled the urge to throw her drink in her face. She counted to five, practicing the training Rune had taught her by spiraling the emotion back deep inside, bottling up that feeling to tap into later when she needed it for a spell.

"Rune, where is that gorgeous girl of yours, Imogen? I had hoped she and I could finish our chat we started last time at the library benefit."

Nadia stiffened. Rune glanced at her out of the corner of his eye.

She suddenly felt self-conscious. She didn't belong there. Imogen did. Who was she kidding?

"Candice, I will tell her you say hello." Rune smiled tightly. "This is Nadia, another one of my employees." Nadia forced herself to smile and nod.

Candice regarded Nadia more closely with a slight sneer on her pinched face. Her eyes darted between her and Rune as if she was trying to figure out exactly how close their relationship was.

Rune extracted them from the situation as quickly as possible.

"I apologize for that. Candice is on the board of the leukemia society. She's rather well-known around town."

"So, you have to kiss her ass," Nadia said dryly. She nabbed a fresh flute of champagne as a waiter passed.

"Something like that."

"So, what's this training? That's what I'm here for, aren't I?" Nadia snapped. Rune's expression hardened.

"Green is not a good color on you, Ms. Winters." His tone was cool. Nadia met his gaze until he turned away.

Rune led her into the corner of the room so they could look out on the guests mingling and dancing, Numinals in tuxedos and fancy dresses mixing with humans in horns and tails. It was already ten p.m. By now, everyone was several cocktails in. The party was in full swing, voices louder, people becoming more boisterous. Laughter rippled through the air. The band increased the tempo of the music to accommodate the mood.

"Let's try some drills." Rune scanned the crowd. "As a Sixer, you have certain abilities. Not only can you sense Numinals, piercing through their glamours, but you can break down their walls or slip in and find an opening without shattering them. Some might even be broadcasting their thoughts if they are untrained. Don't invade anyone's privacy," he warned, "but you need to know how to access another's memories if the event calls for it. You can do this to humans, too, but humans rarely have anything interesting to offer in the way of memories."

Nadia rolled her eyes at his assessment of humans.

"Now, close your eyes—"

"Why do I have to close my eyes?"

"Because you are a novice, and extra sensory input makes it difficult to pay attention. Now, close your eyes."

Nadia huffed but complied.

"Now, focus. Try to drop away everything you hear, smell, touch, taste. Think of it like tuning in to the right radio frequency. You are a single-minded arrow. Find a target and let the arrow fly." His voice was close to her ear. His breath tickled her neck. She tried to ignore that, instead focusing on letting everything else drop away.

At first, all that Nadia could hear was the party, the sounds of laughter and dancing and music. All she could smell was Rune, his aftershave mixing with his natural masculine scent. All she could taste was the slightly bitter taste of champagne on her tongue. And all she could feel was the champagne flute in her hand, the pressure of her feet in her boots, the dress constricting her, and Rune's breath on her neck.

But Nadia let that all slip away, blocking out the sounds, the taste, the smell, the touch, letting the energy of the room wash over her. She focused her sixth sense and psychic abilities, tuning them to different frequencies like she was tuning a radio. Suddenly, everyone's thoughts came into focus.

"Ah!" Nadia clutched her head and tried to block out the sounds. Everything was too loud, everyone's thoughts screaming over one another. Rune touched her temple and her eyes fluttered open, locking on his as he turned down the sound to a manageable level.

He looked impressed. "That was quicker than I would have thought. You're getting better."

Nadia shook her head slightly, trying to dislodge the echoes of the voices still ringing in her mind. "Okay, now what?"

"Close your eyes again. Pick out the individual thoughts. Follow the psychic thread back to a target and look for an opening." He nodded encouragingly and took a sip of his drink. "Get on with it," he urged when she stalled.

"Fine," she grumbled as she closed her eyes. She let the sounds wash over her. She imagined her mind as a heat-seeking missile, picking out a thread and letting the rest fall away. It belonged to an intoxicated pixie who was distracted, dancing and thinking about getting another drink. Nadia slid up to her inner walls and looked for an opening. She tapped slightly. The pixie heard her, shaking her head at the sound, but was too drunk to know what was going on. Nadia found a crack and slid her psychic tendrils inside her mind. Rune had said not to invade anyone's privacy and read their memories, but curiosity got the better of her. She started poking around gently, rifling through her memories like she was flipping through a crate of vinyl. Nadia reveled in the power she was wielding.

"Rune Christiansen, how good to see you."

Nadia's eyes flew open at the voice. The tether to the pixie broke. Standing in front of them was Miles Kirkpatrick, wearing a devil-may-care grin. He looked dashing in a white tuxedo jacket over a black shirt, a pin with the Pact logo on his lapel instead of a boutonniere. Hanging on his arm was a leggy brunette nymph with a lob haircut wearing a short red dress.

Rune put an arm around Nadia's waist and pulled her close. She squeaked slightly, startled, and looked up at him, trying not to let the shock that she felt register on her face.

"Miles Kirkpatrick." Rune nodded at him casually, but Nadia knew better. She could feel how tense he was, pressed close to his body.

"This is Valentina Kurakova." Miles dipped his head toward the nymph at his side, a model Nadia recognized from a recent Gap ad on the side of the corporate headquarters near Myst. Rune took the woman's hand and shook it. She smiled at Rune before looking around at the other guests, a bored expression on her face.

"And this is Nadia Winters. One of my employees." Rune kept his arm around her. Miles took her hand in his and dipped his head down, his lips brushing her knuckles.

"We've met before." Miles grinned boyishly. "At the Kami party. Good to see you again, Nadia. You do look ravishing tonight."

Rune stiffened like a taut violin string. "I didn't realize you two knew each other."

"We only talked briefly," Nadia supplied. "I didn't realize Miles was involved with Pact when we met."

Miles looked about himself like he was looking for someone. "Where is that girl of yours who runs the Foundation? Imogen, was it? Rune, you must let me know the secret to why all your employees are so enchanting."

Nadia turned a bit green again at the mention of Imogen.

Rune's arm tightened around her waist. "Couldn't make it. So tell me, Miles, how goes the business of stealing my business model, customers, and employees?"

Miles laughed, throwing his head back, his white teeth gleaming in the light. But it was a forced laugh, his eyes cold and sharp as they focused on Rune. "Oh, Rune, you do amuse me. In case he hasn't told you yet, Nadia, Rune and I have a bit of a friendly rivalry going on."

"I'm not sure if 'friendly' is the correct term," Rune growled. "Miles here loves to steal everything I've worked for."

"Come now, old man. We've both done pretty well for ourselves. A rising tide floats all boats, as they say." Miles clapped Rune on the side of his arm. Rune looked like he wanted to punch him.

"So, Nadia, what do you do at Myst? Rune keeping you busy?"

Nadia started to answer, but Rune cut her off. "She works with the Foundation."

She looked up at him, surprised, but his eyes were locked on Miles. Nadia adjusted her dress, slipping out from under Rune's arm in a fluid motion. She was tired of being some pawn in whatever little pissing contest they had going on.

"I haven't settled on a position yet. I'm starting with the Foundation, but I'm also working with other departments."

Rune shot her a look. She smiled sweetly at him.

"That's good to explore your options," said Miles. "You should really figure out where and with *whom* you fit best." Miles's meaning was very clear.

Valentina yawned. Rune looked murderously at Miles. Miles seemed to be enjoying himself immensely.

"I hear your user conference is going to be at Moscone Center this year," Rune said, changing the subject smoothly.

At that moment, a woman wearing a heavy velvet cape with the hood pulled over her head approached them. She threw back the hood dramatically, revealing a handsome, done-up face. She appeared to be in her mid-fifties, though she had some plastic surgery touch-ups. Her ears dripped with diamonds.

"Diane," said Miles as he moved over so the woman could join their circle. "You remember Rune Christiansen."

"Yes, of course." She nodded at Rune and gave Nadia a quick, dismissive glance. Nadia shook her head slightly, amazed at the woman's microaggressions.

"Diane. Good to see you again," said Rune, lifting his glass to the woman. "Diane Robbins is Pact's CTO and heads all their current projects," he explained to Nadia.

"Rune here was just asking about Impact," said Miles.

"Ah yes. The user conference is going to be the highlight of the year." Diane took a large sip of her martini, looking around the room.

"If I remember correctly, you usually host it in the spring. It's going to be in October this year, I heard. Why the change?"

Diane flipped a hand about, her large rings catching in the light. "Scheduling with Moscone. We wanted the entire space this year. You know how those things go."

"Rune, when you have a moment, I'd love to speak to you about presenting at Impact," said Miles. "The conference last year was such a success, and this year we are expanding, bringing in some outside speakers from peer companies to let our users know about any partnerships and developments from a community perspective."

"What a lovely idea. We don't have any partnerships with you, though. In fact, I would say our relationship is more like that of a rival or competitor, wouldn't you agree?" Rune took a sip of his drink. Everyone laughed politely. Miles looked like he was thoroughly enjoying Rune's animosity. Nadia wondered if it was all just one big game to them.

"There is always room for change, don't you think?" Miles met his gaze. "I would say the current landscape is ripe for disruption."

The corners of Diane's mouth twinged in a wan attempt at a smile. "I agree. Hacksilver is going to be the future of the crypto-currency movement. You really should check out what we've been working on recently, Rune, especially with our partnership with Portl. You might get some fresh ideas. I heard you pushed back the release again on your new VR game? Such a shame. Any specific reason for that?"

Rune's smile was icy. "As you know, we have several projects. Veil is just one of them. It doesn't take priority over the many other important divisions on which we focus. Recently, we've been work-ing on several new initiatives, doing outreach, and partnering with various volunteer organizations to help the Numinal community in the city."

"Good for you," said Miles. "Someone needs to do something about the state of things around here. Take all these recent attacks on humans—it isn't safe out there. Someone should do something. Perhaps we should make all the demons register with the Council so we can keep track of them."

"No one wants to talk politics at an event like this," said Diane with a laugh. She placed a controlling hand on Miles's arm, and he stopped whatever he was about to say next.

"You think the solution is to make a demon registry?" Rune's pulse fluttered in his temples. "I had no idea you had such unin-formed and ignorant sensibilities. What's next, internment camps? Why stop at demons? Why not lock up all the Numinals in the city? That's where you're going with this, right?"

"I didn't say that," said Miles reproachfully. "But you have to agree that something should be done to address the demon prob-lem. I mean, come on, man! You have humans getting attacked left and right. I would think with your company's mission to integrate

Numinals into human society, you would be the one *most* interested in presenting a better image of Numinals."

"To be honest, it isn't just demons," said Diane. "The vampires are out of control too. They think they run the city." She smiled a fake smile and waved at someone across the room.

"I think it's a bit more complicated than that," said Nadia. "Shades of grey."

All eyes turned to her.

"Fifty?" Miles grinned. Rune scowled at him.

Nadia cleared her throat. "I just mean that you're looking at things in black-and-white terms. I think things with Numinals are much more nuanced and complicated. Orange-and-blue morality," she added, thinking back to Maya and Carson's discussion about demons.

Rune nodded, looking impressed. "I agree. Thinking about demons on a black-and-white spectrum is regressive."

An elderly couple bumbled over, interrupting them, and grabbed Rune to take him off to introduce him to someone. Rune looked like he didn't want to leave Nadia, but he allowed himself to be led away. Valentina took this moment to slip away to "powder her nose"—Nadia was pretty sure she knew what kind of powder she was talking about. Diane spied someone more important than Nadia to talk to and excused herself.

Nadia was left alone with Miles.

He snagged them a couple more glasses of champagne. This was Nadia's fourth. She wobbled in her boots but steadied herself on Miles's arm as he led her over to a secluded bench to talk.

Miles told her about his childhood growing up in DC. It was so similar to hers. They talked about their favorite bars and restaurants, places to hang out. There was something oddly comforting about him. She understood his upbringing and his family. He was an East Coast prep kid like she was. He certainly looked the part, with his boyish good looks and sun-kissed, wavy hair. In a way, he reminded her of her ex, Keith. But smarter and wittier.

She found herself flirting with him a bit. Nothing too overt, but just a little. He noticed and responded in kind, sending her little signals with his eyes, leaning into their conversation more. He seemed to appreciate her intellect. Their banter back and forth was so easy, so natural. Nadia lost track of the time.

"Nadia, it's time to go." Rune appeared, looming over them like a hulking shadow.

Nadia looked up at him, annoyed at his presence. "Already! We just got here."

"It's late. We've both had a long week."

"I'm not tired." They had been at the event for several hours, but if he was going to treat her like he was an overbearing dad, she was going to act like the petulant child.

Miles seemed to be enjoying their back and forth immensely. "If you need to leave, old man, I can make sure Nadia here makes it home safely." He winked. Rune looked like he wanted to throttle him.

Nadia stood up quickly to prevent any bloodshed. "Rune's right. It's getting late." Miles stood as well. They faced one another, an awkward triangle. Nadia wondered where Valentina had gotten off to.

Miles took her hand and kissed it. "It was an absolute pleasure talking to you, Nadia. I do hope to see you soon."

"Likewise."

Rune wrapped an arm around her and ushered her away.

Rune was silent as they walked outside. He was silent as the valet pulled the McLaren around. And he was silent as they both climbed into his car.

Rune drove. Nadia stewed. She snuck glances at Rune, mentally willing him to say something. It didn't work. After a bit, she couldn't take the silence any longer.

"Why are you acting like this?" she shot out, immediately biting her tongue and cringing at her behavior.

"Like what?" Rune asked, his voice sharp and cutting.

She refused to give him an answer. She turned on the stereo. Another dark metal song blasted out.

Rune turned down the volume. Nadia glanced at him. His jaw was rigid, his hands clenched the steering wheel. Nadia felt her face grow hot, uncomfortable with the obvious tension between them.

"What were you two talking about?" he demanded. "You looked pretty cozy over there."

Nadia could not believe he was insinuating what he was. She glared at him. "Nothing. We were just talking about growing up in Washington, DC."

"It didn't look like nothing."

Nadia gaped at him. "Where is this coming from? I didn't do anything wrong!"

"When I take someone out, I expect them to—"

Something inside her snapped. "To what? Hang on your every word? Prop up your delicate male ego? Is that what Imogen does? Well, news flash: I'm not that girl. I'm not some pawn or prop. And also, when did all this"—she waved her hand around at her dress and face—"become part of working at Myst, *boss*? I wasn't aware that being dressed up and toted around as your arm candy was part of the job description." She crossed her arms in a huff. This was bullshit.

He was silent for some time. A heavy metal song played quietly in the background. They slid silently through the streets of San Francisco, the McLaren gliding through like a lethal shark. The mood in the car was tense.

Rune pulled up to Marina's house. There was something still

hanging in the air between them. Some unspoken words. Nadia wanted him to say something. She certainly wasn't going to speak first.

She unbuckled her seat belt and started to open the door.

"Ms. Winters," Rune started. "I . . . apologize for my behavior."

Nadia stared at the side of his face. He was a statue, refusing to look at her.

"Look who's green now." Nadia climbed out of the car and slammed the door.

Chapter 15

On Monday morning, Nadia texted Rune that she wasn't feeling well and had to skip training. She knew she was being a coward after their argument, but she just wasn't feeling up to a grueling session under his intense scrutiny. She couldn't believe she had said those things to him. After drinking too much, she had finally buckled under the pressure of the night and lashed out. She needed to be more careful. After all, he could fire her, and then where would she be? She felt guilty about ducking training when he responded right away, telling her no problem and to rest up.

When she got to her habitat, there was a small silver box with a red bow propped up next to a card on her desk.

Green isn't a good color on either of us.—R.

Inside the box was a necklace with a small amulet—an evil eye symbol made from blue-and-white glass to ward against jealousy. Nadia brought it up to the light, a small thrill going down her spine as she examined the piece. She wasn't immune to the lure of apology jewelry. Her mother's jewelry box was filled with it.

"Your father might be an idiot, but at least I got a good piece of jewelry out of it," her mother had said on more than one occasion.

Nadia clasped the amulet around her neck. A small chime

sounded in her mind. The amulet was charmed. All angry and jealous thoughts she had about Imogen disappeared.

"What's that?" Piero asked as he strolled up to Nadia's workstation. He leaned in and examined the amulet. "An evil eye. Where's this from?"

Her cheeks burned. "It's nothing."

"Uh-huh." Nadia had a feeling Piero knew everything. Gratefully, he changed the subject, instead piling loads of work reviewing more resumes and drafting proposals for Mystos on her.

After he had given her the assignments, Piero lingered at her desk. "You know, there *is* something different about you. Have you been working out?" He said it like he already knew the answer and was fishing for something.

Nadia looked down at her body. While she had always thought of herself as average, thanks to the grueling drills and martial arts training Rune put her through each morning, she was building muscle and toning up. She hadn't lost any weight, but her body composition was changing, her body firming up as she became strong and capable. Nadia now understood how Rune maintained the body of a gladiator in peak physical condition. He spent hours a day training, periodically disappearing from his office to burn off excess energy in the gym.

Carson called out for her from across the room. "Nadia! Do you have a minute to discuss a new project?"

"Be right there!" She looked back to Piero and the stacks of files he had just dumped on her desk.

"Remember that I'm your supervisor," said Piero. "*My* projects come first. Don't let wolf boy over there monopolize all your time on his little game."

"Prioritize your work first. Got it."

He patted her on the cheek. Nadia swatted his hand away.

"Remember the pecking order here. I'm Rune's second-in-command. Don't forget it."

Carson was deep in conversation with his team of engineers when she made her way over to the group.

"What's up?" she asked, notebook and pen in hand, ever ready to take notes on any assignment he might give her.

Carson handed her a piece of paper. "This is a list of artifacts we need from the vaults." Nadia glanced at the list, which contained generic descriptions like "scroll," "shield," and "sword."

"There's a problem with gamers not believing the artifacts we're overlaying in Veil are real. We need to use real ones, not ones we just fabricated. We need one of each type of those things listed, and we will 3D scan them and program them into the game."

"Okay. I just pick whichever ones I want?"

He nodded. "You've played video games before, right? Just make sure the ones you pick look impressive. You know, like with lots of detail and color. Visual patterns, color changes, and depth are good too for making realistic models."

An idea struck her. "You know what would be cool? If there was a way to give the gamers more information on the artifacts. Sort of like a museum exhibit label that gives you a narrative about each piece."

Carson grinned, a broad smile illuminating his handsome features. "That's an excellent idea! I like it. Can you write up informative stories about each of the artifacts?" He turned to his team. "We can program in another screen on the hover pop-up, right?" They nodded.

Nadia's pulse quickened. "There's like two hundred items on this list."

"Yep. That's the preliminary list too. We're planning on expanding once we finish this round of beta testing."

She swallowed, thinking back to the stack of files Piero had dropped on her desk.

Carson must have seen the look on her face. "You should

prioritize this before anything that Piero currently has you doing. This is way more important. We're on deadline for the release."

"All right," said Nadia, her voice betraying her uncertainty.

"Don't worry about Piero. I'm Rune's second-in-command here, and these are his marching orders to get Veil ready for the release on time. If Piero gives you any shit, send him to me and I'll deal with him. He knows that the release takes precedence above everything else right now."

Nadia took the list back to her habitat. She wondered how on earth she was ever going to finish all this work.

The next few days fell into a pattern. In the morning, Nadia trained with Rune before starting her job rotation helping Piero meet with prospective talent for Mystos consulting projects. In the afternoons, she worked in the vaults on Carson's artifact narrative project. In the evenings, she stayed late, meticulously studying the foundations of magic books that Rune had assigned her while also searching for any information on removing Blood Oaths and breaking pacts without consequences. She hadn't found much, though she did learn the difference between vows, oaths, and pacts. Vows were merely promises, pacts were magical contracts between people, and oaths were made to the Numinous and were woven into the very nature of reality. Blood Oaths were the most powerful type, changing a person's DNA and passing down through the generations. She wished she had known all this *before* she had ever met with Mercurio.

Nadia was burning the candle on both ends. Every day she was exhausted and mentally and physically sore from the morning training sessions. At first, Nadia hadn't understood the necessity of physical training to grow and control her powers. But as she gradually got physically stronger, her mental stamina improved as well. Rune moved on from Sixer training to Septer training. Each day he reviewed what she was learning through self-study before he taught her to control her magic—with and without the use of spells or ingredients. While at first her efforts at controlling her powers were met with piddly little sparks or just nothing at all, she soon could tap into her powers and call them forth. It was painstakingly frustrating. She wanted to just use her powers without going back to the basics of energy manipulation. It was like being able to write symphonies in your mind, but only being able to plink out a couple of notes of "Chopsticks" when you tried to play your masterpiece.

"You're going to have to learn how to crawl before you can learn to fly," said Rune, noting her frustrations.

The awkwardness between them had improved a bit, just by the sheer amount of time they were spending together. Though sometimes, it was still like talking to a brick wall. After the disastrous episode at the gala, Rune stayed carefully controlled around her and barely showed any emotion. Now and again, some of her more pathetic efforts at energy manipulation were met with a tiny smile or chuckle from him. Nadia was tempted to mess up more just to make him laugh. She still thought he saw her as a charity case, but as she was getting the hang of her powers, he had started nodding in respect versus shaking his head in exasperation. Nadia knew how patriarchal and backward it was to have a man bolster her self-confidence, but she couldn't help herself—she had little in the way of a support system otherwise. Marina's lack of interest in doing anything more than the bare minimum for Nadia's training wasn't exactly giving her legs to stand on as she tried to navigate her strange new world. And Avery—well, Avery was a conundrum. He seemed mildly curious about her but clearly thought Nadia shouldn't be impeding on his and Marina's happy little life together.

Thomas kept popping up like an annoying cousin, pestering her and asking her questions about the various projects she was working on and the floorplans of Myst's headquarters. She kept all her reports vague and general, things that anyone probably could have gleaned from careful outside observation. When he pressed for certain insider details, she tried to twist them, changing them so that she wasn't actually passing on any proprietary information he couldn't find out himself through other channels. She was walking a fine line, but she felt this way, she wasn't crossing it and betraying Myst.

She felt guilty for telling Thomas any information, but she had no choice. Memories of demons feeding from her would occasionally escape from their box in her mind and grip her in an irrational panic—not to mention worry about any unborn child she might be condemning if she didn't abide by Mercurio's wishes. That threat was less immediate and worrisome. It was hard to imagine life with a baby. Changing diapers and wiping noses never had figured heavily into her life plans. She supposed she would have a kid someday, but she figured the baby flowed naturally after finding the man. And she definitely wasn't anywhere near that.

Nadia thought her attempts at work-life balance were going okay considering the circumstances, but others started noticing that she was slipping.

"I don't know what you're up to, but this isn't going to cut it," said Piero. He crossed his arms over his lime-green coat and looked her up and down. They were going over resumes in one of the glass-walled conference rooms on the ground floor, trying to put together a team to handle a new consulting bid for a telecom company. Resumes, coffee cups, and the remnants of their morning pastries covered the conference table.

Nadia was beginning to understand that snacks were a big part of startup life.

"This"—he held up a hand and made a circle gesture at her— "this whole situation isn't working for me."

Nadia stifled a yawn. "What do you mean?" She looked down

at her rumpled T-shirt and ran her hands over the wrinkles to iron them out.

"Don't give me that, missy! You know you aren't bringing your A-game here. This is like the third day in a row you've worn yoga pants to work. And what is *that*?" He peered at a stain on her shirt. "Is that wine?"

It was true. She wasn't bringing her A-game. Nadia was stretched thin, distracted. She needed to focus on work. But between learning to control her powers, handling all the projects that she kept being pulled into, and searching for a way to break the Blood Oath, her work was suffering.

Nadia realized that Piero had said something else, and she snapped back to, shaking herself out of thought.

"Sorry, what?" she asked as she rubbed her eyes.

"Hello! Earth to Nadia! I said that whatever extracurricular activities you have going on have to stop. You're exhausted every day. You walk around here like a zombie. Earlier, you called the kitsune 'Mr. Fox.' Do you know how offensive that is to a kitsune?"

Nadia cringed. Earlier that day, she had met with a prospective candidate, a snowy white kitsune with nine tails. The meeting hadn't gone well. The kitsune already worked with Pact and was taking issue with Myst's "No Hexes or Curses" policy. They were trying to smooth over the issue and come to an agreement on the terms and scope of employment. Nadia's calling him "Mr. Fox" had only alienated him further.

"I'm sorry. I'm just dealing with some personal stuff, but I will get it together."

"Good." Piero eyed her. "I've seen this before with new hires. I get it. San Francisco is a great city. There is always something going on, and you don't want to say no to anything. You want to experience it all. And you should! You're young and pretty, and I'm sure the boys are all lined up to take you out. But get your shit together at work first. Got it?"

"Okay, okay."

"One more thing," said Piero, dropping his voice a bit. "People have noticed that you and Rune are coming out of the gym at the same time each morning."

Nadia flushed.

"Just as I thought," he said knowingly. "Best keep those extra-curriculars to a minimum."

To make matters worse, Maya even pulled her aside to talk to her. They were taking a break in the lounge area one day, having a mid-day coffee and watching music videos on the big-screen TVs so Maya could show Nadia her latest music video on the charts.

As they sat on one of the couches, waiting for Maya / The Mighty Troglodyti's new single to play, Maya leaned over, keeping her voice low. "Hey, just so you know, it's best to keep a low profile around this place. The gossip mills can be brutal."

"What are you talking about?" asked Nadia, suddenly worried someone had seen her with Thomas.

Maya took a deep breath and then dived right in. "I'm going to give you a bit of unsolicited advice. Bear with me. I love Rune, but he is not a guy a girl like you should get involved with. People have noticed your interactions. How your eyes follow him when he walks across the floor. How you blush, like, every time he says anything to you."

"I do *not* blush," said Nadia, mortified.

"Yes, sweetie, you do. You're even doing it now. So whatever little thing you two have going on, whatever little infatuation you have with him, know you are getting in way over your head. He's intense. He has his demons. You've seen how he is around the office, with the mood swings and the brooding."

"I appreciate the concern, but I can handle myself." Nadia took a sip of her coffee, wishing Maya would just drop it.

Maya's expression softened. "I know you can. I just don't want to see you get hurt, that's all. I think everyone here has had a crush on him at some point. It never ends well. I just had to say something since there seems to be something going on between you two."

"Well, I can guarantee you nothing is going on. That would be . . . inappropriate. He's the boss. You know that I'm a mess with my Septer abilities. He's just training me, that's all."

Maya looked skeptical. "We have trainers on staff. Why would he spend the time to personally train you?"

Nadia shrugged. "Because I'm that hopeless?"

"Maybe," said Maya. "But just be careful. Okay? Rune doesn't do easy breezy."

"What about him and Imogen?" Nadia felt her jealousy rise and fingered the amulet around her neck. The feeling dissipated.

Maya shook her head. "Who knows? She's like the Rune whisperer or something. Only person who truly gets him and speaks his language, apart from Carson. No one is sure how it's going to be around here when she leaves."

The video on the TV changed, and Maya nudged Nadia. "Hey, check it out." They watched the video, which started with atmospheric nature shots of clouds, forests, and glaciers set to a dark beat. The melody started up, and the video cut to The Mighty Troglodyti DJing to a huge music festival in the snow, glaciers and snowcapped mountains in the background, as the crowd danced wildly.

"Is that Iceland?" asked Nadia, impressed.

Maya nodded. "It was the biggest shoot I've done. It was totally wild."

"By the way, I was wondering if you had that list of charms I should know."

"Oh, sure." Maya held out her hand, and Nadia took off her Psionic and handed it to her. Maya clicked through to her profile and starred one of her curated, public lists, called "Fuck Off,

Creeper," so Nadia could access it from her launch page later. "Hey, what's this 'For Nadia' list?" she asked as she handed the watch back to Nadia.

Nadia clasped the watch back on her wrist. "Oh, Rune made a list of spells he thought I would need while working in the vaults. Like finding lost objects, the ability to read any language, checking whether an object is cursed. Stuff like that."

Maya's mouth dropped open. "Rune made you a spell list?" She grabbed Nadia's wrist and scrolled through the list in the app before she clicked through to other various windows. Her complexion paled, and she opened her mouth like she was about to say something but stopped herself.

Nadia shrugged as she took her wrist back. "Yeah, so?"

"You don't think that's a little weird?"

"I'm talking to an elf. I don't know what's weird anymore."

Maya tucked her hair behind her ear and turned to face her on the couch, pulling up her legs underneath her. "I'm just saying . . . Rune helps a lot of people, but I've never heard of him making anyone else a *spell list*."

"They probably aren't as hopeless as I am."

Maya looked dubious. "If you say so."

Chapter 16

Nadia kept in mind Piero and Maya's warnings about the gossip mills around Myst as she and Rune continued training in the mornings. She wasn't sure how to quell any burgeoning rumors other than quitting training with Rune altogether, and that wasn't an option even if she had wanted it to be.

If Rune knew about the gossip, he said nothing to her.

"Ah, there you are," said Rune as Nadia entered the gym. Once again, he had beaten her there and had been working for some time before she arrived.

Nadia yawned as she made her way over to the mat where Rune had assembled an array of training materials. He quickly ran her through a workout until her heart rate was elevated, and she had a light sheen of sweat on her brow.

"Let's switch gears a bit today," said Rune. "Have you had a chance to explore the extra modules I added to your Psionic?"

"Uh, a little bit."

"Well, you really should explore the extra material I added. I put it there for a reason."

"I will, I will."

Rune frowned slightly but said nothing. He gestured to the center of the blue mat. Nadia walked over and stood, facing him with her hands on her hips.

"Now what?" she asked.

"To be an effective spellcaster, you need to exert your will on the world. Magic is an expression of the true will of the individual. Magicians must believe they are entitled to change reality in accordance with their desire."

Nadia snorted. "Magic must be the true millennial calling."

"Winters . . ." warned Rune.

"Okay, okay. I'm listening. Exerting one's will on the world. Got it."

"As I'm sure you are aware from your extensive self-study"—Rune looked at her pointedly and Nadia fought the urge to roll her eyes—"there are numerous ways to cast, all depending on the ability of the witch or magician. You appear to have a natural affinity for Thelema—magic through visualization. Not to be confused with Aleister Crowley's religion and philosophy of the same name. Thelema is the most complicated and difficult type of magic, not requiring the use of rituals, spells, incantations, or tools to manifest intent. Of course, the use of these will only heighten and concentrate your powers.

"Now, Numinals stem from the Other Realms, where the same laws of physics do not bind them as in the Earth Realm. Numinal magic evolved under different conditions. The vast majority of humans cannot see the infinite possibilities that exist in reality. Numinals and Septers have the ability to see these possibilities and reweave the threads of reality into new forms."

Nadia scrunched up her nose. "This sounds like quantum mechanics."

Rune nodded. "Quantum mechanics is just starting to touch on this, but ultimately it is a human construct and theory. It will never fully encapsulate the Numinous and the underpinnings of reality, the way humans will never understand the universe and create a scientific system that explains everything."

Nadia shook her head in exasperation. "I'm human. How am I supposed to understand all this?"

"You are *not* human. You are parahuman. You are a Septer. You have an innate ability to understand the Numinous and magic. But that's all you have right now—the innate ability. We need to turn that ability into a useable skill."

Rune magicked a tiger's eye marble out of thin air and placed it on the ground in the center of the blue mat.

"We'll start with something small. Go ahead."

"What do you want me to do?" asked Nadia.

"Whatever you desire. But you must truly want it."

Nadia stared at the marble, biting her lip. She held her palm over the marble before she quickly snatched it back, feeling foolish. She didn't know what she was doing. Rune gave a slight nod of his head, like he was urging her to get a move on.

She held out her hand again and focused on the marble. She let her mind detach from what she was seeing—the tiny marble sitting on top of the training mat—and thought about the infinite possibilities of reality and what she could be seeing instead. A mini black hole. A mountain of marbles multiplying and multiplying. The marble sprouting wings and flying away. Her mind bounced from option to option as she tried to focus on one.

The marble twitched and rolled slightly to the side and back up in a crescent path.

"I take it you intended for more to happen?" Rune's expression was kind and understanding, but she still felt like she had failed.

She nodded.

"Try again. You must *truly* want it. Focus your emotion."

She returned her focus to the marble and imagined it gently floating up in the air to meet her outstretched palm, like a tiny hot air balloon bobbing in the wind. She pushed through her doubts and believed she could levitate the marble. In her mind, reality untethered itself, and she picked out the strands and rewove them into a new reality, one where she could make the marble fly. The marble twitched again and slowly began to rise.

"Yes, that's it!" said Rune. The Psionic pinged at her sudden elevated heart rate, but she was unable to control her excitement. This was the first time she had performed intended magic apart from basic energy manipulation. The rush of power was intoxicating, a heady surge that made her feel alive. She glanced at Rune and licked her lips.

The marble dropped back to the floor.

"You lost your concentration. What were you thinking about?" asked Rune.

"Uh, nothing." Nadia lowered her hand, blushing. She was not about to tell him that she was thinking about how perfect his face was.

"You need single-minded focus to cast. You can't let other thoughts distract you. Once you master your skills, magic will come to be second nature, like breathing. But until then, you must focus. Again."

Nadia repeated the drill over and over and over, the marble floating, slowly at first and then gaining speed, up into her outstretched palm. Rune circled her as he critiqued her form and offered advice. After a bit, Nadia wanted to move on to a new drill, but Rune refused, urging her to keep practicing until it became second nature.

"Where did you learn about all this, anyway?" asked Nadia as she raised the marble to her palm again.

"I studied for many, many years."

"How come you think I'll be able to pick it up quickly if it took you so long?"

"As a Septer, you have a natural affinity for all types of magic, as long as you can overcome your human instinct. I had to overcome my own natural instincts, which limited me more than they do you."

"What are your natural instincts?"

The corner of Rune's mouth turned up. "Are you always this inquisitive?"

Nadia floated the marble back up again and clasped her hand around it. "Only when I think there is more there than meets the eye."

Rune didn't respond. They fell into silence as Nadia repeated the exercise. Nadia dropped the marble and then levitated it up again from the floor.

"So how was your weekend?" asked Nadia after a bit.

"Fine."

"Did you do anything fun?" she asked when Rune didn't offer more.

"Why are you asking?"

Nadia caught the marble again. "I don't know. Just making conversation."

"Why?"

"Because that's what people do when they hang out."

"We are not 'hanging out.' We are training."

They lapsed into silence again. The marble rose to her palm, and she dropped it to the ground before levitating it up once more.

"Do you watch movies?" asked Nadia.

"For the love of God, woman." Rune's voice was tinged with irritation.

"What?"

"Enough with the questions. You need to focus."

Nadia shook her head slightly, exasperated at Rune's stoicism. "Oh, come on, give me a break. I can do this in my sleep now. Look." She raised the marble to her palm again and then snatched it out of the air before dropping it back down to the mat. She repeated the drill.

"I watch TV and movies," said Rune after a bit. The marble wobbled a bit in midair, but Nadia corrected it, raising it at a steady pace.

"What do you watch?"

"*The Real Housewives.*"

Nadia looked up in surprise. The marble fell to the ground.

"Just kidding," said Rune. "Again." He jerked his chin at the marble on the floor.

Nadia focused on the marble, trying to hide her smile at his joke. She wanted to ask him more questions, discover his tastes, find out what made him tick. She hoped he wanted to know things about her, as well.

"What was the last movie you watched?" Nadia asked.

"*Bringing Up Baby.*"

"Really?"

"I like classic movies." He shrugged.

Nadia tucked that snippet of knowledge away. She also liked classic movies. *Some Like It Hot* with Marilyn Monroe was one of her favorites.

"What was the last book you read?" Nadia asked next.

"This isn't Twenty Questions."

"Just answer."

Rune chuckled. "Fine. It was a book of Middle Persian poetry, in the original language."

"You read Middle Persian?"

"Among many others."

Nadia fell silent, thinking about that as she raised and lowered the marble for several more minutes. She tried to focus, but her mind kept trying to wander, pulled aside by thoughts of Rune like the moon's gravity pulling on tides. She couldn't stop her thoughts from circling, caught in his orbit. They pulled her concentration away from the marble.

She needed to break the monotony. Nadia caught the marble and tossed it to Rune. He caught it out of the air.

"Carson says you have a lot of power," said Nadia. "Come on, show me something good."

The corner of his mouth turned up. "I'm not here for your amusement."

Nadia circled him, and Rune turned to face her like they were squaring off for a fight. "I know, but just show me something. I know you can do awesome things. C'mon, do something cool. Make me think I'm somewhere else, or make it seem like it's snowing inside or something."

"Illusion magic is not very difficult. It's a trick of the eye, like glamour."

Nadia stopped circling. "Then show me something real."

"Like what?"

"I don't know. I don't even know what's possible."

"Anything is possible," said Rune with a grin. He tossed the marble into the air before quickly waving his hand in a stream of gestures. As the marble reached the pinnacle of its trajectory, it erupted into dozens of snowy white doves that scattered in all directions. Nadia gasped and turned about herself, astonished at the birds that flapped and fluttered around them like they were caught in the middle of a blizzard. Rune waved his hand, and the birds transformed into dancing white butterflies in a cloud around them. Laughter bubbled out of Nadia as the white butterflies coalesced together above her like tiny pearls or pixels to create the 3D image of her face, expressions of awe and wonder on the porcelain face mirroring her own. One of the butterflies broke away from the others and came to rest on the tip of her finger.

Rune waved his hand again, and the butterflies evaporated into thin air like wisps of smoke.

"How can I learn to do that?" asked Nadia, in awe at Rune and his power.

"By learning to focus," said Rune. "Walk with me. I have an idea."

*   *   *

In the emerald-green glass-walled conservatory adjacent to the main warehouse headquarters, Myst housed a botanical garden where rare herbs, plants, and flowers could grow for use in various Mystos engagements. It was an indoor jungle, stone walkways weaving through lush vegetation, big leafy trees and exotic flowers blooming and filling the warm, moist air with a rich, earthy odor.

Nadia couldn't help but marvel at the strange flora and fauna as Rune led her deeper into the garden, pushing giant leaves to the side as he wound them through the maze of otherworldly plants. Oversized insects and butterflies and Numinal creatures that Nadia had never seen before—tiny winged Pegasi and mischievous, pink and purple pixies—flew about the verdant trees and colorful flowers. Others frolicked in the waterfalls of a lotus pond covered with lily pads and crisscrossed with little bridges like a miniature Japanese tea garden. Giant pink-and-green pitcher plants with their heavy, bulbous sacs full of nectar hung on vines the size of Nadia's wrist. Strange, glowing jellyfish-like creatures with tentacles waving like sea grass floated in the air, twinkling like dawn fireflies in the muted morning light that fell down on them through the green glass enclosure.

In the middle of the garden was a labyrinth: a huge winding stone walk similar to the one at Chartres Cathedral, a mosaic pattern of twisting, enveloped passages leading to the center. "You should incorporate walking the labyrinth into your practice," said Rune. "It will help you focus and clear your mind. I often walk the labyrinth when I need to work out a problem or unwind my mind."

Nadia entered the labyrinth and followed the pathway to the center, moving slowly. Rune stayed outside the circle and watched her.

"Tell me what magic is to you," he called out to her.

Nadia thought for a minute before answering. "Magic is a tool. One that I need to learn how to wield by practicing and memorizing and focusing."

Rune had taken a seat on a nearby marble bench. He picked a light-pink flower bud from a bush next to the bench and twirled the stem between his fingers. "That is why you must repeat drills and memorize spells and herbs and ingredients. You believe that magic is something that you must learn to master, so that is how it works for you."

"What is magic to you, then?" She looked over at him.

The bud in Rune's hand continued to rotate as he twirled it. It started to bloom, quickly transforming the flower from a bud to a heavy, full-blown blossom. The strange plant's petals darkened to a dusty-pink color tipped with ruby as they opened, slowly arching backward like ballet dancers.

Rune stared at the flower. "To me, magic is the unseen forces in the universe. It isn't merely a tool but is an innately personal relationship—a dance of sorts—to the Numinous. It's a mirror that reflects true nature through the manifestation of one's will. Magic is a wild, living force that is within everything and everyone. A magician knows how to pull on the strings of this force, to press the invisible levers, to effect the change he desires and imprint his will on reality.

"Take attraction between two people, for example. Sure, there might be discrete scientific phenomena that you could use to explain why two people are attracted to one another. Pheromones, chemistry, biology, and the like. But for anyone who has ever been attracted to someone else, isn't there something indescribable, inscrutable, and ultimately ineffable about it? What else is the totality of this attraction except for some unseen force or magic? How else can you describe attraction except as some sort of push and pull, magic and counter-magic, a type of dance between two people?"

Nadia was fully aware of her body and how it was responding to his words. A heated flush rose from her core and spread, sending tendrils of desire over her skin. She kept walking, trying not to let the emotion overcome her. There was a strange magic filling the space between them, a spell starting to weave all around them, drawing them closer together. Nadia thought about his words as she walked along the stone path. She had always thought of attraction between two people as a sort of art piece, a cocreated work full of passion and vibrancy, where each brushstroke of one artist was measured and balanced against the other.

In a way, it was like Rune said, a dance. Perhaps she innately knew magic better than she thought.

Rune continued, "But for that dance, for that magic to ever happen, someone had to think it was possible. Right now, your mind, and therefore your magic, is limited by what it believes. You believe that you can only do magic through rote memorization and repetitive practice, so that's how it works for you. But what if I told you that anything is possible? You could be a master magician if you stripped away all those limiting beliefs and instead looked at the potentiality of any situation."

Nadia shook her head. "I can't just jump off a building and fly just because I think I can. What about the laws of physics?"

"Nadia, you just spent the better part of an hour levitating a marble against the laws of physics. Give yourself a little more credit and expand your mind. You mustn't doubt yourself. Doubt cripples magic. If you doubted yourself, you would fall to the ground like a rock."

"Okay, so how do I learn to not doubt myself?"

"You must learn to master your mind. If you can master your mind, you can master reality."

Nadia sighed, growing frustrated with Rune's cryptic Yoda-esque statements. "I don't even know what that means. You sound like a fortune cookie."

Rune chuckled. "It appears that with you, hearing the words of the theory isn't going to be enough." He paused a minute, watching her navigate the labyrinth. "I have an idea." Rune stood and walked over to Nadia. She stopped in the center of the maze. The sunlight shining in from the green glass walls hit her eyes, and she blinked suddenly in the bright light before her vision cleared and focused on Rune.

"I can't guarantee that this will work, but it might accelerate your understanding." He started reaching a hand over to her temple before he stopped himself. "I need you to lower your defenses for a minute. I promise I won't read your mind."

"All right." Nadia hesitated, worried he might glean something about Mercurio, but she chose to trust him and closed her eyes. With a deep breath, she lowered her outer walls. She felt exposed, naked, but she pushed through the fear and uncertainty and knew that Rune wouldn't pry into her mind.

Rune touched her temples gently, barely making contact. He counted down from seven, her entire world narrowing down to the sound of his deep voice reverberating into the core of her being, like she was a cork bobbing along in a sea of heady champagne, waiting until she could completely submerge herself into him. She sank deeper, the champagne turning viscous and thick as Nadia lost herself in the golden, molten-honey lava that was Rune. And then she was nothing, a malleable piece of flesh and consciousness that he could imprint his will and magic on.

There was a brief discontinuity, a stinging pinprick in Nadia's mind. A wrinkle formed as her mind fought the sudden intrusion, but it was smoothed over as the memories were assimilated into her own. A single heartbeat pulsed in the center of her bottom lip. Nadia's eyes fluttered open, and she took a sharp intake of breath as her eyes met Rune's.

"What the hell was that?" she demanded.

Nadia struggled to assimilate the foreign memory into her own.

The memory was like recalling a dream, coming back in quick flashes or feelings:

Walking the streets of a bustling city, much like New York. Blaring horns, pedestrians hastening down the sidewalk. Feeling familiar, yet entirely foreign. Rune's hand grabbing hers and pulling her out of traffic and into a grassy park.

"I planted a seed of an idea," said Rune. Nadia fought the rising bile in her throat, the panic that threatened to choke her. The Psionic pinged.

"You *Inception*-ed me," she accused.

Rune stifled a laugh. "If I had done that, you wouldn't even be aware of it. No, I planted a memory in your consciousness, not your unconsciousness. Since you are aware of it, you can recall it at will and use it as a learning tool about how to change your reality."

Nadia shut her eyes again. *The city, spinning on its axis, buildings flipping upside down. Rune and Nadia, walking the streets of San Francisco instead of New York.*

The false memories rubbed up against her real ones, wearing them down and smoothing the edges so that she no longer fought them.

Entering a stone fortress on a hill. A wall of flashing lightning rods. Pulling apart and rewiring limiting beliefs. Paradigm shifts shaking the ground like earthquakes, breaking apart and rearranging her own personal truths. Rune grinning at her as she breaks apart an old belief and builds a new one: Anything is possible.

Nadia took a deep breath and opened her eyes.

"All I did was implant an idea," said Rune. "The way a book or a person might implant an idea through words. Since you have an affinity for Thelema, it will be easier for you to understand a memory, something personal and recognizable and visual, rather than mere words. Whatever you are experiencing is your interpretation of the seed of the idea."

"Isn't this cheating or something?"

Rune shook his head. "Think of it more like hacking the system. Attempting to fast-track results by personalization. You have the lesson now. You have a memory, a visual representation of how to mentally rewire beliefs. What you do with it and whether you learn from it, well . . . that is up to you."

Chapter 17

By August, the city's weather turned to the pleasant mid-seventies, which was practically balmy as the city was mostly covered in fog the rest of the year. It was the perfect weather for happy hour and drinks, something the other Mystics reminded Nadia of quite often.

On a Friday, Nadia yawned as she packed up her bag at her habitat, getting ready to go home for the evening. Marina had texted her that Avery was picking up Thai food, and they had planned an evening of catching up on their Netflix shows and drinking Marina's magical margaritas.

During college, Nadia used to go out every weekend with friends or dates. Her social life now consisted of take-out and watching movies with her grandmother and her weird roommate. How the mighty have fallen, thought Nadia, though she didn't mind. It was nice to finally have a relationship with her grandmother after all these years. And Avery was warming up to her, though he still acted like she was a huge imposition on his life and his relationship with Marina.

Maya strolled up to Nadia at her habitat. "What is this? You aren't going home, are you? The gang is going out for drinks to celebrate Imogen's last day."

"I thought we already celebrated today?" Earlier that afternoon, they had a farewell party that included a cake that Grudax and the goblins had made, balloons, booze, and impromptu speeches that ended with Piero standing on a desk and singing Sarah McLachlan's "I Will Remember You" before Rune had pulled him down and yelled at everyone to get back to work.

"That was the entire office celebration. A smaller group is going for drinks." Maya spied Piero and gestured him over.

"What's happening? What's the emergency?" Piero looked back and forth between them. "Spill it."

Maya bumped Nadia with her hip. "Nadia here is trying to skip drinks."

Nadia made a face at her for ratting her out.

"No, she isn't. She's coming with us," Piero proclaimed. He straightened his tie and brushed an invisible piece of lint from his purple coat.

Nadia shrugged on her cropped red leather bomber jacket. "You don't care if I'm there. You just want this to be enough of an employee outing that you can charge your drinks to Rune's credit card." Nadia lifted her hair out from under the jacket as she put it on and finger-combed the tangles in the waves. Marina had told her that a witch's hair started tangling the more her powers grew, the body reacting to extra energy in the air during spellcasting. Nadia had taken to regular deep conditioning treatments, as well as Marina's special herbal salve that helped hydrate to keep her dark locks looking shiny.

Piero waved a hand, shaking his head in dismissal. "Lord knows, I try. But seriously, I'm going to fire you if you don't come."

Nadia grabbed her bag from under her desk and threw it over her shoulder. "You say that every week. Sorry, guys. I would totally go grab a drink, but I'm exhausted. This week kicked my ass." She gave Piero a pointed look.

"Hey, bitches! Are we doing happy hour, or what?" Sophie bounced up to them, the fringe of her leather jacket and cowboy boots swaying as she moved. Her hair was now lavender blonde, feathers and beads woven into her locks. She looked like she was off to Coachella.

"Miss Grumplestiltskin over here is refusing to come out with us," said Piero.

Sophie smirked. "'Fraid you can't hang? It's okay. We understand not everyone can cut it in the fast-paced startup world. As Mystics, we work hard, play hard."

Nadia felt the cattiness rise inside her. "Actually, I'm not as tired as I thought."

Sophie's smile was wintry. "Great. The more the merrier."

Nadia followed Piero, Sophie, and Maya over to the lobby, where Imogen, Carson, and Rune stood around chatting. Anya had already left for the evening, her spot at the reception desk vacant.

Piero's eyes lit up as he saw Rune. "I knew we could get you to come out sooner or later. Had to take Miss Imogen here leaving to get you to do it. Drinks on you?" He grinned cheekily at Rune, who regarded him in mild amusement.

"Sorry, guys," said Rune. "I'm not going to make it."

"Why not?" Sophie stuck out a bright-pink lip, pouting.

Imogen gave him a playful nudge. "It's my last night here. Sure you don't want to come out?"

It looked like Rune might say yes, but he merely shook his head. "I have some work. Maybe I'll catch up with you all later."

As they headed out the door, Nadia looked back over her shoulder. Rune stood like a statue in the lobby, watching her. His eyes locked with hers, and she held his gaze, the Myst Psionic emitting a small beep on her wrist. A small sense of hope surged to life within her heart. A tiny flame fanned by his smoldering look. Rune had told her that anything was possible.

Nadia held on to that thought, her steps light, as she caught up with the others.

*   *   *

Classic rock was playing over the loudspeaker when they arrived at the food truck park near Myst headquarters. The atmosphere was loud and boisterous. Numinals and humans were taking advantage of the happy hour specials, eating kabobs, pizza, and various other fusion dishes from the food trucks, some roasting s'mores around the fire pits scattered throughout the park.

After they found a wooden picnic table big enough for their group, Carson and Maya went to go get drinks and tacos while the rest of them settled in.

"I wonder why Rune didn't want to come out," said Sophie.

"He never comes out," said Piero. "I wish he would loosen up. He's such a stick in the mud sometimes."

"Oh, he's not so bad," said Imogen. *Of course she would say that.* Nadia fingered her amulet.

"I bet we won't ever get him out again now that you are leaving," Sophie said. She jerked forward slightly like she was startled and pulled out her cell phone from a back pocket. "Goddammit," she muttered as she read her email. She held up her phone so Piero could read it. He scanned the email and whistled.

"Vega is going to go crazy," said Piero.

"What is it?" asked Nadia.

"Another incident with Veil that is going to require a lot of hazard pay." Sophie tucked her cell phone back into her pocket. "Carson needs to look into this. There have been so many big treasure payouts recently that it's causing all these harassment issues with the actors."

"Hey, no work emails," called out Maya as she and Carson returned with trays of tacos and beer.

Carson's ears pricked forward. "What about the treasure payouts?" He looked at Sophie questioningly as he unloaded the food and drinks onto the wooden table.

She shook her head, shrugging. "I don't know. Vega emailed that there's been another harassment issue because of the treasure payouts. That's like the third one this month. I thought the big payouts were supposed to be rare?"

Carson frowned. "They are. The winnings are tied to a random number generator, like a slot machine."

"Maybe it's a bug," suggested Piero.

Carson growled. "My code does not contain errors."

Piero rolled his eyes.

The music over the loudspeaker changed to a dark, melodic rock song. Sophie jumped up, squealing. "Oh my God! I love this song."

"Is this the new Tommy Lightning?" asked Piero. "You know, I hung out with him once. When I was playing Hedwig at the ACT, he was in the audience, and I totally fangirled all over him after the show. I should be embarrassed. But I'm not."

"You liar. What happened?" Sophie's dark eyes were envious.

"Who's Tommy Lightning?" Nadia asked.

Sophie's mouth dropped open. "You've never heard of Tommy Lightning?" Nadia shook her head.

"His band is Buckskin Voodoo. He's a vampire. Totally rad. He doesn't even wear glamour. People think it's a costume."

"He's amazing," gushed Piero, his eyes gleaming through his rose-tinted sunglasses. "He does all these acrobatics. Flips through the air, hangs from the rafters."

"Guys and girls alike line up trying to get him to bite them," added Sophie. "I would totally let him bite me."

"Ew, gross. You'd let him bite you?" asked Maya. "That's sick." She stuck out her tongue and pretended to gag.

"Less permanent than a tattoo," Carson teased, his canines descending as he grinned.

"I heard he's playing at Screamforce this year," said Imogen.

Nadia had no idea what they were talking about. "Screamforce?"

Carson nodded. "Sorry. Impact. Pact's user conference is on Halloween this year. We've been calling it Screamforce. It's the second biggest user conference in the city each year after Dreamforce."

"And I'm going to have to skip it this year," said Imogen. "Something I don't feel too bad about. Rune always gets so moody. But I am going to miss you guys when I'm back at Trinity." She pressed a hand to her heart, looking at each of them. "Truly. You guys have been my family. My home away from home." She looked out of place in the food truck park, wearing her knee-length skirt, tight sweater, and heels.

"Here's to Imogen. We're going to miss you around here." Maya raised a plastic cup to her. They all followed suit, bumping their plastic beer cups together to cheers before they dug into the trays of carne asada and carnitas tacos, the sizzling aroma of the grilled meat and onions wafting up.

"These are the best tacos I've ever had," Carson said. He grabbed another soft taco and shoved the entire thing into his mouth, wiping his closely trimmed beard with a paper napkin as he swallowed. "I didn't have these growing up. I don't think they came to San Francisco until the turn of the century."

"They had tacos here before the year two thousand," said Nadia, glancing at Maya like, *what is he talking about?*

"I meant the turn of *last* century." Carson sprinkled cilantro on the top of another taco before he popped it into his mouth. He grinned wolfishly and winked at her shocked expression. She hadn't realized he was that old. She looked at the others, wondering if they were older than she had thought.

"If you choke, I'm not going to save you," said Maya, grinning and nudging him.

"I would." Sophie smiled coquettishly at Carson. Maya frowned and looked away.

"Have you heard about the latest attacks?" asked Piero, smoothly changing the subject. He shook his head in disgust. "Horrible, just horrible."

"I read about those. There's something odd about them," said Imogen before she daintily took a bite of her taco.

"It's demon-related for sure," said Carson. "But low-caste. Body snatchers, if I had to guess."

"Body snatchers? Like pod-people body snatchers?" Nadia hoped this wasn't a new thing that she had to worry about now. San Francisco was turning out to have more layers than she could have ever imagined.

Carson shook his head. "I'm talking about the type of demon who possesses. They aren't corporeal enough generally to survive in this realm for too long without a body. They're mindless soul-suckers. Barely sentient. They just feed on instinct and drive humans to madness to feel the emotion they seek."

"I thought when the Realm Gates shut Numinals couldn't travel between the realms." Nadia glanced at Imogen. "That whole Collapse thing?"

Imogen patted her red lips with a paper napkin. "That's true. The Gates are closed. But sometimes teeny tiny portals can spontaneously open, allowing low-caste Numinals with no physical body to slip through."

"They sometimes manage to jump into the Earth Realm and latch on to a body, like leeches. You'll see them like a dark shadow over someone's aura." Maya shuddered.

"This is like Numinal 101." Sophie took another sip of her beer, glancing at Nadia over the rim of her cup.

Nadia ignored her. "So low-caste demons can slip in to Earth, but no Numinal on Earth can travel to the Other Realms?"

Maya nodded. "It doesn't even happen very often that demons get enough power to even jump realms. It is super strange that there have been so many. Something is going on. Someone is calling them or letting them in or something."

"Who would do that?" Nadia asked.

Imogen shrugged. "No idea. But it would take some seriously dark magic."

"Like, *exceptionally* dark magic," interjected Piero. "Like, I don't even know anyone in our talent pool with enough power."

"I bet Rune could. The guy's a beast." Carson stood up. "I'm going to get more tacos. Anyone?" He pointed at each of them with his index fingers like he was shooting a gun.

He returned several minutes later with two trays full of tacos and a small paper bowl of chopped peppers.

"You're good at balancing all that," Nadia commented, watching him balance each heavily loaded tray with one hand.

"Spent some time in Hawaii bartending after 'Nam." He set the trays on the table and started unloading the tacos.

"What are those?" Maya wrinkled her nose at the pile of peppers that Carson placed on the table.

"Carolina Reapers. The guy at the taco truck said they are the hottest peppers in the world." Carson rubbed his hands together as he sat back down at the picnic table. "Who wants to challenge me?"

"Um, no thanks." Piero held up a hand. "You might be used to panting and drool, but I certainly am not."

"What? No takers?" Carson caught Nadia's eye. "What about you, Nadia? You look like you can handle some heat."

She grinned, shaking her head. "Pass. I'd like to keep my taste buds intact, thank you very much."

Carson looked crestfallen. "No one? Sophie?"

Sophie shook her head. "I like to gamble, but not with my own money, and definitely not with my life."

"I will take another beer, though." Imogen wagged her empty cup.

"Get another round for the table." Piero fished through his wallet and pulled out the company credit card. "What?" he asked, seeing their faces. Piero loved to spend Rune's money. "He isn't here, anyway. What he doesn't know won't hurt him."

"What don't I know?"

Nadia turned to the sound of Rune's deep voice behind her. He stood, his hands in his jeans pockets, watching them. His eyes flicked down to meet Nadia's. There was the slightest hint of a smile on his lips, and her heart did a weird little flutter thing.

"You made it." Imogen grabbed the credit card from Piero. "Drinks on you." She winked at Rune before she and Maya went off toward the bar to get more beer.

Carson pointed at the pile of red peppers in the paper bowl. "Rune, dude. Check it out. The guy at the taco truck said they're the hottest in the world. Want to go, one for one?"

A smile broke out over Rune's face. "Remember what happened last time?"

Carson shook his head and smiled wolfishly. "Nope."

Rune chuckled. "You, my friend, are a Pavlovian Fail. Loser has to clean the communal fridge . . . sans magic or help from the goblins." The others cringed and groaned at the bet. Nadia scooted over on the bench to make room. As he sat, his leg brushed her thigh, and she jumped, flushing.

Sophie had seen that interaction. She took another sip of her beer before her eyes flicked toward Rune and then back to Nadia. She wagged her eyebrows, grinning evilly. Nadia met her gaze, and she shook her head slightly as if denying something. She did not need Sophie spreading gossip about her.

Rune and Carson squared off, facing each other on either side of the picnic table. Each had a cup of the peppers on their side and several beers lined up for them to try to cut the burn.

Carson pointed two fingers at his eyes and then Rune's eyes. "I'm looking at you, buddy boy. You might be the boss, but tonight, I'm going to own you."

Rune grinned. It made him look younger. "Bring it."

"Countdown from three," said Piero, acting ref at the end of the table. "Three, two, one. Go!"

Nadia cringed as Rune and Carson each picked up a piece of

the pepper and dropped it in their mouths. Imogen turned her head, gripping Maya's hand.

"Not so bad." Carson chewed a few bites. "Barely feel it."

Rune's eyes sparkled in amusement. "Not a thing." He swallowed and jerked his chin toward the pile of peppers. "Ready for the next?"

Carson swallowed as well. "Absolutely." They each took another piece of the pepper and dropped it into their mouths.

"How's this one?" asked Rune, his eyes locked with Carson's.

Sweat beaded at Carson's temple, and he brushed it away. "Fabulous." He gritted his teeth. "Couldn't be better."

Rune swallowed. "Ready?" He hadn't even broken a sweat yet, looking entirely unflustered.

Carson swallowed and sucked air over his tongue. "Born ready." He grabbed the beer next to him and swallowed it in several gulps.

"You guys don't have to do this, you know," said Maya. "We get it. You're macho men. No need to kill yourselves."

Carson glanced at her, panting. "Oh yes, we do. I am not about to clean the fridge. Have you seen what grows in there?"

Rune and Carson ate another piece of the Carolina Reaper. By this time, Carson was flushed and sweating, the wavy hair at his temples soaked with sweat. Rune, on the other hand, looked calm and collected. The only indication that the capsaicin affected him was a slight fluttering at his temple.

"You sure you can handle the heat?" challenged Rune. "If you can't handle the heat, get out of the kitchen."

"Them be fighting words, son!" bit out Carson.

When it came to the fifth piece, Carson finally conceded. "You win. I'm done." Carson gagged like he was going to vomit and gulped down another beer.

"It looks like Rune here is a ringer." Imogen raised her beer in salute.

They all cheered and clapped and hit their palms on the table.

Carson was beet red and looked like his head was about to explode. Rune gestured for him to stand up, and they bumped chests and hugged in a masculine, bro-y way. Rune grabbed Carson by the nape of his neck and put him in a headlock.

A flash of healing light energy hit the back of Carson's neck. Nadia felt the slight reverberation, a small vibration that dissipated like ripples on water after a stone was dropped. Nadia looked around at the others. No one else had noticed.

Rune let Carson up. They stared at each other, some wordless conversation passing between brothers, and they hugged, slapping the other on the back.

Carson, his complexion returned to normal, sat back down between Maya and Sophie and draped each arm around their shoulders.

"What do you think, ladies?" he asked.

"Ew, get off. You're all sweaty." Maya threw his arm off. A flash of hurt registered on Carson's features, but he quickly returned to his normal self. He grabbed a beer and took a sip as he turned to Sophie, who seemed enthralled with whatever he was talking about and didn't seem to mind the sweat.

Nadia watched Rune, who still was standing up next to the patio table, separated from the rest of them. He saw her watching him.

I saw you help Carson, she didn't say.

And he didn't say, *I let you see.*

"I'll get us another round." Rune gestured toward the bar.

Imogen jumped up. "I'll help you." They walked off toward the bar, Imogen smiling up at him.

"Are you excited to get back to Trinity?" Maya asked when Rune and Imogen returned with more drinks.

Imogen bobbed her head. "I am. I really will miss you all"—she glanced at all of them, her gaze resting a little longer on Rune than the others—"but I miss Dublin, and teaching, and my fiancé, of course."

Nadia inhaled suddenly and coughed loudly. Rune glanced at her. She was sure he knew what she was thinking. Imogen had a fiancé? She sure didn't act like it. Nadia wondered if it was an open relationship.

Maya passed Nadia a beer. "Here, take a sip."

"Are you okay? I know humans are fragile. You aren't going to keel over or anything, are you?" Piero looked concerned and patted her on the back. "Vega made all the managers and execs take CPR, but I'm not sure it applied to humans. You bunch are so *delicate*."

"I'm fine. I think I got one of Carson's peppers!" Nadia exclaimed. Sophie smirked.

"Well, we will certainly miss you here." Rune held Imogen's gaze before she turned away, two red dots on her cheeks.

"We definitely will." Piero bumped his shoulder into Imogen's as she sat next to him. "But who else is going to help me find the perfect amulet at two a.m. the night before a bid is due?"

Imogen laughed and gestured to Nadia. "That's Nadia's job now. No more two a.m. phone calls for me!"

"We're screwed," said Sophie.

Imogen scoffed. "Nonsense. Nadia is extremely knowledgeable. I am leaving you all in capable hands."

Rune's eyes flicked to hers.

I am in your hands now, Ms. Winters? He didn't ask.

And she didn't respond, *Do you want to be?*

They spent the rest of happy hour getting comfortably tipsy on beer. Carson started doing impressions, Sophie explained her plans to manifest a tulpa, and Piero regaled them all his latest dating adventures from Tinder. Nadia and Rune continued whatever little game they had going on, not talking to each other directly but sending smoldering gazes that the entire group must have seen.

Only Imogen seemed oblivious. Or maybe she noticed but was happy that Rune appeared to have taken an interest in Nadia. She had a fiancé, after all.

The sun set, streaking the sky with purples and oranges. The world was awash with color, and Nadia felt slightly giddy as she waited at the bus stop near the food truck park to go home. It was the feeling of anticipation, like something really, really good was about to happen. Things finally seemed to be going okay. She was settling into her job, making friends, and now Rune was acting like there could be something there between them. She had felt it when she first met him, but had squashed that idea down after they started training. There had been no room for a girlish infatuation when she needed to focus on controlling her Septer abilities.

But now, that had all changed. Rune had changed. It was like he was thawing to the idea of her. She had been a distraction that he pushed away, but now he was warming to her. It was too soon to really hope, but she tucked away that flame of potential, kept it close to her heart, occasionally touching it to remind her it was real, and she wasn't imagining things after all.

Nadia reached for her cell phone, had a moment of panic when she couldn't find it, and then realized she had left it back at the picnic table. She headed back over, hoping that it was still there.

The others had left, but Carson and Rune were still seated at the table, drinking beers. Nadia caught a bit of their conversation as she approached. They hadn't seen her yet.

"—going on with you and Nadia?" asked Carson. Nadia quickly ducked behind The Falafel King food truck. Pressed close to the truck, she could hear the rest of their conversation.

"Nothing," said Rune.

"Doesn't look like nothing, bro. You guys were eye-fucking the shit out of each other all evening."

"I'm telling you, nothing is going on."

"Well, you should hit that. She's hot." Nadia rolled her eyes. Men. They were all the same, no matter what species.

"Nah, not my type," said Rune.

Nadia's little flame of hope flickered and died. Her shoulders sagged, but she kept listening. She should walk away, but sometimes, she liked to hurt herself. She liked the pain.

"You two are spending an awful lot of time together. People have seen you leave the gym at the same time. You sure you're not into that?"

"Hardly. The girl is a walking hazard. I'm merely trying to protect the company. Teach her basic magic, so she isn't quite such a nuisance."

Nadia's blood started boiling. She felt the magic and anger flowing through her veins, and she clenched her fists, fighting the urge to do something rash.

"If you say so," said Carson. "Wasn't she your date to that gala? Instead of Imogen? What's going on with that, anyway?"

"Nothing there to tell. She's going back to Dublin to her fiancé."

"So, now maybe you need a little brunette distraction to keep you busy."

Rune chuckled. "She's a nice girl and all. I can tell she'd go for it if I tried. But I'd just be leading her on. It wouldn't be fair to her."

"But what if she's the one that the seer talked about? The raven—"

Rune cut him off. "Drop it."

"But, dude, what about the—"

"I said drop it. It's not her."

"Okay, okay. But even if it's not her, doesn't mean you can't have a little fun in the meantime. You need to get laid."

"I get laid plenty."

Well, then. Nadia felt the heat rush to her cheeks. She had been right. He thought of her as a charity case. He had called her a nice girl, like he pitied her crush on him. She let herself have a moment of being embarrassed and angry before she stood up a little straighter, refusing to give in to the self-loathing. Fuck him. She was awesome, and if he couldn't see it, that was his loss.

She stepped out from behind the food truck, smiling brightly. "Have you guys seen my cell phone? I think I left it here."

Rune had the manners and grace to look guilty. She gave him a *fuck you* smile and picked up her cell phone from under the picnic table. "Later guys," she called out over her shoulder as she walked away.

Only when she was out of sight and away did she let herself feel the sting of disappointment and hurt. On the bus home, she slumped over next to the window and watched the sights on the street go by. But she did not cry. She wouldn't let herself.

Chapter 18

The following evening, Nadia ran around Marina's house, quickly tidying up and getting ready. In the kitchen, she artfully arranged a tray of appetizers, labeling the artisanal cheeses she had bought earlier at the Ferry Building with little toothpicks and signs before she carried the tray into the living room. Avery was kicking back with his feet up on the coffee table, reading a *Lapham's Quarterly*. Nadia looked pointedly at him before he rolled his eyes and lowered his feet so she could set the platter down.

Avery plucked a cracker from the tray. "When are your friends getting here?"

"Any minute now. You could help me clean up a bit, you know." Nadia shooed Monday from a pile of magazines and stuffed them behind some of Marina's throw pillows on the couch. Monday glared at Nadia and stalked over to Avery, who idly rubbed under the cat's chin.

"You seem to have it all handled." Avery was wearing another one of his loud Hawaiian shirts, unbuttoned, and men's jogger pants. Nadia wished she could ask him to change or at least button his shirt, but she knew it would be fruitless.

Nadia scanned the living room, looking for anything else that might be incriminating or embarrassing. She waved a hand toward a row of pillar candles that sat on the mantle above the fireplace, and they flamed to life. She lit some incense as well, pushing her magic to the top of the incense cone until it started smoking, letting a fragrant, citrusy odor waft up from the burner on a side table. She plugged her cell phone into a speaker and put on a random chill music playlist from Spotify. Satisfied for the time being, Nadia headed back to the kitchen.

Marina was pulling out a blender from the upper cabinets next to the stove. "Grab the bag of ice from the freezer, will you?" she called to Nadia over her shoulder. Marina had broken out one of her beaded kimonos from her touring days and had feathered her long dark hair. It gave her a bohemian-rocker look. Nadia and Marina had spent the afternoon oohing and aahing over the pile of caftans and kimonos and jewelry from an old steamer chest in Marina's bedroom, and Marina had given Nadia a long-sleeve black lace dress that she was wearing with a pair of combat boots she had picked up at a thrift store on Haight Street.

Once they assembled the ingredients into the blender, Marina added a pinch of something from a small vial from the spice rack, winked at Nadia, and waved her hand in the direction of the blender, muttering incantations. The blender roared to life. Nadia grabbed glasses from the shelf and lined them up.

The doorbell chimed.

"They're here!" said Nadia.

"You get the door. I'll get the margaritas."

Nadia rushed down the hall to the front door and yanked it open. Piero and Maya stood on the porch. She ushered them inside.

Piero held up a bottle of wine in either fist. "We brought booze."

"Great! My grandmother is mixing up some of her magical margaritas in the kitchen."

"Wow, I love your grandma's place!" said Maya as she entered, looking up and around herself. "Very boho chic." She was wearing a faux leather jacket that had patches all over it, including one on the center of the back that said NLA below a fiery red-and-orange phoenix. Nadia had seen stickers with that symbol up around Maya's habitat.

"Thanks for coming over," said Nadia.

"It was a little short notice, but luckily for you, my Saturday night plans fell through." Piero handed Nadia his checkered suit jacket and the bottles of wine. He eyed a taxidermy boar hanging in the hall and crinkled up his nose. "How . . . quaint."

Nadia led them into the living room and placed the wine and Piero's jacket on a side table. Avery stood up slowly as they entered.

"Piero, Maya, this is Avery, my grandmother's roommate. Avery, Piero and Maya." She waved a hand between them. Everyone nodded in greeting. Piero seemed to perk up at the sight of Avery and his bare chest.

Marina entered from the kitchen's side door, carrying a tray full of glasses and a pitcher of her margaritas. "And this is my grandmother," Nadia said, introducing her. "Marina, this is Maya and Piero from work."

"Ms. Nichols, it's so nice to meet you," said Maya, stepping forward. "Can I help you with that?"

"Please, call me Marina." She placed the tray next to the cheese and crackers. "Grandmother makes me sound so old, don't you think?"

Piero nodded in agreement. "My nonna refused to let me call her that. Said it aged her ten years just thinking about it. Of course, she didn't really age . . . but you know how it is."

Once they were settled in the living room with drinks, the conversation died. Nadia, sitting on one of the side chairs she had pulled around the coffee table, took a big gulp of her margarita. She immediately felt the buzz of Marina's secret ingredient. They all smiled at one another, but no one said anything. Nadia had the sinking suspicion that inviting her work friends over for drinks was going to be a big mistake. She should have known it would be weird with Marina and Avery hovering around. But after Rune's harsh dismissal, she had felt the need to reach out and try to make friends of her own. She spent too much time with Rune as it was. She needed her own life.

Maya cleared her throat. "This drink is very good. Do I detect a hint of grapefruit and jalapeño in here?"

"Oh yes, it's my secret recipe," said Marina.

"It's very good," Maya repeated.

They fell into silence again.

Piero's gaze roved over Avery's torso. Nadia recognized that glint in his eye. Avery magicked his ukulele into his hands and started strumming it, refusing to look at Piero. The cat meowed.

Nadia jumped up. "I think we need more drinks. Maya, want to help me in the kitchen?" She rushed over to the side table and grabbed the bottles of wine.

"I am so sorry," said Nadia, once they were out of earshot and in the kitchen. "This is so awkward. Marina and Avery insisted they stay home and meet you guys when I asked if I could invite you over."

"Don't even worry about it. I don't have any family, so you're lucky they even care enough to hang out and meet us. Your grandma seems cool. Kind of an aging rocker chick vibe. And Avery seems . . . nice enough. He's High Fae, right? They're always a bit standoffish at first. Well, everyone except Imogen. She's like the anti-High Fae."

Nadia rummaged in a drawer for a corkscrew and tossed it to Maya, who started opening the wine.

"I just think we all need to drink more," said Maya as she pulled out the cork.

After a pitcher of margaritas, several bottles of wine, and several shots of liqueur, which Piero insisted on after learning that Avery had never had Sambuca, they were all sufficiently sloshed. Nadia sat on the floor with Maya next to the coffee table, eating the remains of the cheese and crackers and making a mess of crumbs.

"We should order a pizza," announced Marina. She was standing next to the fireplace, swaying to the music. After learning that Marina had been in a band, Maya and Piero insisted she play one of her records. Marina had dug up one of her old vinyl singles and was playing it again on the record player in the corner. It was a folksy blues song about traveling and being lonely, and Marina's distinctive voice carried the melody out through the room.

"I second that." Piero hiccupped. He was sitting cross-legged on the couch next to Avery, who was plucking out notes along to the music on his ukulele. Nadia crawled over to her cell phone and managed to pull up an app for delivery. She ordered three large pizzas and a salad for Maya from a local slice shop.

"Marina, can I ask you a question?" slurred Piero.

"Go for it." She swayed back and forth, her eyes closed.

"What is up with witches and your crazy nondisclosure agreements? Y'all are driving me batty with what you will and will not divulge."

Marina opened her eyes and nodded knowingly. "I'm sure you're working mostly with coven witches? Each coven's individual spells are how they exert power and control in a territory. The stronger the bank of spells, the more power."

"I get each coven is entitled to their IP, but come on! The paperwork is killing me."

"Are you in a coven?" Maya asked Marina. "Nadia's never mentioned one, but I assume if you were in one, she would be too." She leaned back on her elbows, kicking her legs out in front of her. Nadia wondered if she should join a coven. It sounded nice. Like a magical support group.

Marina shook her head. The music stopped, and she bent down to the record player before she placed the needle on the edge of the vinyl and started the song over. "I used to be, back in the day. But not anymore."

Maya started stretching and doing some yoga. "Nadia told me you bound her powers when she was younger. Can I ask why? It seems a little extreme."

Marina's eyes widened slightly like she was surprised at the question, but she kept swaying to the music. She took a big sip of whiskey from a glass in her hand as if fortifying herself. "I had a falling out with my coven. I was mad. I didn't want my grand-daughter involved in all that. It seemed like the right decision at the time."

"Coven drama is crazy," drawled Piero. "I mean, completely nuts. The things I've heard would shock you." He shook his head. "Sophie was keeping a file for a while. She said it was for HR pur-poses, but you know she's obsessed with that sort of thing."

"Really? Why's that?" Nadia started stretching as well. Her muscles were tight and sore from Rune's workouts.

Piero threw a small square throw pillow at her. "Duh! Because she's only a Sixer." Nadia ducked, and it sailed over her head.

"She's always trying to cast spells," said Maya, "but of course, none ever actually work. It's sad, really. Her dream is to do magic, and she just . . . never will be able to. She pretends like she doesn't care, but I can tell it just eats away at her."

"Wow, I had no idea," said Nadia.

"Well, that's why's she so jealous of you," said Piero as he hic-cupped. "I told her not to be, that being a Septer has its own set of problems. But the Light knows that girl does not listen to me. Her parents are famous magicians or warlocks or something back in London. She grew up in their shadows."

"Wait, what?" asked Nadia dubiously. "Sophie. Jealous of me?" Sophie acted like Nadia was a total noob. Why would she be jeal-ous of being that?

Piero topped off Avery's drink. "Before you came along, she was our token Sixer. And here you come along, all cute and competent, and a Septer at that! I thought her head was going to explode when she found out you could do magic."

"Plus, she's always had a thing for Rune," Maya fake-whispered loudly. "And now Rune spends all his time helping to train you. She's totally jealous."

Avery snorted but said nothing.

Piero eyed him playfully. "What? What does He-Of-So-Little-Words have to say about Rune Christiansen?"

Avery looked guarded, like he didn't know if Piero was actually making fun of him. "It just seems strange that an esteemed Numinal is taking such an interest in a human."

"I'm human, and you like me!" Marina called over her shoulder as she put a new record on. Janis Joplin's scratchy voice filled the room.

"That's different," said Avery. "There is just something . . . off with him. I can't put my finger on it."

Nadia suddenly felt defensive of Rune. "You just don't like him because he's actually doing something with his life."

"Knock it off, you two," warned Marina.

Nadia downed her drink and wiped her mouth with the back of her hand. "Fine, fine. I'll be nice. But seriously, Rune has been really helpful. I don't know what I would have done without his training. It's not like you two have exactly prepped me for all . . . this." She waved her empty glass around herself.

"What's going on with you two, anyway?" asked Piero.

"What do you mean?"

Piero gave her an exasperated look. "Oh, come on, dish! What was going on with you two yesterday at happy hour? I wish someone would look at *me* like that." His eyes darted over to Avery.

"Nothing's going on." Nadia poured herself another drink. "Abso-fucking-lutely nothing."

Marina sidled over to Avery, her bangles jangling as she danced. It sounded like bells.

Maya sat up from her twisty stretch on the floor. "What happened?"

"Nothing. Not. A. Thing."

"If you say so." Maya raised her eyebrows and looked at Piero like Nadia was being delusional.

"What's that look?"

"Nothing."

"That look isn't nothing. What were you going to say?"

Maya's pointed ears quivered. "I don't even know if I should tell you this."

"Spill!" Piero climbed down to sit next to them on the floor. They sat, cross-legged in a circle, like they were in grade school during storytime.

Maya glanced over to Marina and Avery to see if they were paying attention. They weren't. Marina was draped over the back of the couch, discussing something or another with Avery. They were in their own little world.

Maya leaned in toward Nadia and Piero. "Okay, remember when I looked at your watch, and you told me Rune had made you a spell list?"

"Yeah, I think so."

"Well, I saw something. I didn't tell you at the time, but . . . Rune put his personal grimoire on your Psionic."

Piero whistled. "That is some heavy shit."

Nadia glanced at her watch, frowning. "He did? How do you know?"

"It's a link in the list. I helped Carson program the back end."

"So what?" asked Nadia. "What are you getting at?"

"A magician's grimoire is *extremely* personal," explained Piero. "Remember how earlier we were talking about coven secrets? It's like that, but even more secret. It's a magician's source of power—you can tell a lot about them from the ways the spells work. You can find out their strengths and weaknesses. That's why it's so secret."

"So . . . what's that mean?" asked Nadia. "Maybe he just used an abridged version to teach me or something."

Maya grabbed her watch and scrolled through the interface. She tried to click on it, but it wouldn't open. "See? It's locked. You'd still have to figure out how to open it to find out."

"So, it's like some weird test or something?"

"Nadia, will you check on the pizza?" Marina called out. "I'm starving."

They all started at the sound of Marina's voice. Nadia leaned over and grabbed her cell phone, squinting at it. "It says the guy is here in twenty minutes."

"Perfect," said Marina. "I'll go whip up some more drinks." She walked over to the front of the couch and grabbed Avery's hands, hauling him up. Marina danced off into the kitchen with Avery following dutifully behind.

Once Avery and Marina were out of earshot, Maya leaned back into Piero and Nadia. "I have no idea what it means. Maybe it's a test; maybe it was just a mistake when he was loading apps and spells onto the watch."

"Rune doesn't make mistakes," said Piero. "At least, not ones like that."

"Well, I don't know," said Maya. "I just think it's really strange, that's all."

"Should I ask him about it?" Nadia wondered if this was the reason Rune kept asking her if she'd explored all the modules he uploaded onto her watch. Maybe he was waiting for her to find this one.

"No!" said Maya and Piero in unison.

"If it was a mistake, he might get mad that you potentially have access to all that," said Maya. "If it is a test, then he probably wants to see if you can open it, and asking him about it isn't the way."

Nadia tapped on the screen on her watch, trying to open the grimoire. "I think it was definitely a mistake. Rune doesn't think I'm very capable." He'd said as much. He'd called her a walking disaster.

Piero rolled his eyes. "Oh, stop it. False modesty is so unbecoming. We all know Rune sees something in you."

Nadia just wished she knew what it was.

Chapter 19

"Nadia, pay attention," said Piero sharply. She snapped to. Piero glanced over his shoulder to where Rune was walking past the co-working desks. Several Mystics followed after him, taking notes as he talked. Nadia kicked herself for slipping and thinking about him. Ever since she had overheard how he really felt about her the previous week, she had made a point of ignoring him. She was a busy woman; she didn't have time to sit and moon over some guy who missed his shot with her. She had been largely successful in avoiding him, except for those morning training sessions. For those, she went through the motions, learned what he taught her, and remained entirely professional. She had cut herself off from feeling anything more for him. She couldn't. That ship had sailed. Not everything was possible, as it turned out.

"As I was saying, our ten o'clock is Madam LeRoux. She's unhappy with the lack of work. She's been doing mostly one-off gigs with WishSeed, love spells couched in relationship advice, that sort of thing. But we haven't been able to fit her talents into any Mystos consulting projects yet. I need to jump on a call, so I'm going to need you to take this one yourself."

"Are you sure? I haven't taken a meeting by myself yet."

"You'll be fine! Now, scram. Get in there." Piero jutted his chin over to the conference room where Madam LeRoux was waiting.

Madam LeRoux was a voodoo healer from Haiti. Nadia wasn't

sure what she had expected, but it wasn't this well-dressed woman sitting politely in the conference room. Her dark hair was pulled back in a twist. Her legs were demurely crossed in a skirt suit. She looked like a court reporter or a paralegal.

"I'm Nadia, one of the talent managers. Nice to meet you." They shook hands and then took a seat at the conference table. "I understand you're having some concerns recently. What's been going on?" Nadia picked up a pen, ready to take notes.

"I just want to start by saying how much I love working with Myst. Your company is so much better than Pact. I love the work I get with WishSeed. The clients are the best part of the job. I love helping people." The woman sighed. "But that is the thing. I get three times as much work from Pact doing curses. Myst only allows me to do healing spells or love spells. There just is not that much of a demand for healing."

"You know our policy on that," Nadia started.

The woman held up a hand, stopping her. "Yes, yes. I know. Only white magic is allowed. Absolutely no black magic. But if Myst would allow me to do more work in the grey magic zones, it would help me tremendously."

"I'll have to check with HR."

"I understand. But I already have permission to use grey magic with the love spells. I just want to expand that scope a bit."

Nadia jotted a few notes down on her pad. "Could you send us a list of the potential grey magic spells you want to incorporate into your work with us? That would help us understand and assess the risk for each one."

"Yes, yes. Of course."

They chatted a bit more about the scope of her work, both with Myst and with Pact. Madam LeRoux wouldn't give Nadia many details about Pact, citing the nondisclosure agreement employees signed when they started working. She seemed highly knowledgeable, though, about a wide variety of magical issues.

"Can I ask you a question?" Nadia asked her as they were wrapping up the meeting.

"Of course."

Nadia took a deep breath. "Do you know anything about Blood Oaths and how to remove them?"

The woman looked suspiciously at Nadia. "Who made the Blood Oath?"

"This is all hypothetical. Say, a human and a vampire made it many years ago, and it has passed down through the family. Is there any way to remove it?"

Madam LeRoux looked like she didn't believe it was hypothetical, but she played along, picking her words carefully. "Blood Oaths are very powerful, very dark magic. They call on the Blood Laws."

"What are the Blood Laws?"

"They're the natural laws by which the Numinous works, sort of an operating system. Blood Oaths call on the Blood Laws, writing the Oath into the very nature of reality. To make it, the human and the dark creature drink each other's blood, sealing the Oath in their very life essence. That is why it passes down through the generations. The only way to remove a Blood Oath is to have the creature release the human from the bind, to rescind the agreement. But the Oath will still pass to any heirs. There is no way to break the Oath so that it will not continue in perpetuity. Removing the Oath is like removing a link from a chain. The chain will continue as long as the lineage continues."

Nadia leaned forward. "I heard there is some sort of spell or ritual that might get around it. Like a loophole?"

The woman shook her head. "I've never heard of such a thing. But I do not know all the mysteries of the universe, so it is possible."

"What about pacts? Can you remove a pact without consequence?" asked Nadia before stopping herself. "Hypothetically speaking, of course."

A confused expression crossed her face. "Of course. There are spells, very strong ones, that can sever a pact without repercussion on the parties."

"Do you know those spells?"

She shook her head. "I'm afraid not, no. But I'm sure Myst has something in their libraries. They are rather extensive. Have you asked the CEO, Rune Christiansen? I'm sure he is at least familiar with them."

Nadia stood up quickly and started packing up her papers. There was no way in hell she would ask Rune. "Thank you, Madam LeRoux. I will see what I can do about the parameters of your services and get back to you."

When Nadia emerged from the meeting, the office was abuzz. She walked Madam LeRoux out and quickly hurried back to where everyone was gathered around one of the giant flat-screen TVs on the wall in the lounge. It was turned to the local news. Everyone was silent, watching.

"What's going on?" Nadia whispered to Maya.

She leaned in, whispering back. "They found three bodies in the Tenderloin this morning."

"What?" Nadia exclaimed.

"Shhh!" A turquoise-haired gnome turned around with a glare, hushing them.

The reporter on the screen turned to the camera. "Police say the other recent attacks around the city are all connected and that we are experiencing a crime wave unlike any other. Police have the suspect, twenty-four-year-old Chester Charles Smith, in custody. Smith is a grad student at San Francisco State University, studying psychology. Classmates and friends say they are shocked by their friend's actions and that he would never have done something like this."

The screen showed a map of the Tenderloin, with the location of that day's attacks starred. An arrow moved across the map, tracing the attacker's path and the location of the murders.

The camera cut to a young man with tears running down his blotchy red face. "Chester was my best friend. He wasn't like this. He wouldn't have hurt a fly!" The man rubbed his eyes. "Something must've happened. This wasn't him."

It cut back to the reporter walking on the sidewalk in the Tenderloin, passing SROs and liquor stores. In the background, a man in a wheelchair waved at the camera and made gestures to others who started waving their arms in the air, trying to get the reporter's attention. "Friends of other recent attackers have shared similar statements: that their friends seemed preoccupied in the weeks before the attacks, that they weren't acting like themselves. Some have had very colorful theories about what is causing the uptick in violence."

The camera cut to an old lady wearing a ratty pink bathrobe as she sat on the dirty sidewalk in the Tenderloin.

"I tell you, it's demons," spat out the woman. "I saw that man's eyes. Glowing red. The end times are coming!"

The camera cut back to the reporter. "Police have made a call to the public for any information regarding the attacks. This is Tina Nguyen. Nancy, back to you."

Everyone started talking all at once about the murders.

"I heard they're only going after virgins," said Sophie.

Piero snorted. "Guess you're safe then."

Nadia snuck a glance over to where Rune was standing off to the side. He looked deep in thought.

Carson walked over to him, looking grave, and held his laptop up for Rune to see. Rune peered down at the computer. Nadia took this opportunity to sidle over and eavesdrop.

"You know how we switched the Redcaps to be virtual treasure faeries instead of real?" Carson glanced at Nadia as she idled near someone's habitat, pretending to look at pictures of their kids, and she took that as an invitation to join them. She peered at the screen. It was a map of San Francisco with various locations marked with pin drops and numbers.

"With both the Redcaps and the new, virtual treasure faeries," Carson continued, "when users find them, a random number generator kicks in to give the users the amount of the pot they win. We use a true random number generator powered by atmospheric noise versus those pseudo-random number generators that are in slot machines and the lotto." Nadia knew that Carson was explaining this all for her benefit. Rune clearly knew how his tech worked.

"Go on," said Rune.

"Well, I track the locations of the pots the users win so we can move the gaming locations around the city to make users explore different areas. But, after the latest attacks in the Tenderloin, I noticed that the locations of the attacks almost exactly coincide with several of the locations of the large pots the users have been winning. I thought that was strange, so I looked into it more."

"Cut to the point, Carson," snapped Rune.

"Okay, okay. For whatever reason, those locations—the payouts that coincide with the attacks—are generating patterns instead of randomness in the random number generator."

"What are you saying?" asked Rune.

Carson looked grim. "I think our app is involved with the attacks."

Nadia looked back and forth between them.

"Shit," Rune muttered, running his hands through his hair. "Are you sure about this?"

"One hundred percent. I triple-checked. They're all large pots, too. We're hemorrhaging money."

Rune thought for a minute, rubbing the stubble on his chin as he looked distractedly off to the side. "Okay. We need to call an emergency board meeting." He spied Anya. "Anya! Call the board. We need to have a meeting. Now." She nodded and quickly walked back toward the front reception area with her long gazelle legs. Rune sent Carson off to create a presentation outlining his findings. Then, he turned to Nadia. She was sure he was going to dismiss her for inserting herself into the conversation. "Nadia. I need you to sit in during the meeting."

"Me?" she asked, surprised.

"I haven't seen a Sixer before, even trained, with your level of ability. And I need to use it. There is something off about these board meetings."

"What do you mean?"

His eyes flicked up briefly as he took a deep breath. "I've suspected for a while that there is a mole at Myst. At the last board meeting, we discussed confidential information that somehow ended up in the hands of Pact. I'm not sure if it was someone on the board or just a coincidence, but I want you to see if you can pick up on anything. There might be something you could tell from their clothing or the objects in their pockets. Some connection to Pact. I normally wouldn't ask this of you, but I'm desperate. If Pact suspects that Veil is causing the attacks, they would launch a campaign to tank us."

Earlier that week, they had been practicing psychometry—reading the energy signatures on physical objects to tell about their past or where they'd been. Nadia had proved to be rather talented in this arena and had impressed Rune with how quickly she picked up the basics. While the board members most likely had mental shields Nadia couldn't get past, she might be able to pick up on who they'd been talking to or what they'd been doing from the objects they carried. It was a reach, but it was something.

"Okay," she said slowly.

Anya rushed back over.

"I got a hold of everyone except Simon," said Anya. "His assistant says he just got on a plane to Tokyo."

"Fuck," muttered Rune. "Get a hold of the pilot. Send emails. Smoke signals. Something. Whatever you need to do, just get him here as soon as possible."

"You got it," said Anya.

"Plan to stay late," said Rune to Nadia. "This could go all night."

Chapter 20

When Nadia entered the conference room that night at nine p.m., the board had already assembled. Five sets of eyes turned to her as she pushed open the glass door. She gave a bright smile and took a seat next to Rune, smoothing down the pencil skirt she had changed into as she sat. She placed her notebook and pen on the table.

"Who's the bird?" asked a British gentleman in his early sixties. Nadia recognized him as Simon Davies from the band Lazy Susan, which had been popular in the '80s. He was wearing his signature look—a fitted suit jacket over a T-shirt—although his once-blond hair was streaked with grey at the temples. Nadia realized he must be Sophie's uncle, the one who had gotten her a job at Myst.

"This is Nadia, my assistant," said Rune. The group shared knowing looks. "I asked her to sit in on the meeting to run errands or get us food or drinks if we need it," he continued. Nadia shot Rune a dark look. Even though she knew this was just an act, she bridled at being called his assistant and his insinuating that she was just an errand girl or a pretty face.

"Lovely. I'll take a cup of coffee, dear," said a glamorous woman with short dark hair in her early fifties. "Two sugars, no cream."

"I'll take something a bit stronger, thanks," said Simon, not bothering to look at Nadia. "Meredith, I urge you to join me. Sounds like we're going to need it."

The woman shrugged. "Curtis?" she asked a middle-aged man with dark skin, wearing a blue polo shirt with a NASA logo on it.

"I'll take a drink as well, thanks," said Curtis.

"Water, please," said a Fae man with a shaved head. He pushed up the sleeves of his saffron-colored monk robe.

"Don't be a pussy, David," called out Simon.

David gave Simon a withering look.

Rune shot Nadia an apologetic smile. "Could you get the bottle of Mars Single Malt in my office, please? The Komagatake twenty-seven-year-old?"

Nadia wondered if he was trying to get rid of her for a minute as she knew he could have just magicked the whiskey over himself. Or maybe he didn't want the board to see his powers.

After she had returned with the bottle, she poured everyone a drink, including herself. She shot it back and poured herself another. Rune raised an eyebrow at her. She returned the look, challenging him to say something. The corner of his mouth twitched before he turned back to the group.

"All right, I'm sure you are wondering why I called this emergency meeting of the board."

"Damn straight we are." Simon took a sip of his drink. "I had to reroute the jet over here. I'm supposed to be in Japan right now."

"I understand," said Rune smoothly. "But I assure you, this is a matter of grave concern for Myst."

"How grave?" Meredith asked primly, adjusting her silk blouse. "If this is another false—"

"Meredith, please. I will explain everything." Rune pulled up Carson's data on the screen on the wall. Nadia took a deep breath and pictured her mind to be a satellite dish as she tried to read the room's mood and look for any anomalies. Everyone's thoughts blasted her at once, and she cringed with a small gasp. Rune shot her a look, and she adjusted her mental receiver to a manageable level.

"As you are aware, we have been beta testing Veil with much success. One of the perks of the game is payouts, much like a lottery, that users receive when they find treasure faeries. The amount of the payout is determined through a random number generator. The engineering team has been tracking the payouts and the locations to move them around the city." Rune showed the map of the city with points marked. "See here. These are the locations of the biggest recent payouts." Rune clicked to another screen, which superimposed a map on top of the current one. "And these are the locations of the recent murders and attacks in the city, which we believe are demon-based due to their violent nature."

The room was silent. They all glanced at one another. And then they all started talking at once.

Rune yelled for everyone to calm down. "One at a time! One at a time!"

"How do we know that Myst is somehow involved with the attacks? That data is circumstantial, at best." Curtis rubbed a hand over his closely trimmed goatee.

"We don't," said Rune as he leaned back in his chair. "But the data cannot be ignored. If demons are somehow slipping into this realm and possessing those humans who are attacking people, which does appear to be the case, the random number generator is picking up on it and spitting out patterns—causing exceptionally large payouts—at those locations. Even if Myst is not the cause of the attacks and is just picking up on an energy surge when demons slip into this realm—or something similar in nature—it could look to the authorities that Myst is involved if this got out. Like something in our tech is calling to them, or somehow some location data about the users has been leaked or hacked. We have no idea what the potential scope is of all this."

"We don't have any duty to take this to the authorities," chimed in Simon. He downed his glass of whiskey and pushed the glass toward Nadia.

"We might not have any legal duty at this point, but we do have an ethical and moral one," countered Meredith. "Not to mention a duty to the company. This could be another Cambridge Analytica data breach situation. If the press got word that we knew about it and did or said nothing, it could ruin Myst."

Simon scoffed.

"What do you think, David?" Rune asked. Unlike Avery, who dampened his Fae appearance almost completely down to human, David let his otherworldly nature radiate from his skin, casting a golden glow from his body. He was dampening it for the meeting, human minds unable to fully comprehend Fae in their true glory, but it was still riveting. Rune caught Nadia staring and gave her a look that said, *stop acting like a dumb mortal and keep it together!*

"The Fae are concerned about the recent attacks," David said slowly, looking about the room. "There is talk about dark forces aligning, the Dark Court going on the offensive after so many years. The Fae are concerned that this is an indication that the Dark King and Queen are planning something . . . how do you say? Monumental."

"People have been saying that for years," said Rune tightly. "The Dark Queen and King and their Horde are trapped in the Other Realms and cannot escape."

Nadia stared at Rune. She wasn't sure what he was talking about, but it sounded fantastical. Dark Queens and Kings? She suddenly had the sensation of being out of her body, like she was in a simulation or a game and was looking in.

"We, too, have been hearing things," said Simon. "The Brotherhood has foretold of a great prophecy—"

"Enough with you damn Illuminati and your prophecies!" Curtis pounded a fist on the table, causing Nadia to jump. "When was the last time one of your so-called prophecies proved to be true?"

"Even a broken clock is right twice a day," Meredith declared.

"The Sisterhood, on the other hand, has been keeping vigil, and we have not found any disruption to the natural order of things."

"Your sisterhood can suck my—"

Rune cut Simon off. "Okay, okay. That's enough. We need to make decisions. Do we take any sort of action now, or do we wait for more information, knowing that we don't have any concrete proof? All we have are some correlations that appear to show our user base is involved."

"We should inform the Council," said David. His saffron-colored robes fluttered from an invisible breeze.

"We should not," said Rune, his voice clipped. "I don't want the Council anywhere near Myst business."

"Now wait, Rune," cut in Simon. "Just because you detest the Council doesn't mean we can neglect our duties."

"To hell with that." Rune's eyes narrowed, his voice low. "I will not throw away everything I've worked on to appease a group of tyrannical Numinals and their antiquated rules. Besides, San Francisco is outside Council domain. They have no authority here."

"But they still hold power and influence in this region," said David, thoughtfully.

Rune shook his head. "I do not want to be involved in any Council business, and I do not want them involved in mine."

Curtis sighed and crossed his arms over his chest. "I still will never understand why you left the Council, Rune. You could have done so much good there. A tempering factor to advance Numinal and human relationships and understanding. The Council now is just an empty echo chamber holding fast to those antiquated rules, as you put it."

"What's in the past is in the past," said Rune, his voice gruff.

The corner of Simon's mouth turned up, and he sat back in his chair, regarding Rune. "This whole thing is awfully convenient, don't you think?"

Rune stared at him. "Don't mince words, Davies. Spit it out."

"We've been asking you for weeks now for the year-end projections, and you keep delaying. Always something about Veil, a new issue that took priority. And now, a whole new crisis just appears out of nowhere—one that indicates potentially huge financial losses. It just seems rather suspicious."

"Are you implying that I am making this up?"

"Now, Rune," cut in Curtis. "I don't think Simon here is saying anything of the sort. But we have been asking for those projections for a while now."

"Thank you," said Simon. "Finally, someone is the voice of reason here."

"I'll get you a report by the end of next week," said Rune. "Can we please get back to the issue at hand? The financials won't mean anything if Veil somehow is linked to the attacks."

"Let's put it to a vote," suggested Curtis.

"All in favor of informing the Council?" asked Rune. David and Simon were the only ones with their hands raised. "All against?" Curtis and Rune raised their hands. After a moment, Meredith's hand crept up as well.

"I move that we conduct a confidential, internal investigation to determine if Myst is involved before going to the authorities," said Curtis.

"I second that," said Rune. "All in favor?"

All five members of the board raised their hands.

After the meeting was called, the board members sat around the table for a bit longer chatting. Nadia started clearing away glasses.

Meredith regarded Nadia as she worked, her cat-like eyes narrowed. "You are goddess-blessed, aren't you?"

Nadia flushed. "I'm not sure I know what that means."

"The feminine energy is strong with you. You know, the Sisterhood is always looking for new recruits. If you ever want to talk about the path of the goddess or need anything"—Meredith passed Nadia her business card—"please do call."

Simon threw up a hand in disgust. "Leave the girl alone, Meredith. Your little cult has enough members."

Rune watched the exchange, looking thoughtful.

While Nadia cleaned up the conference room, Rune escorted the board members out. Nadia's mind raced from everything that she had heard, and she tried to make sense of it all. As she finished tidying up the glasses and notepads that had been scattered across the conference table, she saw Rune head up the staircase in the back. She hurried after him into his office.

"Okay, what was all that about?" Nadia demanded as she took a seat across from him at his desk. "What are the Light Court and the Dark Court? Who are the Dark King and Queen? What is this prophecy and this Council?"

Rune sighed. "I apologize for that. I didn't know we would be discussing the Prophecy."

"What is the Prophecy?"

"It doesn't concern you."

"It does now."

His expression was unreadable. "There are forces in the universe bigger than you or me or any of us. The Realms of Light and Dark have been in constant battle for as long as anyone can remember. There is a prophecy that the Dark will tip the Light. Some believe it will happen soon, and some are afraid that the city's recent attacks are precursors to the Dark taking over. What happens in the Other Realms could bleed over into the Earth Realm. The vibrations and patterns might play out here as well."

"Who are the Dark King and Queen?"

"Do you really want me to give you a history lesson right now?"

"Now is as good a time as any." Nadia shifted, making herself comfortable.

"Fine." He sighed heavily. "Once upon a time, there was only one race of Numinals, spirits born of the Numinous. There was no good or bad, no evil. There just *was*. Something happened, and the Light split from the Dark, creating two courts. You are familiar with the Seelie and the Unseelie, yes? Those are Western-centric terms that don't quite capture the members of the original courts, but it's close enough for now.

"The Seelie have ruled for millennia in the Light Court, and the Unseelie ruled in the Dark Court, though now there are no more Unseelie. Now, a race of demons rules the Dark Court. Eventually, the other races of Numinals evolved from the two courts. Demons, Fae, shifters, elves, and all other Numinal creatures are descended from the two branches. The separation of Light and Dark lost meaning except for those closest to the original branches of the tree as the bloodlines started mixing and creating new races."

"Why did the Dark and the Light split?"

He waved his hand in dismissal. "Immaterial. This is the reality we are in now."

"So, the descendants of the Unseelie who are still in the Dark Court want to take over the Light Court, and the Prophecy says that they will?"

"Some say so. I, on the other hand," he said dryly, "do not take much stock in so-called prophecies. They are little more than the ramblings of broken minds, trying to comprehend things far greater than themselves."

"Aren't you concerned about the attacks in the city? What if this is the Prophecy coming true?"

"For as far back as there have been humans, there have been demons attacking them. No, I am not concerned about that. I am concerned, however, about how this affects Veil."

"That seems a little callous."

"Ms. Winters, the world will chew up and spit out bleeding hearts. You would do well to become a little bit more hardened to the world, lest it comes after you next."

She stared at him and wondered how the world had chewed *him* up and spit him out for him to make that statement.

"Did you discover anything in the meeting?" he asked finally.

She thought for a second. "Simon is hiding something. I'm not sure what, though."

Rune nodded. "I suspected he might be the cause of my uneasiness. Did you pick up anything specific?"

She shook her head. "Just feelings. They all had strong mental shields. Inanimate objects are way easier to read. They practically blast you with information."

"The mind is constantly changing and adjusting and protecting itself. Inanimate objects are static and wide open unless they've been spelled."

"I didn't sense anything about Pact, but Simon's been hanging out with someone with a lot of psychic energy. The remnants were all over his clothes, like a musty scent." Nadia shuddered. "It wasn't a good feeling."

"I know he runs with some powerful people."

"Back to my questions," Nadia cut back, "what is this Council? And did I hear correctly you used to be on it?"

"The Bifrost Council is a group of Numinals who have made it their mission to open the gates between the realms once more. As you may have heard, the Realm Gates have been closed for nearly seven hundred years, and no one has been able to pass through back to the Other Realms. Some Numinals believe that it is not possible to open the Gates again, while others believe they can find a way."

"What do *you* believe?"

"I'm not sure if it is possible, so that's why Myst focuses on assimilating Numinals into human society."

They stared at each other for a minute before Rune turned back to his computer and got back to work.

But Nadia wasn't done. "Can I ask you a personal question?"

"No." Rune didn't even look up from his computer. Typical. She ignored that.

"Have you been to the Other Realms?"

He paused and glanced up at her. "Yes. I have."

"How old are you?" asked Nadia. She didn't care if that was rude or not. She was dying for any scrap of information about him. He revealed so little about his personal life.

Rune's dark eyes bore into her, and she suddenly felt very young. "I was born in the eleventh century. Any more questions?"

Nadia definitely had more, but she bit her tongue.

Chapter 21

To comply with the board's resolution, Rune tasked select members of the Veil team with investigating Myst's involvement with the attacks in the city. Composed of Nadia, Carson, Maya, Sophie, and Piero, they spent hours poring over the app data and news reports, trying to figure out what was going on. They looked for any sort of pattern: any indication Veil was causing the attacks versus merely picking up on an energy surge, like lesser demons slipping into this realm. Nadia was surprised that Rune included her in the group, but he told her that her mental flexibility and powers as a Septer would be useful for examining things from angles that the others couldn't see.

It was slow progress.

"Okay, if I have to look at one more sequence of code, I'm going to explode," said Piero. He threw his head down on the table in mock despair. "I don't know how you people can do this day in and day out. I feel like I'm going cross-eyed. Seriously, look at my eyes. Are they turning inward?" He peered over at Sophie, who shrugged.

"Easy, princess," said Carson. "Don't blow a gasket."

It was after hours, and they had taken over one of the conference rooms as a war room, scribbling notes on the whiteboards on the walls, pinning up news reports they had found online about the attacks. The wall looked like one of those crazy person investigation walls on those crime shows, full of newspaper clippings, maps of the city pinpointing the attacks, sticky notes with clues, and lines of Veil code and outputs from the random number generator.

Maya glanced at the clock. "Should I order Postmates?"

"I don't know about you kids, but I actually have a life away from the office," Sophie said without looking up from her cell phone.

"I'd be down for some Postmates," Nadia told Maya. Maya grabbed her cell and scrolled through a list of restaurants.

"Thai?" asked Maya. "I know a place with a really good vegan curry."

Carson groaned. "You women and Thai food. How about barbeque?"

"Way to be original, cowboy," said Piero.

"Count me out," said Sophie.

"Hot date?" asked Piero.

"All my dates are hot," Sophie retorted. She batted her eyelashes with what Nadia assumed was her attempt at a provocative smile. It made her look slightly deranged.

"If you're going to lie, at least be creative," said Piero. "I've seen these cavemen you go out with. Tepid, at best." Sophie scowled at him.

Nadia stood up, stretching as she walked over to the crazy board and stared at it. Her mind kept churning over the data, rotating the Rubik's Cube, looking for the answer . . . looking for anything that would show whether Myst was causing the attacks. So far, nothing had been conclusive.

"I know what we need." Carson bolted and returned a minute later with a bottle of whiskey and a wolfish grin. "Rune's secret stash."

"Now that's what I'm talking about!" Piero whooped and grabbed glasses from the sideboards. They stood around the table and clinked their glasses before taking the shots. The whiskey was a good burn and warmed their empty stomachs.

Carson started pouring another round. Maya shook her head. "You know he'll kill us if he finds out." She accepted a refill anyway.

"If I find out what?" All heads swiveled to the doorway, where Rune was leaning with his arms crossed.

"Uh-oh, busted," said Piero, grinning.

"If you find out that the party got started without you. Here," said Carson as he handed Rune a drink. He accepted, and they all took another shot.

"How's it going?" asked Rune. "You all look very hard at work."

"Working hard, or hardly working?" joked Piero.

Rune walked over to their crazy person wall and looked at the attempts at patterns and connections. Nadia followed him, standing next to him as they studied it.

"You find anything yet?" he asked.

"We just can't seem to figure it out."

"Some things take time. You can't expect the answers to just fall in your lap. The universe rarely works that way." He paused. "Most of the time, if something seems easy and too good to be true, it is."

Nadia wondered if he was still talking about the app.

Her cell phone pinged. She fished it out of her back pocket and checked her text messages. It was from Marina, asking if she was going to be home for dinner. She shot off a quick text to let her know that she was working late.

Nadia's phone pinged again as she was tucking it into her pocket. This one was from Thomas.

HOW'S IT GOING? NEED UPDATE.

Of course, he would text in all caps. Idiot.

"Everything okay?" asked Rune.

Nadia shrugged nonchalantly and quickly put her phone back away. "Just my grandmother."

Rune knocked back his drink and placed the empty glass on the table. "Keep up the good work. I'll see you all tomorrow."

"We were about to order Thai. Want to join?" asked Maya.

Rune glanced at Nadia and cleared his throat. "I can't. Thanks, though." Nadia felt an irrational sense of disappointment that he was leaving.

Piero caught her watching Rune leave. "Back to work, you."

The sun shone high overhead as Nadia sat on the porch outside Myst having lunch with Maya, Carson, and Sophie. Around them, the ambient noise of Mystics chatting floated up. Nadia finished her turkey sandwich and sat back. She closed her eyes, enjoying the moment. The East Coast had always been either too hot or too cold, with very few perfect weeks in between. But San Francisco seemed to have perpetually good weather year-round. Especially in the Dogpatch neighborhood. "Hashtag Blessed" rose in her mind, and Nadia smiled inwardly, simultaneously feeling the ridiculousness and the truth of it.

"Guess who has two thumbs and gets to host Myst Assist this year?" said Piero. He maneuvered a packaged salad into the crook of his elbow and pointed two thumbs at himself.

Grinning like an idiot, Piero nudged Sophie over and plopped himself in the middle of the group at the picnic table. He placed his salad down and opened up a plastic fork.

"Wait, really?" asked Carson, a tinge of envy in his voice. "I thought we always get a celebrity to host."

"Negative, Ghost Rider. Budget concerns this year with the launch. But thankfully, yours truly graciously offered to step in, and our esteemed and enlightened CEO agreed I was the natural choice and has bestowed me with the honors of MC."

Carson grunted.

"Well, congrats," said Maya. "That's huge."

"What's the event?" asked Nadia.

Piero opened his salad and poured the dressing on, crinkling his nose in disgust. "Gross." He clawed at the salad with the plastic fork, lamely attempting to stir it around. "Every year thousands of Numinals are displaced from their homes because of natural disasters like Hurricane Katrina or the fires in the Amazon. Myst hosts a star-studded charity benefit each year to raise money to help those poor souls affected by circumstances out of their control. Think Live Aid, but for Numinals. It's *the* event of the year."

"Who are you going to get to headline?" asked Sophie. "You should totally get Buckskin Voo—" Sophie's voice cut off, her eyes wide.

"What was that?" asked Maya. She looked around herself.

"What?" asked Carson.

"There! There it was again," said Maya. Nadia felt it that time. A slight vibration in the air, a barely audible sound like a gong had gone off somewhere deep underground. Around them, the wards rippled, the shimmering gold symbols pulsing.

"What's going on?" asked Sophie.

"Something tripped the wards." Maya looked alarmed at the boundary line next to them.

Carson ran off suddenly, leaping over picnic tables and chairs in his haste. Other Mystics called out "Hey!" after him as he plowed through where they were sitting and eating lunch.

"Are we supposed to do something?" asked Nadia. The wards rippled again in the sunlight.

Piero shrugged. "It could just be a drill. A test of the emergency preparedness system." He took a timid bite of his salad and made a face.

"There wasn't anything on the calendar like that for today," said Sophie, a note of panic in her voice.

Piero looked at Sophie, his face full of concern. "What's wrong, baby girl? You look like you're about to hurl. Did you accidentally eat one of the special dishes? The Light knows this isn't much better. I really need to talk with the head chef. He's been taking a cue from humans, and the food is suffering."

After about twenty minutes, Rune's voice came over the Godspeaker. "All personnel report now to the common room for a mandatory staff meeting. I repeat, all personnel report now to the common room for a mandatory staff meeting."

Piero groaned and stood up. "Whatever this is, it's probably better than this lunch."

In the common room next to the Keebler Elf Tree and the yoga area, the Mystics stood around, waiting impatiently. Rune appeared along with Carson, and the employees gathered around Rune in a semicircle.

"If I can have your attention, please," Rune started. He looked a little frazzled, his hair unkempt. But his voice was smooth and unwavering. "Just now, something tripped the wards around Myst." Murmurs rolled through the crowd. Rune put his hand up to calm everyone. "Now, I'm sure it was nothing. Probably just an atmospheric disturbance from all the construction and drilling in the area. Or possibly it was a Numinal-animal hybrid that wandered into the tunnels and triggered the alarm system."

"Are we under attack?" shouted a brownie with large bat-like ears who stood next to Nadia.

"Yeah, is this related to the demon attacks in the city?" another voice called out from the other side of the crowd.

"There is no indication that Myst is under attack," said Carson. He was covered in dirt and grime, his previously pristine Myst T-shirt and jeans covered with mud splatters. He had a streak of dirt on his cheek, and his hair stood up at a weird angle. "I inspected the impact site at the northern borderline of the wards and found nothing to suggest this was intentional."

Rune nodded in agreement. "The seals held, so whatever it was, whether it was a vibration from construction or an animal, it didn't get through."

"How do you know?" called out another voice. Nadia wondered the same thing. Rune's clothes weren't stained the same way as Carson's.

"If something got through, the seals would be broken," said Rune. "I checked them in the ritual room. This was nothing to worry about. If anyone has any further questions, they can take them up with me."

Rune dismissed the crowd, and everyone milled about for a minute before dispersing. There were ripples of unease despite Rune's assurances that everything was fine.

Piero, though, seemed unconcerned and bounded off to go work on his speech for the charity event.

Maya raised her eyebrows at Nadia. "I need a shot of what he's got. Coffee break later?"

"The goblins are trying out new recipes for Firmament Night."

"Those vegan cranberry arugula tarts they made last month were to die for. Meet you around three at the Tree?"

Nadia headed back to her habitat to work a bit on Carson's artifact project, but her mind kept wandering to the breach. Rune had said it was nothing to worry about, but she sensed that it was a bigger deal than he was letting on. Surely it had to be related to the demon attacks in the city, right? Marina had said that there was no such thing as coincidences, only synchronicities that were unexplored. Determined to get some work done and to stop her racing thoughts, Nadia put on her AirPods and listened to some of Maya's new tunes as she wrote up descriptions for several Hindu mythological artifacts from the vaults, including the Kalasha, a vase that contained the elixir of life and symbolized abundance and immortality.

After a bit, she needed a break. She stood up and stretched before she made her way over to the ladies' room, weaving through the other habitats in the main room until she reached the perimeter walkway. The restroom door was labeled with a picture of Cloacina, the Roman goddess of sewers.

Inside the restroom, she walked over to the giant mirror above the row of inlaid sinks and washed her hands. She inspected her face, turning it this way and that, and tucked a strand of hair behind her ear. She took a mint from the bowl on the counter, popped it in her mouth, and headed back out.

From one of the stalls came a soft, crying sound. Nadia paused. The person was trying to be quiet, snuffling slightly, but a sob escaped. Nadia bent down, trying to get a look at the shoes of the person crying. Black Doc Martens. Sophie.

Nadia stood back up. Whatever Sophie was crying about wasn't her business, and she was pretty sure that Sophie wouldn't want her to pry, considering how awful she'd been to her ever since she started working at Myst. But as she reached the restroom door, another louder sob escaped, almost like Sophie wanted someone to check on her. Nadia stopped, conflicted, wondering what she should do. Sophie let out a small wail. With a sigh, Nadia turned back.

She rapped her knuckles lightly on the stall. "Hey, Sophie? It's Nadia. Are you okay?"

"I'm fine," sniffled Sophie through the closed door.

"Okay . . . can I get you anything?"

Sophie paused. "Can you get me some tissues? There's no more toilet paper in this stall."

Nadia went over to the counter, plucked out a couple of tissues from the box on the sink, and then passed them under the door.

"Thanks," said Sophie in a small voice as she took the tissues.

"Well, whatever it is, I'm sure it will be okay."

Another sob escaped Sophie. Nadia cringed.

"I think I fucked something up." Sophie's voice was barely audible.

"Well, we all make mistakes." Nadia turned to leave, trying to make an escape.

"It wasn't just a mistake. I think I did something really bad."

Nadia stopped. "What happened?"

Sophie was silent for a bit. Nadia leaned her ear toward the door, not knowing what to do. She couldn't imagine what Sophie considered "really bad." The girl was the poster child for nepotism and misplaced entitlement.

"I can't tell you."

Oh, for chrissakes. This was ridiculous. Sophie obviously wanted to tell her, or else she would have told her to piss off. Nadia didn't have the patience for an extended back and forth. She considered just walking away, letting Sophie just cry it out, but curiosity got the better of her.

Nadia slid her psychic tendrils up to Sophie's mind. In her anguish, Sophie had loosened the hold on her mental shields. Nadia found the memory that was tormenting her.

Nadia's eyes went wide.

"Sophie, open the door. I know what you did."

The stall door unlocked, and Nadia pulled it open. Inside, Sophie sat on top of the toilet seat, her eyes puffy and red and angry. Mascara streamed down her cheeks. She held the wadded-up Kleenex in her hand.

Sophie shot daggers at Nadia. "You aren't allowed to read other Mystics' minds. It's in the company policy. I'll report you."

"And then you'd have to tell Rune that you told some random guy at the bar all about Myst's wards and how they're weakest at noon." Nadia knew a game of chicken when she saw it. There was no way in hell Sophie would willingly confess what she did.

Sophie pushed past her and went to the mirror. She grabbed some tissues and wetted a handful before she started wiping away the streaks of makeup on her cheeks.

Nadia stared at Sophie's reflection in the mirror. "Seriously,

Sophie, why would you do that? What were you thinking?" She didn't want to lecture her, but this was not just "really bad." This was catastrophic. The wards and seals around Myst were the only things protecting the headquarters. Now she was sure that whatever happened earlier was no atmospheric disturbance.

"I wasn't, okay?" Sophie snapped. "I was drunk. He was cute. I didn't know he was playing me. I wasn't getting a con artist slash burglar vibe."

Nadia looked at Sophie with her Tik Tok-model outfit, her fake eyelashes, her spoiled It-Girl persona that she worked so hard to cultivate, and felt sorry for her. Underneath all that bravado and attitude was a miserable person, living an unfulfilling life. She would never be a Septer. It just wasn't in her cards. And instead of trying to be happy with what she did have, she squandered it and almost lost it completely. If that guy had managed to break in, Rune would figure out how and fire Sophie for the betrayal.

Nadia could go for the jugular here, really hit Sophie hard where it hurt, but she chose not to.

"Listen, we've all done stupid shit because of a guy."

Sophie's eyes flicked to Nadia's in the mirror's reflection. She was listening.

"Before I moved out here, I was dating this guy, and he ended up cheating on me with my best friend and I caught them in bed together. I went ballistic. Threw a brick through her window, slashed his tires. I know, extreme for me," she said after she saw Sophie's raised eyebrows, "but I felt so used. So tricked. How did I not notice the signs? How could I have been that delusional? But you're like me. We're trusting. We believe people are generally good and won't fuck us over for no reason. So, maybe the guy at the bar did try to break in, but also, maybe it really is just a coincidence. But the point is that Rune's seals around Myst weren't broken. That's all that matters. It turned out okay, either way."

Sophie wiped away the last of her smeared makeup. Her face

was a little blotchy, her eyes a little red. But she adopted a serene look on her face.

"You're right. It turned out fine." Sophie tousled her hair in the mirror. Gave a big sigh. "You know, the more I think about it, the more I think I overreacted. Jumped to conclusions. It was just a coincidence. That guy wasn't trying to scam me. It was an atmospheric disturbance, like Rune said."

Ah, the lies we tell ourselves. Well, if that's what Sophie had to do to get through the day, Nadia wasn't going to stop her.

The door to the bathroom opened, and a Korrigan entered, her wings trailing behind her. Sophie took one final look in the mirror and glanced at Nadia. It was a look that said, *if you tell anyone about this, I will destroy you.* Nadia dipped her head slightly in silent agreement.

Chapter 22

Over the next week, there were several more attacks, random break-ins, and lootings that appeared to be demonic in nature all around the city. The Veil team continued to comb through the data to find out if there was a connection between the attacks and their tech. They couldn't figure out if the app was involved, but the attackers who had been caught were all Myst users. It seemed like there were two types of murders: violent and seemingly nonviolent. With the nonviolent attacks, the bodies of the murder victims were discovered in dark alleys, dead but with no outward signs or markings of struggle. Numinals knew that demons had drained the murder victims' life force, but the local authorities and general human population were stumped about why people were dropping dead in the streets.

But with the violent attacks, the victims had been hunted and killed, many fighting for their lives before being brutally clawed to death. In some instances, the apparently human killers had been found at the scene of the crime, some of them going so far as to ingest the human flesh. The newspapers and local activist groups called for the mayor to issue a state of emergency in the city until the cause of these violent outbursts and strange cases of cannibalism could be determined.

The entire city was on edge. Strangers would glare at one another in passing as if expecting to be attacked at any moment.

More than once, random passersby snapped at Nadia on the BART or Muni for bumping into them. Avery took to picking her up and dropping her off from work if she didn't get a ride home from someone or take a Lyft. Marina was adamant that she should not walk home alone or take public transportation late at night.

Rune was on edge, as well. After the Veil team failed to quickly find the connection between the game and the attacks, he had withdrawn into himself, as if contemplating something in the back of his mind even as he went through the day-to-day motions of being the CEO.

He still trained Nadia in the morning, but he seemed distant and distracted. Part of her wondered if he missed Imogen. The other part of her, the rational part, tried not to care. She had bigger fish to fry. Thomas became increasingly annoying, popping up almost every other day to check in and prod her for information, most often on Rune. Nadia wondered why Mercurio had such a preoccupation with him. She suspected there was some history between them that she didn't know about.

One evening, when she finally emerged from the vaults to go home, everyone had already left. The habitats and lounge area on the main floor were empty. From the goblins' Keebler Elf Tree came the sounds of light snoring; Grudax and crew had already turned in for the evening.

As she approached her habitat, Nadia looked up to the second floor. There was a light on in Rune's office, illuminating his figure. He was pacing back and forth in front of the glass walls as he talked on a Bluetooth headset. Nadia didn't feel like dealing with him after a particularly brutal training session that morning where he had been snappish and surly toward her. She had tried to show him the witchlight spell that Marina had taught her, but he had called the glowing golden globe of light a "juvenile party trick." She gave him a cursory wave, anyway. He watched her pack up her bag as he talked on the phone. Nadia gave him one last glance before she slipped out into the night.

Even though it was a half-moon, the night seemed dark and ominous. Yellow moonlight illuminated strange corners of the buildings at Pier 70, casting inky shadows on the pavement. There was a chill in the air, a slight howling in the wind through the trees. Nadia buttoned up her red leather jacket against the fall air. After she summoned a Lyft, Nadia stood at the corner near the office waiting for her ride to arrive. Only a few cars were out on the street this late.

And then a strange light caught her eye. It was a small glowing orb, about the size of a baseball. It danced along the sidewalk halfway down the block, beckoning her toward it. It reminded her of the witchlight that Marina and Avery had made her practice over and over, but it was perfectly round, flickering a translucent white light; very unlike Nadia's attempts, which were more like Flubber. But this light was perfect.

She wanted to see what it was, but it started moving away. She felt a strange tug. She tried to dig in her heels, but the impulse to know about the light was too strong. She followed the floating orb down toward the docks near the water, but it kept skipping away, almost like it was playing with her. And then it turned and disappeared down a dark alley between two buildings near the pier. Nadia's feet seemed to move on their own. She had to catch the light!

There were no streetlamps in the alley, but the moonlight partially illuminated the trash cans and dumpsters and crates that lined the side of the narrow path. Garbage littered the ground. She stepped on something squishy and hoped it wasn't a dead rat. In front of her, the little light paused, waiting for her, bobbing up and down a bit, almost like it was tied to someone's breathing.

And then Nadia saw something move.

A figure stepped out of the shadows. He looked harmless enough, wearing a hoodie and sneakers, but there was something wrong with his eyes. Even in the low light, they looked bloodshot and dilated, burning red. The man stepped toward her, moving strangely, like he wasn't entirely in control of his faculties—all herky-jerky, like a puppet on strings.

She backed away slowly, not wanting to take her eyes off him. The Myst Psionic beeped at her increasing anxiety, and she cringed at the sound, knowing he heard it.

He held something out. A knife. Moonlight caught on the blade, reflecting its sharp, glistening edges and the darker blood that stained it. Nadia looked down at his feet. What she had initially thought was a trash heap was actually a prostrate body. A dark pool spilled out beneath it.

And then the man lunged.

Rune's training kicked in. Nadia dodged the weapon, grateful for the first time for all the hours that she had spent with him in the gym. She tried to run, but he was too fast. He leaped onto her back and sank the knife into her shoulder as he pushed her down. With a scream, she toppled to the ground. She tried to turn over so that she could kick and punch at him, but he pinned her down, his weight on top of her. His nails raked into her back like claws, tearing her shirt and skin to painful ribbons. She screamed. She started conjuring up a spell to fight back, quickly thinking through the incantation for summoning fire, but the man pressed a knee into her back, wrapped his hands around her face, and slammed her head into the ground, stunning her. Her mouth filled with the metallic taste of blood. The dirty pavement and gravel scraped her cheekbone raw. Her jeans were tugged down, the night air cold on her bare skin.

In a desperate, last-ditch attempt to save herself, the fear and panic she felt threatening to paralyze her, she screamed in her mind, unable to do anything more with the man's large hand covering her mouth as he tried to suffocate her. She sent out a telepathic flare to the universe, sobbed, begged for help, prayed that someone was listening. She had no shame crying for help when she was about to die. Some people might accept their fate with a calm demeanor, but Nadia wasn't one of those people. The instinct to live, for survival, far outweighed her pride.

Something hard pressed against her back and ass as he tried to push into her. Instead of stilling her, it kindled a resolve to fight even harder. She thrashed, threw off his hand from her mouth, and screamed again.

Suddenly, the weight on top of her was gone. Stunned, it took her a second to flip over, but she sat up, her shoulder and back burning. She scooted away to hide next to a dumpster and pulled up her pants. Her breath was ragged, her hands shaking.

Rune had the man by the throat up against the brick wall. His legs dangled in the air, kicking. The man's eyes blazed red, his face contorted into a grimace. Rune punched the man in the chest with a sickening crunch of bone and squelching of blood and forced his hand into the man's torso, twisting and turning his arm. The man screamed. Rune roared a guttural, primal sound as he pulled something that looked like a squirming, soot-covered rag with legs out of the man's chest and flung it to the side. He muttered an incantation, and it dissipated into the air like grey smoke.

Rune dropped the man into a heap on the ground, panting. He looked over at Nadia, rage in his eyes. They were black for a second, and her breath caught in her throat. She blinked, and his eyes were back to normal.

"Are you okay?" he demanded.

"What are you?" Her voice was small. She felt a pang of fear looking at him.

He didn't answer her. Instead, he pulled her to her feet and crushed her to his body. Nadia winced in pain, in shock at what had just happened.

"Are you hurt?" He stepped back, still holding her by the shoulders. His eyes raked over her as he assessed the damage.

She then remembered that she had been stabbed in the shoulder. Pain flooded her body, overwhelming her so that she wobbled, her knees buckling. Before she could crumple to the ground, Rune scooped her up. Everything went black.

Nadia's eyes fluttered open. Shapes and colors came in and out of focus, and it took her a minute to realize that she was lying on her stomach on the couch in Rune's office. She tried to sit up, the leather of his couch stuck to her cheek, but pain and a wave of nausea struck, and she stopped moving, breathing heavily.

"Just keep still," said Rune.

Nadia had never been good at taking commands. She struggled up into a half-seated position and took stock of her body. He had cut away portions of her shirt. A big medical bandage was taped to her shoulder over the stab wound.

For a second, she wondered if he had seen her topless.

Rune looked flustered. "I can't believe you think I would do that."

She hadn't, not really. Rune wasn't that kind of guy.

"Are you reading my mind?"

"Ah, no, but the look is plastered all over your face. You're very easy to read, you know."

He was sitting at his desk, his gaze intense. He looked exhausted and worn out, with dark circles under his eyes, unkempt hair, and a five o'clock shadow.

"I took the liberty of healing you while you were out. It was preferable to waiting. There was a lot of blood. I prioritized the wounds on your face. He did a number on you, but I think I got there before . . . *more* happened."

Nadia closed her eyes, taking big calming breaths. Memories of freshman year in college flooded her mind. How she hadn't been able to fight back. How she had said no, but Keith's frat brother—Cody, she thought his name was—had shushed her and pushed her up against a wall. How she had frozen up in fear and let him drunkenly paw at her skirt, pull aside her panties, and push himself into her under the wooden porch at the frat house. She had gone numb and barely remembered the actual sex. It hadn't lasted long.

After, she had stumbled away, vomited pink jungle juice into a bush, and made her way back to the dorms. She never told anyone what had happened. Nadia told herself she had wanted it, that she could have fought him off if she tried, so it must have been consensual. Now, she wondered if she really could have fought him off.

She touched her face gingerly, expecting pain. "Shouldn't I go to a hospital or something?" The skin on her face felt slightly tender but otherwise intact.

He leaned back in his chair, his gaze steady on hers. "And say what? A demon attacked you? Your back is clawed to hell too. I did my best to stop the bleeding, but healing is not my strongest skill. I've called a professional to finish. She should be here soon."

Nadia paled. "A demon? That guy was a demon?" His expression hardened at her exclamation.

"Possessed by one."

Her gaze flicked about his office as she thought about the demon, settling on the various Numinal pop art pieces on the walls picturing demons and other creatures from various cultures. A shiver ran through her, and she shuddered, goosebumps breaking out over her skin. She looked back at Rune. He was watching her intently.

"Was that grey thing the demon?" Nadia asked. Rune nodded. She looked away. "What happened to the human?"

"The human died."

"Oh." Her voice felt small and hollow.

Rune shuffled some papers on his desk. "What were you doing in that alley?"

"I saw a light, so I followed it."

"For fuck's sake, Nadia!" he exploded. "Don't you know anything? Why on earth would you follow a will-o'-the-wisp into a dark alley? Do you have a death wish?"

Jesus, he was pissy. She knew he was just worried about her, though, and lashing out from the stress of her brush with death. "I thought will-o'-the-wisps were just swamp gas or strange light in marshes?"

"It continually surprises me that you haven't died yet." He paced back and forth next to his desk and ran a hand through his hair in frustration. There was blood on his shirt. Nadia wondered if it was hers.

Rune's expression was serious and full of concern. "A will-o'-the-wisp is a bit of light that Numinals use to lure humans to their demise. Sometimes faeries use it, sometimes demons. Why didn't you fight the compulsion?"

"Wait, I thought faeries were 'good.'"

"There is no good. Just lesser evil."

Nadia tried to sit up further but felt dizzy. Her back stung. She took several deep breaths, trying to work through the pain. "I tried to fight it, but it was too strong. I don't know how to describe it except that I had to find out what it was."

Rune tossed her a wallet. "I went back and got rid of the body while you were passed out. I took his cell phone and wallet. Jonathan Murphy. Name ring a bell?"

She shook her head and looked at the wallet. It felt wrong, like she had committed some crime, even though she was the one who had been attacked. He had been a person with a life. And now he was dead.

Rune looked at her reproachfully. "You're lit up now. What happened to the defensive shield training we've been working on?"

Nadia winced. "I—I was working on some sigils for Veil in the vaults and found one for a boost of energy. I was tired and thought it would be like having a cup of coffee. I must have charged myself up too much."

"Well, that explains why it went after you. You're lucky there wasn't more than one. You're like a siren's call to them right now." Rune sat back at his desk and looked out the window. They sat in silence for a bit. She tried shifting, but her body was in pain. Rune looked over, noticing her discomfort.

He came over and took a seat on the sofa next to her. He placed a hand on her shoulder. She flinched.

"Sorry," she muttered. She wasn't sure why she was apologizing.

He closed his eyes. Nadia felt waves of energy entering her body, and she realized he was healing her. But it was taking a toll on him. He looked exhausted. She stopped him, placing a hand on his to stop him.

"I'm okay. Really."

He opened his eyes. "I heard you. I heard you . . . screaming. I'm sorry I wasn't there sooner."

"You could hear me?"

"I-uh, think we are entangled." Rune looked at her intently, like he was gauging her reaction.

"What does that mean?"

"Our brainwaves are synced to send thoughts to one another without being in telepathic range. I suspected we might be at that happy hour." He looked down. "I should have known something like this could happen. I should have protected you, I—"

Nadia cut him off, taking his hand in hers. He looked back up at her. She smiled a small smile, that small flicker of hope slowly rekindling in her heart. "You did more than enough. Thank you for saving me."

The corners of his mouth turned up slightly. "You're welcome."

He glanced down, finally noticing that they were holding hands, and stiffened. Nadia took her hand back, her breath catching. He cleared his throat. "We'll have to work harder on your shields." The moment was broken.

That small flicker of hope sputtered . . . but it did not die.

Chapter 23

It seemed like half the people in San Francisco had gone off to Burning Man during the first week of September. Many Mystics had tickets for the weeklong festival and had taken off for the desert, leaving the company working with a skeleton crew. The Veil team, however, had all opted to stay to work on the release and continue investigating the game's connection to the attacks, though not without complaint.

"This is shit," said Sophie as the gang ate lunch on the patio under one of the large umbrellas. "I should be out at Black Rock City finding a playa boyfriend."

"You and me both, sister," said Piero as he looked over the top of his Tom Ford sunglasses. As she sat at the wooden picnic table, Sophie scrolled through her social media accounts, looking at the pictures, videos, and reels that burners were posting of the desert rave. Nadia felt a pang of FOMO. She had wanted to go to the desert too but hadn't felt it prudent given the state of her life recently.

Although now that everybody was posting amazing pictures of the art installations and costumes and art cars, she realized a week in the desert on hallucinogens probably would have done her a world of good. Her life was already a surreal head trip, with all the magic and Numinals and supernatural startups. Drugs probably would straighten everything out.

Next year, she promised herself.

"Yo, Nadia," said Maya. "What do you have going on this afternoon?"

"Just working in the vaults. Why?"

"We're short-staffed in the lab. Care to help out with the beta testing today? I have a hard time interpreting human reactions and could use another set of eyes on the data."

"Absolutely," said Nadia quickly.

Carson chuckled. "Sounds like someone needs out of the library."

Nadia wadded up a napkin and threw it at Carson, who ducked and flashed his fangs at her. "Hey, I wouldn't be so eager to get out of there if you didn't keep piling on more artifacts I have to pull."

"Those can wait," said Maya as she stood up. "I have to get a report to Rune by the end of the week, and I'm so far behind. Meet me downstairs in an hour or so? I'll get Kevin hooked up, and we can run the new rounds of tests."

Nadia readily agreed. The isolation in the vaults was starting to get to her.

Later that afternoon, Nadia made her way down to Myst Labs, located several floors underground in the headquarters. The lab was filled with various magical and technological equipment where employees conducted experiments, tested weapons, and worked with game testers to beta test Veil. Except with most people on vacation for Burning Man, the normally bustling workspace was nearly empty.

Nadia wound her way through the floor, weaving in and out of strange equipment and magical projects. Piero and Carson were deep in conversation with a Redcap who was hooked up to a bunch of motion sensors. It looked like they were working on the motion capture sequence for the virtual treasure creatures in Veil. Piero flashed her an exasperated look before returning to whatever argument he was in with Carson. Whatever they were talking about was making him agitated, and he gestured wildly at the Redcap, who was dutifully moving through the choreography for the sequence.

Rune was there as well, working with a fire sylph who was brewing an alchemical mixture in a steaming vat. Rune looked deep in thought, and he absentmindedly ran his hand through his dark hair as he pored over a large spell book with the chemist.

Ever since the attack in the alley the previous week, Rune had been paying extra close attention to her defensive fighting skills. Luckily his quick work with healing had prevented any major damage, and after the professional healer—a centaur that Rune had explained was a pledge to the Mystery Cult of Asclepius—finished the healing, they were able to resume training immediately. Nadia was still sore, but she was grateful that there was no permanent damage to her face. Her back was a different story, though. She would always have the scars.

Nadia didn't mind, though. She liked having scars. Whenever she looked at her naked back in the mirror, the silver lines of claw marks shining from where the healer had knitted her torn flesh back together, she was reminded of her favorite Hunter S. Thompson quote: "Life should not be a journey to the grave with the intention of arriving safely in a pretty and well-preserved body, but rather to skid in broadside in a cloud of smoke, thoroughly used up, totally worn out, and loudly proclaiming 'Wow! What a ride!'"

In the center of the lab, Maya, Kevin, and Sophie were running tests on a mat that looked like a giant treadmill that simulated walking around the city. Kevin, looking ever like the lab rat, was hooked up to some sort of brainwave monitoring machine. Little stickers were placed around his temple to collect data and send it over to Maya's computer, which was monitoring his emotions and reactions. As he moved through the adventures, faeries and dwarves and talking rabbits jumped in front of him, moving through the scripted role-play.

Maya's eyes lit up when she saw Nadia. "Oh good. You're here. Take a look at this." She gestured at her laptop. "I can't tell if his reactions are authentic or not."

Nadia peered at the computer and tried to make sense of the data. Various charts and graphs were plotted out on the screen, similar to a vital sign monitor at a hospital.

Maya pointed to one of the lines on the screen. "See this? I can't tell if Kevin is reacting to the faerie or the dust she emits in the sequence."

Kevin had stopped walking on the treadmill mat and was instead picking at a scab on his elbow, oblivious to their conversation.

"Kev, mate, keep going, okay?" Sophie called out.

Kevin grinned and gave a thumbs-up before continuing to walk, holding out his iPhone in front of him. They watched for a bit as Kevin continued playing the game, interacting with various Numinals in the assigned quests. As each new bit of data beeped on the screen, Maya frowned, glancing at Nadia and Sophie to help interpret the human data.

After a bit, Sophie stopped Kevin and handed him a Capri Sun. "Good work. Take a break, okay?" She turned back to them, shaking her head. "We need a way to distill down Kevin's reactions. We're picking up too much random noise in his brain."

"You know, a Resonance Stone would help with that," Nadia said.

"How do you know about Resonance Stones?" Rune's deep voice asked behind her. Nadia jumped, startled by his sudden appearance so close to her.

The Myst Psionic pinged. "Jesus, you scared me." She calmed her thudding heart and took a deep breath.

Rune crossed his arms over his chest. She tried not to notice the way his bicep flexed in his T-shirt. Her face flushed. Apparently, all that careful telling him to go fuck himself in her mind didn't stick after he had rescued her from the demon attack.

"I read about them in a book in the vaults," Nadia lied.

He nodded slowly. "I think you might be on to something. Resonance Stones can clarify and distill emotion. If we could filter Kevin's responses to Veil through a Resonance Stone, it would strip away all the 'noise,' as Sophie put it."

"It would be brilliant if we could do that," said Maya, leaning back against one of the tables. "I spend hours each test trying to normalize the data. Even with the program that Carson wrote, it takes forever. It would save so much time if I had an artifact to do the work for me."

"Do we have one of those in the vaults?" asked Sophie as she jumped up to sit on a nearby table. She dangled her fishnet-covered legs over the edge.

Rune shook his head. "They're difficult to come by unless you are in the right circles."

"What circles are those?" asked Nadia.

"Not ours," said Rune as he moved on to check on the next group and their experiments.

Nadia let out the breath she was holding and mentally kicked herself for not being more careful about hiding her ties to Mercurio.

The next day, the Veil team met to update each other on any progress they'd made on their investigation. They sat around the patio outside, basking in the fall sunlight, a bit of crispness in the early September air. They had hit a wall when it came to the demon attacks, so they just started throwing out ideas—the crazier, the better. Piero thought they should use demon bait and trap one for questioning. Sophie wanted to seduce a city diener at the morgue and see if they could examine the bodies for clues. Carson scoffed at their suggestions, instead pulling up the latest blog posts from the friendly neighborhood conspiracy theorist to see if that guy had any tips.

"Most of his stuff is total wackjob nutcase ideas, but he occasionally gets some things right," explained Carson as he typed on his laptop.

"Yeah, like what?" asked Nadia. She and Maya were poring through pages of data relating to the amounts of treasure payouts, looking for patterns in the amounts. Unfortunately, almost anything looked like a pattern the longer they looked at it.

"Looks like he's on to the fact the attacks are demonic in nature," said Carson, "but he thinks it's some sort of organ harvesting ring."

"Are we sure it's not?" asked Sophie. "At least we'd have a motive. Right now, it's just random violence."

"I just can't shake the feeling that something is causing the demon attacks. That it isn't random," said Maya. She pulled out a pocketknife and an apple from the pocket of her jacket and started peeling the apple. "It feels like a spell."

"You think someone hacked the app?" Carson's fangs extended a bit as he frowned. "The security on Veil is flawless. I designed it myself."

"I'm not saying that! But what if someone was spelling the random number generator to give big payouts, and somehow it went wrong and was calling the demons into the Earth Realm? I don't know. I'm just thinking out loud."

"Do Numinals ever win the lotto?" asked Nadia. "If someone could cast a spell to win, why don't they do it all the time?"

Piero inspected his nails with a sniff. "They sometimes do. It's super hard to do, though, and only a very skilled Numinal or Septer could pull it off. It takes an enormous amount of energy because of the number of people who want to win. You have to overcome every other person's desire for the outcome. It's all very complicated, and few Numinals even understand how it works." He shrugged. "I don't really understand it myself, but I do know it's easier to sway something small, like the outcome of a local bake-off, than something like the California Powerball."

"Remember a few years ago when that bookie was fixing all the local horse races and sports games?" asked Sophie. "The whole city rioted when the Giants lost the World Series. What was that guy's name?"

"Andreas?" offered Carson.

Sophie snapped her fingers. "That's right! Andreas the Hedge Wizard. I wonder what happened to that guy."

"What's a hedge wizard?" Nadia asked.

"Aren't you a witch?" asked Sophie, a note of aggression in her voice.

"I'm not up on my magic terminology, okay?"

Piero took pity on her. "A hedge wizard—or witch—is a Sixer masquerading as a Septer. They're basically self-taught and don't have any true power. Most are charlatans, scamming people into believing they know what they're doing. They can get away with it, to an extent, if they know the right spells."

"If he doesn't have any true power, then how was he fixing baseball games?" Nadia wondered.

Piero nodded approvingly. "Good question." Nadia glanced smugly at Sophie, who stuck her tongue out like a bratty teenager. Piero continued, "He was basically running a Ponzi scheme, borrowing other people's power and ritual energy that they thought was being used for a good purpose. Experienced Septers and Numinals need tons of energy for some of their rituals and spells, and so they sometimes store it up in talismans or other power stones, using it for later when they need it. A lot of Numinals got left holding the bag when he finally got caught."

"Do you think this Andreas guy has anything to do with the random number generator being not quite so random anymore?" Nadia asked.

The others looked at one another. "He might know something," said Maya slowly. "But it could be anyone really, if someone was trying to get the game to give big payouts."

"But wouldn't he know if anyone else was trying to pull a scam?" pressed Nadia. "Don't these guys usually keep their ear to the ground so they can get in on things if the scheme is good enough?"

Carson nodded. "Let's go find Rune."

They found Rune in the gym, lifting weights. After they told him about their suspicions that the demon attacks could be related to someone casting spells for lotto payouts in the game, Rune agreed that a trip to see Andreas could be beneficial to see if he'd heard of anything like that going on.

"Field trip!" shouted Piero, high-fiving Sophie after Rune reluctantly agreed to let them all join him. Rune looked like he realized too late that he had made a mistake.

In the Mission, Sophie and Piero stopped for gelato while Maya, Carson, and Nadia got cups of pour-over coffee at a local coffee shop. Rune watched them from the sidewalk with growing impatience as they paid inside.

"Next time, the Scooby Gang stays back at the office," grumbled Rune as he herded them down the street.

"Don't be such a Squonk," said Piero before he took a bite of his pistachio gelato.

"Company field trips are a proven way to boost employee morale," added Sophie, smiling coyly at Rune as she walked next to him. She held her cherry gelato up. "Want to try my—"

Rune cut her off quickly. "No."

"—gelato," she finished. Piero elbowed her. "What? I was going to say gelato."

Maya, Carson, and Nadia followed behind them, sipping their coffees. It was a beautiful day, the late-afternoon sun casting a warm glow over the Mission. Along the street, people shopped at bodegas. Fresh oranges and grapes and pumpkins littered the side-walk in a maze of crates as shoppers weaved in and out of taquerias and pupuserias, check cashing stores, pawnshops, and dollar stores, their wares overflowing into storefront displays on the sidewalk like at a flea market or swap meet.

The others had filled Nadia in about Andreas as they had headed over to the Mission. Before running a Ponzi scheme and bookie hall, he had been a Santeria priest, holding mass at small churches he made in basements and warehouses. Except all the rit-ual energy created by his parish went to fueling his Ponzi scheme, instead of for prayer. Apparently, tricking people like that was a huge taboo in the Numinal community, and he had been black-listed for many years. Rune had made a few phone calls to track down his whereabouts and had learned that he was operating a hot dog food truck, deep in the heart of the Mission.

When they got to the food truck, Andreas was outside, talking to an elderly Latina as he showed her a briefcase full of what looked like religious artifacts. Andreas was short and squat, with dark curly hair and a cherubic face. His eyes went wide when Rune descended on him, and he snapped the case shut quickly, shooing the woman off.

"Still peddling your fake relics, Andreas?" Rune growled. "I thought you had been forbidden for holding yourself out as a priest anymore."

"Mr. Christiansen! You do me a great honor by visiting my humble establishment. Please, can I get you and your friends any-thing?" He gestured at the sizzling grill. The smell of the cooking hot dogs, onions, and mustard drifted toward them.

"I'll take one. No, wait, two," said Carson, whose wolf fangs had elongated as he watched the hot dogs cooking. Rune shot him an exasperated look, but Carson merely shrugged. "Well, we are here, aren't we? Might as well."

Andreas rushed inside his truck, wrapped up two hot dogs, and handed them to Carson over the counter. Carson squeezed a thick line of mustard on his hot dog and took a bite, growling in pleasure at the taste. Maya looked like she wanted to throw up.

"I don't know how you can eat that," she declared. "That's disgusting."

"It's delicious." Carson took another bite and grinned. "You elves are missing out."

"Oh, *some* elves eat meat. Just not that processed crap. Seriously, that's probably like pig intestine. It's barely meat."

"Can I try your meat?" asked Sophie. She opened her mouth and Carson fed her a bite. Carson's eyes glazed over a bit as she sucked on his finger. Maya glowered as she watched them. Nadia shot her a small smile and rolled her eyes. *There goes Sophie being a dumb flirt again.* Piero grabbed Maya's hand.

"Come with me to the market," said Piero, as he dragged her away from Carson and Sophie. "We have some duendes coming in tomorrow to check their abilities, and I'm sure they'd love some fresh fruit as a snack during their break. Help me pick out some lulos and mangoes?"

Piero dragged Maya away, and Carson and Sophie strolled off to look at a nearby thrift store together. Rune was talking to Andreas while the others had scattered, too preoccupied with themselves to help Rune with questioning the disgraced priest.

"Hey man, I'm not into that stuff anymore." Andreas looked around himself nervously, wringing his pudgy hands together. "I don't know anything about spells to fix game winnings."

"Come on, Andreas. You must have *some* idea of who could be running that kind of scam." Rune's voice had a seductive tone to it. Nadia wondered if he was gently nudging Andreas with magic to answer his questions.

Andreas ran a hand through his greasy hair, his eyes darting around as he thought.

"I mean, it would take an enormous amount of energy. Like,

massive, man. The only guy in town who could even try to pull it off would be Mercurio. But I don't think he runs those sorts of tricks, man. He's gone legit."

Nadia paled at the mention of Mercurio, and the watch pinged. Rune looked at it questioningly.

"What do you mean, he's legit?" Rune asked as he looked back at Andreas.

Andreas glanced about himself furtively like someone might be listening and leaned in, keeping his voice low. His eyes were big, giving him a kewpie doll look. "He's still amassing energy, but he makes Ambrosia now. It's all sanctioned, man. Aboveboard. But that's all I know, man. I can't help you more than that." Andreas scurried off to help a customer who had just walked up to the truck.

"Do you think that guy Mercurio has anything to do with the attacks?" asked Nadia as they waited on the sidewalk down the street for the others to get done in the bodegas and thrift store.

"I don't know," said Rune. "But I intend to find out."

Chapter 24

A few days later, as they sped along in the McLaren toward Alchemy, Rune told Nadia what he knew about Alexander Mercurio.

"He's a business mogul," said Rune. "Dabbles in venture capitalism. But he has ties to the mafia and trades in illicit Numinal and magical artifacts. Not much is known about his history, though some say that he was an Ottoman corsair in the 1600s before he was turned. How he became a vampire is anyone's guess. He's completely self-serving, driven entirely by profit, greed, and the desire for power. He has a moral compass, but it always seems to be pointing toward himself."

"Sounds like you two have crossed paths before."

Rune's mouth was a grim line. "He and I aren't fond of each other, if that's what you are asking. A few years back, we kicked around the idea of going into business together. The venture started out great but quickly went downhill."

"Why's that?"

"Irreconcilable differences in our views on what are appropriate methods of doing business. Our opinions on Numinal artifacts are also somewhat . . . at odds. This is the first I'm hearing that he's manufacturing Ambrosia."

"What's Ambrosia exactly?" Nadia asked. "I assume you aren't talking about the drink of the Greek gods."

Rune side-eyed her. "It's, uh, a substance that some Numinals take. It's a bit of a delicacy."

"Like a drug?"

Rune nodded, keeping his eyes on the road.

She let that line of questioning drop. It was clear Rune didn't approve of Ambrosia. "So, what kind of artifacts are we talking about? Like the stuff in the vaults?"

"Not exactly. Most of what we have in the vaults are Numinal-*made* artifacts. Mercurio trades in . . ." He paused, searching for the right expression. "Artifacts *from* Numinals."

"Artifacts from Numinals?" she exclaimed. "Like, artifacts *made of Numinals*?"

"Selkie pelts, unicorn horns, elf ears—you name it, he can get it."

"That's disgusting. That's like trading in scalps or human bones or something!" Nadia cried, horrified at the thought of someone skinning Carson or cutting off Maya's ears.

"Unfortunately, there is quite a bit of magic in Numinal artifacts, and they can help people obtain more power and cast bigger spells than they could with their normal ability. It's a real problem in the Numinal community."

"That's horrible," said Nadia, shuddering.

"When we get to the club, let me do most of the talking," said Rune. Nadia understood the subtext: Play the part of the arm candy and keep your Sixer senses open.

Rune had set up a meeting with Mercurio under the pretense of pitching a possible business venture between him and Myst. "I tried to set up the meeting at his office like an adult," Rune had explained to Nadia, "but he insisted that the meeting be more casual and said that I needed to check out his nightclub."

When Nadia heard this, she had insisted on accompanying him. "Listen, I can be useful. While you're off talking business, I can use my Sixer powers and see if I can glean any information about the attacks or his involvement."

Rune initially told her no, it was way too dangerous. "This isn't exactly a work-appropriate outing," he said, trying to dissuade her. Eventually, Nadia wore Rune down, and he agreed to let her accompany him.

Nadia wondered what it would be like to see Mercurio again. She loathed his genteel mannerisms, his terrifying gaze, and the way his cronies all looked at her like she was dispensable. Being around him was like being in a cage with a great white shark or a cobra. He was unpredictable, and it made her feel very mortal, like he could snuff her out at any minute. She was sure he had no qualms about disposing of a body. But like how people wanted to swim with the sharks, Nadia wanted to feel that rush, wanted to live dangerously near the edge. She knew it was reckless, but she didn't care.

She was worried that Rune would somehow realize that she and Mercurio had met before, but that was a chance she would have to take. She wasn't worried that Mercurio would out her as his spy. He wasn't stupid. But Rune was perceptive, and Nadia was finding it harder and harder to lie to him. But ultimately, Nadia wanted to keep an eye on Rune. She was sure he could handle himself, but she didn't like the idea of Rune being involved in any way with Mercurio, and if something happened, she could intervene on his behalf and hope that Mercurio was feeling lenient.

That's what she was telling herself to justify her actions, in any event.

Nadia watched Rune as he drove fast through San Francisco's streets, expertly taking corners and hills as he wove in and out of traffic. He drove confidently and gracefully, though she could tell the meeting with Mercurio weighed on his mind. He was somewhere else mentally. She watched as he downshifted and came to a stop at a red light.

Rune glanced over at her. "What are you staring at?"

Nadia gave herself a bit of a shake, realizing she had been staring at his mouth. She quickly fortified her mental shields in case she was accidentally broadcasting any thoughts she shouldn't be thinking. Really, she was doing the best she could. It wasn't her fault that her boss was extremely attractive and she was posing as his armpiece . . . again.

"Nothing," said Nadia. "Just hoping I dressed okay."

Nadia looked down at her bare thighs, pressed together and barely covered by a tight little black dress. Rune had told her to dress up, to act the part of a date at an after-hours business meeting. She had picked a strappy bandage dress that revealed a decent amount of cleavage, teased up her hair, and lined her eyes with kohl, hoping that he noticed her as more than a nuisance he had to personally train so as not to be a liability.

She was a red-blooded American woman, after all. No shame in trying to provoke a bit of a reaction from a decidedly attractive male specimen, Numinal or not.

"You look fine," said Rune gruffly. He kept his eyes on the road, but Nadia caught him glancing at her, sending a thrill down her spine.

They parked the car around the corner from Asylum. Rune threw a couple of quick anti-vandalism and anti-theft charms over the McLaren as they left the car on the street and walked up to the club. It was dark out, the sky a velvety black that blended with the inky shadows on the sidewalk. Nadia would have walked right past the unmarked door if not for the burly djinn bouncer that stood out front like a statue guarding a sacred tomb.

It took a minute for her eyes to adjust as they walked down the narrow flight of stairs and stepped into the industrial warehouse space. Unlike the last time Nadia had been there, the club was going full throttle, evoking gothy, Euro-bondage vibes. Blue and purple and pink club lights lit up go-go dancers gyrating in cages. Men and women slick with sweat from drugs and dancing moved together to the throbbing music. The space inside was thick, a living, breathing space full of dark, festering emotion and desire.

Rune walked up to the bar and ordered shots of Jameson from a shirtless leather boy who had horns under his glamour. The bartender poured them the drinks and slid them over on the counter.

"Tell your boss that Rune Christiansen is here to see him," he said to the leather boy. The bartender nodded and scurried to the back.

Nadia gazed about the room, taking in her surroundings as she sipped her drink. All around her, people bumped and grinded to the music, writhing limbs everywhere. She felt out of place. She'd been to nightclubs before, but they weren't like this. The atmosphere was desperate, hungry for flesh on flesh, people losing themselves in the lights and the music's dark beat.

Nadia leaned back against the bar as she watched the crowd and tried to settle into the vibe of the room. One woman stood out. She looked like the others, wearing gothy leather and chain clubwear, but there was a magnetic draw to her, a sort of hypnotic spell she cast to those around her like a spider weaving a web. Serpent tattoos covered both her arms, wrapped around like chains.

Rune caught Nadia looking at the woman. "That's Ananke."

"You know her?"

He shrugged nonchalantly. "We've met. She's one of the Lost Ones."

"The who?"

"The Lost Ones are Numinals who came originally from the Other Realms. They weren't turned Numinal or born here on Earth from turned parents. There aren't many left. Most were in the Other Realms when the Realm Gates closed, but the few that were on Earth were either killed or died, unable to hide or assimilate into human culture after the Realm Gates closed. Their minds cannot comprehend human existence the same way a turned Numinal who still retains shreds of their humanity can. Ananke's a survivor, though. She's carved out a life for herself. She presides over all manner of slavery and bonds."

"I thought Ananke was a Greek goddess."

"Many of the traditional 'gods' and 'goddesses' of religions around the world were Numinals who amassed a cult following."

Well, the more you know. Ananke danced a seductive dance, her hips swiveling, seeming to be targeting a group of shoe-gazer guys who were standing in a circle dancing. The guys didn't know what hit them.

"What's she doing?" Nadia asked Rune.

"Just watch. It's her ritual. A compulsion. She approaches men and asks them to dance or to help her do something like tie the laces to her boot. If they dance with her or help her, the men live. If they refuse, they die."

"Are you kidding me?"

"Numinals sometimes are under strange compulsions and cannot help themselves. It isn't her fault that she has to do it, not entirely. Magical compulsions are stronger than willpower and cannot be bent."

Nadia's stomach twisted into a tight knot as she thought about the Blood Oath. One day she would be no better than Ananke, under a strange compulsion to do Mercurio's bidding. The thought of losing her free will made her sick.

They watched Ananke as she approached the group of guys and said something. Thankfully, one of the guys dropped down to the ground and laced up her boot for her. After a few minutes of dancing with the guy, Ananke spied Rune and strutted over, leaving the guy wondering what the hell had just happened, a confused expression on his face.

"Care to buy a girl a drink?" She smiled seductively at Rune.

"Of course, my dear," said Rune, greeting the woman with a kiss on the cheek. He turned toward the bar to signal the bartender.

Ananke's gaze swiveled to Nadia. Her eyes were glassy. "When the pawn becomes queen, the board will turn."

"What?" Nadia asked, not understanding at all. Was that some sort of prophecy? Ananke's eyes cleared after a moment, and she looked at Nadia like she saw her for the first time.

Rune turned back to them, Ananke's drink in hand. "Ananke, this is Nadia."

Ananke held out a hand. Nadia wasn't sure if she was supposed to kiss it or bow or something, Ananke being a goddess and all, so she settled for an awkward handshake.

"Rune, when are you going to visit us? We get so lonely without you. Odette has some new gi—"

Rune cut her off. "Soon. I've been very busy with work. You know how that goes."

"Ah, no rest for the wicked, eh?" She smiled coyly at him, toying with the chains on her rather revealing top.

A burly bouncer with horns and the body of a ram spied Ananke and marched over to where they were standing in front of the bar. "Hey, you! You aren't allowed here anymore!" The bouncer grabbed her under her arm and started pulling her away. With a flick of her wrist, she incapacitated him, bending his arm at an unnatural angle. He fell to the ground with a moan.

Stepping over his prostrate body, she winked at Rune. "We'll chat later. You know where to find me."

The dancing crowd parted like the Red Sea as she walked to the front.

One of Mercurio's goons, a slippery-looking weasel of a man, came to find them and motioned for Rune to follow.

"I'll be back in a little bit," said Rune. "Stay here, and don't get into trouble."

"I'm coming with you."

Rune shot her a dark look. Nadia smiled sweetly. "I'm not going to wait outside like some sort of pet. I'm coming with you. Don't make a scene, people are watching."

Nadia slipped her hand into Rune's and plastered a dumb look on her face. With an angry sigh, Rune led her toward the back.

Nadia looked around for Thomas, wondering if he was lurking around somewhere, but she didn't see him. They followed the man through the throngs of dancing people, behind a heavy velvet curtain, down a dim corridor lit with purple and red recessed lighting, and up a flight of stairs to the VIP section of the club.

As they entered the private rooms, Rune put his hand around her waist. A possessive gesture. Nadia stiffened in surprise at his touch but then quickly settled into it. Even if it was all pretend, she was going to enjoy being Rune's date for the evening.

The VIP section was different than the club downstairs. While downstairs was a minimalistic industrial warehouse space made for dancing, the lounge upstairs was a lush, regal abode partitioned off from the main area. Blood-red velvet lined the walls, cushioning the acoustics in the room so that the exotic, slow melody that played over the loudspeaker allowed for more intimate conversations. Rune and Nadia wove in between panels of sheer, tent-like fabric that hung from the ceiling, creating cluster areas with ornate pillows and recliners. Nadia couldn't help but stare at the Numinals and humans lounging in a drugged, hedonistic bliss, touching and kissing one another in writhing masses of limbs and flesh. On several of the tables was a contraption that looked a bit like a hookah pipe, with long tubes protruding from a central spigot. A Resonance Stone sat on the top of each instrument, lighting up with different colors as the guests took long drags from the pipes.

Mercurio sat in the back of the room, lounging on a high-backed chair that looked like a throne, his leg kicked up over the side, a willowy blonde nymph sitting in a posed position on the floor next to him. He was holding court, with several djinn body-guards surrounding him and his posse. They had arranged themselves artfully on the furniture like a Thomas Couture painting. Mercurio took a long drag from the pipe of one of the hookah-like contraptions, his eyes closing in bliss as the Resonance Stone on the top glowed a deep crimson.

Rune and Nadia stopped in front of him. His head rolled forward, and he opened his eyes. There was a glimmer of recognition in them as he saw her standing next to Rune.

"Rune Christiansen," said Mercurio. He cocked his head to the side.

"Alexander Mercurio," replied Rune smoothly.

"I couldn't believe my ears when you called, wanting to set up a meeting to talk about a possible partnership." He smiled, fangs extended. "Last time I saw you, you cost me five hundred grand in a warehouse fire."

Mercurio had been wearing a three-piece suit but had discarded the jacket and rolled up the sleeves of his shirt as he lounged, giving him the distinct patina of a wealthy business mogul confident in himself and his power. His hair was slicked back, but in his relaxed state, a lock had come undone, tumbling over his forehead. He ran his hands through his hair, pushing it from his face.

Rune chuckled slightly. "If I remember correctly, you started the fire yourself when you tried to smoke me out of the building."

Nadia glanced about herself, sizing up the guests. She cautiously sent out her psychic feelers, opening up her mind like a satellite dish scanning the starry night sky to sense if anyone knew anything about Veil or the attacks. Many of the Numinals' and humans' minds were open, but in their drugged state, she wasn't making any sense of the information. It was all muddled and unclear, like trying to find a pattern in a Pollock painting.

Mercurio uncorked a crystal decanter on the low circular table, poured himself a glass of dark liquid, and took a sip. He sat back, regarding Rune for a second before his gaze flicked over to Nadia. He sat up a bit, seeming to notice her now.

"And who might this be?" He walked around the table over to where they stood, his eyes raking over Nadia's short black dress and strappy heels. Rune pulled her closer to his side. Mercurio looked back and forth between them, a wicked smile spreading across his face.

"This is Nadia," said Rune. Nadia smiled coquettishly, playing the part of dumb eye candy.

Mercurio took her hand and kissed it. His lips lingered a bit too long on her knuckles. Rune emitted a low growl.

"The pleasure is all mine." Mercurio held her gaze, his eyes speaking directly into her mind.

You look good enough to eat, thought Mercurio at her.

Nadia coughed, her panic rising. She realized that somehow, she and Mercurio must be entangled. That wasn't good. Not good at all. She glanced up at Rune. He watched them intently, frowning.

How are you doing this? thought Nadia at Mercurio. Luckily, it seemed like her entanglements with Rune and Mercurio were on different frequencies, so they couldn't hear her mindspeak to each of them.

Part of the benefits of being one of my employees, thought Mercurio at her, with a glint in his eye.

Mercurio motioned for them to take a seat around the table, and he returned to his throne across from them. Rune took a seat on one of the high-backed chairs pulled up to the table, and Nadia followed, perching gingerly on the edge of her chair. She gave a wan smile to the demon sitting next to her, a grotesque half-human, half-monster not bothering to hide her warts and pus with a glamour. The demon stared at Nadia, flicking a forked tongue over her lips and rocking slightly forward like she might lunge at her.

The nymph poured them a drink from the crystal decanter.

Nadia took a small sip. The drink had a strange bitter fruit flavor. A cozy feeling flowed down her throat and spread from her back like warm honey.

"So, about the matter at hand," Rune started. "I've heard about your new business venture, and I think there could be an interesting partnership opportunity here. We've been working with various energies to power our wearables and mobile games, and—"

Mercurio waved a hand, cutting him off. "There is plenty of time for business talk later." He grinned lasciviously at Nadia and jerked a thumb at Rune. "Is he always like this? You think the guy would learn to relax and kick back every once in a while. Here, come sample the latest batch. I think you'll be impressed with my methods, Christiansen. The quality is superb, if I do say so myself."

He held out one of the pipes. Rune shook his head. Mercurio looked surprised. "You exhibit such control, my friend. How do you ever manage?"

"Careful practice," said Rune tersely.

Mercurio held the pipe out to Nadia. "Care for a drag . . . Nadia, was it?" Nadia took the pipe.

"She doesn't need any—" started Rune.

Mercurio stopped him. "Go ahead, dear." He leaned back, watching her as he crossed a leg, and took another sip of his drink.

While Nadia was no stranger to party drugs, she suspected this one was like opium, given the state of the other guests, and she wasn't too keen on smoking something if she didn't know what it was. She didn't detect any scent from the drug, but merely touching the pipe was giving her a small euphoric rush up the back of her neck and down her spine and made her want to try it.

Don't do it, Rune thought at her. *Just trust me on this.* His eyes pleaded with her.

Her eyes flicked back to Mercurio.

Go on, thought Mercurio. *Just try a little bit.*

"Is it safe?" she asked Mercurio.

"Absolutely," he said, grinning. *I would never do anything to harm one of my employees.*

Nadia doubted that, but she had come this far already. She took a drag.

Her mind fractured. It felt like a diamond splitting into a million different pieces, light refracting off each glowing shard like drops of dew on a spider's web. Her mind expanded out like an explosion of the cosmos so that she was flung far and wide, no longer inside her body, time and space falling away so that she just *was*. It was incredible, like her entire existence was one continuous orgasm, reaching that peak and falling, falling, falling over the edge down and down, farther down than she'd ever been before. She reached a gate, a barrier. She thought about passing through it, but something stopped her. Rune's voice echoed around her, calling her back. And then everything snapped back like a rubber band, her mind fusing together, harder and sharper than before.

She opened her eyes after what could have only been a few seconds, coming back to, and gazed around the room. She felt euphoric. Her senses were heightened. Colors were brighter, lines crisper, her mind working faster and quicker than before like it had been rewired for efficiency. All the gunk and extra shit that had bogged her down before had been blown out. All eyes were on her. Mercurio looked delighted. Rune looked like he was going to murder Mercurio.

"What a marvelous reaction!" Mercurio clapped his hands together. "I've never seen someone get a grip on themselves so quickly. Usually, humans fracture and take hours to put back together the pieces—if they find themselves at all."

"What was that?" Nadia handed the pipe back to Mercurio. He took a drag and closed his eyes in bliss for a second. Nadia felt a pang of sadness at having to give up the pipe so quickly. She wanted to feel that euphoria again.

"Ambrosia vapor. Come. I will show you." He stood up and held out a hand to help her up. Nadia placed her hand in his and rose. Rune followed.

Mercurio led them outside the partitioned room to the balcony outside, which overlooked the nightclub's main floor. Nadia put her hand on the railing and peered down at the mass of writhing humans. Rune stood behind her, caging her in with his hands on the railing on either side of her body like he was trying to shield and protect her.

"Humans expend so much energy." Mercurio leaned in toward them. He had to speak loudly to be heard over the club music blasting through the room. "Look at them. It's just wasted into the air. Unless we capture it." He motioned toward the ceiling, where there hung a complex array of tubing and pipes connected to giant sacs that looked like pitcher plants. Nadia's mouth went dry. He continued, "Humans are fragile creatures. If they take too much, they die. A proper draining to leave a human with enough energy is an art form—a process that took years to master. I don't want a bunch of dead humans on my hands. Could you imagine the PR nightmare that would be! Instead, we just skim a bit off the surface. Take a bit from the collective. It's just there, rolling off them, ripe for the taking. All it takes is the proper way to capture it.

"Now *bottling* it, on the other hand, is much more difficult. The energy dissipates too quickly to store it for very long. That's why I need a constant supply of humans to keep up production. Hence the nightclub."

Realization dawned on Nadia. She fought the urge to throw up and shot Rune an angry look over her shoulder. Why hadn't he told her what Ambrosia was made of?

Mercurio looked earnestly at her. "Now, as a human, I'm sure you are questioning this procedure. But I will let you know that I'm doing a grand service to humanity. Capturing the energy in this way, no one dies. As I mentioned, we skim a bit off the top, and collectively, they are just a bit more tired than they thought they would be. Danced a bit too hard. Enjoyed themselves a bit too much."

Rune cut in. "You're manipulating people's emotions, stirring them up to feel things they wouldn't normally feel. You're brainwashing them, controlling them."

Mercurio laughed, his dark eyes sparkling, and ushered them back inside to where it was quieter. "My clients do enjoy certain 'flavors,' if you will. It is true that we seed certain emotions. Make humans feel a certain way to capture and distill unusual . . . vintages. Tonight, we are brewing a rather delicious air of lust and desire. But only those with a refined palate can appreciate the more subtle nuances of human emotion and how it affects their energy and flavor." Mercurio sniffed disdainfully at Rune. "If you understood my vision, you would appreciate the art and skill that goes into the proper balance of such flavors."

So, this was Mercurio's business. He used his nightclub to bring about certain emotions from humans and siphoned them from the air so that demons and other Dark Numinals could feed. Nadia glanced back at the Numinals in the VIP section. Most had grown bored with them and had gone back to their hedonistic pleasure and feeding, lounging on the pillows, taking hits from the hookah-like contraptions. Nadia supposed she should be happy they weren't draining humans directly, but it still left her with a horrible feeling that this whole thing was all very, very wrong. Mercurio treated humans like they were grapes ready to be crushed for winemaking.

Mercurio continued to proudly show off his production and facility. Whereas before the room looked like a VIP room in a nightclub to Nadia, she now noticed more details around the edges. It now looked more like a dispensary or an apothecary, with cabinets and drawers spaced around the perimeter of the room. Racks of strangely colored bottles and vials of liquid lined the shelves on the walls, with glass counters full of chocolates and other desserts tucked on the side of the lounge area, on display like colorful jewels.

Mercurio went behind a large glass counter and placed his hands on it like he was Willy Wonka at a candy store. "Care for an edible? Or maybe some sanguine? This is a particularly strong batch of O-negative." He swept his hand toward a spouted absinthe fountain on the counter filled with blood. "I know you won't try the *ousia*—that's a special, extremely potent form of Ambrosia," he added, for Nadia's benefit, "but I could mix up some fresh Ambrosia elixir if you are interested to take some with you. Come on, Christiansen. I know you're tempted."

Rune smiled tightly. "I'll pass, for now, thank you. As lovely and illuminating as this has all been, shall we get down to business?"

They moved back over to the seating area away from the strange vials and Ambrosia edibles. While Rune and Mercurio discussed a potential partnership, Nadia took this moment to open her mind and extend her psychic tendrils again. This time she mentally tip-toed toward Mercurio, careful, oh so careful, that he wouldn't know she was poking around. She slid her mind up to his, hugging into the curve and the shadows, and looked for an opening. She rubbed up gently, praying he wouldn't even notice.

Suddenly, her mind was seized, held fast in a vise. She froze, suffocating and choking. Her mind was in a complete state of shock as the grip tightened around it and pulled, cutting off all thought and ability to fight back. She felt herself moving, not of her own volition.

She was ripped from Rune's side as she fell toward Mercurio. The distance between them closed, a fish almost out of the water, and she fell into his embrace. He caught her, her breasts crushing against his inhumanly cold body, his arms clasped around her back where he held her up. Her mind reeled from the shock.

"What the fuck?" Rune yelled. It seemed far away, like a dream.

Little girl trying to play games with the big boys, Mercurio thought at her, his fangs extending, his eyes twinkling eagerly. *You thought I wouldn't notice you trying to read my mind. I don't take insubordination from my employees lightly. But you already know that. You want to be punished, don't you? Bad, bad girl.*

He licked her neck and found the pulsing vein beneath it. He shuddered as a wave of pleasure overtook him. He started feeding, absorbing her energy into his body through osmosis as it left her body through meridians up to where he had punctured her aura at her neck. He sipped her through his teeth like he was tasting wine, rolling it around on his tongue, licking and kissing her neck. She could feel him becoming stronger, vibrating at a higher frequency as her life essence ebbed out, and she started to feel worn and tired and drained. She tried to push away from him and wondered vaguely where Rune was. In the background, she could hear fighting and skirmishes and spells being shot off.

"Such a unique flavor," he murmured into her neck. "Thomas was right about you."

Nadia wondered why she was still alive. By now, she thought she should be dead, given the amount of energy he was draining from her. With a strange sense of detachment, she wondered if he was going to bite her. While demons generally just sucked off the life force from humans, Nadia had learned that vampires liked the taste of blood, biting their victims and drawing out the energy that way. It was messier, but it was more pleasurable. Mercurio's fangs grazed her neck, teasing her flesh. His erection pressed against her bare thigh.

Just do it already! she yelled at him in her mind. She wanted him to bite her, to get it over with. She was becoming irrational, her thoughts disordered as her imminent demise drew near, the walls caving in.

He fed and fed, gorging himself on her life force. She sensed him contemplating whether to bite her neck, trying to decide whether the mess of her blood was worth it on the floors so he could taste it. His fangs were on her neck, pressing down, so close to sliding into her skin.

Nadia couldn't help herself. She started laughing. His fangs punctured her neck, but he stopped, confused at her reaction.

Nadia knew she was supposed to scream. She was supposed to cower in fear, play the damsel in distress, be scared of the psychotic vampire threatening to kill her. But if the culmination of her entire existence was going to end right there, sucked dry at some human energy hookah lounge upstairs at a SoMa nightclub in the middle of a city crawling with strange creatures, she was going to go out laughing, dancing, shaking a goddamn tambourine. Her world had already been turned upside down. She didn't have anything else to lose. Her carefully planned life, goals, and dreams had already been destroyed.

"Why are you laughing?" Mercurio hissed.

That made her laugh even harder. Blood dripped down her neck from the puncture marks, and every time she laughed, more blood dribbled out. She knew she was dancing on her own grave.

He shook her and slapped her face. "Control yourself, woman! This instant!" This made her double down even more. He had loosened the hold on her mind in his confusion, and she took that opportunity to extricate herself. He backed away, looking at her like she was possessed.

Nadia stood and faced Mercurio, a trail of blood falling over her collarbone and chest. She looked at this vampire, this creature who had tried to drain her and had failed. Without even know-ing how she was doing it, she gathered all the energy around her, sucking it into her body. She thought about how angry she was at him, at Marina, at Keith, at her parents, at everyone, the anger and rage seething and growing and twisting inside her until she felt she couldn't hold it anymore. With a long violent scream, she expelled it all back out, the force blasting through the room like a bomb had gone off. Nadia closed her eyes, feeling the shockwaves radiating from her body.

When Nadia opened her eyes, she saw the destruction she had caused. It looked like a war zone. She stood in the middle of a blast ring, the marks scorched into the carpeting. Bits of fire and rubble littered the ground, furniture thrown haphazardly around, the air smoky. The other humans and Numinals in the room lay about dazed and wounded. Mercurio cowered behind an upturned chair, covering his head.

Rune grabbed her arm and yanked her toward the door. Nadia, stunned, allowed herself to be pulled along. Rune hustled Nadia out of the lounge area, down the stairs, and out through the club's back entrance to the street, practically carrying her to his car. The tires squealed as he peeled from the curb.

They were silent for several minutes before the gravity of the night hit her. She started shaking uncontrollably.

Rune looked over, concerned. "Shit," he mumbled. "Hey. Nadia." He caught her eyes. "Look at me. Breathe. You're okay. Everything is okay."

She took some deep breaths, calming herself, and stared at Rune as he counted "one, two, three, three, two, one." After a few minutes, she calmed down enough to stop shaking.

They rode in silence. Nadia watched the streets of San Francisco blur together as she tried to process what had just happened.

"Fuck!" shouted Rune as he punched the steering wheel. She flinched at his outburst but merely continued to stare out the window of the car, unable to control the tears that slid down her cheeks.

Nadia dug around in her purse for her house keys. Her hand grasped the key chain fob shaped like a four-leafed clover, and she pulled it out. She fumbled with the lock for a minute before she unlocked the door and pushed it open.

She waved to Rune, sitting in his car, waiting for her to get inside. Seeing that she was safe, he tore off from the curb. The taillights of the McLaren disappeared around the corner with a screech of tires.

Once inside, Nadia locked the front door and leaned back against it, closing her eyes. *What a night.* She had been in shock as they drove away from Mercurio's. She had moved through the rest of the evening in a daze. Rune had driven around for a bit, alternating between concern for Nadia and anger at himself.

He had taken her to a twenty-four-hour diner near Union Square, one of those retro ones with torn red leather booths and black-and-white checkered tile on the floor. He had ordered her a strawberry milkshake and had explained that the sugar would help stabilize her and replenish her energy. She hadn't been hungry at all, but he insisted she drink it, and as he sat across from her in one of the booths watching her intently, she slowly came out of shock and returned to her senses.

They hadn't talked about what happened, instead making idle chitchat about the few other people in the diner and the music in the tabletop jukebox. Rune had changed a twenty-dollar bill for quarters and placed the pile of change in front of her, letting her pick all the songs that played over the sound system in the mostly empty diner and gently teasing her for playing Justin Bieber and Drake. Nadia had been grateful for the distraction.

"There she is," said Marina, as Nadia entered the kitchen. Marina was standing at the stove, a spatula in hand. The smells of grilled cheese cooking on a skillet wafted toward Nadia. Avery was sitting on the counter, a half-eaten sandwich in hand. Next to him, Monday sat on the counter, chewing on a piece of cheddar.

"Hey," said Nadia.

"You're home late. Want a grilled cheese?"

"No thanks, I'm fine." Nadia got a cup from the cabinet and poured herself a glass of orange juice.

"You're all dressed up," said Marina. "Were you out with friends?"

Nadia took a sip of her juice. "No, Rune."

Marina and Avery shared a glance. Nadia now knew they were entangled.

"Oh? What happened with keeping your distance from him? I'm not sure I like all this time you've been spending with him."

"He's my boss, okay?" snapped Nadia. "I have to work late if he says so." Avery raised his eyebrows at her and took another bite of grilled cheese. Nadia knew he was wondering what kind of work involved little black dresses.

"Somebody's testy right now," commented Marina. She flipped the sandwich before pressing the spatula down on top of it. The sandwich sizzled in the pan.

"Sorry," said Nadia. "I'm just tired. We went to Mercurio's nightclub."

Marina and Avery looked at her sharply. "Oh?" asked Marina, trying to keep her voice light. "What for?"

"Rune and Mercurio were talking business."

"What kind of business does Rune have with Mercurio?" asked Avery.

"They were talking about a possible joint venture. I'm not sure about the details."

Avery narrowed his eyes at her. "Why would Rune take you?"

"To help out? I don't know."

Avery snorted. "This is why I don't work. No one respects work-life balance anymore. Especially around these parts."

"Are you sure you're okay?" asked Marina, eyeing her. "You seem a little peckish. Did you drink too much? I can whip up one of my anti-hangover cures. Fix you right up."

Nadia bit her lip and considered telling her what happened. But then she would have to put it all into words, and that would make the whole thing real. She much preferred to box it all up and shove it away, next to the other traumatizing things that kept happening to her.

She forced a smile. "I'll be fine. I think a good night's sleep will help. Night. I'll see you tomorrow."

"Don't let that boss of yours work you too hard," called out Marina as Nadia headed up the stairs. "It's all about creating healthy boundaries."

Chapter 25

At their next training session, Rune doubled down, working Nadia harder than ever. He was ruthless, throwing spell after spell at her to deflect while they fought with various martial arts weapons. It almost felt like he was punishing her for what happened with Mercurio. They hadn't talked about it, instead focusing on her training. Nadia was happy not to try to explain what had happened but was confused why he felt the need to drill her so hard.

Rune pushed her, but Nadia pushed back, determined not to let him break her. When they started working with bo staffs, Rune knocked her painfully onto her butt, sweeping her legs out from under her with the staff before he followed up with a magic strike, a hit like an air punch from his fist so that she had to quickly throw a shield up around herself to withstand the damage.

"Up!" he commanded as she lay on her back. He twirled the staff in his hands like a baton. He had barely broken a sweat.

Something inside Nadia broke open. With a primal scream, she leaped up from the mat and swung her stick at him. He caught the strike in his hand, moving with preternatural speed. Even after all their training, his reflexes still surprised her.

Rune yanked Nadia's staff toward him, and she flew into his torso. She felt like she had just run into a wall.

"Something wrong?" He looked down at her, his dark eyes hard. He was entirely too close to her. Barely controlled rage rolled off him in waves. Nadia scowled. She yanked the stick back and quickly stepped away from him.

"Why are you working me so hard? It's almost like you're trying to hurt me."

"If I were trying to hurt you, you would know," he said, his voice cold. "I am working you hard so that you won't be so vulnerable."

"Well, ease up. I need a break." Nadia threw her staff to the side and rubbed her sore shoulders, glaring at him.

"You'll get a break when I tell you that you get a break," Rune said in a low, dangerous voice.

She stared at him. He stared back. It was a battle of wills, and Nadia was too frustrated to win. She preferred a battle of words instead.

"Are we going to talk about what happened?" demanded Nadia.

"What exactly did happen, Ms. Winters?" Rune's tone was icy.

"I don't know!" Nadia exploded at him. "You never tell me anything! I have no idea what's happening to me! And why didn't you tell me what Ambrosia was? Why didn't you tell me Mercurio was skimming off humans to feed?!"

"I didn't want you to be worried about that when you were supposed to be using your Sixer senses to detect anything about the attacks. It would have preoccupied your mind, clouded your judgment. We all know you have issues with focus."

"Fine, but even when we were there, you could have said something! Why did you let me take a hit of that?"

A muscle in his neck pulsed. "I tried to stop you."

"You could have tried harder! I'm working off half-information here. How am I supposed to help if you don't tell me anything?"

Rune clenched his jaw. "So I'm supposed to tell you that all your nightmares are true? That there are Numinals out there who feed from humans? Fine. It's true. The world is a scary, horrible place full of monsters who prey on people. Believe me, Nadia, there are so many worse ways to die than by a Numinal feeding. You don't even know half the terrors that lurk around every corner of this city—this realm! Does knowing that make you happier? Are you content now with the truth that you hid from your entire, sheltered little life? Wake up, Nadia! Open your eyes and stop being a child."

"I don't have to put up with this bullshit!" Nadia threw up her hands in frustration and started to leave.

"Don't walk away from me."

Nadia paused at the dangerous tone in his voice. She gave him a look that said, *Just try and stop me*, and left.

Rune avoided Nadia for the next several days. That was fine. She was sore and in a pissy mood. Plus, she had more than enough to do without worrying about organized feeding zones in San Francisco for demons and vampires and other Dark Numinals. Several times she thought about telling Maya or Piero what had happened at Alchemy, but every time she tried, words failed her. She wasn't sure how to process what had happened there with Mercurio's feeding on her, and her apparent ability to somehow blast his lounge to bits. She felt like a walking freak show, unable to control her magic.

Nadia threw herself into work, continuing to help the Veil team investigate whether the app was related to the attacks while simultaneously trying to stay on track for the launch date. She tried to push thoughts of Rune from her mind, but she failed, her thoughts circling over their last encounter like she was working a sore tooth.

After the fifth day of Rune avoiding her, she couldn't take it any longer. Nadia cornered him in his office, shutting the door behind her as she entered. The walls were glass, and everyone could see them, but she was *going* to have this conversation.

"Ms. Winters," he said, coolly, looking up at her over his designer glasses as he sat in front of his computer.

"Why are you avoiding me?" Nadia marched over to his desk, pulled up a chair, and planted herself firmly in it.

His eyes narrowed. "I'm not avoiding you."

"You are. It's because of what happened at Alchemy. I didn't do anything wrong. I don't know how I did that, with the blast. And I didn't know that Mercurio would . . . do that."

"Do what, exactly? Possess your mind?"

She glared at him. "I don't know how he did that. One minute I was trying to get inside his, and the next, he was inside mine."

"You let him in," he accused.

"I did not. He attacked me. He wanted to feed from me the minute I got there. Even said I was 'tasty' and had a good . . . 'flavor.'" She shuddered.

Rune sucked in a breath. "Are you this much of a damn fool?" he yelled, standing up and placing his hands flat on his desk as he leaned toward her.

Nadia stood up as well, shocked at his outburst. "Apparently!" she yelled back. "Because I have no idea why you are so mad at me!"

She stared at Rune, hating him at that moment. Hating that he had this power over her to make her so angry. She balled up her fists, fighting the urge to lash out and punch him.

Rune stood up to his full height and looked down at her with a contemptuous look. "I don't like when people lie to me. How long have you been a Blood Muse, Ms. Winters?"

She blinked. "A what?"

"A Blood Muse. An unlimited source of energy. Sweet blood to demons."

She crossed her arms over her chest. "Still drawing a blank here, Christiansen." His jaw hardened at her using his last name.

"Are you really this ignorant?"

"Enlighten me, Oh Noble One."

"A Blood Muse is like catnip for Dark Numinals who feed from humans. They can't help themselves around you. There is some mechanism, some biological evolution that gives Blood Muses extra energy, pulling from the environment so that a feeding lasts longer. You are basically a smorgasbord, fun-feast, all-you-can-eat Dark Numinal buffet."

She paled. "What?"

He returned her gaze, a murderous expression on his face. "Exactly what I just said, Ms. Winters."

"You mean, I can't die if demons feed from me?"

"You can, but it will just take longer."

"And Mercurio realized that."

"If he didn't when he was feeding, he certainly did after you destroyed his VIP area. Unless he knew you were a Blood Muse all along and wouldn't die when he was feeding. But then, how would he know that? Is there something you aren't telling me?"

Nadia started laughing and dropped back to her seat. Rune looked at her much like Mercurio had at Alchemy. "What's gotten into you?"

She tried to contain her laughter. A snort escaped, which made her laugh even more. "It's just . . . my life. It's ridiculous."

"Others in your place would be grateful for their powers and ability." He took a seat back at his desk and watched her like he didn't know what she would do next.

She doubled over. Rune, telling her to be grateful that she was a demon buffet! That was like telling the Thanksgiving turkey to be thankful for pilgrims.

"If I were you," he said dryly, "I would think hard about my life. And be happy for that ability to protect myself."

Nadia shrieked with laughter. He looked at her like she was completely batty. Insane. Maybe she was.

And then, as suddenly as she started laughing, her laughter turned to tears.

Rune leaped up and pressed a button on the wall. The glass walls of his office turned opaque. Great big sobs wracked her body. She tried to stop, but the more she tried, the harder she cried. Rune slid a box of tissues toward her and watched her carefully as he sat back down. She took a tissue from the box and blew her nose loudly.

"Please stop crying," Rune begged. He pinched the bridge of his nose, his eyes closed, like he was in pain.

"I'm . . ." She sniffed loudly. "Trying!"

After a minute or two, Nadia got a grip on herself. She dried her eyes with a tissue and wiped away her smeared mascara as she took deep, calming breaths. She felt like a popped balloon, all sad and deflated. Her chin trembled, and she looked up to meet Rune's gaze. If he had suspicions that she couldn't control her emotions, she'd now confirmed them.

"Are you okay?" Rune's voice was strained. "I'm sure this is . . . a lot for you to take in. I . . . want to help you."

"Why? Why do you even care?" She sniffed loudly again and wiped her nose again with the crumpled tissue.

"I care about all my employees, Nadia," said Rune gently. "You are a great asset to this company." Nadia couldn't read the expression in his eyes. For a second he had seemed sympathetic, but now he was walled off again. Cold.

So that was it, eh? She was an "asset." Well, that was fine with her. At least she finally knew. She was an asset to him, just like she was an asset to Mercurio. She was just a pawn they were both using.

Nadia took a second to compose herself, smoothing down her hair and straightening her blouse, wiping away any remaining smears of makeup from her cheeks.

"I apologize for my outburst. It won't happen again."

Rune followed her to the door of his office. "Nadia, listen . . ." She stopped. He was close behind her. She could feel his breath on the back of her neck, the warmth of his body so near to hers. "I'm sorry for putting you in danger. I miscalculated. It was an error on my part. I should have never let you come with me."

Nadia stiffened. Part of her wanted to lean back into his body.

The other part of her wanted to show him that she didn't need his pity. She was a survivor. She would survive Mercurio, and she would survive being a Blood Muse. She wasn't sure why Rune had such an emotional reaction to it, but whatever it was, she didn't need his help or his confusing mood swings.

Rune cleared his voice and took a step back. Nadia pulled her shoulders back, opened his door, and walked out into the hall.

There was a hush over the main floor. Nadia looked down over the hallway balcony railing at everyone's upturned faces.

"Get back to work!" Rune yelled out to the onlookers before he slammed the door to his office. Nadia cringed. Plastering a look of calm poise on her face—her glamour—she headed down to the vaults to look up what in the hell it meant to be a Blood Muse and if she could get rid of it as well.

Chapter 26

The bell above the door to the corner liquor store near Marina's house jangled as Nadia pushed the door open. She smiled in greeting to the cashier, Mehmet. He greeted her back, raising a hand. Nadia made her way to the back through the narrow aisles full of canned food and snacks, toilet paper, cleaning supplies, and cat food, to the wine selection, and browsed the rows of bottles for a label that looked like it was expensive enough that she wouldn't wake up with a sulfite hangover the next morning.

Nadia had learned that lesson the hard way after trying to be frugal and drinking a few too many bottles of Two Buck Chuck the previous week.

While Nadia had drunk socially in college and with coworkers, the stress of Mercurio and the Blood Oath on top of starting a new job at Myst had made her drink regularly. She found herself polishing off a bottle of wine—sometimes more—all by herself several times a week after she learned that wine hangovers weren't nearly as bad as vodka hangovers.

After she found an Australian red blend, she grabbed the bottle and started to walk to the front. On impulse, she grabbed a second bottle, just in case. Tonight, she didn't want to think and she didn't want to feel.

She grabbed packets of Funyuns and Haribo gummy bears from the snack display at the front of the store and placed everything on the counter as she dug out her wallet and reusable grocery bag from her tote.

"Rough day?" Mehmet asked in his husky Turkish accent as he rang up the purchases.

Nadia sighed. "Lately, every day is a rough day."

Mehmet packed up her snacks and wine after she paid and slid her purchases in her reusable bag toward her. "Cheer up, princess. I'm sure things will get better. At least it's Friday."

"Thanks." She grabbed the bag and tucked it under her arm. "See you."

Outside, the late summer sun was low on the horizon, casting a warm golden glow on the trees and sidewalk. Nadia made her way down the residential street lined with old Victorians, watching people return to their homes for the evening. Several people were out walking their dogs.

Nadia turned onto Marina's street, eager to get home and crack open a bottle of wine and kick back with some TV to numb her existence.

"Quite the display of power the other day at Alchemy," said Thomas, as he appeared to her right. Nadia stifled a scream, juggling her bag so she wouldn't drop it.

"Fuck! You are *so* lucky I don't carry pepper spray!" she hissed as she stopped to catch her breath and still her heart.

He chuckled and pulled on the lapels of his leather jacket. "I'm immune."

She shifted the bag to her other arm. "Well, stop doing that. You're giving me a nervous condition."

"Duly noted."

"Leave me alone, Thomas," said Nadia as she pushed past him. The boundaries of the wards around Marina's house shimmered in the distance, and Nadia picked up the pace. Thomas couldn't follow her inside once she crossed the boundary lines.

Thomas caught up to her and easily paced her. "I'm merely

escorting you home to make sure you get there safe. These are dangerous times, you know."

"Yeah, because of demons like *you* attacking everyone in the city."

He tsked. "You know I am nothing like those low-caste demons. I have restraint after all. I haven't bitten or fed from you, have I?"

Nadia scoffed. "But I'm sure you've been known to imbibe some Ambrosia now and again."

"As do most, my dear. Think of it as harm reduction for Numinals, like methadone to the heroin addict. With Mercurio's methods, no one has to die. It seemed like you quite enjoyed it when you tried it."

Nadia crossed the boundary lines to the wards and turned to face him. She shifted the bag of groceries to her other arm and pointed at him. "You're really starting to piss me off. I had a life before all this happened. You royally fucked me over."

He threw his head back and laughed. "Oh, I'm sure by the end of this, you will thoroughly loathe me. I look forward to it."

"Fuck you," muttered Nadia. She turned to walk up the path to the front steps.

"One more thing," Thomas called after her.

"*What?*" she asked impatiently.

"Mercurio is very upset with your insubordination. That little mind trick you tried to pull on him didn't go over well, and he isn't too keen on having to redecorate after your . . . tantrum."

Her pulse quickened. "I didn't mean to. Tell him I'm sorry. I lost control." She didn't want to grovel, but hell if she was going to piss him off. He knew she was a Blood Muse. He might want to feed from her again as punishment.

A slow smile crept up Thomas's face. "Don't worry. I covered for you. I told him that the explosion was an . . . accident—you are a Blood Muse learning about her powers, after all—and that the whole thing was Rune's fault and that you would never, *ever* dream of trying to invade his privacy by reading his mind like that again."

Nadia walked back toward the boundaries. "Why would you do that for me?"

"I told you, Nadia. I'm on your side here. I just wish you would trust me." He took a step back away from the wards. "Until next time," he said and then disappeared into thin air.

Nadia was in a foul mood by the time she pushed open the front door to Marina's house and deadbolted it after herself. She stomped through the house, slamming doors and cabinets as Monday followed her around, flicking her tail back and forth. It was almost like the cat was watching her, making sure she didn't break anything. She wasn't sure she wouldn't. She felt like grabbing all the glasses in the cabinet and throwing them on the floor. She wanted to destroy things the same way her life had been destroyed. The anger felt good. Pure. She'd been pretending everything was fine for way too long.

Marina and Avery were playing dominos in the living room when Nadia flopped down on the couch with her bottle of wine. She drank a long gulp straight from the bottle. Avery shot Marina a look but said nothing, merely returning to the game. He placed snake eyes down on the board.

"I don't understand how you can play games when the whole world is going to shit around you," Nadia huffed. She took another long swig from the wine bottle and considered going for something harder. She wanted to get drunk, fast.

Avery snorted, shaking his head. "Haven't you heard of escapism? When the state of the world is shit, is exactly when you should be playing games."

Marina rummaged through her domino tiles and placed one on the board. "How was work?"

"Shitty. And to make matters worse, Thomas paid me another

surprise appearance. He likes to pop up out of nowhere and scare me, just for the hell of it."

Marina glanced up at her. "That does sound like something he would do, unfortunately."

"That's it? That's all you're going to say? My demon babysitter stalks me and likes to jump out of nowhere, and all you can say is that it sounds like him?" This was too much. Nadia got up in a huff. "Maybe none of this would be happening to me if you weren't so chickenshit to stand up for yourself and figure out a way to break the Oath. I'm going to my room."

"You shouldn't speak to your grandmother like that!" Avery called out after her.

"It's fine, let her go," Nadia heard Marina say as she ran up the stairs, wine bottle clenched in her fist.

Nadia slammed the door to her room, not caring that she was acting like a childish brat. She drank. She flopped down on the bed, face first, and burrowed her head under mounds of pillows. She was tired of plastering on a smile and pretending everything was okay. Things were not okay. She was tired of spying for Mercurio and lying to Rune and her friends at Myst. She was tired of having to glance over her shoulder in case Thomas decided to pop up unexpectedly. And now this whole business of being a Blood Muse. She missed her old life and her friends. She missed having a plan and a future that didn't involve being tied to some psychopath vampire and demon handler for the rest of her life.

Nadia was in the midst of a full-blown, alcohol-fueled, tantrum pity party by the time she heard footsteps on the staircase. With each step, the old wood creaked and groaned.

"Go away," Nadia mumbled into the pillow. She felt the weight of the bed shift as Marina sat on the edge. Marina put a timid hand on Nadia's back and patted her a couple of times.

"I'm not very good at this whole grandmother thing, but I'm here to listen. What happened with Thomas?"

Nadia turned over, removing the pillow from over her head, and clutched it to her chest. Hot tears slid down her cheeks.

"Thomas is such an asshole. Apparently, I'm a Blood Muse—"

"You're a *what*?" exclaimed Marina.

"A Blood Muse."

Marina looked like the wind had been knocked out of her. She opened her mouth and then closed it again, like she was unsure of what to say.

"Well, then," she said finally. "Out of all the things I thought might be wrong, that wasn't one of them."

Nadia put the pillow over her face, fighting the urge to scream.

"Uh—how do you know you are a Blood Muse?"

Nadia removed the pillow. "Remember when I went with Rune to that business meeting with Mercurio, like an idiot? Well, I pissed him off by trying to read his mind, and he started feeding from me. And then I lost control and exploded the fuck out of the place. It wasn't pretty. I didn't tell you when it happened. I guess I was still processing."

Marina's eyes went wide. "Well, that is . . . something." Indeed, she was *not* good at this whole grandmother thing. Nadia wished she had a normal, nice grandmother that baked cookies and spoiled her and always knew the right thing to say.

"I don't want some lecture on needing to practice my mental shields. I get it. You warned me what would happen if a Numinal seized control of my mind, and I didn't listen. Spare me the lecture."

Marina looked hurt. "I'm not going to lecture you. Lord knows we're all doing the best we can here."

"Well, apparently, it's not good enough! What am I supposed to do? Now Mercurio knows I'm a Blood Muse, and he's going to want to feed from me every chance he gets!"

Marina sighed. "I'm not sure that's quite the case, but I understand how upset you are right now."

"How do you know what I'm feeling? You have no idea what

I've been going through these past weeks!" Mostly because Nadia hadn't let anyone know she was struggling, but that was beside the point.

Marina looked out the window and took a deep breath. "You know, I never told anyone this, not even Avery . . . but I tried to take my own life when the Blood Oath passed to me."

That got her attention. She hadn't considered ever doing that, but she could imagine how it could get there with the rate things were deteriorating. She had gone from happy and optimistic about her future to feeling completely trapped by her circumstances and powerless to change them. Nadia wiped away her tears with the back of her hand and listened.

"My mother had just died," Marina continued, "and while I knew about our family's powers my entire life, I wasn't ready for the responsibility of being at Mercurio's beck and call. I didn't want to hurt people, and I didn't want to hurt. I thought if I were dead, then the world would be a better place."

"What happened?"

"Well, I botched it up, is what happened. I had tried to slit my wrists, but the demon Alastor—this was before Thomas started working for Mercurio—found me and healed me. I was so angry! I thought it was my right to take my own life, but Mercurio and Alastor didn't see it that way. Alastor told me I had a choice and could try again, but taking my life was the easy way out. It took me a couple of years to realize what he meant."

Nadia sat up a bit. "What did you do after he healed you?"

"Well, I decided that even if I didn't completely have my freedom, no one did. People all around me were selling their souls in other ways: going to jobs that were slowly killing them, staying in relationships that were bad for them. I started looking at Mercurio's tasks as a job. A shitty, horrible job that I hated, but one that allowed me a lot of freedom in other ways. Sure, I have to do things I don't want to do, but I justify it by telling myself that a lot of people do things they don't want to do."

"But you have to hurt people." That was one thing Nadia just didn't want to do. She could be self-destructive and hurt herself, but she rationalized that at least she wasn't lashing out at others and harming them.

Marina sighed and shifted her weight on the bed. "True. But one thing I have learned is that most Numinals are notoriously fair. There are very few irrational situations. There is balance. The universe sees to it. People don't get hurt for no reason."

"People get hurt for no reason all the time!" Car accidents, cancer, slip-and-falls . . . hell, Nadia had even had a friend from college that got struck by a bus while she was sitting at the bus stop after the driver had fallen asleep at the wheel.

"But not by the hand of Numinals," countered Marina. "Most believe in karma. What you put out can come back to you threefold, sort of like a game of Russian roulette. Sometimes you get a free pass, and sometimes you lose. I learned that the hard way."

Nadia looked at her questioningly. "What do you mean?"

Marina looked sad for a moment, like she was remembering something painful. "I've made mistakes in my life, Nadia, that I had to pay for dearly. I'll tell you about them someday." Nadia wondered if they had to do with her grandfather. Marina kept a bit of a memorial to him in the living room but rarely talked about him.

"What happens if Mercurio wants you to do something you don't want to do? Do you still have to do it?"

Marina nodded. "Unfortunately. The Blood Oath, if broken, reverts as if it had never been made. It would unravel everything, and the laws of the universe don't let that happen. I couldn't disobey even if I tried. But I don't think I've ever done anything too horrible. And if I did, I know in my heart that the human or Numinal deserved it, and I was just helping to deliver justice and karmic retribution."

Nadia sat up and leaned against the headboard, still clutching the pillow. "That sounds like you're just rationalizing what you have to do." Nadia had learned that she was good at justifying her actions and behavior. It was a self-preservation trick she'd learned at a young age by watching her parents. They were always right, and others were always wrong.

Marina shrugged. "There's more than one way to skin a cat."

Nadia fiddled with a lock of her hair, picking at a split end. She was still worried. "So what happens when the Oath passes to me?"

"Well, I'll be dead, so it won't matter to me."

"Marina!"

She chuckled. "I'm kidding. But seriously, it won't be so bad. I don't know what it's like to be a Blood Muse, but you'll learn to manage Thomas and deal with the Oath. Thomas works for Mercurio for now, but he could easily fall out of favor like Alastor did many years ago."

"Oh good. A new demon to contend with," Nadia grumbled.

"Better the devil you know . . ."

"Yeah, yeah. I've heard that one before."

Marina patted her knee. "I know you're having a rough time getting used to the idea, but I promise you, everything will turn out okay. It always does. I'm grateful for the Blood Oath, in a way."

Nadia looked at her skeptically. "How can you even say that?" Nadia was grateful for a lot of things, but this whole mess was not one of them.

"It's true!" Marina plucked idly at a rogue down feather sticking up through the comforter. She looked thoughtful. "I wouldn't be who I am without the Oath. Our powers are tied to it. Our history, our heritage all stem from it. If our ancestor Maria hadn't made the Blood Oath with Mercurio, we wouldn't be here. She would have died, and we would have never been born. Our powers—our

Sixer and Septer abilities—are a core part of who we are as people. Taking that away would be like taking a piece of your soul away." Marina stood up. "I am grateful for my life. I just hope you learn to be grateful for yours, as well. We'll figure out how to manage you being a Blood Muse, okay? The women in our family have found a way to survive this long, and we will find a way to survive this as well. Let me talk to Thomas. I'll get him to give you a break."

"Thanks," said Nadia. "Oh, one more thing. I want to start paying rent." Marina started to protest, but Nadia cut her off. "I know you said I could stay here for free and all, but I insist. I want to take responsibility and not burden you. I have the money now."

"You aren't a burden," said Marina. "And I won't accept your money."

"But—"

Marina held up a hand. "Letting you live here is the least I can do. I want you to have that as a way for me to make it up to you for everything I did. Save your money for something. Spend it. Donate it to a worthy cause. I don't care. But I won't accept it. Got it?"

Nadia nodded. "Got it."

As Marina left her bedroom, Nadia lay back down, buried her head under a pillow, and thought about what her grandmother had said. She doubted very much that Mercurio believed in karma, let alone anything but himself. She didn't want to just accept her fate and learn to deal with it, but she was just so . . . tired. It was exhausting trying to fight. It was exhausting trying to position herself and get out of this mess. Nadia felt her resolve to break the Blood Oath chipping away.

Nadia succumbed to self-pity for a bit until it turned tedious. She sat back up and looked about her room where at least she was safe and secure. With a sigh, she picked up a book she had checked out of the vaults on Arabic magic and started reading.

*　　*　　*

As Nadia crossed the wards' shimmering boundary to Marina's house the next morning to go out for coffee, Thomas appeared on the sidewalk, a bouquet of red roses in his hands. He looked contrite.

Nadia stopped and turned to him. "What do you want?"

He held out the roses in apology as he stepped forward. "Marina let me know what a pain I've been to you. I feel awful. Forgive me?"

Nadia took the flowers from him. They were beautiful, but she wasn't ready to be all buddy-buddy with him. She marched over to a nearby dumpster and threw them inside. When she turned around, he had a new, even bigger bouquet in his arms. He smirked. "How about now? Do you forgive me now?"

"No. Get out of my face." Nadia pushed past him, trying to get away.

As she kept walking toward the coffee shop down the street, Thomas popped up again next to her. "How about now?"

Suddenly, every tree on the street exploded in cherry blossoms. Pink, red, and white flowers dripped from the heavy branches, the blooms erupting with a heady fragrance that almost knocked Nadia off her feet. A soft wind blew through the trees, blossoms falling around her like snowflakes. Nadia reached out a hand, but the flower passed through it. It wasn't real. It was just an illusion. She couldn't help but smile, thinking about how the magic that Rune had shown her was real.

Thomas saw her grinning, and she quickly turned it into a scowl, huffing. "Ugh, fine! I forgive you. Now go away."

"I have a favor to ask."

"Whatever it is, no." She started walking again, her steps passing through mounds of blossoms.

"Listen, Nadia. I'm here to help you. If you play nice and cooperate, Mercurio will mostly ignore you. But if you refuse, he will take it as a personal affront and take it out on you. He'll break you down into a mindless slave. Don't let that happen. I'm rather fond of that mind of yours." Nadia stopped for a moment, and Thomas reached up and touched her cheek gently. He smiled sadly. "You remind me so much of her . . . ." He seemed to catch himself, straightening. "I'm just trying to keep you alive."

"I don't need your help." Nadia continued walking down the street. Thomas paced her.

"Oh, but I think you do. You're now on Mercurio's radar. He knows you're a Blood Muse. That makes you extra interesting to him. I've been shielding you, protecting you. You should thank me."

Nadia stopped short. "Did you know I was a Blood Muse when you first were testing my powers back in DC?"

Thomas grinned. "I had my suspicions. Mercurio didn't believe it. That's why he made you try Ambrosia. To test if it was true or not. He fed from you to confirm."

"Are you fucking kidding me?" Nadia exploded. "You set me up to be a snack!"

Thomas's mouth was a hard line. "There is more to being a Blood Muse than being a snack, Nadia. That's a little bit overly simplistic, don't you think? Blood Muses are highly prized and honored in the Numinal community. It used to be that only Numinal Kings and Queens were allowed to own Blood Muses. It is said that the Dark King himself had an entire harem full of Blood Muses."

"What if I hadn't been a Blood Muse? He would have killed me!"

"I would have stopped him."

Nadia turned on her heel and walked fast to try to get away. "Unbelievable," she muttered.

Thomas paced her. "About that favor—"

"No more fucking favors," she snapped. "Let's just call a spade a spade. What do you want?"

Thomas grinned. "That's the fire I like to see. Mercurio needs a certain spell from the vaults."

Nadia stopped. "What?"

"Rune has a rare text in the vaults that contains a spell called the Wolf and the Ram."

Nadia crossed her arms. "The Wolf and the Ram? That sounds like a hipster clothing company."

"Ah, Nadia, you do always find the humor in things. Yes, the spell does have an unusual name, so it should be easy for you to find it. Mercurio is upset with your attempts at insubordination. Getting this spell for him is a way to prove your loyalty."

"I'm not a fucking thief!"

Thomas grinned. "Think of it as borrowing. Just snap a picture and send it to me. That's all. Half the material Rune has in the vaults is open source or available from a Creative Commons license, anyway."

Nadia glowered at him. "What does the spell do? Why does he want it?"

Thomas waved a dismissive hand. "Something to do with amplifying energy. I'm not sure of the details."

She closed her eyes for a moment, feeling more of her resolve to escape her fate being chipped away.

"I don't want to do this," Nadia protested feebly as she opened her eyes.

"I know. But you have to. Or else." And with that, Thomas disappeared, leaving Nadia standing alone under a canopy of blossoms—all of them illusions.

Later that day, Nadia changed into workout clothes and headed out for a run to clear her head. After she crossed the wards around Marina's house, she synced the Psionic to her AirPods and put on a playlist of high-energy workout tunes from Spotify. She paused for a minute to stretch and then headed north up Castro Street, jogging through The Castro and Lower Haight, continuing on Divisadero Street up to Pacific Heights, Cow Hollow, and the Marina. With each step, she pushed herself harder, running faster, trying to focus and push away all thoughts other than her breathing and the rush of her heartbeat in her ears. The pain transitioned into euphoria, and she lost herself in the rhythm and the sound of her sneakers pounding the pavement, in tune with the music.

When she finally became aware of her surroundings again, Nadia found herself close to the water on Marina Boulevard. She stopped for a minute to catch her breath while she looked out over the bay. Since it was the weekend, people surrounded her, out walking their dogs or playing in the grassy park near the water. Mothers pushed strollers and sipped coffees while couples strolled hand-in-hand in the afternoon sunshine that had burned off the morning fog. In the distance, the Golden Gate Bridge twinkled in the sunlight.

Nadia found a wooden bench that overlooked the bay and took a seat. She pulled out her AirPods so she could immerse herself in the sounds of the seagulls and the ocean and sat for a bit while she watched the little white sailboats and ferries that peppered the surface of the shimmering water. A few carefree, puffy white clouds hung low over the blue sea, the pretty little scene unfolding like a real-life Thomas Kinkade painting, and Nadia thought about all the things that had happened since that fateful night on her birthday when everything in her life had changed.

She was tired. She was tired of fighting, of struggling, of trying to get everything to go back to normal. It had taken these last weeks to solidify her thinking and how she felt about the Blood Oath, her growing powers, and spying for Mercurio at Myst, but she was ready to accept her fate. She had put up a good fight, tried to regain control of the reins of her destiny, but she had lost. She would do Mercurio's bidding and fulfill the Oath as the women in her family had done before her and would continue to do so long after she was gone.

Nadia felt a strange sense of relief, a splash of cool water on a self-inflicted burn as she slowly accepted her fate. Before, her life could have gone so many different ways. It had been overwhelming trying to position herself, leverage herself to reach for more, always struggling to do better. She had spent the better part of her life striving for constant improvement. It had been exhausting always feeling like she was failing, feeling like an imposter who wasn't supposed to be there, never feeling smart enough or pretty enough or thin enough. She had grown up measuring herself against impossible, Instagram- and Pinterest-perfect standards drilled into her from her school, her parents, and her peers, and she had found herself sorely lacking.

But now, she could stop struggling. It wasn't her fault that her life ended up like this. It was like Marina had said: there were powers greater than her out there in the universe, and instead of fighting the oncoming tsunami, she was learning to ride the waves. Now, Nadia could blame the Blood Oath for the fact her life didn't end up as planned. It wasn't her fault. She did everything right. She did the best she could. But ultimately, she never even had a fighting chance. And that was okay. The odds had always been stacked against her. There was only one way her life could have ever ended up. She now understood that.

Nadia's cell phone pinged, and she dug it out from the zippered side pocket in her workout shorts and checked the text. It was from Zoey.

Hey stranger, long time no talk! Is it true how they say West Coast is the Best Coast??? Btw ran into Keith and he totally highlighted his hair. He looks like a tool. U dodged a bullet w that one. Miss u!

Nadia put away her cell phone without responding to the text and looked back over the water. She took a moment of pause.

She could continue pretending that her life was going great, text Zoey a selfie with the Golden Gate Bridge and the shimmering water in the background . . . but ultimately, what was the point? It would all be a lie. A shiny, pretty lie that she would use to cover up her inexplicable and insane life. She felt alienated from her old friends, unable to share anything about Numinals and magic with them. She had stopped returning her mother's phone calls, tired of lying to her and covering up everything that had been going on in the last weeks. She had even stopped checking social media, the sting of reminders of her old life too strong every time she saw her friends out at the bars and restaurants she used to go to, their smiling faces pressed cheek to cheek in selfies that she once had been in. The things that had once preoccupied her—buying the latest fashion or getting the kickass job or trying to get Keith to take it to the next level—seemed so trivial in comparison to her problems now. And compared with the rest of the world, she had it pretty good. Nadia felt guilty even complaining when so many others had it so much worse.

She had accepted her fate with the Blood Oath. Now it was time to accept that this was her new life, a life based in the city of San Francisco and filled with magic and Myst and new Numinal friends. She would do Mercurio's bidding, steal the spell he wanted, keep working on growing her powers, and hope that Rune never learned of her betrayal. She would lean into the discomfort of spying, play the hand that she had been dealt, and figure out how to try to be happy with her lot in life. And really, she wanted this life. She loved Myst. She loved magic. She just didn't love not having a choice in it all.

Nadia stood up, put her AirPods back in, and continued walking along the coast, approaching the harbor filled with sailboats and yachts. All around her, people jogged along the water, walked their dogs, or played in the grass with their kids, and she found solace in this little bubble of normalcy, surrounded by people who had no idea about Blood Oaths or demon attacks. Tomorrow, she would go back to Myst and deal with Thomas and the spell Mercurio wanted, but today, this time was hers.

A movement caught her eye as she walked along the harbor. She glanced at one of the boats, where someone was waving at her and yelling. She slowed to a stop, taking out her AirPods, and peered down about ten feet to the pier to see who was calling to her.

It was Miles Kirkpatrick.

"Nadia! I thought that was you." He grinned up at her, looking ever the East Coast native with his seersucker shorts, polo shirt, and Warby Parker sunglasses. She couldn't help but grin back.

"Hi! What are you doing?" she called down.

He waved a hand around himself at the boat. "I was about to take her out for a bit. Would you care to join me?"

Nadia glanced down at her jogging shorts and sports bra, still soaked with sweat. "I'm out for a run. Maybe another time?"

He pushed a lock of his golden curls back. "It's such a glorious day out. Are you sure I can't convince you to come with me?" He flashed a dazzling white smile. "Plus, a boating trip is always better with a beautiful woman aboard."

Nadia wavered, biting her lip.

Miles saw her hesitation and pounced on it. "Don't make me beg," he said as he shot her another smile.

Nadia was tempted. A day out sailing on the bay did sound wonderful. She imagined the wind in her hair, the smell of salt-water spray, and the crisp taste of champagne, which she was sure Miles had on board.

But something held her back. Thoughts of Rune popped into her mind. He would go ballistic if he found out she went sailing with Miles. Part of her was tempted to do it anyway. He didn't own her. But the other part of her didn't want to hurt him.

She shook her head. "I really can't today. Thanks, though."

He looked like he wanted to ask again, but instead, he merely waved. "I'll take that raincheck then."

Nadia waved back and carried on her way, thinking about Miles as he sailed away in his boat. She really should work on networking more within the startup community. Mercurio wanted her to spy for him at Myst, but if anything ever happened and Rune found out and fired her, perhaps working at Pact was an option.

If this was her life now, she was determined to make the best of it.

Chapter 27

The next day, Nadia arrived at Myst with a large pink box full of donuts. After she gave a donut to Arne, who grunted in thanks and then held the door open for her, she made her way through the first floor, passing out donuts to everyone who wanted one.

"Someone's feeling generous today," commented Piero as he took a rainbow-sprinkled one.

Nadia shrugged. "I wanted a donut this morning and thought, why not?" Since Marina had refused to let her pay rent, she felt the need to pay it forward somehow. Donuts were the least she could do.

"That's the kind of attitude I like to see." Piero took a bite of the donut, and his eyes rolled back in his head. "By the Light, that's good."

"I'll be in the vaults if you need me."

Piero nodded and took the box from her. "I'll just hold on to these for you then."

Nadia made her way to the back of the room to the elevators and swiped her key card to gain access. The doors silently opened, and she entered and pushed the button for the vault level. The subterranean room was dark when the elevator doors opened, but the ceiling lights turned on after detecting her walking through, her footsteps echoing in the chamber. The shiny door to Vault One was locked. Nadia placed her palm on the biometrics reader to the side of the door. With a hiss, the heavy door swung open, revealing the library and vaults inside the room.

Nadia made her way to the back of the library, down the tiled floors, and past the rows and rows of antique books and equipment. She slung her bag over the back of a wooden chair after pulling out her laptop, and she sat down as she booted it up. She pulled up Myst Foundation's search page and started to type in the Wolf and the Ram before she stopped herself. She chewed on the bottom of her lip, watching the cursor blink in the search bar before she pressed the delete key several times to erase her search terms.

If Rune or anyone else ran a report of what she's been searching for, they would immediately know that she'd been looking for that spell. She couldn't take the chance that they would figure out her connection to Mercurio and that she stole the spell for him. She stood up and looked over to the library stacks.

She would have to find the information a different way.

With magic.

Rune had been using Nadia's Sixer sense to try to find information and a potential link between Veil and the attacks. She could try to use her psychometry skills here to sense the books in the room to find the one with the spell she needed. It was a stretch, but it was the only plan she had.

She walked to the center of the room, the rows of books on either side of her, and closed her eyes. She cracked her neck and shifted from foot to foot as she settled into her body, taking several deep breaths. She stilled her mind, emptying it of chatter and noise, and opened it up to scan like a satellite dish like she had at Alchemy. But unlike her experience at Alchemy, there were no other minds here clouded by drugs or walled off from her prying. There were only inanimate objects that she could sense things about by mentally touching them with her Sixer abilities. Shifting into discovery mode, she sent out physic tendrils, creating a mental blueprint of the room. She sensed the stacks of books, the various globes and antiques scattered around the library, the banister that ringed the second floor, and the high, vaulted ceiling with the baroque paintings on it. She crafted a mental image in her mind, turning it around like the outline of a 3D image in digital modeling software. And then she started scanning each of the books, quickly sensing the information contained within them. She felt a rush of power and dark energy, the tang of magic surrounding her like she was inside a thunderstorm cloud.

Her eyes snapped open. Left quadrant of the library.

Nadia rushed over to one of the rows of stacks of books. Holding out her hand toward the leather-bound volumes, she moved quickly down the row, trying to sense the book like she was a dousing rod trying to sense water. She almost passed over the tome, but no. The book pulsed energy, practically screaming *Read me! Read me!*

She pulled the heavy book from the shelves, dusted it off with a brush of her hand, and sneezed. It had been a long time since someone had pulled this book from the stacks.

Back at the wooden table, she glanced furtively over her shoulder, but there was no one else there. She carefully opened the ancient text, marveling at how well it was preserved. The book had to be over five hundred years old, at least.

Nadia paged through the heavy book, her eyes skimming the gold embossing and colored images next to various spells. After a bit, she found the spell she was looking for. She quickly snapped a picture and shot off the image to Thomas before she could second guess herself.

The dirty deed done, she relaxed and turned back to the spell.

The page in the book was blank.

She blinked, hoping that her eyes were deceiving her. Then she opened up her photos to look at the image she had just sent Thomas. The image was blank as well.

She quickly shot off a text. Did u get the image? Page is blank now.

He responded. The spell only exists with one copy at a time. Thanks, kid. You did good.

"Mother-fucking Thomas," Nadia muttered under her breath. She hoped Rune wouldn't notice the missing spell. She glanced back at the book. On the page opposite the spell, the introductory material was still there. It was an old spell, layers of magic from ancient Latin, Arabic, and Greek twisted together. She read the purpose:

Spell is used to break protective seals.

Nadia's heart rate spiked. The Myst Psionic pinged, but she barely registered the sound. She sat back in her chair, her head spinning. What had she just done? This was so, so much worse than she had originally thought. She didn't want to even think it. No, she couldn't. But she forced herself to: She had just given Mercurio the keys to breaking into Myst.

What had she been thinking all these months? She thought she had been walking a fine line, not crossing it, trying to feed Mercurio bits of information and misinformation like she could outwit a centuries-old vampire. This guy knew the tricks. This wasn't his first rodeo. And she had played right into his hand, giving him the keys to the castle. She had accepted her fate to work for him, but that hadn't meant she wanted to destroy Myst and everything her friends had worked for.

She had to tell Rune. The entire company was at risk! Myst was vulnerable, exposed, wide open. But then horror at the conversation she would have to have took over. He would hate her, she was sure of it. She had to tell him, but right then, there was nothing in the world she dreaded more. He would fire her instantly. She knew that much. But would he call the police? Have her locked up for corporate theft? Was there some sort of Numinal or witch prison? She didn't even know what kind of infrastructure Numinals had. She knew she had broken a bunch of human laws. But Numinal laws? She could only imagine.

She was so stupid! She wasn't this person. She wasn't one to sneak around in shadows, stealing secrets and ancient spells from the one place that she was finally calling home. She had fucked up royally, and there was only one way to make it right.

She stood up to collect her things, resolved to do the right thing. She had done the deed, and she would pay the price. She had that much honor, at least, to fess up to her crimes. She just hoped Rune would be lenient on her. Around Myst, he was the judge, jury, and executioner.

Nadia quickly reshelved the book into the stacks and packed up her bag. She started heading out to find Rune when the library was plunged into darkness.

Red track lights on the library floor turned on, giving the library and vault a strange, eerie reddish glow. Nadia sensed movement at the front of the room and realized too late that the heavy vault door was closing.

She dropped her bag and sprinted down the marble floor toward the front of the library, slipping on the floor like a deer on ice, but she caught her balance and kept running. "No, no, no, no, no!" she screamed as she ran into the door, the opening to get out too small for her to squeeze through. The door clicked into place. Nadia was suddenly glad she had slipped on the marble. If she had been half a second quicker, she would have gone for the opening, and the door probably wouldn't have stopped. She pushed that ghastly thought away and leaned back on the door, closing her eyes.

Rune? Nadia thought. *Can you hear me? What's going on?*

Something tripped the wards.

Clearly. I'm standing in the dark.

Where are you?

Library. The vault door shut before I could get out.

Well, you'll be safe down there.

Nadia's eyes flew open. *You can't leave me down here.*

I'll come get you after I figure out what tripped the wards. Probably some sort of underground Numinal hybrid like last time.

But Nadia knew that it couldn't be an animal that wandered in. She had just sent the spell to Thomas and Mercurio, and minutes later, something tripped the wards, sending Myst into lockdown mode, killing the lights and locking the vault. It couldn't be a coincidence.

Rune?

What?

What if it's not an animal? What if it's an intruder?

Well, good thing you got locked inside the vault instead of outside.

You aren't seriously considering leaving me down here, are you?

Vault One is impenetrable. Even if someone managed to break the defensive seals, they would never be able to break into the library. You're completely safe.

There was a boom from outside the vaults, somewhere deep in the rock.

What was that? asked Nadia. *That sounded like an explosion.*

Hold on.

Nadia stood in the dark room. Her eyes jumped around the dim reddish shapes that she could barely make out. She knew that Mercurio must be attacking Myst. But Nadia didn't know what he could be after.

*Okay, Nadia. I want you to listen to me. Something broke

through my defensive seals underground. From that explosion, it sounds like they are going for the vaults.*

What should I do?

Just hang tight. They can't get into the vaults, so you are perfectly safe.

But Nadia knew that Mercurio wouldn't be after anything in the vaults. He already had access through her, so it didn't make sense that he would break into Myst, especially in the middle of the day. If Mercurio was behind the attack, which he had to be since Nadia had sent Thomas the ward-breaking spell, he would be going for something else, using the explosion to cause a diversion or make Rune think he was going for the vaults.

Nadia knew where he was going: Rune's office. Thomas had repeatedly pressed for details on the office layout. And that meant all the Mystics at work upstairs were in danger.

Maybe there was still time. If she could get out of this damn vault, she could fix everything. She could go reason with Mercurio. Make sure that no one got hurt. She was somewhat sure he wouldn't harm her. Maybe she could head him off and get whatever he was after for him, so Rune never found out that Mercurio was the intruder. And maybe Rune would never find out that she had stolen the spell and had been betraying him and Myst this entire time. She had resolved to confess her crimes, but suddenly the magnitude and reality of it all scared her. She wasn't sure she could tell Rune what she had done. She needed to undo the damage she had caused.

But she was stuck inside the locked vault, with no way out.

Rune, you need to come let me out.

I told you, you are perfectly safe. Once I've dealt with the intruder, I'll come get you.

No! You can't leave me down here. Nadia forced panic into her voice. *It's dark and creepy, and you seriously want me to listen to someone try to drill through or break down the door with magic or whatever while I'm stuck inside, completely powerless and just listening to them, counting down the moments until they do get through?*

You're being a bit dramatic, don't you think?

If I die because you refused to come let me out, I'm coming back as a ghost to haunt you.

Rune was silent for a minute. *You know, you're a real pain in the ass sometimes.*

Please just come get me.

Nadia, you're being ridiculous. I will come get you after I secure the boundaries.

No! She had to get out of that vault. If Rune intercepted Mercurio, he might realize her involvement. She needed to get to Mercurio first. She still thought she could fix everything. Rune would never have to know how badly she had fucked up.

Rune, I need to get out of the library now.

Winters, I don't have time for this. I will come get you after.

If you don't come let me out, I will be forced to figure out how to get out on my own. There has to be a bomb or weapon or artifact I can set off.

Rune paused. *Are you joking?*

I'm serious. I will detonate something. You cannot leave me in here like a sitting duck when there is an intruder on the loose in Myst.

What's gotten into you? You're acting insane.

Nadia knew she was being completely irrational, but she didn't know what else to do.

Hmm, looks like I found a spell to make Greek fire. I bet there is an emergency system that would open the vault if everything was going up in flames.

Jesus Christ, okay, okay. I'll come get you. Just don't blow anything up.

*   *   *

Nadia waited in the slightly reddish glow of the library's emergency lights, pacing nervously back and forth waiting for Rune. After about ten minutes or so—which, in the darkness, seemed like a lifetime—she heard a muffled electronic beep and a click, and the heavy vault door opened.

"Winters. Let's go," Rune barked as he poked his head out from behind the thick vault door.

Nadia hurried over and climbed out into the antechamber. Rune shut and locked Vault One's door before he cast a few more defensive spells over the barrier as an extra precaution. She followed him over to Vault Four, which was hanging open on its large metal hinges. After they climbed through into the space beyond Vault Four, Rune shut the door, the hinges creaking like it was rarely opened. The door clicked into place, and Rune and Nadia were plunged into inky darkness. Nadia could sense him casting a spell, half-speaking, half-thinking words while making intricate hand gestures. A torchlight burst into flame. Rune floated it above his head so they could see and then turned to her.

Rune looked like a fallen angel in the dim light, his cheekbones and jaw angle more pronounced, shadows playing on his face from the flickering torchlight.

"Thanks for coming for me," said Nadia.

"Well, I very well couldn't let you blow up the place," he said sarcastically. "Are you ready? Careful, the ground is a bit slippery and uneven in parts. I'll try to go slow."

"Where are we?" asked Nadia as she started to follow Rune through a dirt-packed tunnel. If she reached out on either side of herself, she could touch the walls and ceiling.

"Underground."

"I gathered as much. Why are there tunnels underground that lead to Myst?"

"You really want another history lesson right now?"

"It's creepy down here. Can you just keep talking to take my mind off the fact there is potentially a psycho killer headed our direction?"

They emerged from their dirt-packed tunnel into what appeared to be a larger concrete tunnel about twenty feet in diameter. Drips of water echoed down the cavernous space. Nadia heard scuffling in the distance like mice or rats were scratching on stone.

"You're one for hyperboles today," said Rune. "And the intruder isn't in this section." They continued down the tunnel, old graffiti and piles of garbage lining the edges. Nadia started at a shadow, and her Psionic pinged at her elevated heart rate. She stifled a scream when a rat ran across her foot.

Rune looked back at her, and sensing her agitation, he started talking to calm her. "There are tunnels throughout the city, connecting various points. You know how there were originally seven hills of San Francisco? Well, those hills were important because of their position to ley lines, but they were more important because they were the access point to seven secret passageways that Numinals used to move from place to place in the city and avoid detection."

Rune ducked into a side tunnel, and Nadia followed. She slipped on something slimy and wet and grabbed the back of Rune's T-shirt to steady herself.

"You good?" he asked as he took her hand and led her along. "Over the years, this network was expanded by pedestrian walkways, old storm drains, abandoned sewer pipes, and Muni tunnels carved through bedrock to form a latticework of linked ways to move around underground. After the 1906 earthquake, where half the city burned, officials even created a network of cisterns, many of which connect to the old passageways. Chinatown has one of the largest networks of tunnels that were originally used for human trafficking or when people were Shanghaied back during the Barbary Coast days. Many Numinals still live there underground, away from humans. Whoever tripped the wards came in through the tunnels and is probably down here somewhere."

They turned a corner in the tunnel and stopped about halfway down in front of a metal ladder embedded into the concrete. Above them, a storm drain lid was perched halfway on the opening, pouring beams of light down on them.

"After you," said Rune.

"No, it's fine. Go ahead."

"Get your damn ass up that ladder, Winters," he said gruffly.

"Fine," she grumbled as she grabbed the rungs of the ladder and heaved herself up. She climbed up, stupidly aware that Rune was staring at her butt as she moved rung by rung up to the street. Nadia pushed up on the lid of the storm drain and heaved it to the side to widen the opening and pulled herself up and into the light.

They were next to the old Muni depot, only a few blocks away from Myst headquarters. It had seemed so much more convoluted and far when they were underground. Behind chain-link fences, dozens of buses were lined up, with streetlamps spaced between lanes.

Even though it was midday, there were hardly any people out on that block of the city. A Muni maintenance guy in a reflective yellow vest who was setting orange cones up outside the fence line stopped and stared at them. Rune cast a quick distraction spell toward him. The man tracked a seagull flying overhead, his head pivoting as he watched the trajectory of the flight before he gave himself a shake and carried on his business, ignoring them. A bus rambled down the street and pulled into the lot.

Rune turned to her. "I have to go back to the others."

"I'm coming with you."

"Dammit, Nadia!" exclaimed Rune. He ran a hand through his hair in frustration. "I don't have time to watch after you. If there are intruders in Myst, I need to focus. Stay here."

"No, I'm going with you," she insisted.

Rune shook his head. "You're acting really strange, you know."

Nadia grabbed his arm and pulled him back toward Myst. "Come on, already. We don't have time for this."

"Oh, thank the Light, he's back," said Piero once Rune and Nadia entered the Artemis Room. "Rune, what's going on? Is there an active shooter?"

"Something tripped the wards under Myst again," explained Rune to the group as they assembled in front of him. "I'm sure it's nothing. Probably just an atmospheric disturbance or a hybrid Numinal that sensed the wards, like last time." A small ripple ran through the group. Rune held up his hands to calm them. "But my first priority is everyone's safety. Is anyone underground right now? In the labs?"

"Maya and Kevin and some of the Veil team are down there," said Sophie as she looked up from her cell phone. "They've been texting and emailing. Everyone is marked safe."

Carson busted into the room like G.I. Joe, magical ammo and weaponry strapped to his muscular frame. He tossed a glowing laser rifle to Rune, who plucked the wild throw out of the air with magic, looking slightly exasperated at Carson and the weapons. The ammo didn't jive with Rune's story about atmospheric disturbance. Behind him, Grudax and crew filed in with Arne. They had gone completely into guerilla warfare mode, equipped for battle. The goblins wielded an array of kitchen knives, meat bludgeoners, and makeshift shanks, various pots and pans and strainers strapped to themselves like armor and helmets. Nadia blinked. She hadn't realized that the goblins were useful for more than just making pastries.

Carson stood at attention, his military persona activated. "We've secured the perimeter. Grudax has stationed two crew members at every doorway and entry point."

Rune nodded. "Let's get everyone out from the labs first. Arne, stay here and watch the others." Arne saluted Rune with a grunt.

After they left, Nadia tried to figure out a way to sneak off without someone noticing. There was a light buzz of activity as the others formed small clusters. Piero and Sophie gravitated toward her.

Piero looked at her suspiciously. "What's going on with you? You know something we don't?"

Nadia shrugged, trying to look nonchalant.

"I honestly don't know what all the fuss is about." Sophie inspected her nails. "You heard Rune. He said it was some sort of atmospheric disturbance. Last time this happened, everything was fine. It wasn't anyone trying to break in."

"I've never heard of an atmospheric disturbance tripping wards, have you?" Piero glanced at Nadia. She tried to keep her face impassive and failed. Piero's eyebrows shot up. "Oh. My. God. Spill. What do you know?"

"Nothing."

"You are a terrible liar," said Piero. "Look at you. The guilt is just splashed across your face."

"Shhh," said Nadia, looking about herself. She pulled Piero and Sophie over to a corner of the conference room, away from the others. "You're right. It's not an atmospheric disturbance. There are intruders underground right now. Rune said something broke through the seals."

"What?" Piero screeched.

Sophie paled. "Oh my God! Do you think—"

"Shut up and listen!" demanded Nadia. "Something or someone broke into Myst. I was down in the library, but Rune got me out because something is going for the vaults."

"What are we supposed to do?" Piero looked like he was going to faint.

At that moment, Nadia experienced a strange tingling sensation on the back of her neck. It started on her spine and then spread through, the awareness of what it was growing and multiplying like cells splitting.

"I have to go check on something," Nadia said quickly.

Piero grabbed her wrist. "Where do you think you're going? You just told me that there are enemy hostiles in Myst. Now is not the time to go wandering around!"

Nadia yanked her wrist back. "Just trust me. I need to do something."

"Let her go," said Sophie. Nadia looked at her, surprised, but Sophie pushed her toward the door before she could overthink what that gesture meant. "Go. Seriously, or I will have to punch you for being so fucking boring. I'll cause a distraction." Nadia wasn't sure why Sophie was helping her, but she gave her a quick, grateful smile, and Sophie nodded back, an unspoken truce called between them.

Sophie stood up on a chair. "While we wait for Rune and Carson to get back, we're all going to play two truths and a lie." The others in the room gathered around. "Okay, I'll go first. I speak four languages, I've never driven a car, and I've never showed up hungover for work." Laughs and groans broke out. Everybody knew which one was the lie.

While Piero went next, Nadia backed away quietly from the crowd and escaped from the Artemis Room, heading for the winding staircase in the back. She again felt that tingling sensation on the back of her neck—that awareness of who was there—and hurried to the second floor.

Thomas was hunched over Rune's laptop when Nadia found him in his office.

"What the fuck do you think you're doing?" she hissed.

Thomas's head snapped up. "Trying to break into Rune's computer. What does it look like I'm doing?"

"You tricked me! You told me the spell you wanted was for energy enhancement. I would have never given it to you if I had known it was for breaking the seals on Myst."

He gave her a withering look. "Now is not the time to have a crisis of conscience."

She rushed over to Rune's desk. "What's going on? What's Mercurio after?"

"You've done your part. No need to concern yourself with those details." He turned his attention back to the computer.

Nadia wanted to throw something at him. "Thomas! There are people here. It's the middle of the day. Why would Mercurio do this? It doesn't make sense."

He looked exasperated at her. "I don't know. He wanted to make a big scene?"

Nadia stared at him. He stared back. He shifted from one foot to another. He glanced to the side as he grew uncomfortable under her gaze.

"No," said Nadia, realization dawning on her. "No way. Mercurio wouldn't be this sloppy and wouldn't take risks like this. What aren't you telling me?" She searched his face, trying to read him. She sent out her psychic tendrils to read his mind. Her eyes widened. "You. It was you. *You* did this. *You* broke into Myst. Mercurio has no idea about the spell! About any of it!"

"Listen, Nadia," he said, with mock patience. "You just don't understand the whole situation. This isn't what it looks like."

"Oh really? Because from over here, it looks like you just got caught trying to pull a fast one. I wonder what Mercurio would think of all this."

"Don't you dare tell him!"

She gave him a scathing look. "Or what? You'll come and bring demons to suck away my life force? News flash: I'm a Blood Muse. Bring it."

Another boom sounded, deep underground. The ground shook.

Nadia grabbed the back of one of the chairs in front of Rune's desk for support. Whoever was down there had set off another explosion.

Thomas suddenly looked panicked. He held his face with both his hands for a minute, having some sort of episode, and kicked at the ground. He stifled a scream so that it came out like a muffled squeak. Nadia didn't know what to do. The seconds ticked by.

When Thomas looked up, his face was calm and relaxed. He spoke evenly. Controlled. "Listen, no one was supposed to get hurt. This was supposed to happen in the middle of the night when no one was here. Now that I had the spell to break the seals, we didn't have to try during the middle of the day when the seals were the weakest, like before.

"The guys I hired were supposed to loot the place, make it look like this was just another one of the demon attacks that's been going on in the city, and I could copy the blueprints that Mercurio is interested in. Once they wrecked the place, Rune would have no idea that the data had been copied, and there would be no way to trace it back to you. But the guys realized I was after something and decided to break in early, to try to head me off."

Nadia stared at him, unwilling to believe what he was saying. She moved around the desk so that she stood in front of him. "Who are these guys? Is Rune in danger?"

Thomas's words came out rushed. "They're a group of trained mercenaries. They're luring him into the tunnels to capture him and get him to open the vaults."

"How do I know you're telling the truth?"

"You have to trust me."

"Well, I don't."

Thomas ran a hand through his hair, standing it up on end. His fists clenched. "Goddammit, Nadia! Why don't you just listen for once." He looked about himself wildly and then focused in on her. He leaned in, pleading. "Listen, both of us are at Mercurio's whim.

We can help each other. The mercenaries—they are oni demons. They have a code of honor. They won't hurt Rune if he opens the vault for them. I'm telling you this as a measure of good faith, so you trust me. We're friends, aren't we? Friends help each other."

She slapped him hard across the face. He raised a hand to his cheek, his face registering shock.

"Fuck you!" hissed Nadia. "This whole mess is your fault. You royally fucked up my life by turning me in as a prize to Mercurio to try to curry favor. And now you used me again for some half-baked idea that went south because you don't have the foresight to think things through."

"Now wait a second—"

Nadia cut him off. "Rune has passwords and security protocols on his computer and the network! You never had a chance. And who the hell are these mercenaries you turned loose on the company? You want me to trust you? Even if I somehow was inclined to—which I'm not—you just put me and all my friends in danger. Why on earth would I help you when all you've done is screw me over? Did Mercurio ever even give me all those orders to get close to Rune? Or was that all you this entire time?"

Nadia was fuming. She could barely see or think straight. She fisted her hands at her sides, drawing blood where her nails bit into her palms.

Thomas raised a finger and pointed it at her. "Now you listen here—"

"No, you listen to me," she cut in, slapping his finger away from her face. "We are done. We are not friends." She grabbed Rune's laptop and cast the witchlight spell on it, sending a bolt of electric charge and energy through the computer. The computer smoked, and the smell of burning wire and plastic filled the room.

Thomas's face was a mask of rage and horror as he looked at the smoking mess of plastic and metal and circuitry. "How are you going to explain that to him?" he demanded.

"The truth. I'll tell him I was worried about the intruders getting it." She started to leave, but Thomas grabbed her wrist.

"You owe me, remember?" He squeezed her wrist painfully, refusing to let her go. His eyes were manic. "I protected you from Mercurio. You need me."

Nadia yanked her wrist free. "No, I don't." Nadia couldn't believe she ever thought this guy had power over her. He was nothing more than a shriveled worm, hanging to the end of someone else's fishing pole.

"If you tell Mercurio about this, I'll tell Rune about you," Thomas warned.

Nadia wanted to laugh in his face. "No, you won't. That would go against Mercurio's wishes, and you're bound, just like me. You fucked yourself, buddy. I trusted you when you said the spell was for Mercurio, but it wasn't. You used me. I'm not going to forget this. I don't answer to you anymore. Only Mercurio. Got it?" She turned and ran.

Nadia ducked around a corner and into a supply closet, hoping Arne and the others hadn't seen her. She closed the door, hiding inside the tightly packed space. The room's walls were lined with cupboards and shelves that housed a jumble of spellcasting supplies like herbs and talismans and potions ingredients, as well as office supplies like binder clips and Post-it notes and reams of paper.

Rune, thought Nadia.

Little busy right now.

I have to tell you something.

Winters. Now is not the time.

But—

Not now!

Nadia beat her fist against a cabinet in frustration. She had to do something. This whole thing was her fault. If these oni mercenaries hurt Rune or anyone else at Myst, she would never forgive herself.

The watch. She quickly started scrolling through the interface on her Psionic. When Rune had taken her watch to add spells and training resources, he had mentioned that he had loaded several spells for emergencies. She scrolled through the lists and folders in the app, looking for anything that could help right then.

Spell to locate someone in an avalanche . . . spell to hold breath underwater . . .

She tried to stay calm and think rationally, but her rising panic was starting to cloud her judgment and thoughts. What were all these damn spells? Why did Rune think she would need these?

And then she saw Rune's grimoire. She tried to open the folder on the touchscreen, but it was locked just like the hundreds of other times she had tried to open it before.

"Fuck!" she cried out. "I do *not* have time for this right now."

Nadia closed her eyes and mentally sensed the lock in the Psionic. It was like a riddle, a puzzle she had to solve, a test she had to pass. She could sense Rune's psychic signature in the lock, like a thumbprint. She tried to visualize the data points and encoded information, but it soon became too complicated for her.

Doubt crept into Nadia's mind. Who was she kidding? She couldn't decipher this. It could take weeks or months for her to unwind the spell that was protecting this folder in her watch. All the other times she tried, she had failed, and those times weren't ones where she was under pressure and time constraints.

Anything is possible.

Nadia's mind jumped to the memory that Rune had implanted in her mind, the memory of how to rewire limiting beliefs. What if she truly *believed* she could open the lock? She struggled to recall the memory. It came in bits and pieces, like remembering a dream.

Nadia fought to hold on to the fleeting feelings and images in the memory.

Rune laughing, smiling down at her. Nadia breaking flashing lightning rods, using the sparking material to build new beliefs. Feeling powerful.

But there was something else there, something underneath, struggling to rise to the surface. A spell within the memory. Some deep, unconscious magic was taking root and growing, spreading its tendrils and capturing Nadia's mind, twisting it so she could see a new potential.

Rune leaning down, their lips close together, breathing the same air, desire swirling around them in heady waves. A single heartbeat connecting the two of them the moment their lips touched. Hope in the form of a kiss.

Nadia's eyes flew open, and she looked about the supply room wildly, not really seeing any of it. She was unsure if it was her desire or his that had unconsciously manifested within the memory. Either way, it changed everything. The feeling encompassing that kiss reverberated down to her soul, the very essence of her being.

The ground beneath her feet seemed to shift, an existential earthquake that shook Nadia to her core and toppled the tower of her beliefs. She looked about the rubble and knew that one thing was indeed true, like a kiss. She knew that anything was possible.

She looked back at the Psionic. She could open the lock. Rune had taught her everything she needed to know. He had put it there for a reason, to test her, to make sure she was worthy of whatever knowledge was inside. She hadn't understood that before, but she did now. Nadia closed her eyes again and felt the lock in her mind. She felt Rune's psychic signature, vibrating slightly like music. It was calling to her, a siren song, and Nadia answered, innately knowing the spell.

The folder unlocked.

Nadia's eyes popped open. She scrolled quickly through the interface to the digitized version of Rune's grimoire to the powerful spells he had created on his own. Nadia could sense the underlying patterns in the spells as she read through them. They were all so incredibly . . . Rune. There was no other way to describe it. They couldn't have been crafted by anyone else.

His grimoire was organized by type of spell. She scrolled through the categories: health, curses, protective spells, tantric spells . . . It was like she had broken into his mind. She would feel guilty if he hadn't been the one to load his personal grimoire onto her watch in the first place. He clearly wanted her to have them when she was worthy enough to access the information. She clicked into the battle spells. The first spell was the Ulfberht. She quickly googled what that meant and pulled up the Wikipedia page, learning it was a type of Viking sword. It would have to do.

She grabbed the necessary ingredients for the spell from the cabinets and shelves, including chalk, various herbs, candles, and dragon's blood. After poking her head out to make sure the coast was clear and that she wasn't going to be seen by her coworkers or the goblin guard force, she quickly ran around the perimeter of the main coworking space over to an empty practice room in the corner of the building where she hoped she wouldn't be found.

The practice room was one of the smaller ones, about the size of the sparring mat in the gym. Once inside, she closed the door quietly and lowered the security screens. She then checked the instructions for the spell before she drew the necessary ritualistic symbols on the concrete floor with the chalk, lit the candles, and sat cross-legged in the middle of the circle she had drawn. She tried to still her racing heart. Her hands shook, but she steadied them and focused. She hadn't ever attempted to cast like this, but she knew she could do it. She was a witch, a Septer, a magician. She could cast strong, powerful magic, guided by Rune's grimoire.

She had leveled up, the limiting beliefs about her abilities stripped away.

She felt the power and surge of energy rise and she chanted the text of the spell under her breath as she marked herself with the dragon's blood on her third eye, her throat chakra, and her heart chakra. She found her voice, her confidence growing. She finger-painted runic symbols from the spell on her bare arms, covering herself with the dragon's blood war paint as she continued to chant the strange Viking words to the spell.

With each smear of blood, she felt the power grow all around her and within her as she called forth the Ulfberht. She could barely hear her voice, the air and energy swirling around and drowning out all noise. It was like being inside the eye of a tornado.

The whirling energy coalesced, becoming a great, fiery dragon that rose in front of her. It was massive, nearly taking up the entire room. Its red and orange and gold scales were made of flames, its serpent-like tail coiled around its body, its bat-like wings covered in fire and beating the air. It roared, spitting white-hot fire in burning licks of energy that fanned at her face, distorting her vision with heat waves.

Without knowing how she knew to do this, Nadia stood up, facing the dragon, and opened up her heart to let the creature inside her body. It lunged at her, shrinking as it condensed into an arrow and pierced her chest cavity. Nadia's head and blood-covered arms flew back, her mouth open in a silent scream to the heavens as she was propelled up into the air as if on an invisible string. The fiery beast twisted around like a snake, filling her completely and transforming her. She convulsed, her body struggling to contain both her and the dragon, but the creature settled into her being, a coiled spring ready to strike.

She floated back down gently to the ground. Her eyes fluttered open. She looked at her symbol-covered arms and flexed her fingers. There was a slight awareness of the spell in her body, a slight pins and needles sensation that disappeared as the spell settled into place and the symbols vanished from her body. She glanced at her watch, surprised at how little time had passed. It had felt like hours, but the spell had only taken a few minutes to perform.

She hoped she wasn't too late.

CHAPTER 28

Back in the main coworking space, Nadia spied Maya and the others from the lab as they hurried over to the Artemis Room. Nadia rushed over to them, weaving through desks and bean bag cushions to the walkway around the perimeter of the room. Maya saw her and stopped, waiting for Nadia as the others fled to the conference room where everyone was hunkering down.

"Where's Rune?" asked Nadia.

"He and Carson went into the tunnels to secure the perimeter." Maya looked about to make sure no one could hear, her voice low. "Carson told me the seals were broken."

"There's definitely something down there. A group of them. I think they're oni."

Maya's eyes went wide. "Normally, I would say that the guys can handle themselves, but if there is a bunch of them, I'm not so sure. Oni are no joke. We need to do something. Let me see your watch." She held out her hand.

Nadia unclasped the watch and handed it over. Maya whistled softly when she saw Nadia registered as a Lemniscate.

Maya became extremely focused, looking much like she did when she was creating music, and scrolled through the interface of the watch. She pulled up and cast various quick charms on herself and Nadia for seeing in the dark, speed, agility, and strength, muttering quick incantations or making hand gestures over the Psionic interface, performing the hacks that Carson had programmed to bypass the normally tedious, nuanced, or difficult parts of a spell that required specialized knowledge or skill. The sensation of a chime ringing or a stone making ripples in water reverberated into the air and faded away as each spell or charm settled over the two of them.

Maya handed the Psionic back to Nadia. "That one is over my head with the angle it wants. Can you do it?"

Nadia quickly cast a quick charm for finding what you want when it was lost, snapping the angle between two thoughts in her mind and releasing the potential energy. The charm seeped into her body after she cast it into the air, like a sponge sucking up water.

"I figure Rune and Carson are lost, right?" Maya shrugged wildly.

"Does it even work like that?" asked Nadia. "What if there is some magical fine print, like it only works on inanimate objects like rocks, or it's only for something you personally lost, your car keys or something?" She clasped the watch back on her wrist.

Maya snorted. "Carson can be as dense as a rock. It's worth a shot. Okay, with the elevators out, we're going to need another way in."

"I know a way," said Nadia.

She and Maya quickly hurried out to the street and back over to the storm drain near Muni that Nadia and Rune had used to leave the tunnels. They made sure the coast was clear before they climbed down the rungs and dropped into the darkness.

Once inside the labyrinthine tunnel system, Nadia and Maya activated the charm that gave them night vision so they wouldn't reveal their presence by using a light, and they moved rapidly through as Nadia tried to remember the twists and turns that she and Rune had taken. Every sound, every noise of their shoes crunching on rocks or gravel seemed to echo in the dark chambers as they moved along until Nadia had the sense of mind to pull up a noise-dampening charm. Maya, with her limited casting ability, had depleted herself with the other charms she had used, so Nadia attempted to cast it on her. It took a few tries, but after Nadia finally got the charm to work, it shrouded them like they had wrapped a velvet blanket over their bodies, muffling all noise.

"Almost there," Nadia whispered to Maya.

With each step, Nadia felt certain that they would be too late. They were moving too slowly. As they rounded a corner that Nadia recognized as the first turn away from the vaults, they spied something on the ground. A body.

"Oh my God, Carson!" Maya dropped to her knees in front of him. A moan escaped him. He had been hit over his head, a trickle of blood running down the side of his temple.

"Is he okay?" Nadia crouched down. Maya pulled up his shirt, looking for injuries and wounds on his torso.

"I'm okay." Carson struggled to sit up. He wobbled, woozy, and gave up, instead leaning his head in Maya's lap. "They jumped us. Five of them. They took Rune."

Nadia stood back up. "You get Carson back above. I'm going after Rune."

"Don't be stupid," said Carson. "Rune can take care of himself."

"I'm going after him," snapped Nadia. And then she disappeared, running around the corner. She knew Rune would never open the vault door. She didn't want to know what the mercenaries would do to him when they realized that.

The door to Vault Four was open, leading to the antechamber. Nadia could hear voices in the room beyond.

"*Doa wo akete,*" a gruff voice commanded.

Nadia peered around the lip of the opening into the antechamber. Rune and the five mercenaries were diagonally across from her vantage point.

The oni mercenaries were huge Japanese demon warriors, not

wearing glamours. Their faces were thick, meaty ogre faces, with jutting teeth from prominent overbites. They all had sharp horns jutting from their foreheads, and they were wearing similar-looking black jumpsuits and robes. Each one had a different skin color— ebony, crimson, jade, indigo, and grey—polished and shining in the dim light of their lit staffs. The one with jade-colored skin was holding Rune's hands behind his back, while the one with crimson skin punched Rune in the face. Rune's head snapped back with a sickening crunch of bone.

This was it. It was now or never. Nadia had a momentary pang of self-doubt, but she barreled through it. She charged up the Ulfberht spell, waking up the coiled serpent. She felt the dragon stir within her and then surge up. It erupted out from her core so that she was woman, dragon, and weapon, the fiery flames of powerful energy licking around her body, her hair flying about her face like it was electrically charged. She was a weapon, forged from the crucible of fire.

She stepped out from the shadows.

Her eyes locked on Rune. He looked stunned, his eyes going wide. She felt the power of the spell reach its pinnacle, and then she was working on pure instinct. The oni warriors surrounded her and attacked, jumping on top of her as they tried to subdue her. She fought them off, slashing at their flesh like she had diamond-tipped claws, throwing balls of molten witchlight that spread and burned the oni like she had breathed fire on them, their screams echoing in the cavernous chamber. The runic symbols she had painted in dragon's blood protected her arms, the oni's blows glancing off her. She was only vaguely aware of the pain she felt when the indigo-skinned one slashed her across the stomach with a knife, another one biting into her leg savagely with sharp incisors. She registered flashes of images, their faces twisted into masks of rage as they tried to gut her with their horns or stab her with their spears. She screamed a primal scream, everything coming in bits of rage and fire and power, and she kept fighting. Rune joined in, blasting energy bolts that crippled the oni.

One by one, the oni fell to the ground and stopped getting back up as they lay on the stone in pools of blood and fire. Nadia's energy started waning. The spell was wearing off, her energy spent. She tried to conjure a ball of fire, but all she could make were a few sparks before the last of the dragon left her. She sagged against a wall, trying to stay upright, breathing heavily. There was one oni left, the one with skin like polished ebony, and he struggled to his feet, holding a sword, and limped toward her. Nadia's back was to the wall, and there was nowhere to go. Behind the oni, Rune crawled to his knees, his face bloodied, his shirt torn from battle. He raised a hand. A blast of energy hit the oni in the legs. The demon fell before it could reach Nadia.

The oni looked up, hatred in his eyes. "*Mata aimashō.*" He folded out, disappearing.

Nadia took big gulps of air as she came back to her senses. Her vision, clouded before with rage, cleared. She winced at the cut across her stomach, the pain returning after the rush of adrenaline was gone. Rune struggled to a sitting position. His eye was blackened and swollen closed. Blood poured from cuts on his lip and temple.

"Oh God, Rune! Are you okay?" Nadia rushed over to him and dropped to her knees, fighting the pain of her open wound. Blood stained her tank top, where she had been slashed and cut open. She pressed a hand to her stomach to staunch the blood.

"You cast the Ulfberht spell," Rune said incredulously.

"I know. It was in your grimoire you loaded onto my watch. Let me help you up." Nadia slung one of his arms over her shoulder and hauled him up, sucking in a sharp breath at her pain.

"You stupid, crazy girl." He bit out a laugh that quickly turned to a cough. "You cast a spell without knowing what it would do."

"I googled Ulfberht. It's a type of sword. I thought that was good enough."

He shook his head. "I can't say I approve of your methods, but I must admit, that was a sight to watch. Your power animal is a dragon . . ."

There was a strange expression on Rune's face. He looked at her like he was seeing her for the first time, like she had shattered his view of her. She hoped she didn't look like too much of a fool when she went into the magic battle trance. She wondered if he knew about the spell within the false memory. The kiss.

She looked up at him, questions in her eyes, and hoped he would answer them. He leaned down toward her, his mouth slightly open. This was it. The moment she had been waiting for. Nadia savored the sweet anticipation.

Time seemed to slow. Everything else melted away so that all Nadia could focus on was Rune. The open, vulnerable look in his eyes. His lips . . . so close to hers. Electricity rippled in the air. They leaned closer together, sharing the same breath, millimeters apart. Nadia closed her eyes, lips slightly open . . . but the moment never came. She opened her eyes. Rune stood frozen. He leaned back, a slightly surprised look on his face like he had realized what had almost just happened. The look shifted quickly to anger before he masked it with a neutral expression.

Nadia tried to control her emotions and tried not to register confusion or disappointment on her face.

Rune coughed and wiped a rivulet of blood from his temple. "Is Carson okay?"

"Maya has him."

Rune suddenly looked very tired. "Let's get out of here."

Chapter 29

"Wait, so let me get this straight," said Piero as he glanced back and forth between Rune and Nadia. They sat on either side of him at the long conference table in the Artemis Room. "Rune is captured by a group of five oni mercenaries, and Nadia—the one who almost cried over a paper cut last week—saves him?" He held up a hand to give Nadia a high five. "You go, girl!" Nadia slapped his hand, grinning.

The others sat around the conference table, some on the leather boardroom chairs, others leaning against the side counters. Pizza boxes and beer bottles littered the table. Rune had sent all Mystics home after he and Nadia had emerged from the tunnels, but Carson, Sophie, Maya, and Piero had stayed and had helped Rune and Nadia secure the perimeter of Myst headquarters with emergency seals and wards. After that was done, they had sent for a healer to patch up their wounds. There was no permanent damage from where she had been slashed with the knife across her stomach, but Nadia would have another scar to add to her growing collection.

"I don't understand why they broke in during the day," mused Piero. "It would have been so much easier at night."

"I guess they needed someone here so they could capture them and force them to open the vaults," said Maya. "Do we know who sent them?"

Rune shook his head. "No, but they were definitely hired by someone."

"So, this isn't related to the demon attacks around the city?" asked Sophie.

"Possibly," said Rune. "The attack doesn't fit the pattern, though. But there is one good thing that came from all this."

"What could possibly be good about this?" asked Piero.

"We know for sure now that Veil isn't causing the attacks," said Carson as he grabbed a pizza box from the stack and helped himself to another slice.

"How's that?" asked Maya.

"You know how Veil was picking up patterns within the random number generator?" asked Carson. "Turns out it was picking up on a big energy surge, not causing it. We know the time that the wards were tripped, and shortly after, there was a big energy surge in the area that would have been the energy expended to break the seals." Nadia realized that must have been the explosions she heard underground. Carson continued, "All the users in a five-block radius had treasure payouts at the same time the seals were broken."

"The demons were creating energy surges during attacks?" asked Nadia. "Why?"

"It looks like they were casting some sort of spell that created a surge," said Rune. "Probably to subdue their victims. We suspected the Veil was merely picking up on the surge, not causing it, but we never knew if the attacks occurred before or after the treasure payouts. But now we have hard data that shows the treasure payouts occurred after the attack. This was a much larger surge than any of the previous attacks in the city, which makes sense. They would have needed a great deal of energy to break my seals."

Carson helped himself to another piece of pizza. "Do we know how they broke the seals?"

Rune shook his head again. "I assume they had a powerful spell and enough energy, probably with an amplifier, like a talisman. The seals we put up today will work as a temporary fix, but I'm going to have to completely redo all the wards and seals. It's going to take me a bit of time to do that."

"I still don't understand how Nadia managed to take out five oni mercenaries," said Piero, eyeing her as he held out his glass for Rune to refill with whiskey. "Did you She-Hulk out or something?"

"Remind me not to get on your bad side." Maya grinned.

Nadia shook her head. "Guys, it wasn't me. It was just the spell."

"*What* spell?" asked Sophie quickly. She glanced around at the others. "I mean, in case we need to research it or something."

"It was called Ulfberht," said Rune. "It puts the caster into a psychic battle trance, like a Viking berserker."

"Whoa, where did you learn that one?" asked Sophie, a hint of respect in her voice.

Nadia glanced at Rune. "It was in the digital copy of Rune's grimoire on my Psionic. I just cast the thing. Rune was the one who created the spell in the first place."

Carson froze as he was about to take another bite of pizza and looked sharply at Rune. "Wasn't that locked?"

Nadia watched them share a strange look. "Yeah, I managed to unlock it," she said when Rune didn't respond.

"And we are all grateful she did," said Rune smoothly. "Here's to Nadia." He raised his glass. "I can't say I've ever had a more devoted employee. Thank you."

Nadia bowed her head as the others cheered and clinked their glasses together. She was suddenly overwhelmed by the day's events, fatigue setting in now that the magic and adrenaline from the fight had worn off. That morning in the vaults when she had sent Thomas the spell seemed like a lifetime ago. She had thought that everything was crashing down around her, unraveling at the seams. She had thought that everything—her job at Myst, her new life in San Francisco—was going to go up in flames.

But it seemed like fate had thrown her a bone and given her a free pass, a Get Out of Jail Free card. Not only did Rune *not* find out that she had been spying on him and that she was the reason intruders had broken into the company, but by trying to undo the mess she caused, she had finally understood her powers in a deep, profoundly changing way. She'd been able to cast some serious magic, and she had only just begun to realize what the implications of that were on her life.

She had seriously lucked out. She felt like she had squeaked by, just barely. Next time, she wouldn't be so lucky.

She needed to figure out her next steps. How to navigate Mercurio with her newfound powers and leverage over Thomas and still manage to keep her job at Myst. And maybe she could figure out a way to remove the Blood Oath and untangle herself from Mercurio's web. Now that she knew that anything was possible, she had a resurgence of hope for finding a way out from its morally confusing and sticky constraints.

Nadia glanced up at Rune, who was watching her. She smiled slightly, and he returned the smile. There was something there, some magic between them. The seed of the idea had taken root. Nadia was sure it could eventually blossom into something magnificent, something wonderful and beautiful and messy and real. She could see the potential there for the relationship, one that was complex and dangerous and exciting, one that would fundamentally and definitively change her life and the very core of who she was as a person. But not yet. It wasn't right. Not quite yet. The Blood Oath would always be in the middle, an invisible third, a wedge that would forever separate them unless she was honest and told Rune about her ties to Mercurio. And she couldn't do that. It was too soon. They barely knew each other. Their relationship was too tenuous to risk severing it altogether with the knowledge of a betrayal like that.

So all Nadia could do was wait and see, continue to move forward, try to navigate the strange terrain of her life, and hope for the best. But as she sat back in her chair and gazed around the room at Piero, Carson, Sophie, Maya, and Rune, the new friends who colored her new life, she had a strange sensation of rightness. There was no sense of restlessness, of unease, of wondering if she had made a wrong turn somewhere down the line and got lost. It was like the stars had aligned to illuminate the right path for her just to show her that she had been on the right path all along. With an inward smile, Nadia realized she was exactly where she was supposed to be, right then, at that very moment.

She was home.

Epilogue

Maya, Piero, and Sophie left the Artemis Room to head home for the evening until it was just Rune, Carson, and Nadia. She looked tired, and a couple of times while they were sitting around the conference table, Rune caught her staring at nothing, like she was deep in thought. He worried that the spell had been too much for her. When she started to fall asleep at the table, her head bobbing down before she jerked herself awake, Rune decided to send her home.

"I'll see you tomorrow?" Nadia asked Rune as she paused in the doorway. She rested one slender hand on the doorframe as she turned back to him.

"Why don't you take the day off?" Rune and Carson both had kicked up their feet on the conference room table, the remnants of delivery boxes and beer bottles and soda cans spread over the surface of the table. "You should rest and recover."

She bit her lip like she wanted to say something but merely nodded and left.

Rune poured Carson and himself another shot of whiskey and then leaned back in the leather boardroom chair. He closed his eyes and absentmindedly swirled the amber liquid in the glass.

"She's the one from that seer's prophecy, isn't she?" asked Carson.

Rune's eyes flew open. He took a deep breath, placed a hand behind his head, and stared at the ceiling.

"She opened your grimoire," Carson pressed. Rune glanced over to Carson, who held up his glass, sloshing the whiskey a bit as he spoke. "I know you locked it with your Soul Signature. I helped you program it. In theory, only you or your soulmate should be able to open it. You never told me you wanted a soulmate! I didn't peg you as the sentimental type."

"I don't believe in nonsense like soulmates," snapped Rune. "They are a myth. A societal construct. A fallacy to bolster belief in monogamy."

"The fact she used your Soul Signature defeats that argument. What else could she be?"

Rune shook his head and leaned over, cradling his forehead in his hands. "I don't know. I don't know what to think. About any of it."

"Dude! Be happy! How often does the universe actually send you a soulmate? The rest of us can only dream of being so lucky."

"She's human," said Rune. "What am I supposed to do with that?"

"At least she's cute and nice and has a banging bod. The universe could have sent you some hagfish or some were-rabbit or something."

Rune swiveled his head over and gave Carson a look that said, *Really?*

"You know I'm right. Plus, she's a Septer. You guys can do spells together and geek out over finger positions or chanting or whatever it is you magically inclined people do." Carson shot back his whiskey and grimaced, pulling air between his teeth to cut the burn of the alcohol. "Are you going to tell her?"

"No."

Carson nodded and scratched his stomach. "Probably for the best. You tell a girl that she's your soulmate, she'll walk all over you. Treat you like her bitch. Makes them too comfortable in a relationship. Way better to keep them guessing about how you feel."

"Maybe this is why you're single."

"Hey man, don't hate the player, hate the game."

They lapsed into silence. Carson made himself comfortable, settling back in his chair and closing his eyes. Rune took another sip of his whiskey and rolled it around on his tongue, tasting the smoke and cinnamon flavors. He was spent from the day. Putting the wards and seals back up around Myst so quickly had taken an immense toll on him. It had been a priority, though, with the boundaries of the company open and vulnerable. Rune needed to figure out who had sent the team of mercenaries to break into the vaults and how they had managed to break in past his defenses. He suspected it was Miles and Pact. But his thoughts kept returning to Nadia. He hoped she was okay. If he was tired, she must be exhausted.

He still couldn't believe Nadia was his soulmate, not that he even believed in that sort of thing. But she had to be. Only a soulmate could use one's Soul Signature. He didn't know what to think. He hadn't even wanted to hire her. He couldn't believe the girl he was interviewing could possibly be the one from the prophecy when she cast that ring of fire and had tried to bind him. He didn't know why he had loaded his grimoire onto her watch. It had been an impulse, some nudge from the universe that felt like the right thing to do.

All this time, Rune had been lying to himself. He had been making up excuses to be around her. He had told himself that he was interested in her as an employee. That his top priority was Myst, so he was investing in her to help the company. What a joke. Hell, he forced her to train with him each morning just so he could spend time with her alone and get to know her better.

He had tried to stop his feelings toward her from growing once he had realized what was happening. He had tried to keep her at arm's length, not wanting to complicate things any more than they already were. The poor girl. She had been nothing but open and honest and trusting of him, and he had been pretending to be indifferent, yanking her around. That evening at the food truck park, even though he knew he shouldn't, he had indulged in some non-verbal seduction, catching her eye, holding her gaze too long. But after, he had felt guilty and purposely said those things to hurt her and push her away when he had sensed her listening around the corner. He couldn't risk her getting too close. It was too dangerous.

But there was just something about her that Rune couldn't stop thinking about. He loved the cute way she scrunched up her nose or bit her lip when she was thinking. The incessant questions. The way she pretended she wasn't watching him, studying him, the way he had been studying her, trying to figure her out. He had noticed and cataloged all those moments.

And they had almost kissed! He thankfully had stopped himself in time. There was no telling what would have happened if he hadn't.

Rune knew he needed to tell her the truth. He would figure out a way to tell her about his flawed nature, the dark essence inside himself that he spent so much time and energy keeping locked away. But not yet. She was too young, too inexperienced. She wouldn't understand that he had no choice in his actions. If he told her everything now, she would run in terror. But Rune could wait. He would wait. He would watch her grow and blossom into the beautiful, powerful woman she was destined to be. And she was a Blood Muse. The Numinous was just fucking with him at this point. He couldn't imagine, *wouldn't* let himself imagine, how wonderful and juicy and sweet she would taste if he fed from her. And if they made love during a feeding . . .

Rune shut that line of thought down immediately.

There was no point in unnecessary torture. He'd experienced that quite enough already in his countless lives.

Rune glanced over to Carson, who was nodding off in his chair, his glass empty and fallen off to the side next to his dangling arm. A trail of Cheetos crumbs led from his mouth to the empty bag near his other arm.

With a deep sigh, Rune stood up. He grabbed Carson and hauled him to his feet. Carson wobbled a bit, his eyes still closed.

"Just put me on one of the couches," mumbled Carson.

Rune started walking with Carson to the door. "You know I wouldn't do that. You can crash at my pad downstairs."

"You're the best, man."

Rune shook his head, wishing that were true.

Acknowledgments

Heartfelt thanks to everyone who helped make this book happen, but especially:

My husband Sam Wiley, for listening to me talk endlessly about this story for years and years, for coming up with all the good ideas (that I then have to execute), and for helping me brainstorm my way out of corners I have written myself into. I am so lucky to have you as a partner.

My sister Chrissy Casey, for always being a champion and cheerleader when the voice of doubt tries to take over.

My mom and dad for instilling an early love of reading and books.

My writing mentor and author Seth Harwood, for the many years of teaching and workshops, and for creating a supportive writing community for his students.

The Ground Fiction members and Seth's writing groups for reading and workshopping snippets of my story over the years.

My early readers Leflora Cunningham-Walsh, Katherine Carter, Ali Motlagh, Michelle Schaefer, Christy Wicks, Brett Welch, Jacquelyn Bridgeman, Hazel Garcia, Christina Parker, Gaby Manchester, Siobhan Goodwell, Susan Wiley Sanchez, and Gale Wiley for their invaluable feedback and encouragement.

My longtime writing pals Cherryl Chow, John Hartsell, Connie Howard, Norm Crawford, and James Harris for their critiques and conversation over lunch.

My Burning Man camp Dustfish and friends in San Francisco, whose unique personalities inspired me to create Numinals.

And finally, my baby daughter River, the littlest Numinal, whom I can't wait to make up stories and play make-believe with one day.

ELIZABETH COLEMAN lives in San Francisco with her husband, daughter, and two extremely spoiled cats. She writes across genres and mediums, but her stories all delve into what it means to be human, and because life is better with a little bit of magic, they usually contain elements of the fantastic. *City of Sevens* is her first novel.

Connect with her at www.thelizcoleman.com and @thelizcoleman.